"What do you want, Mace?" Rhett's question was soft, guarded.

She skewed her lips to the side as if trying to find the right words. "I'm just wondering where the boy I knew went."

Rhett crossed his arms. "He grew up."

"That's a pity," Macy said. "He had this amazing ability to dream big but plan well—something this place really needs. That boy could have shaped the ranch into something beyond what his father possibly ever could have."

He clenched his teeth and reminded himself that Macy was just being Macy. She'd been known to kick a hornets' nest before—literally.

He pressed his palms against the armrests. "You finished?"

"For now, sure. Forever?" she asked. "Not a chance."

Rhett couldn't hold in a chuckle. "I don't doubt it one bit."

This was the Macy he remembered, *his* Macy— someone who would stand against the wind and glare at a coming storm. Someone who didn't flinch.

Well, not his Macy. He wasn't quite sure where that thought had come from…

Avid reader, coffee drinker and chocolate aficionado **Jessica Keller** has degrees in communications and biblical studies and spends too much time on Instagram and Pinterest. Jessica calls the Midwest home. She lives for fall, farmers' markets and driving with the windows down.

A seventh-generation Texan, **Jolene Navarro** fills her life with family, faith and life's beautiful messiness. She knows that as much as the world changes, people stay the same: vow-keepers and heartbreakers. Jolene married a vow-keeper who shows her holding hands never gets old. When not writing, Jolene teaches art to inner-city teens and hangs out with her own four almost-grown kids. Find Jolene on Facebook or her blog, jolenenavarrowriter.com.

The Rancher's Legacy

Jessica Keller

&

The Texan's Secret Daughter

Jolene Navarro

LOVE INSPIRED
INSPIRATIONAL ROMANCE

LOVE INSPIRED®
INSPIRATIONAL ROMANCE

Recycling programs
for this product may
not exist in your area.

ISBN-13: 978-1-335-46129-2

The Rancher's Legacy and The Texan's Secret Daughter

Copyright © 2021 by Harlequin Books S.A.

The Rancher's Legacy
First published in 2019. This edition published in 2021.
Copyright © 2019 by Jessica Koschnitzky

The Texan's Secret Daughter
First published in 2019. This edition published in 2021.
Copyright © 2019 by Jolene Navarro

This edition published by arrangement with Harlequin Books S.A.

For questions and comments about the quality of this book,
please contact us at CustomerService@Harlequin.com.

Love Inspired
22 Adelaide St. West, 40th Floor
Toronto, Ontario M5H 4E3, Canada
www.Harlequin.com

Printed in U.S.A.

CONTENTS

THE RANCHER'S LEGACY

Jessica Keller

For the ladies in my Psalms 23 study.
Thanks for being my sisters.
Thanks for yanking me back on the path.
Thank you for being there. Always.

He restoreth my soul: he leadeth me
in the paths of righteousness for his name's sake.
Yea, though I walk through the valley of the
shadow of death, I will fear no evil: for thou art
with me; thy rod and thy staff they comfort me.
—*Psalms* 23:3–4

Chapter One

"I don't know why you're here." Rhett Jarrett rested his elbows on the large desk. It was too large—too grand—and he'd never look right behind it. Never be able to fill the spot his dad had. "I mean, other than it's always nice to see you. But you know where I stand on this."

Uncle Travis pushed more papers across the desktop. "With time, maybe you'll see his reasoning."

Rhett opened a drawer and slid the papers unceremoniously inside. Rereading the will wouldn't suddenly make him appreciate the choices his father had made. All it would serve to do was remind Rhett his dad had found a way to control him after the grave.

Late afternoon sunshine poured through the wide windows filling the west-facing wall of the office. March had begun unseasonably warm, even by Texas standards.

Upon entering the office a few minutes ago, Rhett had immediately cracked a few of the windows in an attempt to banish the musty odor of too many papers and books collecting dust in one cramped place. No doubt the wood paneling lining the lower half of the walls hadn't helped his mood either. It only seemed to add to the dark heaviness that had settled on Rhett's life since his dad's sudden passing. Unsaid words, missed opportunities and apologies that would never happen weighed him down.

No amount of fresh air would clear his chest of those things.

Air gusted in, carrying with it the smells of the horses in the nearest enclosure and the cattle in the pastures beyond. They mingled with the scents of Texas Indian paintbrush, bluebonnets and red poppies. Wildflowers quilted the fields on either side of the long driveway leading to his family's property. Spring at the ranch had always been his favorite time of year. He liked the physical parts of the ranch—the animals, the fields, the work.

Just not all the *other* aspects of Red Dog Ranch.

Not the parts his dad had cared about.

"Uncle Travis, listen. I—" Rhett started.

The door to the office clicked open and Macy Howell appeared in the doorway. With her hand resting on the knob, she hesitated for a few seconds. Her long, black hair swayed from her abrupt stop.

Rhett had known he would see his dad's office assistant sooner or later, but after the last few years of carefully visiting Red Dog Ranch only when he had been assured she was busy or away from the property…it was startling to see her so soon his first day in the office.

Macy adjusted the armful of files she clutched. Her

gaze hit the floor like a dropped quarter. "I didn't realize you were busy. Should I come back later?"

But Macy casting down her eyes didn't compute for Rhett. Growing up, she'd been the girl who would spit at a wildfire and dare it to come closer. She'd hauled hay bales in the field at the same pace as Rhett and his brothers had.

When Rhett had scooped Macy into his arms after she'd been bitten by a copperhead, she had told him not to worry because the pit viper had barely kissed her. Even in that sort of pain, she'd been focused on being tough and making others feel better.

The Macy Howell he knew didn't hesitate, didn't look away.

She especially didn't look *down*.

The back of Rhett's neck prickled in a way that made him want to scrub at it. He fought the urge to ask her what was wrong. But they'd stopped asking each other prying questions three years ago. One kiss had changed everything.

Ruined everything.

And he shouldn't care.

Didn't care.

He dug his fingers into his knees.

Kodiak, Rhett's seventy-pound Chesapeake Bay retriever, lifted her giant head and sniffed in Macy's direction. The dog lazily looked back at Rhett as if to ask if this person was a threat.

Oh, she was.

With a gaze that could melt his resolve and her bright smile, Macy definitely was.

Satisfied that Rhett hadn't given a command, Kodiak let out a loud harrumph and laid her head back down. Her front paws stretched so the tips dipped into a spear of sunlight.

Despite Macy seeming to act out of character, the sight of her standing there in jeans and a flannel over a blue T-shirt still hit Rhett with the force of a double-strength energy drink spiked with strong coffee. She had a pencil tucked behind her ear. She looked like... like the best friend she'd once been. Like the person he used to be able to count on.

Like someone who hadn't rejected him.

Looks could be deceiving.

Uncle Travis's bushy gray eyebrows rose as if to ask, "Are you going to answer her, or what?"

Rhett cleared his throat, but it felt as if he'd swallowed a mouthful of summer soil that had baked in the Texas sun for weeks on end. Gritty and dry. "What do you need?"

"These are the files for the teens with internships starting this weekend. You should probably look them over. Know something about each one before you have to train them." She stepped into the room holding the pile of file jackets like a peace offering. "Brock always did."

Brock Jarrett, also known as his father.

Rhett's shoulders stiffened. "There's no one else set up to train them? Dad did it all?"

"I don't think Brock had made plans in case..." Uncle Travis's voice drifted away.

In case he died suddenly.

In case a trip to the library became his last trip.

In case one uninsured teenager sending a text while driving changed the Jarrett family forever.

Macy took another step into the room. "He usually spent the first few days with them, yes. They each get assigned to a staff member, but Brock did the bulk of the mentoring."

Rhett shook his head. "Someone else can do it."

Kodiak groaned and lifted her head, alerted to trouble by his change in tone.

Macy's wide brown eyes searched his. "Rhett." She whispered his name and, for a reason he didn't want to explore, it made his gut hurt. "Please."

Rhett let his gaze land on the painting of longhorns instead of Macy. Meeting her pleading eyes made his resolve shaky and that was the last thing he wanted. His mom had painted the picture years ago, before her mind had begun to fail her. She'd proudly given it to Brock as a Valentine's day gift.

Thinking of his mom made Rhett sit a little straighter. Her well-being depended on how he ran this ranch now. The will clearly stated Rhett was to take care of her and provide stable jobs for his sister, Shannon; Cassidy, the girlfriend of his deceased brother, Wade; Wade's daughter, Piper; and his brother, Boone, and his family. With Boone off at seminary with his wife and daughter, at least that responsibility was off Rhett's list. But the others stood.

However, so did the will's ironclad wording about the ranch continuing to serve foster kids. If Rhett put a stop to the foster programs at Red Dog Ranch, the will stated he would have to forfeit his inheritance. It was continue his dad's work or get none of it.

"Leave them on the table." Rhett jerked his chin toward a small side table near the office door.

Macy did, but she stayed in the doorway. "We need to talk about the spring kickoff event and the Easter egg hunt."

"Put those thoughts on hold. I'm looking into cancelling programs," Rhett said as he turned back to his uncle. "Which means you and I need to keep talking."

Macy's eyes narrowed for a second. She was biting her tongue. Years of knowing her made that clear, but she backed out of the room and closed the door.

As Rhett waited for his uncle to say something, he rubbed his thumb back and forth over an etching near the bottom right edge of the desktop. His dad had made him muck stalls alone for two weeks straight after Rhett had carved the indentation. At all of seven or eight years old, it had been quite a chore.

Uncle Travis offered a tight smile. "She's the perfect one to work with to help you meet the terms of the will. You see that, don't you?"

Rhett pinched the bridge of his nose.

Of course he saw that.

It was half the problem.

Macy had always put the foster programs before everything else, just like Brock had. Before the moneymaking aspects of the ranch, before family, before friendships. She had a passion and knowledge Rhett lacked, but working alongside her would be difficult; between losing his dad, dealing with family drama and being forced to put his business on hold to deal with Red Dog Ranch, Rhett was already past his ears in difficult. He needed to start making hard decisions and taking action to mitigate losses and stress.

Keeping a wide berth from Macy was one significant way to limit stress.

"As executor, don't you have the power to change the stipulations?"

His uncle's shoulders drooped with a sigh. "We've been over this."

And they had.

Many times.

As executor, Travis's job was to make certain all of Brock Jarrett's wishes were carried out to the letter. And Rhett's father had left many…letters. Red Dog Ranch had been willed to Rhett in full—the land and his father's vast accounts. But there were conditions.

If Rhett rejected the position of director, then they were supposed to sell the land and donate the money from the sale to a charity Brock had stipulated. Even in death his dad had placed continuation of the programs offered at the ranch before his family's long-term well-being. The only other option allowed in the will was for the property to pass to Boone, but Boone had been emphatic about refusing the inheritance. He wanted to finish seminary. He had a plan that didn't involve the ranch and no one could fault Boone for putting God first.

Well, Rhett refused to remove his mom from her home, from the land she loved. Even at the expense of his own happiness. His father had effectively tied his hands, making him the bad guy if he backed out.

Rhett lifted his chin. He wasn't backing out. He

would take care of his family's future, would succeed in a way his father never had.

Kodiak made a small sound in her sleep, drawing Rhett's attention for a heartbeat.

He had placed his business, Straight Arrow Retrievers, on hold after getting the call that his father had passed away. But "on hold" might quickly become "closed forever." A burning sensation settled in Rhett's chest.

It was too much to manage. Too much to juggle. There was no way he could keep his business, the ranch and the foster programs all running successfully. One of them had to go.

His jaw hardened. "I'm going to find a loophole out of the foster programs at the ranch."

Uncle Travis frowned. "Even if you could—and I'm fairly certain you can't—talk like that would have broken your dad's heart."

"He knew how I felt about everything when he chose this for me," Rhett said.

While Red Dog Ranch had always functioned as a working cattle ranch, it also existed as a place that served children in the foster system. When Rhett was young, they had started hosting large parties for foster kids throughout Texas Hill Country for every major holiday. That had morphed into weekend programs that taught horseback riding and other life skills. The final addition had been building a summer camp on the property that was free for foster children to attend.

The summer camp had been Brock's pride and joy. It had seemed as if he lived all year for the weeks the ranch swelled with hundreds of kids. His father had poured his time and energy into every single one of the kids. Often as kids aged out of the foster care system, Brock had offered them positions on his property.

Rhett cared about kids who didn't have a home.

He did.

But it would be almost impossible to carry on his dad's mission with the same passion. He scrubbed his hand over his jaw and blew out a long breath. As horrible as it sounded, he resented Red Dog Ranch and all that it stood for. His father had cared more about it and the foster children than anything else.

Especially more than he'd cared about Rhett.

Uncle Travis clicked his briefcase closed and stood up. He hovered near the desk, though. "A gift is only as good as what you do with it."

Rhett stood. Crossed his arms over his chest. "A gift and a burden are two very different things."

But Uncle Travis pressed on. "Your aunt Pearl, bless her, she never knew what to do when someone gave her something really nice." He laid his free hand over his heart. "When I lost her and got around to cleaning out her stuff, you know what I found?"

Rhett pressed his fingertips into the solid desktop and shook his head. Once Uncle Travis got started down a rabbit trail, there was no point stopping him.

"Boxes of expensive lotions and perfumes that our kids had given her over the years." Travis fanned out his hand as if he was showing an expansive array. "She'd just squirreled it all away. Jewelry that I'd given her and the kids had given her." He pursed his lips. "All never worn."

Rhett offered his uncle a sad smile. Aunt Pearl had

been one of his favorite people growing up and he knew, despite her stubborn streak, Travis missed her every day. Letting the man talk would do no harm.

"Pearl grew up poor, you see," Uncle Travis said. "I don't know whether she was waiting for a time she deemed special enough to use those things, or if she just didn't believe *she* was special enough to use them. But in the end it didn't matter, did it? All those things, those pretty things, all of them went to waste. Unused. Rotting and tarnished or full of dust. Pearl never got to enjoy them because she didn't believe she was worth enjoying them."

Rhett looped a hand around the back of his neck and rocked in his boots. "Why are you telling me this?"

"Like I said—" Travis's voice was wistful "—a gift is only as good as what you do with it." His uncle tugged on his suit jacket and made his way toward the door. "Remember, son. 'For unto whomsoever much is given, of him shall be much required.'"

It had been a while since Rhett had cracked the book. "I know the Bible, Uncle Travis."

He paused as he opened the door. "Ah, but do you know the heart of God in this matter? Have you sought *that* out, son? Because that's more valuable than a hundred memorized Bible verses." Uncle Travis shrugged. "Just a thought."

After his uncle left, Rhett fought the urge to sit back down and drop his head into his hands. Fought the desire to finally lose it over his dad's death. Fall apart once and for all. But he couldn't do that, not now. Maybe not ever.

Way too many people were counting on him to be strong.

Rhett mentally packed up every messy emotion in his heart and shoved them into a lockbox. He pretended he was jamming them down, squishing them until they were so small and insignificant they weren't worth thinking about. Or talking about or sharing with anyone.

No one would care about them anyway.

Then he clicked the lockbox shut and tucked it into the darkest corner of his mind to be forgotten.

Macy was going to pace a hole in the floorboards at the front of the ranch's office. Travis Jarrett had left half an hour ago, but Rhett still hadn't vacated his father's office. What was taking so long?

She jerked her hair up into a ponytail.

The second—the very second—he left that office he'd have to listen to her, hear her out.

She'd *make* him.

Macy paused near her desk and picked up a framed photo of her and Brock Jarrett. It had been taken at last year's spring kickoff event for Camp Firefly— the free summer camp Brock ran at Red Dog Ranch for foster kids. She traced a finger over the photo— Brock's smile.

Macy blinked away tears.

After her father walked out of her life when she was ten years old, Brock had stepped in and filled that void. And when her mom died eight years later the Jarretts had moved her onto their property. Rhett's dad had been family to her—*Rhett* had been like family to her too. Now they hardly acknowledged each other, and with Rhett's mom fading fast, Macy couldn't help but feel like she was losing everyone she cared about all over again.

"I'll keep your secret," she whispered to the image. "I promise."

She set the picture down and absently rubbed her thumb back and forth across the raised scar on her pointer finger. A nervous habit she'd tried, unsuccessfully, to break more than once. The scar was Rhett's fault. Six years ago, he had dropped his cell phone when they were out hiking and she'd crawled back over the large rocks on the trail to get it, disturbing a copperhead in her zest. Of course, Rhett had carried her to safety, rushed her to the hospital as her skin swelled and blistered and the pain intensified, and stayed by her side while she healed. The memory caused a rueful smile to tug at her lips. He had lost his cell phone after everything anyway.

She forced her thumb to stop moving.

The scar on her finger wasn't the only one she blamed him for. The Do Not Cross tape coiled around her heart was all his doing too.

Macy whirled toward the door to Brock's—no, Rhett's—office.

Enough.

She marched toward the door and didn't bother knocking before opening it. "We need to—" The words died on her lips. Rhett wasn't there.

The man must have slunk out the never-used back door like the guilty dog he was.

Macy balled her fists.

They would have to face each other—have to talk at some point—and today was as good a day as any. She hadn't been able to get a good read on Rhett with Travis there so she had held her tongue.

I'm looking into cancelling programs.

Not if Macy had anything to do with it.

She grabbed her keys, locked up the office and hoofed it out into the yard. Orange mingled with pink and gold in the sky. A slight breeze carried the chill whisper of the approaching night. The sun had dipped close to the horizon, not quite sunset yet but soon enough.

Various structures peppered the Jarrett property. The office and main buildings serving the summer camp wrapped through the front of their land, including ten camper cabins and a mess hall that was built into the side of the largest hill they owned. The barns and cattle fields took up the opposite end of their holding, and the family home rested like a gorgeous crown jewel at the end of the long driveway. Macy lived in one of the small bungalows tucked just west of the family ranch house. A handful of staff members lived on the property.

Macy passed the small corral that housed Romeo, the ranch's attention-needy miniature donkey, and Sheep, an all-white miniature horse that belonged to Rhett's niece, Piper. Romeo trotted beside the fence line as she walked, trying to coax an ear scratch out of her.

"Not now, buddy." Macy didn't break her stride. Still, his pathetic bray made her heart twist. She loved the little donkey and all of his quirks—maybe *for* his quirks. "I'll bring you apples later, deal?"

Beyond their enclosure, she spotted a horse and rider picking their way through the bluebonnets blanketing the nearby field. She squinted, trying to focus on the rider. Shannon Jarrett, Rhett's sister. Despite the fact that none of the women were related, Shannon, Cassidy and Macy had formed a tight-knit sisterhood. Especially during the last five years.

Macy climbed onto the fence and waved at her friend.

Shannon nudged her horse into a trot so she was within yelling distance in seconds.

"Did you see where your rat of a brother went off to?" Macy called.

Shannon tossed back her head and laughed. "Well, I know you aren't talking about Boone." And neither mentioned the other Jarrett brother, Wade. His death five years ago had been the catalyst that set the Jarretts drifting apart. Being Wade's twin, Shannon had been deeply affected by the sudden loss of him. She hadn't quite regained the wide, carefree grin she'd been known for as a child. Probably never would.

"I could hardly call a man training to be a pastor a rat." Macy joined in the laughter.

Shannon nodded, her short blond waves bobbing. "Rhett walks Kodiak to the lake every morning and every evening. I don't think she can last a day without swimming. Rhett says it's in her breed's blood."

Macy tipped her head in a silent thank-you and made for the lake.

Red Dog Ranch sat on over three thousand acres

of gorgeous Texas Hill Country land and had multiple lakes and ponds. Some of them Macy would need a horse or one of the trucks to reach, but she guessed Rhett had stuck to the one closest to the house. Long ago, she and Rhett had dubbed the body of water Canoe Landing. It was where he'd fished with his dad and where he and his siblings had learned to swim. Macy too.

Embers of memories burned in the back of her mind. She snuffed them out. A million yesterdays couldn't help her solve the problems she faced today.

When Macy hiked over the hill that led to Canoe Landing, she paused. Rhett had his back to her. His shoulders made an impressive cut against the approaching sunset. Rhett had always been taller and broader than his brothers. The Wranglers and starched button-down he wore fit so well, they might as well be illegal. Under his cowboy hat she knew his hair would be naturally blond-tipped and tousled.

He was the kind of handsome that female country-western singers wrote ballads about, but it was clear he had never caught on to how attractive he was or how many hearts he could have broken if he'd wanted to. Rhett wasn't like that.

She fiddled with the end of her flannel.

Kodiak bounded out of the water, dropped a soggy ball at Rhett's feet and then leaned around his leg and let out a low growl. Her yellowish eyes pinned on Macy.

Rhett pivoted to see what had captured his dog's attention. His eyebrows rose when he spotted Macy. His eyes were such a shocking shade of blue and his tanned skin only made them stand out more.

I'm sorry I kissed you and ran off.

*I'm sorry I never returned your calls. I was con-
fused. I let too much time pass.*

I ruined everything.

She swallowed the words rushing through her mind.

Macy tucked her thumb over her scarred finger.
"You snuck out the back?"

Rhett patted Kodiak's head before he lobbed the
ball in a wide arc. It splashed down in the middle of
the lake. The dog became a blur of brown along the
shoreline. She dove into the water, going under before
paddling wildly.

Rhett crossed his arms over his chest. "I didn't know
I was supposed to check in with the assistant before
leaving."

"Listen." Macy squared her shoulders and lifted her
chin a notch higher to hold his gaze. "We need to come
to some sort of a truce here or else work is going to
become very miserable, very fast."

Unless he fired her, of course. Rhett had the power
and ability to do it, so while she wanted to push him
and fight with him over the foster-related events at the
ranch, she needed to tread the subject carefully.

Good thing Macy had cooled down considerably
since she'd locked up at the office.

Rhett shifted his line of vision to watch Kodiak
swimming in circles. "I suppose you're right." He
glanced back at her. "We can't keep acting like the
walls of Jericho to each other if we're going to be sharing office space."

"You're…you're going to let me stay then?"

The notch in Rhett's throat bobbed. His gaze traced

her face. "This is your home, Mace. You love your job."
He looked away. "I don't plan on taking that from you."

"Thank you," she whispered. She tentatively
touched his arm. "Rhett, I'm so sorry about your dad.
He loved you a lot."

His bicep tensed under her touch. " I thought we had
plenty of years left. I never thought—" A harsh exhale
of breath escaped his lips. "What a stupid thing to say.
No one expects these sorts of things."

"I'm here." She squeezed his arm lightly, then let
go. "If you need someone."

His brow bunched as his eyes cut back to her. "We
haven't spoken in three years."

"The walls of Jericho fell down." Macy slipped her
hands into her pockets. "You know that, right?"

A muscle in Rhett's jaw popped, once, twice. "I'm
a… I'm not looking for friendship again, Mace. Not
with you. I think it's important to put that out on the
table."

She knew Rhett hadn't meant the words maliciously;
he was just stating reality. Rhett was a man who dealt
in facts. It was his attempt at being forthright. Chival-
rous even, making certain no one would get the wrong
idea from the get-go.

But, wow, what he said smarted.

Not with you.

Those three words stung her worse than any pit
viper ever could.

After Brock's funeral she'd foolishly hoped she and
Rhett might have been able to let bygones be bygones
and fall back into the easy, lifelong friendship they had
once shared. A part of her had even wondered if God

was drawing them close for another chance at being together in the way Macy had always wanted.

Well, consider that balloon popped and tossed in the garbage.

"Understood." She kept her voice even. If they weren't going to deal in niceties she might as well get down to business. "We need to talk about the foster programs."

Rhett let out one sharp laugh that held no hint of humor. "Which one?"

"Let's start with Camp Firefly." As if summoned by her mention, a pack of fireflies began to flit over the lake. Kodiak had noticed them too and began snapping her giant muzzle in their direction. The little bugs looped and pitched in oblong circles around each other. Encouraged by their presence Macy said, "You can't cut it."

Rhett cocked his head. "Who said I was?"

"You did." She jabbed a finger in his direction. "Mr. I'm-Looking-into-Cancelling-Things."

Rhett rubbed his finger across his lips. Was he hiding a smile? Was this a *joke* to him?

Kodiak slogged out of the water. She gave a shake, sending droplets flying, and then walked toward her master, her tail wagging the whole way.

"I can't make any promises about next summer, but with only three months left until camp it would be hard to cut it." Kodiak dropped down at his feet. She adjusted to lay her head near his boots, leaving wet marks on the legs of his jeans. "Some of the kids have already gotten letters inviting them. No matter what you think of me, I'm not heartless, Macy." He cut his gaze to collide with hers. "I promise, I'm not."

"I know you're not," she whispered into the growing dark. Rhett had never been a spiteful person. Hurt, but never hurtful.

They both stared out over the water as the sun tucked itself further into tomorrow.

"It's just…" Macy looked up into the sky as if she could find the right words somewhere in the clouds. "Your dad really cared about these programs. He cared about each and every foster kid. I'd hate to see *any* of the programs get cut."

Rhett stiffened. "My dad cared more about those foster kids than he did about his own flesh and blood." There was no trace of a smile left on his features. Only hurt mixed with a hint of disappointment. "You know I'm right."

Bringing up Brock had been a mistake, but it had easily slipped out. Brock and Rhett's relationship had been tense since Wade's death. They'd fought over blame instead of helping each other grieve. Macy had never understood how the fault of a boat capsizing in the Gulf of Mexico could belong to either of them.

Rhett tapped his thigh, causing Kodiak to rise and follow after him.

"Rhett, please," she said. "The foster programs, they're important. They were started because—" Because of you, she almost said. *Right or wrong, they were supposed to be Brock's love letter to you.* "There has to be a way to make it all work."

"It's late, Mace. We can talk about it tomorrow." He

tipped his hat and walked past her up the hill in the direction of the Jarrett house.

Macy stared after him, watching Kodiak's tail bob in rhythm with Rhett's footfall—the whole time wanting to call after him, wanting to spill her secret so he could understand once and for all. So she could help him work through the hurt he felt over his father.

But she could never tell Rhett that he'd once been one of those children in need.

That Brock and Leah Jarrett had adopted him.

Chapter Two

When Rhett padded into the kitchen at the family ranch the next morning, Shannon offered him a cup of coffee with a sad smile.

He declined. Shannon consumed at least six cups of the stuff a day, but Rhett had never taken to it. That hardly stopped his sister from trying to get him to drink it whenever she could.

However, he wished he was a coffee drinker because it had been a long night.

Rhett bit back a yawn. "Does Mom walk the halls yelling like that often?"

Shannon nodded, swiping at her eyes. Then she took a long swig from her mug.

Guilt stabbed through Rhett's chest. Strong and palpable.

For the last three years he'd been gone, running Straight Arrow Retrievers, his dog-training business more than a hundred miles away from Red Dog Ranch. For his mom's sake, Rhett had made a shaky truce with his dad and had visited the ranch a few weekends a year. It had been difficult to find days to visit when Macy wasn't going to be on property or he would have visited more often. Foolish now that he thought about all he had missed. All for stubborn pride. He had missed his mother's decline, missed so many days when he could have been spending time with her. Rhett rubbed his jaw.

He had kept in touch with Shannon, Cassidy and Piper with phone calls and video chats and they had often made the trip out his way for visits when he hadn't been able to come home.

But he hadn't been around when his mom had started showing symptoms. Hadn't gone along to the countless doctor appointments. Hadn't been a part of the discussion when her plan of care was decided. And having only been back living in the family house for three days, Rhett scarcely knew how to speak to his mother any longer.

Dementia.

Such a small word for such a life-altering disease.

Before now the extent of his knowledge had sadly been gleaned from TV ads that rattled off more about the dangers of the marketed drug than actually showing the truth of the illness. Commercials that depicted smiling elderly people watching their grandchildren play or sitting hand in hand with their equally elderly spouse.

All lies.

Rhett hadn't been at Red Dog Ranch to watch his mom's mind deteriorate, but Shannon had. Boone had too, up until he had enrolled in a divinity school last year, moving his wife and daughter out of state in the process.

Rhett opened his mouth to say something to Shannon but closed it just as quickly. What was there to say? "I'm sorry" sounded small. Too little, too late.

Six months ago Brock had hired a nurse to be with Mom during the day while he was working and he managed her care at night, but now with Brock gone… they needed to figure something out. Rhett made a mental note to pull out his mom's insurance information and check over the plan to see what it would cover. The day nurse always arrived before breakfast every morning, but Rhett needed to look into the possibility of having someone with her at night, as well.

Ever present, Kodiak followed him to the fridge.

"Not much in there," Shannon offered. "You'd do better to head to the mess hall. Cassidy does most of the staff meals there." She jerked her chin to indicate the direction of the mess hall. It was located where the biggest hills began to roll through their property. Their father had insisted on building the dining hall there so that a huge, long basement could be constructed into the hill. All the nonperishable bulk food used to cook staff meals and feed the kids who came for summer camp could be stored there in a cooler environment without wasting tons of energy. The concrete basement also served as a great spot to find momentary relief from the heat of summer. Brock had searched for a contractor who would build into the shape of the land like that for a long time. Basements were rare in Texas.

His mom shuffled into the room, her hand resting on her nurse's arm. Rhett had seen plenty of his parents' wedding photos and snapshots of their dating history to know that his mother had always been a beautiful woman and maybe even a touch regal in how she carried herself. Now in her midsixties, he thought she looked a bit like the actress Helen Mirren. Outwardly she appeared healthy, but her pale blue eyes told the real story…she looked through him vacantly. She smiled pleasantly at him, almost blandly, as the red-haired nurse helped her into her chair.

A large common room made up the heart of their home. Vaulted ceilings with exposed beams gave the house a grand bearing, and a stone fireplace in the sitting room only added to that feeling. Every stone had been mined from Jarrett-held land. The kitchen flowed directly into a dining room and the large sitting area. In the sitting area, the wall without the fireplace boasted two-story-high floor-to-ceiling windows. From Mom's vantage point, she could gaze out to the wide lake where he took Kodiak for her swims and beyond into a field of bluebonnets.

Her chair looked as if it was about to swallow her petite frame. As she gazed around the room, her eyes never really landed on anything in particular. It struck Rhett that she looked lost.

Lost and scared.

His throat felt as if someone had stuffed a bale of hay down it, followed by some of the pebbles that made up the driveway. Rhett swallowed hard, once, twice, three times before he could get any words out. "How are you this morning?"

She pursed her lips. "Do you know where Brock is? I've looked everywhere but, by the cat's yarn, I can't find him."

Rhett glanced at Shannon, who gave an infinitesimal shake of her head. *Don't tell her. Don't correct her about Dad. Don't correct her at all.* Shannon had gone over the rules with him in regard to how to deal with Mom a handful of times in the days since he'd been back. But every time Mom asked… Well, someone might as well have kicked him in the stomach while wearing steel-toed boots. And then sucker-punched him in the jaw for good measure afterward.

Their mom had been present at the wake and funeral. She'd wept with Boone and Rhett each on either side of her, holding her up. She *knew.*

But right now, she didn't. Her mind was living in the safer Land of Before.

He wouldn't lie to his mother, but he'd learned quickly there was no reason to cause her undue emotional trauma either.

Rhett cleared his throat. "I haven't seen him in some time."

True. Far too true.

His mother dipped her head. With shaking fingers she traced a swirling pattern into the armrest of her oversized chair. "He's probably off somewhere with Wade, don't you think? It feels like forever since I saw my baby boy."

Shannon's coffee mug clattered against the kitchen island's stone countertop. She braced a hand on the counter and the other was pressed against her heart. "She mentions him—" her whispered voice broke "—all the time. I can't…" Her shoulders trembled as she hurried out of the kitchen.

Rhett wanted to go after her, but what comfort could he really offer? The family had lost Wade when he was only nineteen years old. Nothing he would say to his sister could change the truth of what had occurred. Wade was gone and Rhett couldn't make the anguish of losing her twin disappear.

Grief over Wade threatened to swallow Rhett in equal measure to what he felt over losing his father. Wade had stormed off spewing hurtful words at the whole family the day Rhett had cornered him, confronting Wade about every horrible thing Wade was involved in.

You know what? Don't worry. You'll never have to see my pathetic face again. Wade's final words came back to bite Rhett. His brother had left the ranch and headed straight for the Gulf of Mexico and boarded a small party boat. When the boat capsized everyone on board had been too intoxicated to get off in time, to radio for help.

Wade had been right. They never got to see his face again.

Brock had blamed Rhett for Wade's death. Rhett shouldn't have spoken to his brother that way. Wade would still be with them if Rhett hadn't confronted him. But Rhett had shot back that it was Brock's fault for allowing Wade to flounder for so long, allowing him to go down a wrong path years before he drowned. For investing more into the nonprofit at the ranch than his own son.

Rhett and his dad had never completely patched the bridge between them after that. Rhett walking away from the ranch had only solidified the tension in the relationship. If given the chance, Rhett would have handled both Wade and his father differently.

There were things Rhett would take back if he could. So many things.

But right now he could only move forward. Do better. Be present.

Rhett shifted from one foot to the other. "I believe you're right, Mom, about Wade and Dad being together." His voice caught on the last word and he prayed she wouldn't notice.

She folded her hands in her lap and looked toward the lake. "Just as I thought. Still…" Her voice trailed off for a heartbeat. "I'm looking forward to when Wade comes back. I long for the day you and him are in the same room together again."

"Mom," Rhett said, keeping his voice even. "Wade may never come home."

"Don't you say something so horrible." His mom met his gaze. "He will. My boy will."

Before he left the house Rhett pressed a kiss to his mom's forehead, made sure she didn't need anything else and checked in with the nurse, Louisa. He should have headed straight to the mess hall, but his boots pointed south of there, in the direction of the little white chapel his father had built soon after he started Camp Firefly.

Rhett checked his phone. He was so used to having it on silent because the ring tones and even the vibrate setting interfered with training dogs. Most of them he trained using whistles and other noises so distractions were unwelcome. He had texts from a few of his clients who had been in the middle of sessions when his dad had passed so he'd put them on hold. They'd been patient, but training built week by week and he needed to either continue with them or send them to a new trainer, or else the dogs would lose their momentum.

Rhett made a split-second decision—offering them time slots if they were willing to come out to the ranch and refunding them if they didn't want to drive so far. One client texted back immediately, confirming a time slot for the next day. They were eager because they already had their dog signed up for contests. Two more asked for refunds and referrals to other trainers.

As he approached the church, he noticed that someone had used large white stones to outline a path leading to the chapel's front door. It was set up on the hill nearest to the mess hall. A wide cross had been erected on the hill years before the chapel's creation. At the end of each camp session, his father had the kids write on rocks the last night and lay them at the foot of the cross—usually a word symbolizing something they were trusting God for.

Distantly, he wondered if they'd kept up that practice after the church had been built. Would he have to lead that ceremony this summer?

Rhett tested the door. Open. He slipped inside, slid off his hat and stooped to dodge the end of the bell rope. Sunlight streamed through the stained-glass windows, painting the dull brown carpeting with a brilliant prism of colors.

Do you know the heart of God in this matter? Have you sought that out, son?

Of course he hadn't. If he sought out what God wanted…it wasn't worth it. If the Bible was true— and Rhett believed it was—God seemed to ask for dangerous, impossible things. Rhett was trying so hard to keep himself together, he couldn't afford dangerous faith right now.

Rhett gripped the edge of a pew. He hadn't willingly set foot inside a church in five years. Not since learning about Wade's death. His father's funeral had been held in a church, but he didn't count that time. He had entered that church out of duty, not choice.

If Rhett's own father—his flesh and blood—hadn't cared enough to know about his dreams and worries, he couldn't imagine God would either. Much like Brock had been, God was busy with far more important things than Rhett and his heart. After all, God had a universe to run. Rhett's small slice of the world hardly measured up to that. And he couldn't blame God for not concerning Himself with what must be Rhett's miniscule burdens in the very grand scale of human history. But it sure made Rhett want to keep his distance.

Rhett considered himself a Christian, but he certainly didn't like to bother God.

"You may not care about me, and that's fine." A wash of embarrassment flooded through Rhett at the idea of talking out loud, but he pressed on. "But Shannon… Please…could You be there for Shannon? She's been through a lot and I don't know how to help her. And Mom, God, please. It's hard. Seeing her that way."

The weight of so many new responsibilities sagged onto his shoulders. His father's death hadn't only made the ranch his obligation, but in a very real way Rhett had become the head of the Jarrett family. A role he wasn't sure he was cut out for. Between worrying over what his mother needed and his concerns for Shannon, he already felt stretched thin.

And then there was Macy. Macy touching his arm by the lake last night. Macy saying she was there if he needed her. Macy studying him with those large brown eyes that seemed to know everything about him. Rhett swallowed hard. Working alongside her was going to be difficult because the truth was, he missed his friend.

But he couldn't forget that he'd offered her a job at his business and when she'd showed up on his doorstep it was to turn him down, to pick the ranch—to pick his dad—over being near him. Worse, when he had tried to usher her inside so they could talk things over she had grabbed his shirt and kissed him—a kiss he had never known he had wanted until that point but afterward had never been able to get out of his head.

Then Macy had run off.

Rhett had left messages for two weeks. Messages she hadn't returned.

Now he had to see her every day and it was hard to forget their old friendship, the jokes they had shared over the years. That kiss.

Kodiak whimpered behind him.

Attempting to alleviate the tightness building in his chest, he blew out a long stream of air.

It didn't help.

Macy wrapped her fingers around the mug in her hands and prayed she wasn't making a huge mistake.

From the wide bank of windows in the mess hall, she had watched Rhett veer off the walkway and head toward the chapel. Witnessed him duck inside. The minutes had ticked by and curiosity had gotten the better of her.

Patience might be a virtue, but it was one that Macy sorely lacked.

Now in front of the chapel, she rested her hand on the doorknob and sucked in a fortifying breath.

Rhett did not want her friendship—he'd made that crystal clear last night—but coworkers should be civil to each other. An employee could check and see how her boss was doing without it meaning friendship, right?

Besides, she knew him too well to ignore the fact that he was obviously under a lot of stress. Her heart went out to him. If only she could convince him to share his burdens. He didn't have to manage everything alone. He wasn't alone at all.

She opened the door and let it close with a thump behind her so as not to startle him with her presence. He swiveled around in his seat. His hair was sticking out in adorable angles, reminding her of old times when he'd been a sleepy, hopeful boy swapping secrets with her around the campfire instead of the serious man he'd grown into. An awful twinge of longing stirred through her. She missed the Rhett who had been all dreams and optimism. He had changed once he hit high school, closing up a little more with each football game his father failed to show up to. Each broken promise.

But his hair wasn't sleep mussed. The particular style he was sporting at the moment had been caused by him grabbing the tips of his hair and yanking as he thought through something. She'd seen him do it enough times to recognize the signs.

"I can leave." He rose and put his hat on. Ever beside him, the large dog stood when he did. "It's all yours."

She held her free hand up in a stop motion. "I came to see you."

His left eyebrow arched.

"Here." She extended the mug and walked down the aisle. "A peace offering."

"What are we making peace for?"

"Last night at the lake."

His large dog edged to sit a few inches in front of the toes of his boots as if the beast was concerned that Macy might try some ninja-attack move on Rhett at any second. As far as Macy could tell, the animal had appointed itself as Rhett's personal guard.

As if a man with muscles like Rhett needed one.

"Is that thing safe?" Macy looked down at the dog.

He nodded. "She won't do anything unless I tell her to."

She handed Rhett the mug. "Earl Grey Crème black."

His features immediately softened and he cocked his head as he accepted the mug. "You remembered my favorite tea?"

"Your favorite *drink*," she corrected. Unlike most of the cowboys and staff at Red Dog Ranch, Rhett had never taken to coffee. After she'd tried the Earl Grey Crème black tea that he preferred, she had to admit it was delicious. It was a perfect balance of milk, sugar, vanilla and bergamot flavors while still delivering a welcome kick of caffeine.

My dad cared more about those foster kids than he did about his own flesh and blood.

Regret formed a lump in her throat. She glanced at the light bleeding through the stained glass windows, then glanced back at Rhett. "I'm sorry. Last night when I brought up the foster programs and your dad… I know that still hurts."

He blew out a long stream of air, looked away. Nodded to accept her apology.

A part of Macy wanted to tell Rhett that Brock had loved him and the rest of his family. Maybe Brock had been bad at showing it, but they had been his life. His passion for foster kids had bloomed from his love of family—he'd wanted to give kids without homes the same opportunities and security that his children had been afforded.

But right now wasn't the time.

With Brock gone, it might never be the right time.

Macy searched for a way to connect with Rhett, anything that could encourage conversation. She needed to establish easy communication between the two of them so they could work alongside each other for the best of the ranch. And if she was being honest, her heart squeezed at the sight of her oldest friend looking so… lost. Despite what he had said last night, she wanted to connect—wanted him to know he wasn't alone.

Her gaze landed on his dog. *Perfect.*

"So, when did you acquire your ever-present shadow?" She smiled, hoping he could see the words were kindly meant.

"Kodiak." The dog perked up when he said her name. It was a good name for her because the dog's coat was the same red-brown color of a Kodiak bear. Her fur went slightly curly near her neck and back haunches.

Rhett grinned down at Kodiak and stroked behind

her ears. "She was a training failure." His voice was warm. "Weren't you, girl?"

"She looks well trained to me."

His smile dimmed when he looked away from Kodiak to meet Macy's gaze. "What I mean is, her owner brought her to me to be trained and then she bonded to me and refused to go back with her owner." He crossed his arms over his chest. "It's not generally seen as a good thing."

"Well, she seems happy with the arrangement," Macy said.

"Her breed is extremely loyal." Kodiak let out a groan, protesting at the absence of his pets. "So once they pick their person it's an almost impossible bond to sever." He relented and tapped his fingertips on her head. "The breed can be hardheaded."

"Her breed?"

"She's a Chessie." He must have noticed Macy's confusion. "Sorry, that's dogspeak for a Chesapeake Bay retriever. People hear the retriever part and think they'll be like Labs or goldens, who love everyone and everything, but Chessies aren't like that. They're affectionate with their family but are extremely protective and don't warm to strangers easily."

As if to demonstrate what Rhett was talking about, Kodiak butted her head against Rhett's knee but kept her yellow eyes trained on Macy the whole time. The dog was definitely suspicious of her.

Macy inched back a half step. "Does that happen a lot? Training failure?"

"Thankfully, she was my only one. But her owner was my first client when I started the business so failing on the first one…" He rubbed his chin. "Well, let's just say that was like a bull kick to the ego. I almost thought about turning tail and coming home." He cleared his throat. "Back here, I mean."

She'd never known he considered returning to Red Dog Ranch.

"Rhett, that last time we saw each other…" Macy said.

When I kissed you.

Rhett held up a hand. "We're different people than we were three years ago, Mace. I don't see the point of backtracking down that road."

When her boyfriend had broken up with her, she'd driven the hundred miles. She'd shown up on Rhett's doorstep. He had thought she was there about the job he'd offered her, but she had grabbed his shirt and yanked him into a kiss. She would never be able to forget how his body had gone rigid. He hadn't returned the kiss and, when she broke away quickly, his eyes had been wide, horrified. "Why did you do that?" he'd asked. Repeated it twice.

And she had turned around and run back to her car. Too mortified to face him for months afterward. It had been the action of a woman who had read a man wrong.

So completely wrong.

Rhett had never cared for her. Not like that.

Not like she'd wanted him to.

Macy rubbed her thumb over the jagged scar on her pointer finger. "Why didn't you come back home? After Kodiak, I mean?"

He lifted his shoulder in a half shrug. "There was nothing to come back to."

I'm not looking for friendship again, Mace. Not with you.

Macy tugged her inner shield closer in an attempt to make his words bounce off of her harmlessly, but they went around her defenses and struck the tender places left in her heart. She'd thought she had walled off the part of her that cared about Rhett—about all men—because she knew there were no romantic relationships waiting in her future. Not now, not ever. If Rhett, who had known her better than anyone in the world, could see her completely and find her lacking… could not want her…then no one would.

No one wanted Macy Howell. Not for the long haul. Not her father, not the ex-boyfriend who had started the fight between her and Rhett three years ago and not her closest friend.

Why didn't anyone ever fight to be with her? What made her not worth it?

Because something's wrong with you.

Hot shame poured through her body.

Macy took another step back and fought the warring desires to slam her finger into Rhett's chest as she gave him a piece of her mind or to turn and run so she could go lick her wounds in private. But if she wanted to help the foster kids, she couldn't do either. She needed to be able to work with him, talk to him.

Relax. This isn't personal. It will never be personal again.

She forced a long drag of air through her nose.

Macy might not matter to anyone, but she could make her life matter by fighting for the kids. By making sure Rhett didn't end up cutting the programs they all looked forward to.

She let a breath rattle out of her. "Kodiak's a good fit here." *There, back to a safe topic.* Macy gestured toward Kodiak. "Red dog. She could be the ranch's mascot."

Rhett frowned. "She's brown."

Macy narrowed her eyes, pretending to examine Kodiak. "It's definitely a reddish brown." She wrapped her fingers over her opposite elbow.

Kodiak looked up at Rhett with such adoration.

"You were always fond of dogs," Macy said. "I guess training them was a given."

"Dogs make sense." He shrugged. "You don't have to be anyone special to gain their loyalty. A dog is simple to figure out. They only ask for kindness and time spent together."

"And treats."

He smiled. "And treats."

She hugged her stomach as she watched him walk out of the chapel, her mind roiling with so many emotions it was difficult to sort through them. But one thing was certain: it was going to be near impossible not to fall for Rhett Jarrett all over again.

Chapter Three

Kodiak snored near Rhett's chair as he sifted through the files Macy had left in his office yesterday. Each name and picture made his heart twist.

Gabe Coalfield, seventeen, wants to be a veterinarian someday.

Harris Oaks, eighteen, would be happy to do anything to have a job.

Deena Rich, seventeen, just wants to feel useful for once.

Rhett pushed the papers away and covered them with one of the financial ledgers. As he made decisions he wanted to continue being able to think of all the children involved in terms of a faceless, nameless group—not as individuals with hearts and dreams.

With ambitions in their lives he might crush if he closed the ranch's doors to them.

He pinched the bridge of his nose.

Why had he been put in this situation?

Going over the calculations in his father's books had only solidified Rhett's decision to cut programs. Brock had neglected the cattle business that went along with the ranch, among other things. While the Jarretts enjoyed the cushion of an ample bank account for now and healthy investments in a few other areas, the ranch hadn't turned a profit in years, which meant Brock had been slowly dipping into the family's savings in order to keep the daily functions of the ranch running.

Fine to do once in a while, but the records showed it had become the way of Red Dog Ranch. That couldn't stand any longer. If they kept operating in such a manner, eventually funds would run out. Money Rhett needed to pay for his mom's medical care. Funds he needed to use to compensate staff dependent on the ranch for their livelihoods.

Additionally, he wanted to be able to leave Wade's daughter, Piper, and Boone's daughter, Hailey, something someday. As well as any other nieces and nephews who might come into the family down the road.

His father may not have cared about the Jarrett legacy—about providing for the long-term future of their flesh and blood—but Rhett did.

And there was nothing wrong with that.

Rhett dug his elbows into the desktop and sat straighter in his chair.

He would not allow himself to feel guilty for doing the right thing.

One of the teenager's photos had slipped loose when he shuffled them under the ledgers. Rhett picked it up and studied it. The girl had crooked teeth; her smile appeared forced. The look in her eyes—lonely and beaten by life—gutted him. She would have an internship, but she represented so many kids waiting for an opportunity, a break. One he was considering taking away.

He turned the picture over.

A soft knock on his door. Macy, more than likely.

Rhett massaged his temples. Earlier in the chapel he had opened up way too much to Macy. How did she do that to him? They'd been around each other for twenty-four hours and his resolve to stay distant had already crumbled.

And she lived a stone's throw from his house, so even when they weren't in the office he couldn't escape her presence. They hadn't spoken in three years and yet she *knew* him. Knew how his mind worked. Knew how he ticked. It was unnerving.

He dropped his hands to his desk and studied the spot on his arm where her fingertips had rested.

Since they were little, Macy had always had a way of cutting through his nonsense and zeroing in on pieces of Rhett he thought he'd hidden from the world. Then again, he'd always been terrible at playing hide-and-seek.

When they were young, it had been one of Macy's favorite games. She'd never failed to find him and find him quickly. However, she had also possessed a knack for unearthing the most unimaginable spots to hide in. Once they were a little older it had become near impossible to ever locate her. Most times she ended up having to reveal her spot, no matter how hard he'd searched.

It would seem he was still terrible at hiding from her.

"Come in."

She opened the door, clipboard in hand. Her smile

was tentative. "Have you had a chance to go over the files I left?"

He nodded.

She took the chair on the other side of his desk. "Great. Let's decide who each of them will be placed with."

"Do you know what a liability it is having them here? Our insurance rates are sky-high with all the minors on the property." He had spent a chunk of his morning reading legal nonsense and now his head felt foggy with all the information.

"The social workers have signed off on the waivers," she reminded him.

Rhett sighed and slid the files to her side of the desk. "You can go ahead and make all the placement decisions. You've been at the ranch all this time and I'm only just back, so I'm deferring to your knowledge here on what's the best fit for each of them."

She didn't move to pick up the paperwork. Macy opened her mouth. Closed it. Looked toward his mom's painting and then back at him. "I'm more than happy to help." She spoke each word deliberately. "But your dad always wanted to be a part of the process. He said it was—"

"Mace," he cut in. "If you haven't noticed by now, I'm not my dad."

"I realize that. I should have phrased that differently." She hugged her clipboard to her chest. "No one is asking you to be a replica of Brock."

Wasn't that *exactly* what everyone wanted him to be? His dad's will had set him on a lifelong course where he'd have to hear again and again and again how he didn't measure up to Brock. If he succeeded with the ranch he'd have to hear how he was following in his dad's steps, and if he failed he'd have to hear how disappointed his dad would have been.

"Aren't they?" He hated how hoarse his voice sounded.

She offered him the hint of a smile. Her wide brown eyes studied his face. "I'm not."

Wasn't she though? After all, wasn't she the one who kept bringing up how his dad had done things?

"I really promise I'm not." She gave a small shrug. "It's just really hard to strike him from all conversations when I'm missing him."

Understandable. Talking about Brock was clearly healing for her, but the same thing opened Rhett's wounds deeper.

"Then what do you want, Mace?" His question was soft, guarded. "Because when you look at me like that…"

She skewed her lips to the side as if trying to find the right words. "I'm just wondering where the boy I knew went."

He sighed. She might as well have said she didn't like the person he'd become.

Not that it mattered. He shouldn't care about what an old friend thought of him.

Rhett crossed his arms. "He grew up."

"That's a pity," Macy said. "He had this amazing ability to dream big but plan well, stay rooted and focused—something this place really needs. He had the heart and determination to grow Red Dog Ranch into an amazing place if he'd wanted to. I think that boy could have shaped the ranch into something beyond what his father possibly ever could have."

He clenched his teeth and reminded himself that Macy was just being Macy. She'd been known to kick a hornets' nest before—literally. She'd treat him no differently. It was her nature to push and he had loved that about her.

Just…not right now.

He pressed his palms against his armrests. "You finished?"

"For now, sure. Forever?" she asked. "Not a chance."

Rhett couldn't hold in the chuckle that escaped from his lips, though it had an edge of desperation in it. "I don't doubt it one bit."

This was the Macy he remembered—his Macy— someone who would stand against the wind and glare at a coming storm. Someone who didn't flinch.

Well, not *his* Macy. He wasn't quite sure where that thought had come from.

Macy ran a slender finger down the to-do list on her clipboard. "Now, about the Easter egg hunt…"

"Wait. That's still on?" He flipped through a stack of paperwork in his dad's inbox. "I'm sorry, I'm not caught up on everything. I thought we still had time to alter things." And he had figured his father was waiting until the last minute to reach out to previous vendors like he always had. His father had possessed a huge heart, but he hadn't been much of a planner. Rhett had been considering his father's lack of planning a blessing for once because it would make the event easier to cancel if nothing had been set in stone yet.

Her eyebrows shot up. "Of course it's still on."

Rhett rubbed his forehead. "How much do we usually spend on it? In total."

She thumbed through a few pages on her clipboard. "At least ten thousand. We always have a huge turnout," she added quickly.

Some people might have thought she was estimating high, but Rhett didn't believe she was. The Red Dog Ranch Hunt had become an event that drew many foster families from far away. People booked every room at nearby hotels in order to attend. The event had taken on a life of its own, complete with his father hiring a private helicopter pilot to drop candy over the fields as the children watched. When it came to these events his father had been nothing if not excessive. They also provided a full ham supper for around a hundred people who stayed afterward. The dinner was a ticketed event that raised money specifically for a college scholarship program for foster kids. Not to mention purchasing the eggs and prizes, paying staff to run various games and do setup, hiring a company to put up and tear down decorations and seating. Renting outhouses and paying for random other items.

Honestly, she was probably guessing low.

Rhett flipped the ledger to the latest financial records and twisted the book in Macy's direction. "Tell me how we can afford to host any event with this kind of bank account?"

Macy sucked in a sharp breath. "I had no idea he'd let it get this bad." She held up a finger. "He would sometimes mention that we should cut expenses here and there and then never did it so I figured we were fine. I never pushed the issue."

"Seriously?" He cocked an eyebrow. How could she not know? She'd been his assistant.

Macy waggled her head. "I promise you, I had no idea. You know how your dad could be about these things. He managed the accounts himself. I entered the bills into the finance software and entered payroll, but I only handled submitting those expenditures for his approval. I didn't balance the accounts. I never *saw* the actual money in the account." She pulled the ledgers closer. "Oh, Rhett. What a mess."

He believed Macy. Brock had been a man who kept many things close to his chest. Judging by how she had responded, Rhett knew she had never seen these books. Hadn't realized the foster programs were draining the family's personal accounts.

Rhett pressed his fingers against his forehead. "My dad had a big heart."

She looked like she might cry. "He had a *huge* heart, but that doesn't excuse this." She gestured toward the ledgers.

Rhett nodded. "Huge heart. Not a lick of business sense."

Macy snaked her hand across the desk to cover his. "You have a better sense for these sorts of things than he ever had." She gave his hand a pump.

Rhett slipped his hand from under hers and it instantly felt cold, lacking. He could have so easily turned it over and leached comfort from her, but he had to keep his head on his shoulders when it came to Macy. Uncle Travis was right. Macy could help him— but Rhett had to stay focused on keeping their partnership about working toward what was best for the business.

"So you understand why we have to nix the egg hunt this year?" Rhett asked. "Can you double check the recent bills to see if the ranch has made any deposits to secure vendors? I doubt it, but a quick check can't hurt." His dad had been notorious about scrambling at the last minute to get things done. Rhett tucked the ledger away. "That's potentially thousands of dollars we can immediately save."

Macy held up a hand. "I think recouping as much as we can is the right step. But, Rhett, we can't outright cancel the egg hunt." She tugged a newspaper clipping from her stack of papers and shoved it toward him. "It's already run in the paper."

Of course his dad would set up the announcement while procrastinating on the actual work of pulling together the hunt.

Instead he groaned. The sound made Kodiak's ears twitch. "This is bad."

Macy set down her clipboard. "What if we can run the event without touching your family's money? Or at least, minimally touching it. We can do this. We just have to think it through."

"I don't see how that's possible."

"If we work together, I think we can secure donations and get others to pitch in. I'll look through the bills and see if we can get refunds on the few things he might have secured, and if not refunds maybe we can renegotiate the contract terms." Her eyes lighted with excitement. He could practically see the wheels turning in her head. "If we can do this without too much expense, are you on board?"

"I'm tempted to say yes." Rhett was worried it would be hard to throw an event together so quickly, but his dad had done it all the time. Besides, Rhett knew not to doubt Macy's tenacity. "Though it will be a lot of work in a short amount of time."

"We've faced bigger obstacles together," she said. Macy sent him an excited smile. "I don't doubt what we can accomplish if we both commit to this."

He couldn't say no. Not to that smile. "All right, then. Let's do this."

"Great." She popped up. "In that case, I've got a lot of work to do so I'm going to dive in right away." She reached to grab the clipboard she'd forgotten in her exuberance. "We can do this."

He gave her a thumbs-up.

When she was about to leave, Macy hesitated in the doorway, her back to him. "You know, you don't have to be your father." She slowly turned to face him, her hand braced on the frame. "But you do need to be the best Rhett you can be. You need to live up to the potential God's placed inside you." She moved her hand from the frame so she could hug her clipboard to her chest. "Understood?"

Standing there with her chin held high, her eyes slightly narrowed at him and pure challenge lighting her features... Rhett had never seen anyone more beautiful.

The realization forced all the oxygen from his lungs.

"Mace, I—" His voice cracked.

"I'm going to be here, beside you in this." She

pointed at him. "And I'm going to keep challenging you."

That's what he was afraid of.

In the following days, Macy tossed herself into researching how to plan a charity event and began to make a list of all the companies and local residents she could call. She made a second list that she dubbed her pie-in-the-sky list that was made up of actors, famous singers, news anchors at the big stations, radio deejays—anyone she believed was worth reaching out to. Even if one or two of them chose to give a monetary donation, it could make a huge difference. Texas was home to plenty of celebrities and many of them were proud to support Texas-based events.

Hey, a person could dream.

It was something she'd learned from Rhett when they were young. Too bad he'd lost his wide-eyed belief in chasing after big dreams somewhere along the way. Though his dog-training business had been a bit of a dream chase for him, hadn't it? Maybe there was still a part of the boy she knew somewhere inside the jaded man. Deep, deep inside.

Macy found herself praying while she worked— often more for Rhett than anyone else.

Please help me help him. Give me the right things to say when we interact. I know he's hurting and he probably hasn't talked about it to anyone.

A boy with freckles and a wide grin ducked his head into her office. "Hey there, Miss Howell."

She rose from her desk and smiled at the teenage boy. Gabe had attended Camp Firefly for the past four summers and he volunteered hours at the ranch, mucking stalls and helping feed the horses, already. Making him an official intern had been a no-brainer.

The interns were starting today.

Rhett was working with one of his dog-training clients in the far field again, so they had agreed that she would give the kids a quick tour and then hand them off to their appointed mentors to shadow for the day. Macy was happy Rhett had started seeing his clients again and wanted to do whatever she could to encourage him to keep his business alive. It had only been two appointments so far, but she knew he loved training dogs and didn't want him to have to lose Straight Arrow Retrievers.

Initially Macy had challenged Rhett about working with the foster kids, but she had promised herself she would stop forcing Rhett to do things the way his father had. Just because Brock had insisted on training the interns himself, it didn't mean Rhett had to. With that in mind, she had told him she would help run things—help take the load—so it was nice to see he was willing to trust her to do just that.

Macy joined Gabe outside and introduced herself to the seven other interns. She rattled off the speech she'd heard Brock recite multiple times but knew she wasn't doing it justice. Normally Brock spent the first two or three days showing the interns the entire ranch and explaining every part of its workings. He introduced them to every staff member and made sure they knew what to do in an emergency. He got to know them and made sure each one felt valued at the ranch. But with plans for the egg hunt looming over her, each day—

each hour—was an imperative for Macy to seek donations and coordinate every aspect of the event. She also had to start devoting time to mapping out the plans for Camp Firefly because summer would be here before they knew it.

So for the first time in the history of Red Dog Ranch, Macy handed the interns over to each of their appointed mentors right after the tour and headed back to her office. She worked on drafting letters to some of the people on her second list—the dream-big list—and emailed them before her nerve waned.

Less than an hour later, Gabe banged open her door. He was panting and his face was tomato red. "There's been an accident. Miss Howell, you've got to come quick!"

Macy sprang from her desk. "What type of accident?"

Gabe was already at the front door, motioning frantically. When he saw she was following he headed out the door and started running for the closest horse enclosure. "This way."

Judson, one of the ranch's field hands who had been assigned to be Gabe's mentor, was crouched over Piper, Rhett's four-year-old niece. Piper was curled in a ball sobbing, her tiny shoulders shaking.

Rhett came tearing across the opposite field, Kodiak at his heels. Rhett's face drained of color as he dropped to his knees beside Piper and lightly brushed her long brown hair from her forehead. "What's wrong, sweetheart?" His chest heaved. No doubt Judson had radioed him and Rhett had sprinted the whole way.

Kodiak whimpered as she pranced around the pair.

"M-m-my aarrrrm," Piper wailed.

It was then that Macy noticed Piper's arm was twisted at the wrong angle. Broken. Macy's stomach threatened to pitch.

And suddenly, as she watched him crouch over Piper, Macy noticed the back of Rhett's neck turn red. "How did this happen?"

"Uncle Rrrrhett. It hu-hurts." Piper's whole body shook. "Huurrrts." Kodiak crawled forward and gave Piper a tentative lick on her cheek.

Macy hadn't noticed Judson take off when they appeared, but he must have headed for the barn. He came back, sprinting in their direction with one of the red emergency totes full of medical supplies that were stowed all over the ranch.

Judson panted. "I called Cassidy. She was in town getting groceries but she's on her way back. She should be here in minutes."

Wordlessly, Rhett took the medical bag and found the sling inside. Since Piper was so small, he knotted the top to shorten it. Then he helped her sit up.

"I'm so sorry, baby girl. This might hurt." He gingerly lifted her broken arm and set it in the sling. She let out a yelp of pain and started to cry harder, her cheeks going red.

Rhett pressed a quick kiss to the top of her head. "You're so brave. That will help your arm not move around too much until the doctor can see it."

She bit her trembling lip and nodded. Despite him living far away for much of her life, Uncle Rhett was her favorite person in the world and it was obvious that she trusted him completely. He'd given her Sheep, the miniature horse, for her birthday and her mom, Cassidy, had often talked about the weekly video chats Piper and Rhett had when he lived far away.

Cassidy's van rounded down the driveway.

Rhett scooped his niece into his arms, avoiding the injured arm.

He turned toward Macy. "Find out what happened and call me."

He gave both Judson and Gabe a significant look. Then he charged toward the van with Piper in his arms. Seconds later they watched Rhett, Cassidy and Piper head off toward the hospital.

Macy prayed that Piper would be okay and that nothing else was wrong with her, and she prayed for Rhett too. The man was fiercely protective when it came to his family and he was bound to want consequences for whoever had let Piper get hurt.

Thirty minutes later, once Macy had calmed down an upset Gabe and a profusely apologetic Judson, she called Rhett. She'd already texted with Cassidy, but she knew she needed to talk to the boss. "How's Piper?"

"Broken arm and a sprained foot." He sounded tired. "She says the kid put her on one of the big horses bareback. Is that true?"

Macy sagged into the chair at her desk. "Judson went into the barn for a minute. He knows he shouldn't have left Gabe on his own with one of the horses, but we know Gabe well. He mucks the stalls for us all the time." Macy pressed on.

"Piper knows Gabe so she ran out to see him. Gabe said Piper told him she wanted to ride the big horse so he let her sit up there. He turned his back for a second." The teenage boy had been so upset about the little girl getting hurt. He had teared up in Macy's office. "He didn't realize the horse was only green broke. He thought it was one of our calm trail horses. He didn't know, Rhett. He's just a kid himself."

When Rhett didn't say anything, she continued, "Judson was going to teach him how to work the green broke correctly, so he went to get a longer lead line. That's the only reason Gabe was out there alone." She was rambling, but Rhett had to understand that it was an accident, pure and simple. "It could have happened to any of us."

"And if Piper had said she wanted to light the mess hall on fire—" Rhett's words were clipped "—would he have let her do that too?"

Macy dropped an elbow onto her desk and pressed her forehead into her hand. "This wasn't his fault."

"So is it Judson's?"

"It was an accident, Rhett. Accidents happen." She knew it wasn't wise to get into this on the phone, but Macy had always had a hard time biting back her words. Frustration was hard to pack away for later. While Rhett lived by facts, she was fueled by emotions.

"An *accident* took my brother. An *accident* took my dad. I'm done with accidents, Mace."

Ouch. He was right. But facing losses, facing accidents, didn't mean a person should never take a risk again. "Next time—"

"There won't be a next time. Our intern program ends today."

That immediately cooled her thoughts. "You don't mean that."

"I already sent messages to all the teens."

"Rhett, please. Just hear me out," she said. "The intern program doesn't cost the ranch a cent, but it provides free labor. It makes zero sense to cut it when we're trying to save money."

"If a kid other than my niece gets hurt and someone sues us, how's that saving money? Or if an intern got hurt? Managing interns divides the staff's focus. It's really not as mutually beneficial as you might think."

"Rhett—"

"I'll talk to you later, Mace." And he was gone.

Couldn't he understand that even with a mentor nearby things could happen? People got hurt every day. It was called life. Piper was a perfect mix of curious and courageous, which meant she was always taking risks. Rhett wouldn't be able to protect his niece from every bump and bruise in life no matter how hard he tried.

He loved his family fiercely. It was a quality Macy had always found attractive about him, but she found herself wishing he cared about the foster kids too. Maybe it was wrong to put that on him—he wasn't Brock and she didn't want him to be Brock. Really she didn't.

But she was so torn between the family she loved and the children she was dedicated to helping. Macy needed to decide where her loyalties lay. With the man who had once stolen her heart? Or the kids who desperately needed an advocate?

If only the answer could be both.

Chapter Four

Rhett entered the kitchen section of the mess hall where he knew he'd find Cassidy and Piper. It had been a few days since the accident, but he still wanted to make a point of checking on his niece first thing each morning. Guilt clung to his shoulders as he spotted Piper in her cast. If Rhett hadn't been in the far field with all his attention on the dog he was training, he might have prevented her injury.

It confirmed what he had feared all along. He would never be able to run the ranch, the family's charitable foster programs and Straight Arrow Retrievers at the same time. Not well. Not successfully.

Something had to give.

And unless he could find a loophole in the will, it was clear which of the three he would have to let go.

"How's my little soldier holding up?"

Piper rounded one of the wide metal islands in the industrial kitchen. Her hair was back in her normal braided pigtails. She had on jeans, tiny boots and a button-down shirt speckled with pink flowers. "I am *not* a soldier."

The little pout she wore reminded Rhett of Wade so much it made his chest ache. He would do anything to take care of these two ladies—for the brother he had lost. The brother who might still have been around if Rhett hadn't pushed him away.

Rhett cleared his throat.

"Tell him, Mom." She spun toward Cassidy.

Cassidy used the back of her hand to shove light red hair away from her eyes. "It's cowgirl or nothing, Uncle Rhett. You know better."

Rhett dipped his head. "Of course. My mistake. How's our little cowgirl holding up then?"

Piper straightened her spine and held her head higher. "I'm not *that* little anymore."

He bit back his smile. At four years old, Piper barely came above his knees. She took after her mother, petite for her age. Wade had also been the shortest of all the Jarrett siblings. But what Piper lacked in height she made up for in personality tenfold.

Rhett narrowed his eyes, making a show of examining her. "Now that you say it, you do look taller today."

Cassidy hid a grin as she filled a metal pancake dispenser with batter. It looked like a large funnel, but when she pressed the handle it released the perfect amount of batter onto the huge skillet, making it easy to dish out hundreds of pancakes in very little time.

At least, Cassidy made it look easy, but then she had always had a knack for cooking even at a young age. Rhett was sure he would make a mess of everything if he tried to use the contraption. Set him in a pen with five growling dogs? No problem. Ask him to fix breakfast for a crew of thirty workers? Not a chance. Cassidy was the expert here.

Fresh pancake batter sizzled as it cooked. Glass containers full of maple syrup rattled in a pan of boiling water on the nearby stove, permeating the air with their overly sweet scent.

Piper pushed away the sleeve on her right arm, revealing her hot-pink cast. "Look at how many people signed it." She grinned at him as she tapped an inch of blank pink. "I'm saving this spot for Gabe though."

Rhett lightly set his hand on her head. "Gabe isn't going to be back at the ranch, honey."

Her eyebrows went down. "How come?"

Cassidy glanced over her shoulder from her spot near the griddle. "You didn't make him leave because of what happened, did you?" She went back to flipping pancakes, moving the done ones onto a large platter. "Rhett?" she dragged out his name.

The hum of people talking in the mess hall told him that the staff was starting to pile in for breakfast. No time for long explanations. Even if there had been time, he wouldn't have the talk in front of Piper.

Rhett pushed his fingertips against the cool metal of the island. "She got hurt because of him."

And because of me.

Piper tapped on his leg. "He didn't push me."

"I know, but—"

"So it's not his fault." Piper folded her arms and locked onto him with a hard stare. Had she been taking lessons from Macy? All Rhett knew was he was steadily losing to a four-year-old.

"But—"

"Accidents happen." She looked toward Cassidy. "Right, Mom?"

Cassidy directed the kindest, most loving smile at her daughter. "Sometimes an accident can turn out to be the best thing that ever happened to us."

Rhett knew she was talking about becoming pregnant with Piper when she was only eighteen. About the gift that was his niece—a piece of his brother that lived on even though Wade was lost to them. But surely Cassidy hadn't forgotten that Wade had died in an accident of all things.

"Sweetheart." Cassidy motioned toward Piper. "Can you go put the butter on the tables?"

"I can even do it with my cast. It doesn't stop me. Nothing stops me." Piper collected two small plates from the counter and headed into the mess hall. She was used to helping her mom in little ways, especially with the morning meal.

Rhett shoved his hands into his pockets. "She's a lot like her mom."

"Flattery isn't going to get you out of this talk," Cassidy said.

He waited until Piper was long out of earshot before responding, "The fact is most accidents have consequences. Bad ones."

"Don't you think I know that? After what I've been through? Come on, Rhett." Cassidy scooped the last of the pancakes onto the wide platter. "I want Gabe to still have a chance." She passed a platter to Rhett. Her rule had always been every person taking up space in the kitchen had to help. Looked like Rhett would be serving the food at the meal. When she picked up the second platter he reached to take it from her.

She didn't let go right away. "He needed the internship. The boy wants to be a veterinarian and those schools are hard to get into. Scholarships are even harder to come by. He needs to be able to put us on his résumé. If he can show he interned with the animals here, it'll give him a better chance at succeeding. Remember being like that? Like him? Needing a start?"

Of course he remembered. Rhett had been that boy not that long ago.

Chest deflated, he broke eye contact. "I already cancelled the program."

She let go of the platter and folded her arms. "Then uncancel it."

"I can't."

"Being the boss around here you're the one person who can do just that." She sighed, unfurled her arms and dusted her fingers off on her apron. "Everyone deserves a second chance, Rhett. Everyone."

"What if I can't manage the program adequately?"

"Then accept some help." She pinned him with a stern look. "No, I'm not talking about hiring people. Even though you refuse to acknowledge it, you have a huge support system here. So many people willing to help you. But I think you have to learn to be willing to accept help first."

He wasn't really sure he understood what she was getting at and he told her so.

"You know how I said everyone needs a second chance?" Cassidy arched an eyebrow. "Well, that includes forgiveness. Sometimes I think you're holding

yourself back for something you think you did wrong.
Some sort of penance that maybe you don't even realize
you're forcing on yourself. I wish you would forgive
yourself for whatever you think you did. You deserve
a good life, Rhett. Don't be burdened by something
you're forcing yourself to carry, okay?"

Rhett swallowed hard. Cassidy had always been a
straight shooter.

"Promise me you'll think about it," she said.

He nodded. "I will."

"But not for too long." She pointed a spatula at him.
"You Jarretts can be the worst type of overthinkers."

This time he didn't fight the smile. "I would love to
say you were wrong."

"But you know I'm not." Her voice was an odd mix
of hope and disappointment all in one. There was more
on her mind than their current conversation.

She shooed him toward the door leading out to the
mess hall. "Now get breakfast out there before it goes
cold."

"Will do, sis."

He knew she was right about people needing second
chances. Although, if it was up to her, sweet-spirited
Cassidy would give everyone in the world a tenth and
eleventh chance. Everyone would have unlimited opportunities to turn their life around for good. But having a sympathetic nature had gotten her into trouble
in the past.

He couldn't afford to make the same mistake.

The fact was, Piper's injury rested heavily on his
shoulders. The accident wasn't Gabe's fault. No, Rhett
was to blame. He had thought he could set aside his

responsibilities at the ranch for a few hours a day to continue working with clients. He had been wrong.

Macy finger combed her hair as she rushed up the steps to the mess hall. She shoved through the front doors to discover the dining area empty save for the cloying smell of maple syrup and bacon lingering in the air. She'd missed the staff meal completely but perhaps Cassidy had some leftovers tucked away.

Cassidy stuck her head through the wide serving window that connected the kitchen to the eating area. "If you're looking for Rhett he left down the back stairs a few minutes ago. Said he was making a call. He might still be down there."

"Rhett?"

"Tall, handsome guy." Cassidy held a hand in the air demonstrating how tall he was. "Partial to dogs and cowboy hats. Runs the place," she teased.

"Huh." Macy played along. "You mean the one stubborn as sunbaked cowhide?"

Cassidy winked. "Same guy."

"Not here for him." Macy splayed a hand on her stomach as she entered the kitchen area. "I'm here for food."

"Tough break." Cassidy wiped down one of the metal islands. "I'm fresh out of pancakes."

"That's terrible news." Macy wasn't exaggerating. She had a soft spot for breakfast foods and Cassidy was an excellent cook. Cassidy's pancakes deserved sonnets written about their greatness. "I overslept."

Cassidy stilled. "You?"

"I know." Macy held up a hand in defense. "I was up late working on details for the Easter egg hunt."

"How about this? You come in here and help me with dishes and I'll whip up a batch of chocolate-chip pancakes just for you." Cassidy motioned toward the wash area. "We can talk while we work."

Macy wasted no time rolling up her sleeves and heading to the deep sinks. She fished the scrubber out of the warm water and went to work on the first pan she found. "When I suggested to Rhett that we could plan the egg hunt without using much money, I might have bitten off more than I could chew," Macy confessed. "I've been racking my brain trying to think of businesses we could approach as sponsors and I could ask them, but I know they would be more willing to donate if the pitch was coming from Rhett, you know? Everyone always dealt directly with Brock."

Cassidy carried a few more dirty dishes over to where Macy was stationed and plunked them into the sudsy water. She paused nearby. "So why don't you go and ask him to do just that?"

Cassidy had always been so matter-of-fact about things and Macy appreciated that character trait. Though not a Jarrett by blood, Cassidy was very much a part of their family—more so even than Macy, who had spent her whole life with the Jarretts. Macy's mom and Mrs. Jarrett had been friends since high school, so Macy had been visiting Red Dog Ranch since she was one week old. Where there had been cracks and brokenness in Macy's family, she had seen what she thought was perfection in the Jarretts. They were kind, they loved each other, they spent time together.

Despite everything, she would never be connected to the Jarrett family in the way Cassidy was. Never connected in the way she had always wanted to be. Accepted, but not one of them.

Suds splashed onto Macy's shirt as she forcefully scrubbed a pan. "Rhett has a lot on his plate right now. Besides, I'd love to demonstrate that I can take care of something like this on my own—prove that he can trust me."

"First, refusing help doesn't necessarily mean capable." Cassidy pursed her lips. "Second, Rhett already trusts you completely."

Macy knew Cassidy had a soft spot for Rhett. When the family had finally accepted Wade was gone, Rhett had been the one to track Cassidy down and offer her a place at Red Dog Ranch. Her parents hadn't been supportive of her keeping her baby—they told her doing so would ruin her life. But Rhett had convinced her that she was as good as family to the Jarretts and she and her child would always have a place here. He had been the protective older brother Cassidy had never had.

Macy sighed. "He trusted me at one point in life, but that was a long time ago."

"All right. That's it." Cassidy tapped a finger on the counter. "Out with it, already."

"What—"

"Don't play coy with me," Cassidy said. "It's time you shared what went down between the two of you— because all I know is that one day you two were thick as thieves and then he left the ranch and you two suddenly started avoiding each other. It's boggled my mind for the last three years and I'm never going to get a peep out of Rhett, so you're going to have to be the one to spill."

He didn't want me. I made a fool out of myself.

Macy blew dark strands of hair from her face. "What's there to say? We grew apart."

"Oh, don't feed me that line." Cassidy shook her head. "You won't get out of this that easily." She tossed a dirty dish towel into a laundry basket they kept near the sink. "We're friends, aren't we?"

Macy pulled the plug from the sink, letting the water drain away. "Of course we are."

"Then tell me the truth."

"I want to." Macy trailed her thumb over the scar on her pointer finger. "I just don't think you understand how hard it is."

"Here's what I do understand. If I could turn back the clock to when Wade and I had our last fight—" Cassidy's voice clogged with emotion "—I would have done anything to stop him. To go after him. To get him to come home. *Anything.*"

Macy wiped off her hands, making sure they were dry, and then rubbed Cassidy's back. "I know you'd do anything to have Wade back. Wade loved you. I know he did. But what happened between Rhett and me… it's not the same."

Cassidy turned so her hazel gaze connected with Macy's. "You have a chance to make things right between the two of you," she whispered. "A second chance, Macy. Don't squander it. I'd give anything to have that with Wade."

Macy wrapped her arms around her stomach. "Did Rhett ever tell you he offered me a job? He wanted me to leave the ranch with him. Move away. Not together, of course." Macy flushed, hoping Cassidy didn't get the wrong impression. "He offered a high enough salary to cover rent in the area and things like that. An option so I wouldn't be dependent on Red Dog Ranch for a home."

Cassidy popped up so she was seated on the counter. "He never said a word. I'm assuming you said no."

Macy nodded. "I did, but… I went to turn him down in person. Remember I was dating Jim? He broke up with me. Over Rhett. He accused me of being in love with Rhett and not him, and I'm ashamed to admit he was right."

"I honestly don't know why Jim held on for so long. Anyone with eyes knew where your heart was." Cassidy batted her hand. "And we don't need to feel bad for Jim. He's happily married and all that jazz now, so it's all a good ending for him."

"I drove to Rhett's new place right from the breakup and thought about how much I cared about Rhett the whole way there. When he opened the door… I don't know what came over me." Macy wrung her hands and looked away. "I literally clenched my hands in his shirt and yanked him down for a kiss."

Cassidy pumped a fist in the air. "You know it, girl!"

Macy covered her face with her hands. "He froze. He didn't kiss me back."

"He was probably just taken by surprise," Cassidy offered.

Macy swallowed hard. "When I stopped he said 'Why did you do that?' all horrified. He said it a couple times."

"What did you say?"

"Nothing," Macy said. "I turned and ran back to my car."

"Oh, no."

"Oh, yes." Macy shrugged. "He called and left messages for the next few weeks saying he wanted to talk, that—" she put her fingers up to make air quotes "—we needed to discuss what had happened." She lowered her hands. "But I was mortified. I avoided him." After a lifetime of rejection from her father, then the breakup with Jim, which she realized was right but had still hurt, Macy hadn't been able to face Rhett's rejection maturely. If she could turn back the clock she would handle it all differently, but turning back the clock only ever happened in children's bedtime stories. "By the time I decided to swallow my pride five months had come and gone. I called him once, all those months after. He never called me back. And that was it."

Cassidy arched an eyebrow. "You two have talked about this since though, haven't you?"

"It was three years ago." Macy repeated what Rhett had said. No matter how much she wanted to make things right, if Rhett wasn't willing to talk there was nothing she could do about it. "Everything's changed now. It's not worth rehashing."

"Macy." Cassidy hopped off the counter and took her hand. "That man loves you. He always has."

"Yeah." Macy released a long stream of air. "Like a brother."

"You're wrong and I know you don't believe me." Cassidy offered a sad smile. "But I loved one of the Jarrett boys. I know how they think."

Macy needed to steer the conversation away from anything that would make Cassidy think of Wade. "It's later than I thought. Can I take you up on the pancakes another day?"

Cassidy nodded. "You never responded to my text —are you coming to our girls' movie night tomorrow night? Shannon picked out *To Catch a Thief.* Come on, you can't say no to a Cary Grant movie."

"You know me too well," Macy said. "Of course I'll be there."

Cassidy gave her a thumbs-up and then headed toward the back room. She paused when she reached the threshold. "You should talk to him, you know."

"I'm actually going to track down the man in question now." Not that she was going to talk to him about their awkward moment three years ago, but she didn't need to get into a circular argument with Cassidy over it.

Macy checked her watch.

She also had an appointment to keep in town and an idea simmered at the back of her mind. If she could convince Rhett to go along, maybe, just maybe the meeting could be the first step of his softening toward the ranch's mission as far as foster kids were concerned.

Lord, please help me convince him.

"I think he's still downstairs." Cassidy jutted her chin toward the stairwell located along the side of the kitchen which led to the basement area. "I never heard the door open down there. It's heavy and makes a loud sound whenever it closes."

Macy nodded and headed toward the stairs. She

knew about the loud door and hadn't heard it slam either. She paused at the top of the steps. When Cassidy was out of sight, Macy tugged out her phone and typed in Straight Arrow Retrievers. Macy had never gone to his website or sought out information about his business because doing so would have been like tearing open stitches for her emotionally. She had avoided all mentions of Rhett in order to protect her heart. If she could pack him away she wouldn't have to hurt.

But he was here now.

She might as well know.

Listing after listing popped up, revealing articles written about the awards that dogs he'd trained had won. One about a dog who now starred on a television show. Another dog he'd trained was being considered for induction into the Master National Hall of Fame—one of the highest honors a hunting dog could obtain.

"Oh, Rhett," she whispered. Her throat felt thick with both pride and sadness. He had accomplished so much in such a short amount of time. And while he had scheduled a few training appointments at the ranch, how much had he truly sacrificed in order to return home and meet the terms of the will so his family could keep the property?

The low timbre of his voice drifted up the stairs. From where she stood, she couldn't make out his words, but she was happy she wouldn't have to go out searching for him.

How many hours had she and Rhett spent as teens, and even into their twenties, hanging out in the mess hall's basement? They had often run to the basement for their breaks during the summer and fall working hours in order to escape the heat and sun outside. Built into the hillside, the large basement area stayed cool even on the hottest day. They used to sit on the pallets, knee brushing knee, and talk about everything.

She pushed cherished memories away. They only hurt. What was the point of reliving memories when she had no hope of ever making more with her old friend?

Macy tucked her phone into her back pocket, rolled her shoulder and took a deep breath as she headed down the stairs.

Chapter Five

Rhett huddled on a pallet in between a stack of industrial-sized cans of tomato sauce and boxed pasta. He stared at his phone's screen, willing his friend Hank to return the voice mail he had just left. He had discovered he got surprisingly good cell reception in the basement the other day, no doubt because a neighbor rented out land to a company to place a cell tower on his property.

For a second Rhett considered joining Kodiak outside. After he had seen to her breakfast, Rhett had left her basking in the sun by the door that led outside from the basement with a bowl of water nearby. But as peculiar as it sounded, something about the cement walls and low ceiling brought Rhett comfort. Made him remember easier times.

The edges of the long basement were lined with pallets balanced on cinderblocks, a way to keep the non-perishable food stored in a cool area away from the floor. The back end of the basement curved, providing a nook at the end that was great for hiding. Even with all the splendor outdoors, this had always been one of Rhett's favorite spots on the property. He and Macy had called the back wall home base. If they'd needed to meet or got split up while working or during a game, this was where they'd always found each other later. Their meeting spot.

Something he hadn't thought about in a long time.

Something he probably shouldn't think about.

Still, an image from their talk in his office flashed to mind. Macy with her head held high and a spark of pure stubbornness lighting her face. In that moment, she had taken his breath away and he couldn't get it out of his thoughts. Since then ideas kept pestering him. Why hadn't he come to terms with his feelings for her sooner? That day when she'd kissed him, it had been an unexpected—albeit not unpleasant—shock. Never good about surprises, he had reacted poorly. His mind had started overthinking, making his body freeze... pretty much the worst thing he could have done in the situation.

If he could do it all over again? He would have wrapped his arms around her and he would have kissed her soundly, senselessly. Then he would have begged her to never leave his side.

But he had botched his chance at happiness with Macy. She had called him after the kiss, once. It had been five months after everything had happened, but Rhett had been bitter about her ignoring all his initial calls five months before. He hadn't returned her call, figuring it was her turn to try calling for weeks without an answer. But she had never called again. He

always wished he had just swallowed his pride and returned her call.

His life could have been so different if he hadn't
been petty in that moment.

A part of him wanted to reinstate their friendship.
He missed having her as his closest confidant. But
when she had tried to broach the subject he had shot it
down, if only to not have to hear her say they should
disregard what happened and go back to being friends.
The fact was he didn't want only friendship with her
and never would. He *couldn't* only be her friend.

But what about the very small chance that she
wanted that too?

No. He had to stop that train of thought. Rhett didn't
have time for a relationship with Macy or anyone. If he
ever entered into a relationship, he would want it to be
at a time in his life when he could give his partner the
attention she deserved, which was definitely not now.

Not that he wanted one. He was fine alone. Great,
even.

He scrubbed his hand down his face.

In another part of the basement they stored extra
bedsheet sets and items staff or guests to the ranch
might need. His father had wanted to meet basic needs
for anyone staying on their property and never wanted
any of the kids to feel embarrassed or ashamed if they
didn't have necessities required for overnight stays.

It was something Rhett might not have thought
about. Scratch the *might*—he certainly wouldn't have
come up with keeping toothbrushes and new stuffed
animals on hand. His mind simply didn't work that
way. Yet another reminder he had no right attempt-

ing to run the foster programs at the ranch. Even if he could right the boat in a financial sense, he would never do Camp Firefly or any of the other programs justice. He lacked so many traits that had been second nature to his dad.

Rhett dropped his head into his hands.

He needed to let go of the grudge he harbored against the foster programs and the kids involved. It wasn't their fault his dad had chosen them over his son. Rhett wanted to let go of his resentment. Truly. But how does someone cut out a piece of their heart that's hurt for thirty years? What would be left if he did let it all go?

Maybe he shouldn't have sent the will to Hank. Maybe the only way to get over his grudge would be to forge ahead, embracing all the foster programs. But they couldn't feasibly keep it up without affecting the long-term security of his family's finances. What a mess. If only he could separate the hurt his father had inflicted from how he felt about the programs.

He stared at the phone again. Should he call Uncle Travis? He closed his eyes. His uncle would tell him to make his dad proud or utter something along those lines. Give Rhett a one-way ticket for a guilt trip he hardly needed, considering he was already good at taking that trip on his own time.

His phone vibrated. Hank.

Rhett answered immediately. "Thanks for calling me back. Were you able to review the files I sent?"

Hank chuckled. "Well, hello to you too, buddy."

"Sorry. It's just—"

"Kidding with you, Rhett. Lighten up."

Rhett used his free hand to rub at a kink on the back of his neck. "Words one rarely hears from a lawyer."

"Oh, now, we're not all bad. You wouldn't be calling me if you thought we were."

"True." Rhett had trained Hank's German short-haired pointer, Riptide, who had gone on to title in the American Kennel Club's National Hunt Test. After Riptide's training was complete, Hank and Rhett had remained in touch, becoming friends. Being an intellectual property lawyer, Hank had assisted Rhett with trademarking his business.

"I will say—" Hank blew out a long breath "—that's one hefty will."

"I really appreciate you taking the time to look at it for me."

"No problem."

"I haven't had any guidance on it," Rhett confessed. "My family doesn't understand the risks involved." He paused but when Hank didn't jump in Rhett kept speaking. "Tell me you found a loophole in it. There's a way to get out of the part about the extra programs if I need an out, right? I would think the part about serving foster children could be interpreted in different ways." Rhett knew he was rambling but he couldn't help it. Uncle Travis had said the terms of the will were very clear: Red Dog Ranch had to continue being used to serve foster children or Rhett lost the inheritance— meaning his family would lose their home.

The floor above him creaked, making him glance upward. The beams supporting the kitchen and mess hall floors had to hold quite a bit of weight. All the machinery and sometimes hundreds of people. If something broke—how much would it cost to fix any issues? Even replacing pieces of flooring and subfloor here and there added up. The camper cabins all needed work before the camp session, as well. The horse barn had some long-standing issues he needed to address. Maintenance was a constant. More money. More needs.

Rhett's chest felt tight.

"If I need to prove the financial burden or whatever it takes, I can certainly do that."

The fingers on Rhett's free hand had fisted, resting on his knee. He deliberately uncurled each finger. *Relax.*

"Slow down." Hank spoke in a calm tone Rhett had heard him use before when he was in lawyer mode. "I looked over everything and at first glance it seems fairly binding. However, as you know, this isn't my wheelhouse."

Rhett's gaze bored into the gray cement wall opposite him. How had that comforted him minutes ago? Now it reminded him of a cell. Trapped. Cold. Alone. "So you don't think there's a way out for me?"

"Now, I didn't say that."

"Then what are you saying?"

"I'm saying lawyers know lawyers. I have a friend from college—he specializes in estate law," Hank said. "I haven't spoken to him in a few years, but let me reach out to him and see if he's willing to take a look at it for us. I can't promise you anything but I'm certainly willing to try."

"I owe you." Rhett asked about Riptide and Hank promised to call if he heard back from his friend. Rhett shoved his phone into his back pocket and rose. He was too tall to stand straight in the basement so he had to crouch somewhat. It was time to get on with his day. He rounded the corner and came toe-to-toe with Macy. His boots shuffled back a step. Loud and clumsy on the floor.

Macy's dark hair hung over her shoulder, free of its usual ponytail, and Rhett couldn't help but stare. Other than at his father's funeral, lately she had worn it up. Even under the dim basement lights it had a shine to it, like a raven's wing in the sun. Rhett had the odd desire to tuck her hair behind her ear just to know what it felt like.

Instead, he shoved both hands into his pockets.

When he finally met her gaze her left eye twitched.

Rhett's mind raced back through his talk with Hank. How much of his conversation had she overheard? He swallowed, trying to find words. Why was he having a hard time speaking?

But all she said was, "Found you."

Rhett forced his shoulders to relax. "You always could."

She cocked her head and studied him for the space of a few heartbeats. "Physically, yes."

He scuffed his boot on the floor, a nervous habit. All the long days, all the years spent with Macy, and he had never been flustered around her.

He cleared his throat. "Remember when we used to play hide-and-seek all the time?"

"I do. You never could find me." She crossed her arms over her chest.

He sighed. "I guess you were just too good at hiding."

She shrugged, but he knew her too well to miss the tense set of her shoulders and her inability to maintain eye contact for more than a few seconds. Macy was keeping something from him.

"Maybe you should have looked harder," she said.

They weren't talking about a child's game anymore, were they? Was it foolish to hope she was talking about their kiss? About what might have happened between them? Rhett hedged with, "Next time, I will."

The barest hint of something that looked as if it wanted to be a smile played across her features.

Moving on.

"How long have you been standing there?" Had she pieced together he was enlisting legal help to outsmart his father's will? If she had, Rhett expected her to be furious. But Macy didn't look upset. Maybe a little confused.

Her brows furrowed. "I was hoping I could convince you to drive into town with me."

He rubbed at the back of his neck. She hadn't answered his question. "There are calls I have to make and I need to check the pole barn and do you know we still haven't hired a veterinarian since Lyle retired?"

Tentatively, she touched his forearm. "Those things will all be waiting for you this afternoon. I promise. We could split up those calls. Divide and tackle together."

"I don't know." Had Macy missed him as badly as he'd missed her that first year? How many times had she picked up her phone to call him, finger hovering over his contact? Because he'd done so daily for longer than he would ever admit. He had grieved their friendship.

Grieved what could have been if only he had realized he loved her sooner.

But she had been fine, hadn't she? Happy here with the people and place she had chosen.

She hadn't mourned their friendship. At least, that's what he told himself.

All Rhett knew was after the kiss he'd called her at least twenty times and she had called him once during the three years.

Once.

Letting her in—even for a morning together to do errands—was a risk Rhett wasn't sure he was willing to take. Then again, what could it hurt? It might help if he could get a better sense of her—understand her passion for the foster programs and maybe see them in a light other than what it had done to his relationship with his father.

"Trust me," she said. "Take a leap and trust me on this."

Curiosity made his resolve waver. He crossed his arms. "Persistent much?"

"You know it." Macy tugged keys from her pocket. "We're going into town to secure donations for the egg hunt. When we decided to go forward with the event you agreed we'd do this together, remember?"

"I did, didn't I?" And there went his resolve completely.

She popped a hand onto her hip. "I'm not taking no for an answer."

"Now that right there. That's the Macy I know." He pointed at her. "I know that's true." He rolled his shoulders. "All right, let's head out."

* * *

Macy fiddled with the buttons that controlled the radio station.

"How about I do that so you can watch the road?" Rhett's fingers brushed against hers as he reached for the controls. He stopped on a popular country song being played on the local station.

As Macy scanned the road, she could see her scar in her peripheral vision where her hand rested on the steering wheel. Rhett's fingers had just traced against that scar. Did he ever think about the day he saved her from the copperhead?

"I saw this guy in concert last year," Rhett offered. "He sounds this good in person."

The voice on the radio came from Clint Oakfield— one of the biggest touring country-western stars at the moment. His first album had gone platinum and the next two had obtained the same distinction even faster than the first.

"It would be great if we could rope someone like him into donating toward the egg hunt." Rhett's statement was delivered in just a matter-of-fact manner; Macy did a quick double take to be sure he wasn't joking. He wasn't. Who was this guy, dreaming big? He almost reminded her of the boy who had once been her best friend.

"How huge would that be?" Macy whispered.

Rhett's laugh was warm and welcoming. "If anyone could do it, you could."

Macy made a mental note to go to Oakfield's website when she got back to the office and see if there was an option to contact his agent or whoever handled his publicity. People had successfully reached out to celebrities on social media before, as well. What would it hurt to try? If he said no they would be no worse off than they were now, but if he said yes? If Clint Oakfield helped in any way at all…it could be a game changer for Red Dog Ranch and all the foster programs. Even if he donated some signed merchandise that they could raffle off, that would be helpful.

"Speaking of donations." Rhett held the clipboard with the list of businesses Macy had wanted to stop in and talk to. He ran a finger down the first section of the list. "All right, we're six for six on places promising donations. Should we try for seven before heading back?" He caught her eye and the grin he sent her way made her stomach somersault. For the last hour in the car he had been her buddy again, joking, smiling and seemingly excited about the challenge of winning over business owners.

A few of the businesses had promised monetary donations; another two were going to donate candy and small prizes to use in the egg hunt. Yet another promised to rally volunteers to help man the event.

Macy glanced at the clock on the dashboard and her heartbeat ratcheted. Fifteen minutes until she was supposed to meet the Donnelleys at Scoops and Sons for lunch.

And she had yet to inform Rhett about the meeting. Hence the erratic heart.

She snuck a glance at him. Okay, the man's jawline and eyes alone could cause her heart to go out of control, but that wasn't today's reason. Besides, Rhett had already made it clear that he should never be the reason for anything in her life.

The Donnelleys had two adopted children and two foster kids. Often they had more. Mr. Donnelley had grown up in the foster system and had been a teenager when Red Dog Ranch launched many of its programs. They were supporters of the ranch, but more than that, they were friends.

Last night springing a lunch date with the Donnelleys on Rhett had sounded like such a good idea. Now? Not so much. Especially not after they'd stopped by a few local businesses and worked as a team to secure donations.

She and Rhett—a team again.

Macy's mouth felt dry. She needed to tell him. Had to be honest.

Suddenly, Kodiak stood in the back seat and pressed her muzzle into Rhett's ear. Rhett had insisted on bringing her along. Supposedly she didn't do well if she was apart from him for too long, and she had already been outside alone for a chunk of the morning.

Macy couldn't fault Kodiak there.

However, she had the distinct impression that the dog wanted to place herself in between Macy and Rhett as often as she possibly could.

Macy probably should have held her tongue, but she had never been particularly good at doing so. "Ever afraid she might nip you?"

"This brute?" Rhett chuckled and gently nudged Kodiak so she would lie down across the back seat again. "I'd trust her with my life." He held up a hand. "And let's say—theoretically—she did accidentally nip someone. Chessies aren't like other dogs. They're known for their gentle jaws."

"Gentle jaws…on a dog?"

He nodded. "That's why they're perfect birding dogs. They can carry a duck back to you without getting a scratch on it. In fact, a Chessie can be trained to carry an egg in their mouth without breaking it." He jutted his thumb toward the back seat. "Kodiak can."

Macy flipped on the blinker, turning the car in the direction of Scoops and Sons. "You're serious?"

"Of course." His blue eyes lighted with excitement. "With Cassidy's permission, Kodiak has started to learn how to do a water rescue on Piper. She can take an arm or a part of Piper's clothing in her mouth and tow her back to shore. It's pretty amazing. I mean, we only got to try it twice before Piper got hurt. But Kodiak had trained with a dummy at our old place."

Macy couldn't hide the smile that crept onto her face. Rhett's enthusiasm was palpable.

"Okay, you're right. That is amazing." It was great to see him so animated.

"Of course, all that's on hold now. We can't do it again until Piper's cast is off." He frowned. "But I've been having Kodiak practice with other objects." He unbuckled his seat belt without looking toward the restaurant. "She's stronger than she looks—able to haul a lot while she's swimming."

"About Piper." Macy sucked in a sharp breath as she parked the car in front of the tiny restaurant. "I haven't had a chance to apologize for what happened." She twisted in the seat to face him. "I'm sorry she got hurt and I take full responsibility for what happened."

"Are you trying to convince me to reinstate the interns? Because—"

She touched his wrist. "It was my fault. Mine alone."

"While I appreciate you saying that," he said, shifting the clipboard onto the dashboard and then scrubbing his hand over his face, setting his hat off balance, "I think the fault rests with me. I shouldn't have tried to keep my business going. I should have known continuing to train dogs would only divide my time and attention. I should have been there overseeing the interns. I shoved off that duty—"

"Onto me." Macy pressed her hand against her chest. "And I failed you."

"I doubt you could ever fail me." His voice was so low, so full of emotion, it stirred feelings in Macy's heart she had convinced herself she was doing a good job locking away.

Apparently not.

While Rhett's words threatened to unbind a piece of her heart, she couldn't let that happen. They weren't true. Rhett hadn't wanted her.

He shouldn't say such things.

Her mind suddenly latched onto something else he had said. "Wait. You said you 'shouldn't have tried to keep your business going.' Does that mean—"

"Yes." He tugged his hat off and shoved a hand into his hair. "I have to give up Straight Arrow Retrievers. I don't see any other way around it."

She twisted in her seat, grabbing his arm. "Look at me. You are *not* giving up your business. You care about it too much. It's your passion, Rhett."

"Well, it's not humanly possible to run the ranch, the

foster programs, and manage my family and Straight Arrow Retrievers at the same time. Not well. Not successfully. Something has to give and I don't see what else I can cut." He tipped his head back against the headrest.

Her heart went out to him. If only she could convince him to share his burdens. He didn't have to manage everything alone. He wasn't alone at all.

"You have a staff, Rhett. Delegate the ranch duties. We can make this work."

He turned his head in her direction. "You know, you make me believe it could almost work. That's dangerous, Mace."

She smiled. "I've never been a fan of safe."

Rhett swallowed hard. While they'd been able to make progress for the egg hunt, spending time alone with Macy was messing with his head. Oh, he wanted to keep talking with her. Wanted to keep making her smile and laugh. Wanted to keep hearing her encouragement.

That was the problem.

Friendship with Macy was far too risky.

Macy was determined and hardworking and positive. She was passionate about important things and was willing to fight for what mattered to her. She was beautiful, but then she always had been. He had simply been too bullheaded to allow himself to notice for fear of what it would do to their friendship.

How many things had he lost because of choices made from fear?

But fear—caution—kept a person safe. In the horror movies it was always the brave person who went out to investigate a noise who got the ax first, not the vigilant ones hiding inside. They were smart. They stayed safe. Alive.

Walls and hiding were good things. No one could tell him differently.

Because the truth was Rhett could very easily lose his heart to Macy for good if he wasn't careful. So he would be careful. He had to be. He had too much to juggle, too much riding on his shoulders without additional complications.

Besides, she had rejected him before.

He had to keep reminding himself of that. It was the one thought that could protect him. He stole a glance at her as she used the rearview mirror to fix her hair.

Perhaps the only thing.

He looked through the window, finally taking in where they'd parked: Scoops and Sons, a great diner off the beaten path of town. While out-of-towners more than likely assumed the place was simply an ice cream shop, it was so much more. Scoops was a mom-and-pop eatery that served up some of the best brisket sandwiches and corn cobbler Rhett had ever eaten.

"I like this place." Rhett plucked the clipboard from the dashboard. "But it isn't on the list."

Macy sighed. "Okay, don't be mad."

Never a good way to start.

"Why would I be mad?" In response to his tone, Kodiak sat up in the back seat and let out a low whine.

Macy nervously looked from his dog to him. "I should have said something sooner. We're meeting someone here for lunch. I didn't think it would be a big deal."

Rhett scooted the clipboard back onto the dash. The metal clip caught the sunlight, sending a prism onto the car's ceiling. "That someone being…?"

"Do you remember the Donnelleys?"

Of course he did. Jack Donnelley was a few years older than Rhett and had grown up in the foster system. Jack had been one of the first kids Brock had ever taken under his wing. Rhett's dad had probably spent more time mentoring Jack than he ever had Rhett. Jack had gone on to do well in college, marry a great woman, adopt children from the foster system and continue to foster more. In Brock Jarrett's eyes Jack was as successful as a man could be.

Everything Rhett wasn't.

Rhett narrowed his eyes. He had a hard time believing Macy had forgotten about the animosity between him and Jack. For senior night at Rhett's final football game, Rhett had begged his father to attend. *Just this once, Dad. Please.* Everyone else's parents had come to all the games, but Brock rarely had. *I would, son, but I have to meet with this family…this other kid needs me.* There had always been a million reasons why he couldn't be there—good reasons, ones that made Rhett feel bad about himself when he looked out into the stands, didn't see his dad and tasted disappointment. His dad was tied up with something more important than football.

More important than him.

Rhett shouldn't have been hurt. He was supposed to be old enough to understand that the needs of others were more important than his silly wants and desires. Whatever Rhett was doing was insignificant in his father's eyes. Always had been.

Probably still was.

Rhett rubbed at his jaw.

The last game? Brock had chosen to help Jack Donnelley pack his apartment and move to Red Dog Ranch instead of attending. His dad had missed the awards ceremony. Missed all the nice things Coach had said about Rhett.

Not that it would have mattered.

Rhett's focus snapped back to Macy.

"If you did this to try to convince me to reinstate the intern program," he said, "I already decided to do that." After talking with Cassidy he had realized she was right. He had sent emails to set up meetings to go over new safety protocols with all the staff members who had been appointed as mentors, and after those meetings took place tomorrow he would send emails to all the student interns inviting them back to the ranch.

Macy's eyebrows went up. "You—you did? Why didn't you say something?"

"I tried to tell you earlier, but you cut me off."

She cringed. "I do that a lot, don't I?"

He suppressed a good-natured laugh because he was certain that wouldn't have been appreciated during the type of conversation they were engaged in. But, honestly, Macy had been cutting him off since she had been old enough to learn to speak. It was a part of her personality—overexcited, passionate, always charging ahead. That was… Macy. It was who she was and he would never want her to be anyone different.

He shrugged. "You always have. Usually it's endearing."

Her eyes went wide. She opened her mouth to say something.

But he couldn't go down that road. He shouldn't have admitted that he found anything about her endearing. Life was far too complicated at the moment to let anyone in.

Especially Macy Howell.

Before she could respond, Rhett hooked his fingers over the handle and pushed it open. "Well, let's get on with it then. We don't want to keep them waiting."

She rounded to his side of the car while he was letting Kodiak out.

"You'll still go in and have lunch?" she asked.

Rhett forced a smile. "As long as the Donnelleys are good with eating on the patio where Kodiak is allowed."

"You're sure?" she pressed.

"Listen." Kodiak stopped when he did. "Recently I asked God to help me get over this…this grudge, for lack of a better word, that I've had against the foster programs." He shrugged. "Maybe this is part of it. A step in the right direction."

"Rhett, that's—it's huge."

He jerked his chin toward the restaurant. "Let's go."

Jack and Sophie Donnelley welcomed Rhett and Macy with hugs. Their children, Ashton, Ella, Will and Vicki, were instantly enamored with Kodiak.

"Can we pet her?" Ella's gap-toothed grin reminded him of his nieces.

"Sure." Rhett gestured toward Kodiak. "She loves kids."

After quickly eating, the kids took Kodiak out to a large grassy patch that ran alongside the restaurant. The patio overlooked the area so the four adults were able to keep an eye on them. Sophie had unearthed a tennis ball from somewhere in the recesses of their minivan and Kodiak was living the retriever's dream with four kids willing to play fetch with her.

Jack leaned back in his chair. "I have to tell you, we were worried about what would happen to the ranch after your father passed. You know, I always thought of him as my father figure too."

Rhett worked his jaw back and forth. He forced out a breath. "Yeah, I hear that a lot."

"Oh, I'm sure." Jack's smile was genuine. He had always been kind, which only made Rhett feel worse about himself for ever having disliked the man. "I haven't seen you in a while, but it feels like we haven't missed a beat. I guess that's because your dad spoke about you all the time."

Rhett caught Macy's eye. "He—he did?"

Jack nodded. "I know he loved all his kids equally, but you held a special place in his heart."

"He was so proud of your dog business," Sophie chimed in.

Rhett's throat felt raw.

Was it all true? Rhett had a hard time wrapping his mind around the idea. When Brock had given him the ultimatum and Rhett had chosen to leave, Brock had been red-faced, yelling. Brock had been the complete opposite of proud. Even after they had patched their relationship back together for Mom's sake, Rhett and his father had forged a tense truce at best.

Not once had Brock looked him in the eye and said he was proud.

Not once had he showed up for a competition that included one of the dogs Rhett had trained.

Rhett let his gaze drift to the field where the kids were playing with Kodiak. His heart twisted. Seeing their joy, their innocence—no, he couldn't harbor a grudge against the foster programs any longer. The kids were blameless in all that had happened to him.

"Ashton's looking forward to his first year at Camp Firefly." Jack rose from his seat to lean on the patio's railing. "We were worried you might end some of the programs your dad had started. New leadership sometimes has different priorities." Jack almost sounded like he was apologizing for judging Rhett incorrectly.

If only he knew how close he had come to striking the truth.

Rhett sighed. The Donnelleys were good people who deserved honesty. "Programs remain the same for now, but we are looking at possibly cutting back." Rhett rushed on, "These things are expensive. Take the egg hunt for example. We've been all over town this morning soliciting donations—and we did well—but it will probably need to be downsized."

Jack turned to face them. "If you still need one, I could probably get you a helicopter for the candy drop, free of charge."

Macy had been reaching for her sweet tea and now her hand froze. "Are you for real?"

Sophie looked as if she might burst with pride. She

leaned toward Rhett and Macy. "Jack just got promoted to sergeant in the Aircraft Operations Division. He's one of their pilots now."

Rhett had forgotten Jack was an officer with the Texas Department of Public Safety. He certainly hadn't known the man could fly a helicopter though. "If you're sure, I won't turn down an offer like that."

"It shouldn't be a problem," Jack assured them. "My department encourages us to participate in charity events."

There were hugs when everyone finally decided to part ways. Rhett invited the Donnelleys to stop by the ranch whenever they wanted to, and Sophie promised they would take him up on the offer.

Sophie laughed. "Now that the kids have met Kodiak you know they're going to be begging to see her again."

Chapter Six

Rhett left the office early the next day to check on
the interns. Yesterday, after he and Macy had returned
home, they had made quick work of the phone calls on
his to-do list and had been able to meet with all the
staff mentors before dinner, making it possible for the
interns to come back today.

Gabe and a few of the others had been assigned to
help on the maintenance crew, so Rhett drove one of
the four-wheelers out to the fence line where the crew
was trimming the long grasses and weeds. Staff had
to keep them short so gates between pastures would
be easier to use.

Normally he would have walked out to the spot, but
at the last minute Rhett had decided to strap a cooler
filled with ice-cold water bottles to the back of the four-
wheeler. It was only March, but the afternoons got hot.

Rhett found Gabe and the others were working hard
under the direction of an aged ranch hand. After confirming with the older man, Rhett had to admit Gabe
was a good kid.

Gabe used the back of his wrist to swipe sweat from his brow. "Boss, if you don't mind me asking, how's Piper doing?"

Rhett handed the youth a fresh water bottle. "Nothing fazes that little girl." He pointed at the teenager. "Speaking of, make sure you swing by the mess hall and sign her cast before you leave today."

Gabe saluted him.

"And, Gabe?" Rhett cleared his throat. "I know you have your heart set on becoming a veterinarian." The teenager nodded. "Come see me after you're done here and we can talk about putting you on rotation with everyone who works with the animals so you get a chance to see all sides. I'd be happy to show you what I do for dog training, as well, if that's something you'd be interested in."

Satisfied that the teenager was in good hands, Rhett headed back toward the house. Kodiak happily bounded beside his vehicle the whole way. He left the four-wheeler in its usual place near the pole barn and was about to make his way to the ranch house to see how his mom was doing when he spotted Shannon crouched where they stored the hay bales.

As he entered the barn his boots crunched on gravel, alerting Shannon to his presence. Her head snapped up and her blotchy red cheeks gave her away. Rhett's stomach clenched. She'd been crying, sobbing by the looks of it. Seeing her that way made his heart feel wrung out.

What had he missed?

"Hey." He hastened his steps. "What's wrong?" He sat beside her, his arm instinctively going around her shoulders. Every protective impulse flared inside of him. Were the tears because of her boyfriend, Cord Anders? And if so…was it horrible that Rhett would be happy if they had broken up? Rhett had noticed Shannon changing, shrinking into herself ever since she had started dating the man. If he had his way, he would ban the guy from the ranch. He shoved the thought away. Right now all that mattered was Shannon was upset. He needed to be empathetic no matter the reason for her tears. His sister deserved nothing less.

She dropped her head into her hands and her shoulders shook a few times. "Nothing. I don't know." Her voice pitched higher. "Everything."

Not knowing what to say, he rubbed his hand in a circle against her back.

"I'm so stupid," Shannon breathed out.

"Shh." Rhett pulled her to his side in a hug. "No one talks about my favorite sister like that. Not even my favorite sister."

A watery laugh escaped her lips. "I'm your only sister."

"What's wrong?" he whispered the question again.

She shoved her blond curls away from her face. "I'm losing everything." She looked away, out the barn doors. Her eyes focused on something far in the distance or maybe nothing at all; Rhett couldn't tell.

His gut clenched. He had never seen his sister despairing.

Help me, Lord.

"First there was Wade—" her voice strained over her twin's name "—then Dad." She wiped at another tear. "Now it's Mom."

Rhett's fingers tightened over her shoulder. The Jarretts had experienced their share of losses over the last few years, but they would weather them together. Shannon had to know that. He would always be there for her, no matter what happened.

"Mom's still here," he said. "We still have time with her."

Shannon's head swung back around, her gaze latching onto his as if he could save her from drowning. "Not really, Rhett. You and I both know that. She's not usually *there*. Not anymore. I can't go talk to her. I can't—" Her face crumpled. "I feel like I'm losing myself. I'm so—" A sob broke from her chest. Loud and full of long pent-up pain.

Kodiak pranced nearby, her low, sharp whimpers joining Shannon's tears.

Rhett gathered his sister to his chest. If only there was something he could say to make everything better for her. But he knew words didn't have that type of power. In his life words had always caused far more pain than healing. Only actually being there for a person helped, and if he was being honest, he had failed Shannon in the past on that count. He hadn't been around to support her during the most difficult days at Red Dog Ranch.

He refused to fail her now.

She clung to his arms and shoved her forehead into his collarbone. "Nothing makes me happy. Nothing makes me smile anymore. Everything keeps changing and I hate it, and I hate that I can't handle it."

His sister's words gutted him completely. Rhett

wrapped his arms more securely around her. "I'm here," he whispered over and over.

She slammed her palms against him and scooted away. "For how long this time?" Her eyes blazed. "You'd sell it in a heartbeat and leave us again if you could. Walk away and never once look back. Never check on us. Never call. Just like before. The only thing keeping you here is Dad's will. We all know that."

"That's not true." His words came out quietly. He would never walk away from his family again, but he couldn't blame her for making a logical jump based on his past actions. He had left her to bear the burden of their mom's illness and deal with their parents alone after Boone and his family left for seminary. She had been the one the police made a death notice to—alone. How secluded she must have felt, entirely deserted by all her brothers. Rhett could never repay her and now it was evident how much it had taxed her, how much he would forever be indebted to his sister. The knowledge hollowed out his chest.

"You don't care about me. Not really."

"I love you. You know that. I'm sorry for—"

She shot to her feet. "You're trying to get out of the will. I know you are."

"Shannon." Rhett slowly rose to his feet. He put his hands out, the same way he would have approached a scared animal. "When I left? That was an issue between me and Dad. I had a beef with him—no one else." He took a step closer. "You have no idea how sorry I am about the past. I ask your forgiveness for not being here, not supporting you better in all the ways I should have."

"Cord's right." Shannon crossed her arms. "None of you care. Not really."

Cord. Of course.

Rhett's movement stilled.

"Is that where this is all coming from?" he asked, hoping for the truth. Praying he could get through to her about her boyfriend. "That guy is bad news. You've been hurting ever since you got with him. That's not love, Shannon. Love heals people—it doesn't destroy them. I don't think he's right for you."

"He's the only good thing in my life right now." Her voice rose. "And now you're trying to take that away from me too. He warned me this would happen."

"That's absurd." Maybe not his best, most caring word choice. Rhett started again, more kindly. "There are so many people here who love you. If this guy has made you think differently then—"

She let out a derisive laugh. "Cord was right. The whole family is against me. I should have known better than to even bother to try to get you to understand." Shannon turned.

Rhett followed after her. "We're not done."

She sliced him with a glare. "Do you think you're Dad now? Because that's hilarious, Rhett." Her voice was ice. This was not any version of the Shannon he knew. It made a creeping sensation go up his back. "You don't have the right to step into our lives and think you can solve all our problems or be some makeshift patriarch now. If you think that's what we want, well, you're wrong. You could never fill Dad's shoes. Not even close. So don't even try."

"I know that," he said quietly. "I'm not trying to be

Dad, but I do want to do the best I can by you. By me. By God. I can't undo the past but I can promise that I will never walk away from you again."

She left and this time he didn't follow her.

While he stared after Shannon's retreating form, Kodiak shoved her nose into Rhett's hand. Shannon was right—Rhett had failed them in the past. All of them, but especially Shannon. He pushed his fingers into Kodiak's coarse fur. Resolve forming.

He had a chance to right the wrongs both he and his father had committed.

For far too long the Jarretts had placed Brock on a pedestal because he was a good man with a big heart. But in a way, their dad had failed them most of all. He had put so many things—admirable things—ahead of his family. From Wade's attention-seeking youth, which had led him down a bad path, arguably resulting in his death, to Rhett's constant struggle with rejection and to Shannon's obvious emotional pain, which had driven her to a man like Cord, it didn't take a genius to see how much Brock's lack of attention had cost their family. Happily married, Boone seemed to be the only one to have escaped a measure of dysfunction, but then again, maybe Boone just hid it better.

Rhett would stay and make the ranch a success. If the lawyer could find a loophole in the will, he would be able to show his family that they—not any program or charity—came first. Rhett would figure out the balance between caring for them and helping people in need, because he was starting to think it was possible to do both. It had to be.

He would prove Shannon wrong on another point

too. He would be there when Cord Anders broke her heart. He was willing to weather years of her barbs and pained words if that was what he had to do to prove to her that he was no longer the man who walked away.

Even though the path was well illuminated by a flood lamp hanging near the barns, Macy could have walked the path from her bungalow to the big house with her eyes closed. The door to the Jarretts' house had been open to her since she was a baby and it had become her favorite place when they warmly welcomed her after her mother's sudden death. Macy had only been eighteen and would have been left utterly alone in the world if the Jarretts hadn't ushered her into their fold.

If they hadn't made her a part of their family.

At one time, she had believed she might really become a Jarrett. Until the bottom fell out and she tasted bitter reality about her friendship with Rhett. Friends, only ever friends.

For so many years, their home had been her home... except she hadn't set foot inside since Rhett had been back. It was his domain now and she had not wanted to encroach.

Cassidy had texted Macy twice during the day, reminding her about the planned movie night in the big house. Why had she agreed to go in the first place? Sure, it would be nice to spend time with Shannon, Cassidy and, if she was feeling up to it, Mrs. Jarrett, but there were things she could be handling in the office. More work to get done.

A dog's bark made her jump. With a small yelp,

Macy whirled around. When she squinted, she could make out Rhett and Kodiak walking up from the lake. And was that…she squinted more… Romeo the miniature donkey with them?

Rhett's posture changed the second he caught sight of her, but he relaxed his shoulders a moment later. "Out for a stroll in your pajamas?" he hollered since they were still a ways away, his voice warm.

Macy glanced down, mortified. Her pajama pants were covered with brightly colored T. rexes trying to hug each other but not being able to because of their short arms, and she wore a shirt with big letters that read Surely Not Everybody Was Kung Fu Fighting. Summoning her dignity, Macy trudged through the bluebonnets toward him. At least she wasn't wearing her cow slippers.

"Nice shirt." Rhett handed her Romeo's lead rope. "Where are you headed?"

Macy jerked her thumb to point over her shoulder toward the Jarretts' house. "Girls night. We're watching Cary Grant."

"Ah, yes. Now that you mention it, I seem to recall Cassidy telling me I wasn't allowed in my own living room tonight." His eyes narrowed. "Are those dinosaurs on your pants or are they llamas?"

"No more clothing comments unless you want me to turn this around and make fun of you." She fell into step beside Rhett as they headed in the direction of the nearby barn where Romeo and the miniature horse, Sheep, spent their nights.

Rhett made a show of pretending offense. He glanced down as if taking in his own boots, jeans and button-down. "All right, do your worst. What do you have to say about this?"

Macy stopped and looked at Rhett. The man was all cowboy—broad shouldered, tough muscled, with a shadow of end-of-the-day stubble dusting his chin. She fought the sudden itch to touch his jaw. To run her finger along the planes of his face, back into the hair that curled out from under his hat. His bright blue eyes drew her in and Macy's gaze went to his lips. She sucked in a sharp breath and took a step back.

Even in friendship they had never been forward with each other. Plenty of high fives and backslaps sprinkled with the occasional hugs, but other than the one time he had carried her after the snakebite, there had never been a touch that held meaning beyond "Well done" or "Good to see you."

Well, besides that one kiss.

"I, ah, I can't." Suddenly nervous, she swallowed hard. "You always look, um, really…attractive." Heat flared on her neck and her cheeks.

Attractive. She'd really just said that.

Out loud.

Rhett's laugh was warm. "Attractive, huh? Why do I get the sense you're buttering me up to ask a favor or something? Go on," he joked. "What do you want?"

You. Just you. Even though you're the most stubborn, exasperating man I've ever met. It's always been you. It will only ever be you.

Romeo butted his head into her back, shoving her closer to Rhett. Rhett dropped a hand onto her shoulder, ensuring the small donkey wouldn't be able to push

Macy again. However, Rhett kept his hold even after Romeo started munching at a patch of clover.

Macy tipped her head to meet Rhett's eyes. She licked her lips. "Come on, you have to know by now how handsome you are."

Instead of answering, Rhett cocked his head and studied her.

He was so close and for the first time since returning to the ranch, something about him was different. It felt as if his heart wasn't entirely locked up tonight. She imagined it as a door only slightly ajar, but maybe she could wedge a foot in. Maybe she could make some progress with him. Maybe she could win her friend back.

Kodiak shoved her way in between them. She sat directly on the tips of Rhett's boots and stared up at Macy, her muzzle inches away from Macy's thigh.

Macy groaned. "I get the feeling your dog doesn't like me much."

Rhett's gaze drifted over Macy's features, lingering on her mouth. A shy smile lighted his face, causing the skin around his eyes to crinkle. "She's, ah, jealous."

"Of me?" Macy gripped Romeo's lead line a little harder than necessary. "I can't imagine why."

Rhett's smile widened. "Really?"

A part of Macy wanted to press Rhett to clarify, but a bigger part of her brain screamed a warning. It couldn't be what she hoped. Rhett could never care about her in the same way she cared about him. If he had, their kiss would have gone far differently.

Why did you do that? Why did you do that?

Macy needed to steer the conversation to safer waters for both of their sakes. Rhett was her boss, he had emphatically told her he didn't want to be friends again, and she still wasn't sure if he was on board with saving all the foster programs long-term.

Further talk in this direction would only end with her hurt again.

Macy's thumb instinctively found the scar on her finger.

Rhett sighed, clearly disappointed that she hadn't continued their conversation. But she couldn't go down that road with him. She refused to press him about why Kodiak would be jealous of her. Any chance Rhett and her could have had at a relationship ended three years ago. Besides, Rhett had just started to warm up to her again—to smile and joke with her like the old days. She wouldn't let anything harm the chance to mend their friendship. Not even her desire for answers and closure about *what might have been*.

She had to change the topic and head up to the house. Macy pivoted to face the barn. "Sheep's probably missing Romeo."

Rhett's Adam's apple bobbed. "Right." He scrubbed a hand over his face. "Let's put him to bed then."

With Kodiak on his heels, Rhett fell into step next to Macy. His ever-present shadow made Macy remember something else she had been meaning to discuss with him.

"I looked up Straight Arrow Retrievers," Macy said with all the casualness she could muster. "Why didn't you tell us about all the awards you won? You trained Benny—that dog went to big award shows as a presenter."

Rhett unlatched the barn door and held it open as she led Romeo inside. He took his time catching up. "Would any of it have mattered?" His voice was quiet, almost a whisper.

By the time he came up behind her, Macy had ushered Romeo into his stall. She spun around, finding Rhett closer than she had thought he would be. "Of course it matters. Your accomplishments are worth celebrating. You can't give it up."

"I don't see how I can keep training dogs with everything else I have going on."

"I've watched you out there in the field with them." She poked his chest. "You're happy. Really happy when you're working dogs. I don't want you to lose that."

He pinched the bridge of his nose. "I don't want to talk about this right now. Other things—" his gaze dipped to her mouth "—but not this."

"Then what do you want to talk about?" The second the question passed her lips she wished she hadn't voiced it. She should have said good-night and gone on her way, but his eyes were pleading with her and looking away was near impossible.

He eased the lead line from Macy's grasp, his eyes never leaving hers. "Why didn't you return my calls?"

Unwelcome nerves jangled through her. "You honestly want to have this conversation?" What if they ruined all the headway they had made? Of all the things for him to want to discuss. "Because last time I brought it up you seemed pretty opposed to it."

He stepped back and looped the lead line back on a peg with some other equipment. "I left you so many messages." His back was to her. His shoulders rose on a shaky breath. "For so long you just ignored them—ignored me. I still can't wrap my head around what happened."

"I was embarrassed, Rhett." She threw out her arms. "What did you expect me to do after that?"

Rhett finally turned around. "I wanted you to talk with me." His voice was even. "Friends do that. They talk through things. Do you know how much I missed you the last few years?"

Friends.

And there it was: Confirmation. Friends. Just friends. All he would ever consider her. Why she should have walked away ten minutes ago. Why she had to end this conversation before she was forced to admit to her feelings.

"I wasn't going to take the job," she said, but it sounded lame even to her own ears.

A wrinkle formed between his eyes. "This has nothing to do with the job offer." He took a half step in her direction. "Are you honestly going to keep pretending you don't know what I'm getting at?"

Macy crossed her arms over her chest. "You didn't call me back either. You know, the path goes both ways."

He took off his hat and ran a shaky hand through his hair. "You called once, Macy. Once. *Five* months later."

Kodiak raised her head and whimpered.

Rhett looked at Kodiak, back at Macy, away again. "I shouldn't have raised my voice. I'm sorry, I'm just dealing with a lot here."

"Like what?"

"Shannon hates me." His voice trembled. "She hates

me, Mace." He shook his head when she opened her mouth. "And you? Whenever I think…" He backed away. "I'm sorry. I shouldn't have said anything. There's so much on my mind tonight. Forget all this for me."

He was gone before she could say anything else. Between what seemed like flirtation at the beginning of their interaction to the bombshell about Shannon and his obvious hurt, it was hard to wade through what she should think and feel about it all. She was relieved he hadn't pressed talking about their kiss more. Their friendship was just starting to feel comfortable again and a long talk about why he would never think of her romantically would only make her pull away. As much as she wished it was otherwise, they needed to go on as if the kiss had never happened.

She could be his friend again.

Just friends.

It would be enough.

It would have to be enough.

Macy stood in the barn's doorway long after she lost sight of him.

Chapter Seven

When Macy stretched, her spine answered with a series of little popping noises. Sleeping on the floor as a twenty-eight-year-old was a significantly different experience than all the times she had done so at sleepovers as a teenager. Her joints wouldn't thank her.

After her conversation with Rhett, Macy had gone ahead with her planned movie night with the other girls. If only because she'd known Cassidy was bound to show up at her house and drag her, kicking and screaming, to the Jarrett house if Macy had dared to text to cancel. Even still she had been tempted.

Thankfully, Rhett was safely tucked away upstairs when she arrived and stayed that way the rest of the evening while Cassidy, Shannon, Piper and Macy watched movies and consumed a shocking amount of popcorn and chocolate. As usual, Piper was asleep within the first ten minutes of the first movie. Somewhere between watching *To Catch a Thief* and Macy's favorite Cary Grant movie, *Charade*, they all decided to turn the marathon into a sleepover and added *House-boat* to the lineup.

A wall of windows on one side of the room showed a pink-and-gold wash of sunrise cresting over the hills. Cassidy and Piper were still snoozing together on the large couch, but Shannon's spot in the recliner was empty. Had she gone upstairs to her own room at some point or had she snuck out to meet with Cord? Shannon had been present last night but not engaged.

Rhett and his sister had to have had words yesterday because it wasn't like Rhett to throw around the word *hate*. A sick feeling swam through Macy. She had considered pulling Shannon aside many times throughout the last few weeks, but the time had never felt right. She needed to be a better friend to Shannon in the future.

Keep Shannon safe, Lord. Help her see how much You love her. Help us get through to her. And whatever's going on between her and Rhett—please heal their hurt. She was about to end her plea but then added, *Could You help me with Rhett too? I'm not sure what's going on. I'm not even sure what's happening in my own life anymore.*

Macy had plugged her phone in to charge on the kitchen counter before she had fallen asleep. With all the emails she had sent out recently regarding the foster programs, she liked to check for responses first thing each morning. After getting home from Scoops and Sons, she had sent a message to Clint Oakfield. Was it silly to hope he would respond?

She rose only to spot Mrs. Jarrett peacefully sitting at the head of the dining-room table. The woman looked over at her and smiled serenely. Macy was once again struck by how cruel Alzheimer's was. From the outside, Rhett's mom appeared the same as ever.

It was a shock to see her up and about before her nurse arrived. How long had she been there? Mrs. Jarrett hadn't been well enough to join them last night. But here she was, hands folded over her open Bible, bright and early in the morning, smiling at Macy as if she had been waiting for her. The woman had a way of looking regal, even in her brown robe with her white hair slightly mussed with sleep. Macy crossed into the kitchen, socks padding over the hardwood floor. "Can I get something for you?"

Mrs. Jarrett touched the spot to her right. "Just come and sit with me, dear."

Macy filled two cups with water and brought them to the table. "How are you doing this morning?"

A glass jar on the table held a fragrant bouquet of Texas sage, orange jubilee and gold lantana. Cassidy had told Macy that Rhett picked a new bouquet of flowers at the ranch for his mother every couple of days.

Mrs. Jarrett fanned her fingers over the thin pages of her open Bible. "If you're asking if today is a good day or a bad day for my mind—today I remember. I know myself."

Swallowing hard, Macy glanced toward the staircase and wondered if she should rouse Rhett or Shannon. She knew they would appreciate some time with their mother during a lucid moment. Macy bit her lip. Another part of her wondered if she should broach the topic of Rhett's adoption with Mrs. Jarrett. Every time Macy sat at her desk and looked at the photo of Brock at the opening of Camp Firefly she fought the urge to go into Rhett's office and confess what she knew. Rhett deserved to know the truth about his parentage, but she couldn't break her promise to Brock.

No matter how often she wanted to.

Rhett's mom gazed toward the stairs. "They're both already gone for the day. Rhett left very early. More so than usual. It makes a person wonder why." Mrs. Jarrett trained her focus on Macy. "When will you two give in and get married already?"

Macy choked on the sip of water she had just taken. She covered her mouth.

Unfazed, Rhett's mom continued, "My thickheaded boy may not realize it, but he's loved you his whole life. Still does. I think more now than ever. Some people love each other for a season or while it's convenient, but you two share the growing kind of love—it keeps getting bigger and deeper."

Macy considered acting as if she had no clue what Mrs. Jarrett was talking about, but why? The Jarrett matriarch was lucid, but lately these were rare moments. Macy had always cherished the woman's wisdom and perspective. She wouldn't forsake an opportunity to speak with the lady who had become her second mom.

She filled her lungs with air, let it out. "I'm pretty sure my feelings are no secret, but Rhett never went down that road. I always figured if it was meant to be, it would happen." She shrugged, trying to pretend the admission didn't sting. "So I guess it wasn't meant to be."

"'If it's meant to be'?" Mrs. Jarrett snorted and batted her hand in the air. "What hogwash. Love is work. Hard work. It's late-night tears and fights and forgiving and choosing a person even on their worst days. I've never known such pain as the pain of love. 'Meant to be,'" she grumbled again, as if the words offended her. "Anyone who treats it so carelessly has never truly known it."

Macy's eyes burned. Tears had gathered as Mrs. Jarrett spoke. "When Rhett left the ranch—" Her voice cracked. "He knew me better than anyone and rejected me."

Rhett's mom nodded thoughtfully. "And he will likely hurt you again and you him. That's how living goes." She tapped the table. "That's especially how loving goes."

Macy straightened her spine. "Which is exactly why it would never work for us."

"Sweet child, don't you know?" Mrs. Jarrett covered Macy's hand with both of hers. "God's love is the only one that never lets us down. All others will at some point. We're human, you realize." She cupped her hands around Macy's. "I made mistakes with Brock and the good Lord knows Brock let us down sometimes too. Rhett will do the same and maybe you don't want to hear it, but you will stumble in relationships too— for the rest of your life, my dear. I'm sorry to be the one to tell you these things."

"I know I'm not perfect—"

"*None* of us are." She winked. "But I find that's part of the adventure."

"Do you know he's trying to downsize the foster programs? He would have cut the egg hunt if I hadn't convinced him not to." Macy felt like she was tattling on Rhett. She knew he wouldn't have discussed these

things with his mom, but Mrs. Jarrett had been a driving force for establishing Camp Firefly, among other
things, and deserved a voice in the matter.

His mom released Macy's hand so she could trace
her finger over a highlighted line in her Bible. "I wonder, does your push to save the things Brock started
come from a place of love or do you believe it's your
burden, your badge of honor—your pride at stake?"
She caressed the highlighted page again. "Right here,
'do all things out of love.' It sounds so easy, but it is
the hardest thing that will ever be asked of us because
love…love is sometimes the most painful feeling on
earth, child. But it's worth it. We have the proof right
here." She closed her Bible and tapped the cover. "It's
worth every sacrifice, every arrow sent into the soft
part of our heart. It's worth it."

As the nurse arrived Macy kissed Mrs. Jarrett on
the cheek. "Thank you for your wisdom."

Mrs. Jarrett caught her hand, giving it an extra
squeeze before letting go. As Macy left, she blinked
away tears. She forced down the emotions talking with
Mrs. Jarrett had stirred. But even after Macy had show-
ered, changed and headed into the office, she couldn't
shake the oldest Jarrett's words.

Macy and Rhett had hurt each other, but did that
mean their entwined story had to end? Macy didn't
want it to.

She wished she would have handled last night differently. Been honest. Vulnerable.

If she had been brave and spoken her heart then at
least she would know now. She wouldn't be stuck in

the Land of Maybe any longer. The truth could have been used to guide her.

Macy finally focused on her phone; an email sparked her interest. She let out a long stream of air. She couldn't wait to tell Rhett about this.

Rhett brushed his hand over his eyes, hoping no one would be able to notice the lingering hint of tears later on. He hadn't meant to wake up early and visit his father's grave, but here he was.

Rhett knelt in front of the headstone and traced his fingers over his father's name and the small dash in between the date of birth and date of death. The small dash that symbolized his life. It was in the dash that Brock had raised and loved Rhett despite both men's failings. Brock might have dropped the ball in many aspects of fatherhood, but Rhett had never doubted his father's love.

Humid air draped around Rhett's shoulders, causing his shirt to stick to his back. A light breeze rustled flowers placed on nearby grave sites and a colorful pinwheel twirled in the wind, stuck into the ground near a tombstone with birth and death dates painfully close together. If it wasn't for the occasional gusts it would have felt like a summer morning outside instead of the end of March.

"Why me?" Rhett whispered. "Why did you leave the ranch to me? It makes no sense. You had no reason to trust me, to believe in me after—" His voice broke. "After I walked away. I'm so sorry I didn't make it to the hospital in time to say goodbye." He had immediately gotten into his truck and headed for home when

Shannon had called him about the accident. But a hundred miles was too far. Too long. His father had passed on fifteen minutes before he parked at the hospital. "I'm sorry, Dad. I'm so sorry I didn't get to say goodbye. Hug you one more time." Tears fell now. *Let them.*

His phone buzzed in his pocket and he tugged it out. It was a text from Jack Donnelley—an image of all of Jack's kids with their arms wrapped around Kodiak as they smiled at the camera. His text said the dog was a perfect mascot for Red Dog Ranch.

Macy had once said the same exact thing.

Rhett turned his phone to silent and tucked it back away.

After a few more minutes Rhett found his way to his truck and eased into the front seat. Why had it taken him so long to visit the grave site?

Last night after talking to Macy, Rhett had gone back to his room, but sleep hadn't come. He had stared up at the ceiling watching the fan blades whip around and thought about all that had gone wrong in his life. If he hadn't frozen that night three years ago with Macy they could have been together now. He might have been home years earlier.

But he couldn't force Macy to talk about their past any more than he could fix Shannon's problems. All night one thought kept pounding through his head— with so much of his life spinning out of control, he needed to focus on the few things he had power over. The biggest being his own heart. Hadn't he asked God to help heal his grudge against the ranch? A piece of that was making peace with his father. Visiting his grave had been the only way Rhett could think to do that.

Without turning his truck on, he gripped the steering wheel and shoved his forehead against it. A sudden throb radiated through his chest, making him gasp for breath. Would life always feel like such a mess? Shannon and the ranch and Mom and Macy. Rhett thought of the Donnelleys—how the ranch had helped Jack when he was younger and how much his kids were looking forward to camp. Rhett's heart twisted. Those kids deserved a place like Camp Firefly. Kids like Gabe deserved a safe space too.

He had asked God to help him release his grudge— coming to terms with his mixed emotions for his father was a piece of moving forward.

Here in the graveyard where thoughts tended to drift toward legacies and how important it was to live with meaning, Rhett finally saw his excuses for what they were—thinly veiled childhood bitterness that he had held on to for so many years. A little boy who wanted his dad to look his way and offer a proud smile, who had wanted to know he came first, if only once. It would never happen, not with Brock gone, and Rhett had to accept that or remain stuck forever.

What was the point of hoarding bad memories, allowing them to take up space in his heart and mind— crowding his life so much that there wasn't room for other things?

Happy, hopeful things.

Rhett was tired of the heavy chains that came with resentment. He didn't want them in his life anymore. Someday, when his body would wind up in a plot not far from his father's, he wanted to know his time had counted. If there was a balance between providing for his family and continuing the events of the ranch, Rhett would find it. He would help heal his family too, if he could.

However, he knew it would be impossible to accomplish any of those things outside of God. Rhett had neglected his relationship with God for far too long. He would never get the last talk or hug with his earthly dad, but he could mend things with God the Father. It was time to go back to church again, time to dust off his Bible and time to open a line of communication through prayer. No matter how strange or strained it might feel, he knew God was there, waiting. Always had been.

Maybe Brock had been too. Rhett would never know because he had squandered the chance to truly reconcile. A mistake he wouldn't make again. Not with God or Shannon or Macy. Not with anyone, if it was up to him. Life was too short, too unpredictable, to hold grudges or allow miscommunications to ruin relationships.

Rhett headed back to the ranch. He had only just parked his vehicle when he caught sight of Macy cutting through the field of bluebonnets toward him. Kodiak trotted at Macy's side, a red ball in her mouth. The two of them looked as if they were racing to put out a fire. The dog was probably miffed at being left behind, but it wouldn't have been respectful to have her in the cemetery and it would have been far too hot to leave her in the vehicle. Rhett exited his truck and strolled to the fence line to meet them.

Macy huffed. "Where have you been? When I saw Kodiak was here but not your truck, I freaked out." Her brows lowered. "And you need to start answering your phone."

Rhett tugged his phone from his pocket. Seven missed calls from Macy. He had turned the vibrate function off after Jack's text had interrupted him. "It was on silent." Her scowl grew and Rhett saw the emotion for what it was—concern. He quickly added, "Sorry if I worried you."

Macy grabbed his wrist. "I *was* worried." She searched his eyes. "Are you okay? It looks like…" She left it there. "Rhett," she whispered. "I know what you said before, but can't we be friends again?"

He covered her hand with his. He instantly found the scar on her pointer finger and couldn't help but trace over it.

Friends.

The word was too small to capture his feelings for Macy.

She knew every rough part of his personality and yet here she was, asking to be friends. Wanting to be a part of his life even though he had hurt her and let her down more times than he could count. She stood toe-to-toe with him even when they disagreed and challenged him constantly, but only because she believed the best of him.

She believed in him. He let that sink in.

Rhett had loved this woman his entire life.

The realization roared through him, shaking him like a powerful storm.

There had never been another woman on the planet

in Rhett's eyes. Only Macy. Always Macy. In the past, he had hidden behind their friendship because he had been fearful of losing her if he made a move. Then last night he had come so close to confessing his feelings, but he was glad he hadn't because Rhett was in no position to start a relationship.

Between his father's death, his mother's health and Shannon's anger, Rhett had so much emotional baggage to deal with before he would be ready to be there for a woman.

To be there for Macy.

If she would even want him.

Rhett scuffed his boot into the dirt.

But he could be her friend, couldn't he? They were already acting like friends anyway. "I'd like to be friends again. I'd like that a lot."

The smile that bloomed on Macy's face was the most beautiful thing Rhett had ever seen. "Then tell me what's wrong."

There was no point hiding the truth; he was sure she had already read the evidence on his face. "I visited my dad. His grave site."

"I'm proud of you," she said. "I know how hard that can be." She released his wrist and he wished she hadn't. "About last night…"

Rhett scratched at the spot on his neck where his hat met his hairline. "Can we forget last night? I was a bear." He had snapped at her because he was upset over Shannon and he was frustrated Macy wouldn't discuss what had gone wrong three years ago. Since realizing he would have had to put a relationship on hold anyway while he worked through all the emotional issues he was dealing with, now he was thankful the conversation hadn't gone any further.

She poked him in the ribs. "Bears *can* be cuddly."

"Not all bears." He rubbed the spot she had poked as if she had hurt him.

She blew bangs away from her eyes. "Anyway, your roar has never scared me." Macy plucked the ball from Kodiak's mouth and sent it flying. Kodiak went tearing through the field after it. "I don't think she minds me nearly as much when you're not around."

Rhett braced his arms on the top fence railing. "Stick around and she'll consider you family like we all do." Kodiak sometimes took a while to warm up to certain adults, but once she accepted them they became fully her people.

"Speaking of, Sophie Donnelley texted." Macy came up beside him, her shoulder brushing his arm. "She asked if the kids could stop by and see Kodiak today."

"Of course. I said they were always welcome."

His dog had already returned with the ball and dropped it at Macy's feet. When Macy looked Rhett's way with her eyebrows raised in question he jerked his chin toward the ball. Macy winked and scooped it back up again, lobbing it in the other direction.

Macy squinted and held her hand to her brow to block some of the sunshine. "Kodiak was good with those kids."

"She always is."

"Now, I don't know much about training dogs…" Macy's words were measured. She had obviously been thinking about this and wanting to bring it up for some time. "So I don't know if this is an odd suggestion, but did you ever think of training therapy dogs instead of hunting dogs?" She pitched Kodiak's ball again and pressed a hand to his bicep when he opened his mouth to say something. "Hear me out. How Kodiak was with those kids? I feel like she could be a comfort dog for kids in trauma. She could be the comfort dog for the ranch." Macy spread out her arms, encompassing the whole property.

"Red dog." Rhett smiled, remembering what she had said in the chapel last week and what Jack had texted earlier that day.

Macy wagged her finger at him. "I told you she'd make a good mascot."

Rhett wrapped his hand over hers and tugged her a few inches closer. "I should have believed you."

"You usually come around to my ideas." Macy tapped on his chest. "It just takes some pestering."

"That's because they're good ideas." He stepped back, releasing her. If he had stood there a second longer he might have pulled her closer or said something he shouldn't yet. "Honestly? I'd love to train therapy dogs." Probably more than he enjoyed training hunting dogs. "But I just don't know when I'd have the time, and it takes a different sort of training than I know."

Macy leaned her back against the fence so she was facing him. "What if we got you help?"

Rhett scanned the pasture. "We're trying to save money here."

"Hypothetically, if someone took on more of the ranch's responsibilities?"

"Sure, yes." Rhett laughed at her tenacity. "I'd love that. It's a good dream."

She pushed off the fence. "In the meantime, you should reach out to your clients again and schedule more sessions. I can handle some of your load and I'm thinking we should approach Shannon, give her more responsibility."

Rhett considered the idea. Shannon didn't presently have a position at the ranch. "She seems to be going through some stuff right now."

Macy nodded. "I think having duties, things to occupy her other than Cord, would be a good thing."

"It's a good thought. Let me mull it over some." He motioned toward the office. "As for now, I have some calls I have to make. Are you heading over?"

"I actually have to run into town." She pointed her thumb in the direction of her car. "But I do want to talk with you about something else. Later, of course. I know you're busy."

Rhett felt his eyebrows rise. He fought the urge to press her to talk now, but if she had wanted to talk over something presently she had had an open opportunity and had chosen not to. He could respect her desire to put off whatever she wanted to say until another time. "How about this evening? I take Kodiak to the lake after supper. Would that work?"

She nodded. "That would be perfect."

"Then later it is." He tipped his hat and Kodiak fell into step beside him. He started thinking about ways he could make their meeting tonight special, a sort of olive branch for the new start to their friendship.

"Hey, Rhett," Macy called after him. He turned to

find her a few feet away, her fingers entwined. "If you made a promise to someone, a promise you weren't sure you wanted to keep any longer, what would you do?"

A breeze swept down from the hills, making the bluebonnets bob around them. The field resembled a sea of turbulent waves.

He hooked his fingers on his belt. "Talk with the person who I made the promise to, I guess."

"What if that wasn't an option any longer?" She was clearly talking about his dad. Perhaps his visit to Brock's grave had prompted her questions. Rhett couldn't deny his curiosity was piqued, but after his time at the grave site this morning, Rhett knew he needed to work on trusting. Trust that his dad had had good intentions for handing the ranch to him, trust that God had a hand in all the chaos surrounding Rhett's life. Trust Macy too.

Rhett took a half step in her direction. "The person you made the promise to, were they an upright person?"

Macy had been looking down at her hands but now her focus snapped to him. "One of the best I've ever met."

"Then I'd leave it," Rhett said gently.

"You're sure?" She eyed him. "Absolutely sure?"

Rhett knew she was asking something bigger, something more…but he couldn't figure it out. However, if Brock had told her some secret, Rhett wouldn't press her for it. She would only feel guilt after telling him and he couldn't do that to her.

No matter how much he wanted to.

"I'm sure."

She could keep her old secrets as long as Rhett had the hope of her future.

Chapter Eight

With no time to change or freshen up once Macy got back to Red Dog Ranch, she headed straight to the lakeshore. It was long past the time Cassidy served supper at the mess hall so she knew Rhett would be at the lake by now. Cassidy had texted earlier, asking if Macy had been able to stop for food while she'd been out. Macy had let her know that she was probably going to skip dinner and dive into a pint of mint swirl ice cream waiting back in her small fridge later tonight instead.

Romeo brayed as she passed his enclosure.

"Sorry, buddy, I got nothing. I didn't even get a chance to grab myself food." She reached over the fence and scratched between his ears. He brayed again. "Oh, you impatient little guy, good thing you're so cute. I see you already forgot about the pear chunks I brought you yesterday." Her stomach rumbled.

She left Romeo and continued in the direction of the lake. She hiked up the last hill and paused at the top. Rhett's back was to her as he stood at the end of the long wooden pier with a bundle or some sort of basket by his feet. Kodiak swam after her red ball in the water. A trail of candles burning inside glass jars led the way down the pier to him. The sight caused Macy's pulse to kick up.

Was this…was this a date?

She brushed the thought away. After all, she had been the one to ask him to meet up to talk, not the other way around. Although it was hardly as if Rhett would have set out the candles if he was going to be here alone.

She would not read too much into the gesture.

She would not.

Hopefully, she would believe the statement the more she repeated it to herself.

Kodiak, who had been dropping the ball onto the pier for Rhett to toss out again, swam past the pier to the shore. The dog leapt from the water, gave one great shake and then charged in Macy's direction.

Rhett followed his dog's progress but stayed on the pier. A wide, handsome smile spread across his features as he slipped his hands into his pockets. "See. What did I tell you? She likes you more than me already."

"Hardly," Macy called back with a laugh.

The dog happily head butted Macy's knee and Macy gave her a welcoming pat only to discover that Kodiak felt dry. "How is this dog not wet?" She touched her coarse fur again.

"Double coated," Rhett answered. "Thick under-layer keeps her skin from ever getting wet. The top layer is considered a harsh coat. You know how a duck can go in the water and comes out without being waterlogged?"

Kodiak trailed along beside Macy as she made her way to the pier. "Don't ducks have some special oil though?"

"Chessies have oil trapped between the two layers of their coat. Works the same way."

Closer to the shore Macy accepted the red ball and threw it out into the lake for Kodiak to go after. Rhett's dog had the endurance of a triathlete.

Rhett came to where the planks connected with the shore and offered his hand. "I have something for you," he said almost shyly.

Macy unsuccessfully fought a wary grin as she slipped her hand into his. "What is all this?"

Rhett led her to the end of the pier. "Cassidy told me you were planning to skip supper tonight. She gave me the candles." He gave a nervous shrug.

Cassidy. Of course. Always trying to set them up. It was too bad the romantic ambiance hadn't been Rhett's idea, but Macy would enjoy it nonetheless.

The pier creaked and swayed with their steps. Macy noticed each jar had been filled a third of the way with sand before a votive was placed inside. Flames flickered as they passed by, giving the pier a dreamlike quality. Fireflies drawn to the lights whizzed around their legs. Croaking frogs, the lake lapping the underside of the boards, their steps and the slight crunch of the tethered canoe against the side of the pier were the only sounds.

Well, besides Kodiak's feverish paddling.

When they reached the end Rhett let go of her hand

so he could tug a blanket from the large tote bucket he must have stowed there. He spread the blanket out then looked over at her, turned and looked out at the lake, cleared his throat, scratched the back of his neck.

Was he…goodness, the man was all nerves.

She, of all people, had flustered Rhett Jarrett. Her logical, straight-talking friend couldn't find words. The realization warmed Macy's heart.

"Rhett," she said his name tenderly. "What is all this?"

He cleared his throat again. "Food." He pulled the top off of the tote bucket. "You weren't at the mess hall so I assumed you hadn't eaten. And Cassidy said she didn't think you had and helped me gather some things. I shouldn't just assume that if you're not with us you're not anywhere though, right? You could have been out on a date instead for all I know." He looked right at her, his blue eyes wider than usual. "Were you on a date? Wait." He held up a hand. "Not my business. You don't have to tell me. Unless you want to, that is. If you do, you can."

Macy pressed her hand over his mouth to stop his rambling. Nervous Rhett was by far the most adorable version of Rhett she had ever encountered.

"Cassidy was right. I have not eaten." And at past eight at night she was definitely hungry now. Macy slowly removed her fingers from his lips. Blood thrummed through her veins at a turbulent pace, making her skin feel tingly. "And I wasn't on a date."

She caught the grin he attempted to hide when he ducked back toward the tote to pull out food. "We had a bad start when I came back. I want to start over like two old friends should have." He handed her a small bundle. "Blue-cheese steak wrap."

"My favorite. You remembered?" Macy took a seat on the blanket facing the lake. She unrolled the parchment paper so she could take a bite of the wrap. The bold notes of blue cheese, spinach and freshly grilled steak made her taste buds dance.

"Of course." Rhett produced a glass bowl full of frozen blueberries—a favorite childhood treat. His mom used to sprinkle them over ice cream or hand out bowls of frozen blueberries on hot summer nights while everyone gathered on the back porch to watch the sunset. Next came a thermos and two cups.

"Just Cassidy's sparkling watermelon lemonade."

"*Just* is not the right word." Macy unscrewed the lid and inhaled the sweet scent emanating from the thermos. "She hasn't made this stuff since last summer and I love it. How did you talk her into it?"

Rhett winked. "I have my ways." His bravado fell to sudden nervousness again. "Okay, and these might not be great, but..." He pulled a small tin from the basket.

When he opened the lid, Macy gasped. "S'mores stuffed cookies. You convinced someone to make them? I haven't had these since..." She snagged one from the tin and sank her teeth into it, letting her eyes flutter closed as the perfect balance of chocolate, marshmallow, graham-cracker crumbs and cookie melted on her tongue. "I think it's been at least ten years since I've had one and they're just as good as I remember."

"Oh, good." Rhett rubbed the back of his neck. "Because I made them and I wasn't sure how they would turn out."

Macy's eyes filled with irrational tears. She had to rapid-fire blink to keep them from falling. "You made these? You got the ingredients and mixed them and cooked them…for me?"

His head dipped with acknowledgment. "Your mom's recipe."

"Thank you," she whispered. She wanted to hug him, to kiss him and to cry too. The last time Macy had tasted these cookies her mom had made them. Each time she had unearthed her mom's spiral notebook full of recipes she had started crying, never able to actually make any of the recipes inside. Besides, she wasn't much of a cook or baker to begin with.

Rhett's gesture was an act of love. Plain and simple.

This was the man she had lost her heart to so many years ago.

Rhett hung his legs over the edge of the pier while Macy finished eating. He scuffed his palms along the thighs of his jeans, trying to will them to stop sweating. A lot of good that did.

Macy gently set the tin of cookies down and scooted to sit beside him at the end of the pier. "Tonight… This is…this is so beautiful, Rhett. What you did for me."

I did it because I love you. I'd do this every day if it made you happy. I should have done this a long time ago.

His throat burned with words he had to swallow.

Tonight wasn't the time to declare anything. Tonight

was an olive branch, letting her know he was serious about them being friends again.

A candle flickered in the breeze beside him. Cassidy had forced him to bring those along and had even sent a kitchen hand to set it all up. He thought the candles were a bit much for renewing friendship, but he knew better than to argue with Cassidy when her mind was made up.

He braced his hands at an angle so one was behind her, bringing them even closer. Raven strands of her hair danced in the breeze, the long ends traced across his shoulder.

"That day, when I left the ranch..." The words were out before he could consider them.

She scooped her hair to the side and turned toward him so their faces were less than a foot apart. Waning sunlight backlit her and his breath caught for a moment. She was the most beautiful person he had ever seen. She licked her lips, drawing his attention to how much he wanted to kiss her.

He sat up, pulling away from her a bit in the process. She mirrored his posture, leaning forward now so her shoulder bumped his arm.

"You stopped me, on my way out." An image of Macy with tears streaking down her cheeks played in his mind, unbidden. It tore at his heart.

"I was afraid you were going to leave without saying goodbye."

On that day he *had* planned to leave the ranch without saying goodbye to anyone. He had been so angry after his father's ultimatum—stay and stop questioning Brock's methods or leave for good.

He rubbed his hands together slowly. If only it was so easy to dust off mistakes. "You told me I was wrong. You said I had to see my dad's side," he said. "All I heard was you choosing him, choosing this place over me like he'd done so many times."

"When you said it was you or the ranch, I didn't know how to answer," Macy admitted. "I loved your dad as if he was my father. Your family had become mine. I didn't just want to leave everything. My home. When you offered me the job on the spot, it came out of nowhere."

He turned his head her way again. Had to see her eyes. "There was more to it than that. I… I wanted you to pick me. I wanted someone—wanted you— to choose me." For his entire life, his dad had never picked him. Rhett had never felt as if he was first place in anyone's heart. He had wanted to be the top person in Macy's life that day, but he knew it had been wrong to demand she choose him over everything else. He couldn't hold the eye contact—not after that admission—so he gazed out at the lake. "You had been dating that guy."

"Jim." She scooted closer.

"Yeah, him."

She surprised Rhett by laying her head on his shoulder. "I'm tired. Do you mind?"

Rhett fought the urge to turn his nose into her hair and breathe in her scent. "Not at all."

"Jim didn't like you." She adjusted where her head was, nestling even closer. She sighed. "He told me to stop spending so much time with you and I did."

"I noticed." Rhett slipped off his hat and set it beside him. Then he leaned his head to rest it on hers. They had never been like this before, so easy with their physical contact, but it felt right. It made Rhett wonder why he had never put his arm around her or reached out for her before now. "And I didn't like it."

"You were jealous?"

"Practically bursting with it," he said. He swallowed hard. "Then after you showed up and turned down the job…" He omitted the kiss after how the conversation had gone last night. "Then you wouldn't return my calls. It seemed I had successfully run off the one person who had always been in my corner, so I figured I was meant to be alone. Later, when you called—" he heaved a sigh "—I convinced myself you were better off without me."

Macy sat up suddenly and scooted so she was half facing him. She dropped her hand to his knee. "We may be the two stupidest people on the planet."

"I don't follow."

"That kiss? I wanted to be with you, Rhett." She looked away. "I had wanted that for a long time. When things didn't go well… I was horrified, to say the least."

"Mace." He couldn't let her continue to believe he hadn't wanted her. Hadn't imagined that kiss differently a million times over the last three years. "I was surprised. But it was a good surprised," he rushed on. "And I muddled it completely."

"You kept saying, 'Why did you do that?'"

He had only meant to start the conversation.

"It all happened so fast." But it had definitely been the wrong thing to say. However, he had pushed back his feelings for Macy for so long and hadn't allowed himself to entertain the idea that maybe she cared deeply for him, as well.

"When I finally worked up the nerve to call back and you never responded, I assumed it was because you didn't want me. Your messages had just said that we needed to talk so I had no clue if it was a good talk or a bad talk. This whole time I've been telling myself something was missing, something was—" her voice caught "—wrong with me. First my dad, then you." She swiped at her eyes.

Heaviness settled on Rhett's chest and lungs as she spoke. He'd had a hand in causing these insecurities. Aware of them now, he would fight them alongside of her for the rest of their lives in whatever capacity she would allow him to.

"Mace." He caught her face between his hands. "There has never been, nor will there ever be, anything you can do or say that will make me not want you in my life. My pride kept me away—that's on me and only me. You are perfect the way you are and I'd never want you to change. That was a lot of words, but I mean it. You have been my closest friend—my best friend—for most of my life. I'd like to erase everything that happened between us ever since I left and just go back to how we were for so many years."

Macy shrugged from his touch.

"Go back to how we were," she said robotically. "Of course. Friends." Her smile didn't reach her eyes.

"It's getting late. Is it okay if I share the thing I wanted to talk about now?"

His hands dropped away from her. During his spur-of-the-moment conversation he had lost track of the fact that she had been the one who wanted to talk about something. "I bulldozed this whole night, didn't I?"

"I didn't mind. We needed to hash this stuff out."

His hat still off, Rhett ran his hand through his hair. "Please, what was it you wanted to talk about?"

Macy grimaced. "It's business stuff—but I'm really excited."

He grabbed his hat and set it back on his head. "Bring it on."

"Let's clean as we talk." She motioned toward the basket. Macy started gathering plates and other items and handing them his way to stow in the bucket he had brought. Rhett got up and started gathering the candles.

The sun had finished its dip to the other side of the world and the fields had turned dark. Kodiak lay a few feet away, catching a small nap. If the three of them could have stayed like this then life would have been perfect. Too bad reality knocked hard enough to wake the heaviest dreamer.

They had made their peace, but Rhett still had to make amends with Shannon and chart the best path for the ranch going forward. Running Camp Firefly was a full-time job on its own, and summer was the busiest time with the cattle. On top of that he still had to replace some essential staff members who had left after his father passed. Soon enough Rhett would have to start putting in fourteen-hour workdays just to keep up.

Maybe things would settle down by the time autumn rolled around.

Macy handed him the blanket. "I might have messaged someone about the egg hunt and not told you about it."

He chuckled. The worry in her voice was evident and he wanted to put her at ease.

"So now you have to tell me, huh?"

She rose and grabbed both his hands, giving them one quick pump as she said, "It's Clint Oakfield."

"*The* Clint Oakfield?" Rhett knew he was bound to be gaping but he couldn't help it. The man had recently been inducted into the Grand Ole Opry.

"The one and only. He wants to come to our event and he's bringing all kinds of signed merch to raffle off. He's also made a donation that covers more than half of our expenses. If it's okay with you, of course. He wants to do a few songs and—"

Rhett caught her up in a hug, lifting her clear off the ground. "You're amazing! You know that, right?"

Kodiak bounded to her feet and came over to them, tail wagging, as she picked up on their excitement. When Rhett set Macy down she turned to lavish attention on Kodiak, and he found he was glad for the distraction.

Because without Kodiak's interruption he very well might have kissed Macy and ruined all the steps they had taken toward mending their friendship tonight.

Chapter Nine

The day of the egg hunt had dawned with an overwhelming cloak of muggy air descending onto the ranch. Macy pulled her hair into a ponytail and fanned her face. With all the running around involved for setup and directing others, she was already on her second shirt of the day and was considering changing again or at least freshening up before the candy drop occurred.

She glanced at her watch. There wouldn't be enough time.

Thankfully no one seemed to be letting the unseasonably warm, damp weather affect their attitudes, nor had it negatively impacted the turnout. Kids and guardians swarmed every inch of Red Dog Ranch. The sight of all of them smiling and enjoying their day filled Macy's heart to the point of bursting.

Every fight, every miscommunication, every late night had been worth it.

The staff and interns had cleared out the largest field in preparation for the candy drop and local businesses had banded together to set up a carnival complete with games, prizes, snacks, horse rides and a petting zoo on the opposite side of the driveway. The little goats included in the petting zoo were the talkative type, filling the air with their bleats. Buses lined the fenced area in the overflow parking section. Clint Oakfield was stationed near the mess hall for photos and signatures, and Jack Donnelley had the helicopter parked near Sheep and Romeo's enclosure. The helicopter was open so kids could go inside, pretend they were flying it and have their pictures taken. A tent nearby served as a place where kids could paint eggs to take home.

Macy decided it was the most successful Easter event the ranch had ever hosted. Wistfully she wished Brock had lived to see this day. He would have been so proud of Rhett, proud of her too.

A sudden stiff wind tore down through the row of hills lining their property, sending some of the promotional signs flying. Macy jogged after them, gathering up the mess.

"Here's another one." A man in a red shirt handed her one she must have missed.

Macy thanked him and stowed the rest inside the Jarrett house, using the diversion as an excuse to also check on Mrs. Jarrett. Rhett's mom observed the event through the floor-to-ceiling, two-story-high windows in the comfort of her living room. For as long as Macy had known the woman, she had been this way—watchful, perceptive and thoughtful. Alzheimer's might have stolen her ability to make new memories or to recall what year she was currently in, but it hadn't taken the truest things about her. Not yet.

"Ah, there's our dear lady." A smile bloomed on

Mrs. Jarrett's face when she spotted Macy. "Looks like a good turnout despite the forecast."

"Everything is going really well," Macy assured her. "Last I heard, it's not supposed to storm until later."

Mrs. Jarrett gestured toward the large bank of windows. "I know we have you to thank for this day. And don't tell me this was Rhett's doing because I know you've worked so hard, dear. I'm so proud of you." She reached out her hand.

Macy grasped it. "You're too kind. You always know how to bless me with the right words."

"Bless you? Oh, child, you're the one who has always been a blessing to this family. Not the other way around, Macy Howell. You are our blessing. I want you to remember that."

You are our blessing.

Could it be true? Macy had never considered herself a blessing to anyone. A burden. Forgettable. Not enough.

Never a blessing.

But Mrs. Jarrett was not one to say anything carelessly.

"Send Brock inside if it gets bad, will you?" Mrs. Jarrett twisted toward the windows again. She drew a blanket around her shoulders. "His joints are probably already barking at him. All this moisture will do that."

Macy urged the nurse on duty to make sure Mrs. Jarrett had extra opportunities to rest today as all the additional people and excitement could make for a rough night for the older woman.

With the knowledge that Mrs. Jarrett was in great hands, Macy headed back outside and surveyed the party from the large wraparound porch. She rested her hand on the walkie-talkie and considered calling Rhett, but she knew he was busy giving tours of the camper cabins to local businessmen who had expressed interest in potentially partnering with Camp Firefly. He was exactly where he needed to be and she wouldn't distract him.

No matter how badly she wanted to.

The weeks leading up to the event had blurred together in a whirl of planning, running errands and scheduling. Rhett had thrown himself into helping and had even called in favors from past dog-training clients, all of which had made a huge difference. Through his connections the price of the food had been covered, among other things. On top of that, the man had spent every weekend working on last-minute maintenance throughout the ranch, but especially devoting extra time and attention toward getting the camper cabins ready for the summer. Time and again she had stopped by on a Saturday to find him knee-deep in manual labor, sleeves rolled up and covered in sweat…handsomer than ever.

It had warmed Macy's heart to see Rhett finally stepping up to help with the foster programs offered at Red Dog Ranch. He went about it in a different way than his father had, but honestly, Rhett had a better mind for the big picture when it came to planning. Macy had come to really appreciate his input and insight. She had come to rely on him.

Not only that but he had started seeing his dog-training clients again. Only a few for now, but it was progress. She had left information about courses for people who wanted to train therapy dogs on his desk and he had promised to sign up for something in the fall.

While she had loved finally being able to work toward a common goal with him, side by side, and while it had been exhilarating and encouraging striving in tandem to make the event a success in such a short amount of time, Macy couldn't help the lingering feeling of disappointment that occasionally tiptoed into her heart.

What had happened to the romantic man she had enjoyed supper with on the pier weeks ago? Perhaps she had misinterpreted everything that evening, but whenever she replayed it—his warm gazes and tender words, his kind gestures like the cookies—she found herself bewildered all over again.

Despite his many mentions of the word *friend*, that night she had wanted him to kiss her. More than she ever had before. But he hadn't. Even after they left the pier, Rhett had insisted on walking her to her bungalow and she was sure he had a reason other than her safety. It wasn't as if she hadn't walked alone on the ranch's property a million other times. But he had strolled beside her all the way to the pebbled path leading to her bungalow, wished her good-night and walked away.

In the following days she had expected him to offer some sort of clarification, but it seemed that Rhett had clammed up again, at least where she was concerned. Oh, he had completely gone all out helping with the egg hunt and had begun intentionally mentoring Gabe, as well. He was talking about hiring some of the interns on for the summer. Rhett had risen to the occasion. Macy had no complaints there.

But it left her wondering…

He felt something for her, something more than friendship. No one could have convinced Macy otherwise, but something was holding him back.

Jack flagged Macy down. "We're going to move up the candy drop. I don't like the looks of that." He pointed to the black clouds piling up in the distance. "Rhett okayed it, but he said to check with you."

Macy radioed to Cassidy. "How are the hams? About done?"

Her walkie-talkie crackled a second later. "We can plate as soon as twenty minutes."

Macy nodded and Jack jogged toward his helicopter. The interns helped direct the crowd to line up near the marked off portions of the large field and Macy followed in their wake. As was tradition, Rhett's uncle Travis took the stage to rattle off instructions.

The helicopter lifted off, beating the air in huge waves. Macy shivered, but the children cheered. Jack circled the field once, allowing the rest of his onboard crew to get into position along the open sides of the large craft. When Travis sounded the bullhorn the helicopter crew began dropping candy out of the helicopter until the field was colorful with it.

Although raindrops weren't falling at the ranch yet, the sky just beyond their property had turned pitch-black with rain. A storm would rip through Red Dog Ranch within minutes. As Jack's helicopter left the area kids were allowed to converge on the field to fill their bags. Macy wanted to urge everyone to go quickly, but the kids hardly needed to be told.

Macy ran toward Romeo and Sheep's enclosure. "I

know neither of you appreciate getting rained on." She attached lead lines to both of their halters and walked them toward the barn. Halfway there, Romeo pinned his ears back and started braying. He planted his hoofs.

"Come on, you goof." Macy tried to coax him with a promise of a treat later. "Let's get you inside and everything will be fine." But the tiny donkey balked.

Rhett appeared beside her, his brow creased with worry. "This storm is bearing down quicker than they predicted." His head swiveled in the direction of the approaching storm. "It looks like a wall of clouds. I can't say I've ever seen anything like it."

Macy tossed the lead lines over her shoulder to free up her hands. She grabbed both animals' halters and used the leverage of all her weight to lean in the opposite direction. "We just need to get people inside."

Rhett pushed Romeo's rear end, getting the donkey moving again. "I'll send everyone to the mess hall."

"You deal with the people and I'll get everything else stowed away," she called after him as he headed to the stage.

Kodiak took off after Rhett, but suddenly stopped and looked back at Macy. She whimpered low in her throat.

Rhett glanced back. "Stay with Macy."

Kodiak charged to join her as Macy fumbled with the lock on the barn.

Rain began to ping off the roofs, the dirt. One second it was sprinkling and before she could open the barn door it was pouring down. Cold water trickled down her spine and her legs.

As she secured Sheep and Romeo in their stalls she

heard Rhett on the loudspeakers directing people toward the mess hall. A heartbeat later, a loud crash of thunder had Romeo bucking in his stall. Macy hoped someone had seen to the group of horses that were being used for rides.

Kodiak pressed close to Macy's legs.

"You can stay in here, girl." Macy ran her fingers over the dog's coarse fur. "You'll be safe and dry and don't need to worry about me." Macy made for the door and Kodiak matched her step for step.

"I said stay." Macy made her voice commanding.

Kodiak barked and followed Macy as she plucked one of the shared heavy-duty raincoats from a peg on the wall and made her way outside.

Macy looked down at the dog beside her. "You're just as stubborn as your master, aren't you?"

Kodiak met her eyes and barked again. Her last command from Rhett would be followed to the letter, no matter what Macy told the dog.

Macy tugged the hood of her coat up. "Well, come on then. We've got work to do."

"It's warm inside. And smell that?" Rhett sniffed the air for the benefit of the scared, young kids filing past him. "Nobody makes ham like our cook, Miss Cassidy. And if I were you, I'd snag an extra one of her cheddar-cheese rolls. Believe me." Rhett held the mess hall's front door open until the last person had entered.

Due to the storm, many people had opted to get on the road instead of stay for the meal the ranch always hosted as a fund-raiser afterward. Rhett couldn't blame them for heading out. He prayed they all made it to their destinations safely. It looked as if it was going to be one wicked storm.

He secured the door then shook rain off of his hat. Outside the sky was as dark as midnight despite it only being four in the afternoon. Bright veins of lightning spliced through the black. They lighted up the grounds below the hills for a heartbeat. Rhett frantically scanned the area through the windows along the front porch of the mess hall, looking for any families that might still be out there, but the main fields where they'd held the event were deserted.

The rumble that followed the lightning was immediate and powerful. Inside the mess hall younger kids screamed and ducked their heads under tables.

Rhett lingered in the entryway with his hat still clutched in his hands, waiting for Macy and Kodiak. He wasn't even going to deny that fact. He was fully aware that Macy was smart and capable and did not need him fretting over her because of a thunderstorm.

Yet here he was.

He wouldn't be able to relax until he saw her safe inside.

Rain pelted the building hard. It was as if someone was heaving bucket after bucket of water against their windows. The south pasture near the lake would flood. It always did during bad storms. Thankfully, rain of this magnitude was a rarity. And they had moved the cattle to a different field to get them away from the event, so that wouldn't be an issue.

Wind bent smaller trees sideways. There would be plenty of shingles to fix tomorrow.

Rhett paced the small area and worked his hat

around and around in his hands a few times before
he remembered his cell phone. Because of dog training, he was in the habit of keeping the contraption on
silent. What if Macy had tried to call? What if she
needed him? She had warned him to turn the thing
on occasionally.

He tugged his phone from his pocket and his heart
leapt when he saw one missed call and a voice mail.
He thumbed the screen to unlock it. One missed call
from Hank, his lawyer friend, who had started book-
ing training sessions for Riptide again. Hank had already told him that the will was as ironclad as they had
originally believed, but Rhett didn't care any longer.

Uncle Travis popped his head into the entryway
hallway. "You're needed."

Rhett stopped pacing. "Have you seen Macy or
Shannon?" His sister was usually actively involved
during events, but he hadn't seen her all day. Hopefully she was in the house with their mom.

His uncle gave Rhett a thoughtful look. "I saw Macy
on my way in. She said she was going to gather as much
of the setup stuff as she could before the worst of the
storm rolled in. Good thing too. Stuff from the games
would have ended up all over the ranch with this wind."

Rhett headed toward the door. "She shouldn't be out
there alone. I should be helping her."

His uncle snagged his arm. When Rhett looked back
to argue, Travis jerked his head toward the speaker
system set up at the front of the mess hall. "This shin-
dig always starts with a word from the owner and a
prayer. It's tradition."

"But—"

"Macy is a grown woman who knows what she can handle. You're the owner. These people are your responsibility. You are needed here." Uncle Travis ushered Rhett away from the doorway. "I'll try to get in touch with Shannon if that would ease your mind."

Rhett nodded and tucked his phone away, but he glanced through the front windows one last time. Macy was out there and so was Kodiak. *Keep them safe, Lord. Please watch over them.*

When Rhett stepped into the dining area, a hush fell over the crowd. He dipped his head as he walked. Rhett made eye contact with a few of the children on his way to the front of the room. One little boy flashed him a thumbs-up so Rhett returned the gesture and added a wink for good measure.

The aroma of freshly baked rolls and chocolate cake along with ham and caramelized pineapple drifted through the room. Rhett's mouth watered. Cassidy and her crew of volunteers had spent all day in the kitchen working on the feast. He couldn't wait to taste everything.

The speaker system was used primarily during the summer months for making announcements or telling the campers to simmer down on occasion. They hadn't used it recently and Rhett absently hoped it was still functioning. Rhett picked up the microphone and tapped it twice. It worked just fine.

"Good afternoon and thank you for braving the storm for this event," Rhett started. He hadn't planned anything to say. In truth, he had forgotten about the little spiel his dad had always given. Brock's talk had lasted a few minutes, a sermon of sorts. Often it included the salvation message.

Rhett let his focus slowly trip across everyone in the room. So many kids and all of them either waiting for a permanent home or waiting for their homes to become a safe place for them once again. Seeing so many of them in front of him, it tore at his heart. After visiting with them all day and seeing their hopeful faces, now Rhett knew that he wanted to help them to continue to be the legacy of Red Dog Ranch.

No matter what, he would choose these kids. This life. This place.

The legacy not only his dad had secured for him, but God too.

He would figure out a way to keep all the programs, turn a profit at the ranch and still train dogs on the side. With Travis, Macy, Cassidy, Shannon and many others—there were plenty of them to divide the work between. Together they would make it a success.

For the first time in what felt like years, Rhett finally understood his dad's passion and drive and he wanted to lay down all his past hurts to honor all his dad had built.

Rhett blinked against the sudden rush of emotions. "I know many of you must have wondered what would happen to Red Dog Ranch after my father passed." He found Uncle Travis in the room and for a heartbeat he pictured Brock there too, beaming and happy. Though this wasn't for his dad any longer; it was for Rhett. "A wise man once asked me if I knew the heart of God when it came to this place and I'm ashamed to admit I brushed his challenge off. But God has this funny way of not letting us forget something like that."

A loud rumble of thunder shook the building and the lights browned out for a few seconds. People in the crowd murmured worriedly. He needed to keep this short and sweet.

Rhett began to walk between the tables as he spoke. "How do we know the heart of God?"

"The Bible!" a little girl called out.

Rhett pointed her way. "Great answer. The Bible shows us God's heart. And what are we celebrating today?"

"Easter!" This time a chorus of kids joined in.

"That's right, Easter. The greatest showing of God's heart for this world. Our heavenly Father loves us so much that He wanted to make a way for us to never be parted from Him. He loves us enough to sacrifice His son so that we can have a relationship with Him." Rhett headed back to the front of the room. "So back to my friend's question—do I know the heart of God in this matter? Yes, well, yes I do. The heart of God, the answer to every question concerning what I should do—what each of us should do in our lives—is love. In any situation we have to ask ourselves, 'What is the loving thing to do?' Then we have our answer."

Cassidy stood near the pass-through, ready to hand out the food. Rhett caught her wiping a tear away.

"My father left behind a legacy of love and I mean to continue it."

The dining hall erupted with cheers and applause. A man seated nearby got to his feet and threw his arms around Rhett in an awkward hug. Clearly Macy hadn't been the only person worried about how Rhett would run Red Dog Ranch.

"How about we say a prayer and then dig in to this food?" Rhett smiled at the crowd. "It smells amazing."

But before Rhett could bow his head Jack Donnelley slammed open the side door so loudly it caused people at nearby tables to jump out of their seats. Jack rushed toward Rhett with the intensity of a bomb-sniffing dog on patrol.

Jack reached Rhett, phone in hand. "My dispatch center just called. Tornado warning. It's touched down less than a mile away. It could be on us in minutes, maybe less." Jack's police training showed as he calmly delivered the information. "We need to get people to safety."

Hands shaking, Rhett got back on the microphone. "Change of plans. We're under a tornado warning. I need everyone to proceed in a single-file line down to the basement."

A few people yelled and more started to cry, but everyone got to their feet quickly and headed toward one of the sets of stairs. Thankfully, there were plenty of adults to help guide the children. Jack, Uncle Travis and Rhett each manned the top of one of the three entrances to the basement, directing people to go down and as far back as they could.

Rhett sent Macy a text:

Tornado. Get inside.

He almost typed I love you but wasn't that something that should be said first instead of texted? He loved Macy. The last few weeks had cemented that truth and thinking of her outside in the storm... All the roadblocks he had imagined between them suddenly felt insignificant. He had made peace with his father and let go of his pain and had done all he could to care for his mother. Besides, if he waited to act on his feelings until everything in his life was perfect the time would never come.

Fear had made excuses easy to believe, but he refused to chart his steps by fear any longer. Next time he saw her he would tell her how he felt. She might reject him, but he would deal with it if she did.

But a text stole some of the power away from declaring love. Then again, what if he never got the chance to tell her? What if...

He refused to think like that.

Cassidy had immediately whisked Piper to the basement and Rhett could hear her instructing people to get on their knees and cover their necks.

Keep people safe, Lord. Please protect all these people.

Maybe the tornado would miss the ranch. Maybe it would change course.

The building started to rattle under an onslaught of wind. Rhett instructed people to head down the steps a little quicker. They were almost done. Almost everyone now.

With his phone in his hand, Rhett willed Macy to call him. To tell him she was fine, tucked away somewhere safe. But he couldn't think only of her either. Other people depended on him. Rhett pulled up the number for the phone his mother's on-duty nurse carried and hit Call.

He didn't even let her greet him. "A tornado's touched down. It's close. Get to the lower interior bathroom. Put Mom in the tub. Grab pillows, blankets—anything to protect yourselves. Stay in there until one of us comes to get you guys."

"Understood." The nurse hung up.

Rhett's mind raced. His ears popped, more painfully than on any flight he had ever been on. The deep sink he was standing near gurgled and then the drain made one long, desperate suctioning sound. Rhett hurtled down the steps to join the others in the basement.

While Northern Texas experienced a fair amount of tornados, they were far less common in the hill country. And with Red Dog Ranch so far away from any of the local towns, he had never even heard a siren before and it wasn't as if they had their own alert system.

Tornados happened, but in thirty years Rhett had never seen one, never been in one.

The deafening howl outside told him that was about to change.

Chapter Ten

Even though she was wearing a heavy coat the rain started to pelt Macy so hard it physically hurt to be outside anymore. And it was cold. Horribly, painfully cold now.

The rain suddenly switched to falling sideways. Dime-sized hail clanged on a nearby roof, coming closer, peppering the ground.

Macy's teeth rattled and her legs trembled as she made her way through a patch of mud. She would catch a cold from this adventure; there was zero doubt in her mind about that. She should have headed inside ten minutes ago—should have gone in with everyone else instead of trying to be useful.

Macy turned to head toward the barn. It was a smelly place to ride out the weather, but it was near and would provide adequate shelter from the wind and wetness. A pole barn full of machinery and the Jarretts' ranch house were also within proximity, but both were farther than the solid oak barn where Romeo, Sheep and the other horses were kept.

When hail was part of the equation, Macy would choose close over comfort.

However, she couldn't make out the barn any longer. Darkness disoriented her. It was as if her eyes were closed. Macy pivoted a full 360 degrees, scanning the area, squinting, but it was no use. She couldn't even tell if she was facing in the correct direction any longer.

Dread pooled like a cooling ball of lead in the pit of her stomach. Weighty. Impossible to escape.

Kodiak rubbed against her leg and Macy steadied herself with a hand on the dog's shoulder. Kodiak's body shuddered under her fingers. Macy winced as her ears suddenly popped with an excruciating and sudden change in pressure.

Then she heard it.

A roar.

The sound of a train engine but louder. It vibrated through her whole body, her bones.

Tornado.

The wall of rain clouds had hidden a tornado.

An angry churning funnel headed directly toward the barn Macy had wanted to seek shelter in only moments ago. If the tornado stayed its course the horse barn would take a direct hit. The rest of the horses were in the pasture so they had the ability to get out of the way, but Sheep and Romeo were inside the building. And there was no time to set them loose; she wouldn't be able to make it. Macy's heart slammed into the back of her throat and sickness washed over her. If something happened to them, she had put them in there. She would be at fault.

But she couldn't think about that right now. Macy had to get to safety.

Go. Move. Get out of here.

A tiny piece of debris slammed into Macy's arm and she cried out as if she had been shot. Warmth seeped over the area. Hot and burning. Blood.

Macy grabbed for Kodiak's collar and yanked her toward the ranch house. "Run! We have to run."

She took off toward the house, knowing Rhett's faithful dog would stick close. She could do this. She could protect them. She could beat this storm.

Faster. Go. Faster.

Her legs burned. She slipped in deep mud and fell onto all fours. Her hands suctioned into the mire. Kodiak shoved her head under Macy's chest as if the dog was trying to lift her up. Macy scrambled forward on all fours, trying to get purchase.

Winds ripped a long swatch of fencing up out of the ground with a sickening crunch and tossed it in a tangled heap only yards away. A huge old tree snapped and took flight.

Wood from the horse barn began to splinter. The barn walls buckled and heaved behind her. Macy looked back to see the roof fly off and go up into the sky as if it weighed nothing. Gone.

Gathering additional debris, the funnel grew darker, larger. Its furious howl filled her ears until it was all she could hear, all she could think about.

She found her feet again and started for the ranch house. If she ran fast enough, she could still make it. She could skid inside and go under the huge, heavy table in their formal dining room. The room had no windows and sat almost in the center of the home, next to their interior bathroom where hopefully Rhett's mom was by now.

Macy was close enough. She would make it. Everything would be okay. It had to be. God hadn't brought them this far just to—

Kodiak's high-pitched yelp brought Macy up short. She whirled around to see Rhett's dog on the ground ten feet behind her with a large sheet of metal pinning her back half to the ground. Kodiak's front paws dug forward in an effort to pull herself out, but it was no use. Kodiak collapsed, her yellow eyes seeking out Macy.

If Macy kept moving she could make it to shelter in time, but she would have to leave Rhett's dog behind.

Not going to happen.

Macy plunged back toward the storm. Stiff winds sent rocks and other debris hurtling around her. Something scraped the side of her face. She pressed on. She dropped to her knees beside Kodiak. "It's okay, girl." Macy wrapped her fingers around the edge of the sheet of roofing. "I won't leave you."

She heaved the piece of metal with all her might. It was heavy and awkward. Her back spasmed, her biceps felt as if they were being shredded and her legs shook. Under normal circumstances Macy couldn't have budged the thing with only her strength. Macy grunted, putting all her weight into it, and was able to lift the debris enough for Kodiak to army crawl out of the opening.

Another loud, nauseating groan and the pole barn shattered like a child's art project constructed out of toothpicks. Large sections crashed onto the ground around them. That building was full of machinery—heavy metal and steel machinery that the tornado would toss around like confetti. Macy threw her body over Kodiak and braced her arms over her own neck and head.

They would never make it to the house now.

Get to the lowest point.

It was the only thing she could remember about tornados. Since all the structures that could protect them were too far away, they had to get over the hill to the lower area near Canoe Landing. Doing so might take them out of the path entirely. Macy hoisted Kodiak to her paws.

"Please be able to stand."

Kodiak had to be sixty to seventy pounds so there was little chance that Macy could carry her too far. The dog limped but kept up with her. They rushed down the hill, skidding and sliding their way down. Macy's arm and cheek stung like fire.

The lake was full of junk the tornado had tossed around and the shores were littered, as well. Macy grabbed a large piece of wood that must have been torn from the horse barn and wedged it up so they could get into the ditch under it. At least the board would deflect smaller debris. She reached back and hauled Kodiak to the lowest point, this ditch that fed into the lake, just as the winds increased and the funnel twitched toward them. Macy wiggled into the small space so she was lying across Rhett's dog, then she pulled the wood up over them and prayed.

Kodiak burrowed her muzzle into Macy's neck so

her nose was beside Macy's ear. The noise of the dog's steady breathing mixed with the sounds of destruction above them. Macy braced her arms tighter over their heads and slammed her eyes shut as if that would help.

"I'm here, sweet girl," Macy whispered.

Was this it? After everything, was this how her life ended?

Facing the possibility of death, Macy's mind raced back through twenty-eight years of life. Her father leaving, her mother's death, being all alone at only eighteen. The last ten years living with the Jarretts and her friendship with Rhett. The work she had done at the ranch and the lives she had come into contact with because of Brock's mission. Late nights spent giggling with Shannon and Cassidy. Quiet moments with Mrs. Jarrett.

Her evening on the pier with Rhett.

Macy had never felt truly loved and accepted in her life. She had always believed there was something defective about her. Some reason why no one wanted to commit. Why no one stayed.

But…it had always been a lie, hadn't it?

You're the one who has always been a blessing to this family. Not the other way around, Macy Howell. You are our blessing.

The Jarretts had welcomed and loved her as is. Shannon and Cassidy had become sisters to her. Macy had a place to belong—people who would miss her and mourn for her if this was her end. They hadn't loved her for all the late nights she'd spent in the office or the weekends she'd pitched in with the animals or the programs she had helped launch. It hadn't mattered what she had done or accomplished.

They had just loved…her.

Macy had always been enough, just as she was.

Tears stung her eyes; they leaked onto Kodiak's fur.

She had treated God the same way, hadn't she? Always trying to do enough and accomplish more so she would feel as if she deserved His love.

What an absurd way to live. She had no more power or ability to earn God's love than she had to stop this tornado. The might of the terrible tornado paled in comparison to an almighty God—and He loved her. He had sent His son to die for her.

"Forgive me," she whispered. "I love You. Thank You for loving me. If…if this is when I meet You, I'm ready. Just please take care of all these people. I love them so much. Take care of Rhett."

She prayed the mess hall would be untouched.

Something large slammed into the side of the building and the lights flickered. Someone in the basement wailed uncontrollably.

Seconds after Rhett's boots hit the basement's concrete floor the whole building plunged into darkness. Kids screamed and the soothing voices of many adults followed. Not wanting to step on anyone, Rhett fumbled around. His hand glanced against the doorknob on the door that led to the walk out where trucks made deliveries. It was a sturdy door, but in the end it was only wood.

Not good.

A tornado could wrench that door open and suck

people out. He was suddenly very thankful for his dad's foresight in insisting on an unconventional basement being built at the ranch, but the first thing Rhett would do was make this entrance more secure.

If he made it out.

Rhett braced his back against the door as if that might help and then he groped for the lock, found it and slipped it into the locked position. The small bolt probably wouldn't help much, but Rhett was willing to take every measure he had at his disposal to protect all the people gathered at his ranch.

His ranch.

Not his dad's. Not Brock's mission or dreams.

Rhett's.

All the glass windows upstairs shattered. It sounded like a series of rapid bombs going off in a war zone. The building started violently shaking and the door behind him vibrated like a jackhammer.

The tornado was passing over them.

Please, Lord, please. I don't care what happens to me but protect these people. Protect Macy and Kodiak and the rest of my family.

Metal rattled and crashed in the kitchen above them. If there was a person screaming a foot away from him, Rhett wouldn't have been able to tell. He could only hear the storm—there was only the tornado and it was all encompassing.

The walls of the building creaked and popped, moaning under the storm's violent onslaught. Something boomed against the door. It sounded like someone was smacking it with a huge metal chain. The bottom corner peeled back with such sudden force

Rhett gasped. Wind lashed in. Just as quickly, tiny debris shoved through the crack in the door frame— nails and wood and a mess of other items—until the small opening was plugged.

Then there was nothing. No wind, no pounding. Rhett could hear his heartbeat reverberating in his ears.

"Is it…" a tentative voice said nearby. "Do we think it's over?"

"Gabe?" Rhett reached toward the voice.

Gabe grabbed his arm. "It's me, Mr. Jarrett."

Rhett yanked the teenage boy into a bear hug. "We're safe. I think it's over." He lifted his head away from Gabe's. "Jack? You nearby?"

Jack's face became illuminated by his phone. "It's dissipated." Jack turned toward the expanse that was the long dark basement. "It looks like the tornado is done but everyone needs to stay put. I know it's uncomfortable in here and not fun to stay with the lights out, but this is the safest place."

Gabe shuffled his feet. "But I thought you said it was all done?"

Jack inclined his head. He fiddled with something on his phone that kept it illuminated. "It is, but the aftermath can be just as dangerous as the storm itself. Downed power lines and sharp objects everywhere. It's not safe to send everyone out yet." He typed into his phone. "EMS is on the way." He turned toward Rhett. "I'm heading out to assess. You're welcome to join me."

Rhett had pulled out his phone but couldn't get a signal. "My phone's not working." There was no message from Macy. No calls from his mom or Shannon.

Jack held up his phone. "Department phone. I'm

connected to a different system. Normal cell infra-
structures will be bogged down for the next few hours."
Jack stepped toward the door. "Are you coming or staying?"

Rhett looked back into the darkness that held all the
people who had come to the ranch expecting a fun day.
He had a duty to take care of them, but he also needed
to check on his mom and he needed to find Macy, Kodiak and Shannon. In the rush Rhett hadn't been able
to touch base with Uncle Travis to see if he had made
contact with Shannon.

"Found it," broke in a voice and then a flashlight
came on. Cassidy held it, with Piper beside her. "Go,
Rhett. We'll take care of everyone here."

Clint Oakfield appeared nearby. "She's right." He
sent Cassidy a tentative grin. "We'll take it from here.
For as long as you need." He clasped Rhett's shoulder.
"You go do what you need to do."

Rhett and Jack shouldered the door open and light
spilled in. Clint stacked a few milk crates together to
form a makeshift bench for him and Cassidy, then as
Rhett and Jack left they heard the country entertainer
sing the first few notes of "Amazing Grace" while a
chorus of voices joined in.

Emotion clogged Rhett's throat as he stepped clear
of the mess hall and surveyed the terrible destruction across the ranch below him. The sky was still
menacing, gloomy with a thick fog spreading into the
lower sections of his land, but he could see plenty clear
enough to know that Red Dog Ranch would never be
the same again.

There was a mess of splinters where once there was

a row of ten camper cabins. Hunks of steel hung from the trees they passed while other trees were shaved down to only gnarly bent trunks. One of their largest tractors lay on its side in what used to be the horse pasture. Where had that thing been parked beforehand? Nowhere near where it rested now. A bus had been tossed into the office building and cars that had been parked along the driveway were totaled—on their roof or sides, all windows blown out, frames twisted into odd angles.

"It's pretty messed up, huh?" Gabe's voice made Rhett whirl around.

"What are you doing here? You should be back in the basement."

Gabe crossed his arms over his chest. "You'll need help finding Miss Macy. I want to help. Besides, Cassidy said I could go with you."

Rhett considered arguing with the teenager but Jack broke in. "Stick close. Don't wander anywhere without either me or Rhett. Understood?"

"Understood." Gabe nodded. "I'll be like a shadow."

Rhett, Gabe and Jack picked their way carefully down the hill, stepping over tree limbs and other materials Rhett couldn't make sense of at the moment.

Seeing his ranch ripped to pieces made Rhett's eyes burn. Both of the barns were completely gone. He had no idea how his animals had fared. Did he still have cattle? Horses? The mess hall was still standing but a portion of the roof was gone. The Jarrett family home looked like it had managed to stay together.

Thank You, God.

Rhett began to move a little faster.

Jack kept pace with him. "I'm so sorry."

Rhett swallowed around the lump in his throat. Once, twice, three times before he could speak. "I, ah, for a long time I really didn't like this place." Hot shame poured through his chest but he pressed on. "My father…"

Jack stopped and set a hand on Rhett's shoulder, pulling Rhett to a stop. "He loved you, but he never said it. His heart was divided between his family and the ranch. I know."

Rhett nodded. "But I love this place." He gazed out over the absolute destruction in front of him. "I love— but I realized it all too late. Why am I always one step behind?"

A theme in his life. Too late to say goodbye to his father. Too late to stop Wade from taking off and ultimately getting killed.

Would he always be one step behind in his life? Doomed to not realize or appreciate all he had been blessed with? He truly was as bullheaded as people said. Why hadn't he been grateful about his inheritance? Sprung to action immediately to help kids. *Kids.* How had he missed every clue Macy no doubt dropped about her feelings earlier in their relationship?

Jack's even voice broke through his thoughts. "It's never too late. As long as you've got breath, don't let anyone—even your own stubborn self—tell you it's too late." Jack jutted his chin toward the ranch house. "You guys go check on your mom first. I'm going to head down the main road and do my best to clear a path so the emergency vehicles can get as close as possible."

"Should we come help you?" Rhett felt torn. He

wanted to do the right thing, but fear for his loved ones was eating at him.

Jack held up his hand. "You worry about your family. I'll deal with this. A crew will be here to help in no time. We'll do all we can to search for survivors and secure your area. From the looks of it, Red Dog Ranch took the brunt of this storm."

"Thank you, Jack." Rhett owed the man so much more than a thank-you. He owed him an apology too. "I've never been much of a friend to you and I wish—"

Jack shook his head. "No more worries, man. Seriously. Just take care of this place. It means a lot to me."

"Me too," Rhett said and meant it.

Rhett hadn't yet made it to the steps leading up to the porch when the front door pounded open and Shannon jogged out.

"Rhett!" She was down the steps in seconds and launched herself at him. Breath whooshed out of his lungs as he tried to keep his feet and catch her at the same time.

"I'm so sorry." Her body shook with tears. Her blond curls were wild. "If something had happened to you..." She dug her fingers into his shoulders. "If you had... I've been so cruel these past few weeks. We fought and—" her voice broke "—I've been—"

"Hey," he said tenderly and set her back so he could see his sister's face. "I love you, kid. I'm glad you're safe."

Her face twisted and she started crying harder. "I l-love you t-too. I'm sorry for—"

"Shh." He leaned forward, pressing a kiss to her forehead. "All that's forgiven and forgotten. I should

have been there for you more than I've been in the past.
I will be. That's a promise."

She swiped at her eyes.

"Mom?" Rhett asked.

"She's scared and confused and keeps asking about
Dad, but she's fine. The nurse too. We rode it out in the
bathroom," Shannon said. Her eyes went wide. "The
family room though—the wall of windows is gone and
there's a small tree in there. But other than that the
house looks okay. Out here?" She groaned.

"Macy and Kodiak?"

Shannon's focus snapped back to him and she
shook her head. "Macy wasn't with you?" Her brow
scrunched. "I just assumed. They're both always with
you."

"They weren't with me." The words hurt.

He should have made Macy come inside. He should
have never nodded along when she said she was going
to clean up the event. He had unknowingly sent Kodiak into the heart of a storm. If something had happened to either of them because of things, because of
material, replaceable stuff...

Jaw involuntarily clenching, Rhett fisted his hands.
"I have to find her."

*God, let them be alive. Let them be all right. Help
me find them.*

Chapter Eleven

Macy couldn't tell how much time had passed since the storm had ended, but it had stopped just as suddenly as it had begun. One second the gusts were trying to tear the sheet of wood off of them and the next all was still. Quiet.

She tried to bend to reach the phone tucked into the back pocket of her jeans, but her arms were pinned in front of her body and she couldn't make out the watch on her wrist even though it was inches from her face.

Was it night already? Was anyone looking for them?

A few birds tittered and somewhere nearby a group of cattle bellowed back and forth to one another. Each sound filled Macy with an almost irrational amount of joy because both noises spoke of hope to her. She had witnessed the horse barn and the pole barn being annihilated, but maybe, just maybe, that was the total loss to the ranch. Maybe all of the cattle and horses were fine. Maybe even now Sheep and Romeo were grazing in one of the pastures as if nothing was wrong.

She squeezed her eyes shut. She couldn't think

about the little horse and donkey. Couldn't let her mind go there. As long as she was under the board and couldn't see the totality of destruction, she had hope. She needed to cling to it.

However, no matter how hard she tried to be positive, it was almost impossible to chase all her unconstructive thoughts away.

What if no one came to free them because no one else had survived? What if she and Kodiak had lived through the tornado's assault only to be trapped under rubble, unable to get free? What if they survived the tornado but died because they were trapped in the aftermath?

Macy's heartbeat hammered in her neck and her temples. Her head pounded. A few tears escaped from her closely shuttered eyes.

Stop.

Thoughts along those lines would help no one. Least of all her.

Stay calm. Keep a clear head. Just keep breathing.

Macy could wiggle her toes, her feet. It was dark and muggy, but she could breathe. The only thing she couldn't do was lift the piece of wood from off of her and Kodiak. While originally the door-sized plank hadn't been very heavy, debris had obviously piled up on top of them to the point that Macy wasn't strong enough to push the covering up enough for them to shimmy out.

Maybe if she rested a bit?

God, I know You see us. I know You care. Please, be with me and Kodiak. Help us feel like we're not completely alone.

Her whole body ached and her muscles burned. Rain and mud had soaked her clothes, and her hair was completely waterlogged. A tremor worked its way through her body. Something substantial and sharp pressed against her left ankle. Kodiak let out a low whimper right before her warm tongue traced up the side of Macy's face, ending at her ear.

What would she have done without Rhett's dog along for comfort and company? Macy would be far more panicked without the warm fluff of Kodiak beside her.

"We made it." Macy nuzzled the dog. "Now we just have to get out of here."

As if her words had stirred the dog to action, Kodiak started wiggling. In an effort to get up, the dog's paw came up and scratched down Macy's arm.

"Ouch. Settle down," Macy commanded her. "You did so well. Just a little longer."

But Kodiak tried to switch positions again. She let out a series of whines and then barked. Macy hushed her, but Rhett's dog continued barking loudly. Her hot breath made the already cramped space feel tight and damp. Macy was about to tell the dog to zip it again when a noise above them caused her to still. Items were being moved. Things were shifting off of their board.

Someone was up there.

"Macy!" Rhett yelled and the desperation in his voice made Macy's heart twist. "Mace, are you there? Dear Lord, please let her be okay. Let me find her. Let her be here."

Macy tried to say something, but her voice was so raw there was no way he heard her. She cleared her throat, trying again. "I'm here. Help! We're under here."

"Thank You, God." Rhett sounded close to tears. "You can breathe? You're all right?"

"I think so."

"Don't move. Let us lift the worst of this away." More stuff shifted above them. "I'm here, Mace. I won't leave until I leave with you in my arms. You have my word."

Kodiak barked frantically again.

Macy grew antsy. Now that she knew rescue was close she felt like she wanted to crawl out of her skin. She didn't want to wait. Couldn't wait. She was too closed in. She wanted to shove the board off of them and never see this ditch again. But she knew Rhett was right. She had no idea what kind of mess was piled above them. There could be live wires for all she knew. There could be a car precariously balanced over them.

I won't leave until I leave with you in my arms.

After what seemed like an eternity but was probably more along the line of minutes, light broke over Macy's face as the board was finally lifted away. Macy spotted Gabe first and while she was happy to see that the teenager was okay, she wanted to find Rhett's bright blues. She groaned, blinking hard, and took a shuddering breath.

Rhett was at her side in a heartbeat. "You have no idea. I thought—I feared—" He placed a hand on the small of her back as he assisted her with sitting up. "I've never been happier to see someone in my whole life."

Her lungs ached. Macy coughed a few times. "I heard you praying."

Rhett smiled gently. "I do that now."

Macy turned to say something more but Kodiak chose that moment to lurch toward Rhett so she could cover every inch of his face and neck with happy dog kisses. She whined and then licked, whined and then licked. Her whole body trembling.

Rhett's laugh was pure joy. A tear slipped down his cheek as he kissed the top of Kodiak's head. "Good girl. You are such a good girl, Kodiak. You heard my whistle, didn't you? You barked so well. That's how we found you."

Kodiak inched closer to Rhett and then let out one sharp yelp. Rhett's eyes went wide.

Macy sucked in another shuddering breath. "She's hurt. It's one of her back legs, I think."

Rhett's eyes found hers.

"Rubble fell on her. She was pinned."

Rhett's blue gaze raked over Macy's face, her body. "You're hurt too." He lightly touched her face. "You're covered in blood."

"I'm okay." Macy smiled despite the situation. "I love you, Rhett Jarrett. I don't want another second to go by without saying that. I've loved you—"

Rhett's mouth was on hers before she could finish. He kissed her lightly, tenderly, as if he was afraid anything more would break her. But Macy needed more. She fisted her hands into his shirt and yanked him closer. Rhett's hat slid off his head as they deepened their kiss. Macy had almost died today, but this kiss? This kiss was life and air and love and acceptance—

everything she'd ever wanted. She was caked in mud, blood and sweat. She was soaked through but none of it mattered.

Macy let go of Rhett's shirt so she could wrap her arms around his neck. She loved this man. She wanted to stay in his arms forever.

The sound of someone *loudly* clearing their throat finally broke them apart.

Gabe smirked at them. "I'm sorry to interrupt y'all but…" He shrugged and held Rhett's hat out to them.

Rhett accepted his hat but kept his other arm firmly around Macy's back, supporting her. He shoved his hat onto his head and then slipped his hand under her knees. With Macy snug in his arms he got to his feet. He looked over at Gabe, who was still smiling wickedly at them. "Think you're strong enough to carry Kodiak back to the house?"

Gabe rolled his eyes. "Mr. Jarrett, I don't 'think'— I *know*."

Macy rested her hand on Rhett's chest to get his attention. "I can walk."

Rhett's arms tightened. "I'm not letting you go." He looked back at Gabe. "She tolerates a fireman's carry well. Do you know what that is? Over the shoulders?"

Gabe dropped to his knees and helped Kodiak get positioned around his neck.

"Lift with your knees," Rhett instructed.

Kodiak's brow wrinkled and she looked over at Rhett and Macy as if she wanted to ask them if they were really going to allow this kid to do this to her, but Gabe rose with minimal wobbling and headed up the hill in the direction of the house.

When they were alone Macy studied Rhett's face. She wanted to scrub away the worried crease in his brow. He noticed she was staring and cocked an eyebrow.

"You found me," she said. She wrapped an arm more securely around his neck.

"I was so scared," he confessed in a small voice.

"It was like our old hide-and-seek days."

His arms tightened. "I would have never stopped looking for you. I would have turned over every piece of rubble, searched in every place until I had you in my arms."

She tried to make light of it all, cheer him up. "Well, you won this round."

"Kodiak helped." Rhett took the hill slower. His gaze swept over Macy again. "I'm worried about this blood. Tell me what hurts."

"I'm alive, Rhett." Her laugh had a raw edge to it. Tiredness will do that. "What does it matter?"

Rhett stopped at the top of the hill and set her down on a wooden stool that must have been blown there from one of the barns.

He cupped her face in both his hands. "It matters because I love you. Everything about you matters to me. Every single thing." The muscle in his jaw popped. "When I thought… When I didn't know… When I couldn't find you…" He pressed his forehead to hers and took a long, slow breath. "I was such a fool not to say something sooner. Not to *do* something. I thought I had time. I thought we had time." He eased back again and brushed the hair out of her face that had fallen from her ponytail. "I love you so much, Macy. I'll spend the rest of my life trying to show you how much."

"Rhett." Her voice was barely a whisper. She was entirely overcome by the strength of his words.

"Now tell me what's hurt," he said.

He picked her back up and she told him about the projectile hitting her arm and the scratch on her face. "Other than that I think I'm just really sore."

Rhett had to step over wreckage all the way back to the house. Tears freely flowed down Macy's cheeks. Red Dog Ranch was completely destroyed. Finally unable emotionally to face the destruction any longer, Macy buried her face in Rhett's neck.

"It's all gone," she whispered. "Everything's gone."

She felt the muscles in his arms flex.

"Everything that matters made it," he murmured against her hair.

In the days after the tornado Rhett spent most of his time managing the cleanup effort. He kept a running list of things that needed to be replaced and repaired. The handwritten list currently covered ten pages, front and back. And it kept growing.

Jack Donnelley examined the two-story-tall, boarded-up wall of the family room. "New windows coming this weekend?"

Rhett finished his tea and set the mug in the sink. "Yes, thankfully. It's a cave in here without them."

Jack crossed his arms. "Have you decided what to do about the rest of the property? All the cabins?"

Rhett pinched the bridge of his nose. "Honestly? I have no idea."

"Take it one day at a time," Jack said. "And no matter what you decide, my family and I will be here to support you."

"Even if I did away with Camp Firefly?" Rhett didn't know why he had tossed the question out there. Jack had come to know God because of Camp Firefly. The program meant the world to him. Of course he would want Rhett to reinstate it. But the cabins had been leveled and he'd been told it could take months for the insurance money to come through. So unless someone dropped a bundle of money and a crew of hundreds of workers on their doorstep, the ranch wouldn't be ready to host visitors for a long time.

Summer was only six weeks away.

"Like I said." Jack pulled on the gloves he wore to sift through rubble. The man had been stopping by in his off-hours to volunteer. "Whatever you decide, we care about your family, Rhett. You Jarretts might as well be cousins as far as I'm concerned. I want whatever is best for you guys and only you can make that decision."

Rhett thanked Jack before he headed outside, and not for the first time Rhett regretted how he had treated the man in the past. Jack had proved to be an invaluable help and an even better friend. Because of the man's position with the Texas Department of Public Safety he was able to schedule relief workers, and since Red Dog Ranch had been the hardest hit out of anywhere, many of the volunteers were being diverted to them. Jack had been instrumental in coordinating transportation, food and lodging on the day of the tornado for all the remaining guests who had attended the fundraising supper. He had also opened his house to Shannon and Rhett's mom for the time being. Rhett had chosen to stay in his family's house while the work was being done.

Lives had been lost in the tornado, but none of the casualties had occurred at Red Dog Ranch. It was something Rhett found himself thanking God for multiple times a day. The morning after the storm they had held an impromptu church service in the small chapel near the mess hall, which had made it through the tornado completely unscathed. Rhett and the staff had sung worship songs together and had prayed and thanked God for His protection.

Rhett's property was mostly totaled, seven of his horses were missing, and at least an eighth of his cattle had perished, but Macy's arm wound and a ranch hand with a broken leg had been the worst of their injuries. Much to Piper's dismay no one had been able to locate Sheep and Romeo, which Rhett knew Macy felt terrible about, but they hadn't found their bodies yet either so Rhett kept reminding both of them that there was hope.

When Rhett finally decided to go into the office and assess the damages there, Kodiak tried to limp beside him, but the full cast on her back leg slowed her down considerably. Rhett sighed. He felt sorry for her. She couldn't go in the water, couldn't play fetch, couldn't do any of the things that she loved.

"Ah, ah, you." Rhett picked his dog up and carried her back to the front porch of the family home. "I know it eats you up, but you have to stay off that leg. Don't look at me with those sad eyes. Doctor's orders." He set her gently on the large dog bed he had hauled out there for her minutes ago.

Kodiak harrumphed loudly but she laid her head down.

"Stay," Rhett commanded her. She had undergone surgery the night of the tornado and had had her back leg casted. Rhett had spent the night with her at the emergency vet clinic and hadn't slept a wink.

He still felt drained but he wasn't sure if it was from not enough sleep or all the stress. More than likely it was a hefty mix of the two.

Rhett had worked fourteen-to sixteen-hour days since the storm and during that time he had put off going to the office. He had told himself it was because there were plenty of other physical needs to attend to. Why should he spend time in the books when there were things to fix and repair? The office had been unreachable for the first forty-eight hours due to the fact that the tornado had seen fit to redecorate the building by dropping a bus on the front half of it. Rhett hadn't been allowed in there until someone from the city had approved the structure.

They had done so yesterday morning but Rhett had found other tasks to keep him busy.

In truth, he had avoided it because it had been his father's domain and Rhett had faced so many losses and setbacks, he wasn't sure he could handle seeing the rest of his father's possessions destroyed.

But it was time.

The bus had smashed into Macy's section of the office so Rhett approached the back door, which led directly into his study. It was the door Macy had admonished him for sneaking out through that first night. Rhett sucked in a deep breath and then eased the door open. He was instantly hit with a strong musty scent. His dad's books were scattered all over the room. The large desk was still in its place and for some reason that was enough to coax Rhett the rest of the way into the space. There was plenty of water damage from a large gap in the wall near the roof. Most of his dad's papers were shot.

Rhett's throat burned as he assessed the area.

Each smashed book, every scattered page and broken picture frame felt like another piece of his dad being taken away. He hadn't mourned his father properly when he passed, but Rhett let the full impact of his death rest on him now as he stood in his father's demolished office.

His dad was gone. The thought hollowed him out just as much as the first time he had thought those words. Brock had been gone for more than a month, but knowing and accepting were two very different processes. Rhett would rebuild, but he would make it his own. The traces that had made it feel as if Brock was simply gone on an errand and would return later—all of that was gone.

On the other side of the room the painting his mom had created of a herd of longhorns hung half off the wall, and there was another gaping hole in the wood paneling behind it. His mom had given the painting to his father as a Valentine's day gift and Brock had cherished the thing. When Rhett still called Red Dog Ranch home not a week had elapsed without Brock gesturing at the painting and saying something like, "Look at that picture, my boy. That right there, it holds the secret to the most important thing in my life." Rhett had always assumed his dad meant his wife. Marriage.

Rhett made his way across the room to adjust the painting but the hook was gone. In fact... He lifted the painting away and balanced it on a chair to keep it away from the water. There was something behind the painting. What looked like a small fireproof chamber was built into the wall, perfectly concealed behind the painting. He pulled on the small handle and the door swung open to reveal a shoebox tucked inside. Rhett drew the box out.

Heart pounding, he carried it to the desk and sat down. He opened the lid and the contents made his fingers shake as he tried to make sense of what was inside. A little stuffed red dog that was somehow familiar even though Rhett couldn't remember ever seeing it before. And paperwork. An adoption certificate with his name and the names Brock and Leah Jarrett. His parents.

But it didn't make sense.

Rhett dug into the box again and found pictures. A baby in a blue onesie sleeping next to the red stuffed dog. A baby laughing while he clutched the little red stuffed animal. He carefully flipped each one over and, sure enough, someone had written the dates on the backs. The pictures were of him. There were more papers in the box but Rhett didn't know if he could handle what he might find. He braced an elbow on either side of the box, pressed a hand to each of his temples and stared at the contents. Spots flashed in his vision. He felt like a fish that had just been torn from the water and was left gasping for air.

Brock and Leah weren't his biological parents.

Rhett's head pounded.

The back door to his office creaked on its hinges.

"Rhett!" Macy burst in. "We found them! Sheep and Romeo. They were at the old Tennison Pond."

Rhett never took his eyes off the certificate of adoption. "That's great. Real great." He spoke with no voice inflection.

"Are you all right?" She stopped a few feet away.

Rhett ran trembling fingers over his jaw. "I'm not sure."

Macy stepped closer. She scanned the desk and breathed, "Brock wanted to tell you. He loved you, Rhett."

Rhett's head snapped up. "Did you know?"

Macy held up her hands. "Let me explain."

"For how long?" He ground out the words.

Her gaze darted away from his. She licked her lips. "It's been less than two years."

"*Two years?*" Rhett shot to his feet. He jabbed at the adoption certificate. *His* adoption certificate. "You've known for two years that I was adopted and you kept it from me? How could you do that to me?"

She flinched and took a step back. "I had to, Rhett. Please."

Rhett fought the rash urge to hurtle the shoebox across the room. Did everyone know? Was it some joke, some great prank they thought they could play with his life? He was thirty years old and just finding out the truth.

They had lied to him. His whole life. It had all been a lie.

He wasn't a Jarrett.

Macy's shoe crunched on some of the wreckage in the office and the sound brought Rhett swiftly back into his surroundings.

Rhett released a rattling breath. "I'd like you to leave."

"Hear me out."

"Right now." He worked his jaw back and forth. "Please, just leave me alone."

"Rhett."

"I don't want to talk to you about this. Not now."

He needed some time. Needed to process. Needed to be alone.

He braced his hands on the desk and sank back into his chair. He suddenly felt very tired and very drained and Rhett didn't think he could have kept standing if he had wanted to.

He focused on the chamber in the wall that had hidden Brock's secret.

Rhett heard the door open again. Heard slow footsteps. Then nothing.

She was gone and he told himself it was for the best.

Chapter Twelve

"All right." Sophie Donnelley dried off the last cup, set it in a cupboard then pivoted to face Macy. She leaned against the counter. "We've left you to your own devices long enough. It's time to spill."

Macy hugged her middle as she considered how best to dodge the conversation Sophie clearly wanted to have. "I don't know what you're talking about."

Not true.

I'd like you to leave.

I don't want to talk to you about this.

Rhett's words flew through her mind like they had a hundred times since she left Red Dog Ranch. Guilt had draped itself around Macy, weighing her down. She had held a piece of truth about Rhett's life and had kept it from him.

In thirty-six hours Rhett hadn't called her. Hadn't texted.

She wouldn't blame him if he never forgave her.

That day she had sat in her bungalow for an hour before deciding the only way to give Rhett the space he needed would be to actually leave the property. Red Dog Ranch had been her home for the last ten years and before that it had been her second home. All her friends were tied to the ranch in some way. Most of them lived on the property.

After packing a bag, initially she hadn't known where to go. She could have rented a hotel room in town, but she'd ended up absently driving around for a while. Intermittently switching between praying, turning up her music, pulling over to cry, praying some more. Without really meaning to she had finally ended up pulling into the Donnelleys' driveway.

Macy had almost left but Jack had happened to arrive home at the same time, and he had let her know that Shannon and Mrs. Jarrett had moved back to their property a few hours earlier because the windows had been installed and the power was back on. Then he'd told Macy he and Sophie wouldn't hear of her going anywhere else as he'd ushered her inside.

"Nice try." Sophie draped the dish towel over her shoulder. She eyed Macy the same way Macy had seen her stare down her children when they needed a talking to. "Spill whatever it was that brought you to our door in tears yesterday with your belongings. Let's start there."

She couldn't evade the Donnelleys' questions forever. Talking was inevitable. Besides, Macy had never been one to hold in her words.

Except about Rhett's origins.

Except for the *one time* she most definitely should have talked.

Macy gestured toward the table. "We should sit first."

"Jack and the kids are zonked out already so we can talk all night if you need to." Sophie joined her there a few minutes later with two cups of sweet tea in hand. Macy told Sophie about when Rhett left the ranch and their first kiss. Then she shared about how she and Rhett had been treating each other like boyfriend and girlfriend ever since the storm.

"I've loved him for so long and we've been through so much but…but I kept something really important from Rhett. Something he deserved to know." Macy decided that Sophie didn't need to hear every detail of the secret she'd kept from Rhett for her to understand and give advice. Besides, Rhett had only just learned he was adopted and now it was his right to tell or not tell people as he chose.

There had been a time when Macy had almost asked Uncle Travis if he knew the truth, but she hadn't been able to think of a way to broach the subject without revealing what she knew. If Travis did know, he had never said anything.

When Macy finished telling her story, her chest felt empty, completely hollowed out. It had taken more than an hour and two refills of sweet tea to explain everything.

Sophie tapped a finger on the table. "When he asked you to leave—"

"*Told* me to leave."

Sophie arched an eyebrow. "He told you, like a command?"

"I'm not sure, actually." Macy shoved a hand

through her hair. Her eyes hurt. She hadn't slept much last night. "It happened so fast."

And her guilt might have been adding to the story.

Sophie's head tilted in thought. She pursed her lips then asked, "Did he say he wanted you gone forever?"

Rhett hadn't needed to say forever because Macy had seen it in the way he wouldn't make eye contact, in his broken posture. Trust was hard fought and easily broken in Rhett Jarrett's world.

"He won't want to see me again. Not after this," Macy said. "Last time it took three years before we spoke. With what I kept from him this time around?" Macy hugged her middle again. Maybe she could keep her heart from feeling as if it was slinking away to some cave to hide. Probably not. "This is far worse. This could be forever."

"You only feel like that in the moment. But it sounds like last time around you two didn't talk for three years for no other reason than you were both too stubborn and scared to return each other's calls. How about try being vulnerable this time around and reaching out—with the understanding, of course, that he may need some time to process and that's okay? Rhett taking time is not a rejection. You understand that, right?"

But Sophie didn't know what Macy had kept from Rhett. Macy had stumbled upon Rhett's adoption paperwork when Brock was having the fireproof chamber installed. She had begged Brock to tell Rhett, but Brock had insisted she promise not to tell him. Supposedly he had made a promise to Rhett's birth mother that Rhett would never know he was adopted.

Later Macy had wondered more about the circumstances of Rhett's birth. Why would a mother not want her child to know about his origins? She had approached Brock about it twice more within the first month of finding out, asking him to tell Rhett, but Brock had said he could never tell. He convinced Macy that Rhett would feel betrayed and could leave the family for good if he discovered the truth. With as divided as Rhett and Brock had been after Wade's death, Macy had hardly wanted a hand in driving them even further apart so against her better judgment she had agreed.

Sophie's voice broke through her thoughts. "Did Rhett actually say 'I don't want to see you again'?"

"He didn't have to." Macy's eyes burned. She needed to go to sleep. Needed to stop talking. "I really messed everything up, didn't I?"

"I wouldn't be so sure. Honestly, I feel like you're making some leaps based on assumptions." Sophie's lips tipped up encouragingly. "I know we haven't spoken much about it specifically, but you're a woman of faith, right?"

"I believe in God, yes." Macy uncurled her arms so she could trace a notch in the table. Her other hand moved to cup the cool glass of tea. "Actually, when I was stuck in the tornado I had this moment of revelation. You see, my entire life I've felt like I didn't measure up—not to my family, my friends or to God—but during that storm I realized that God's always loved me and I didn't have to do anything to earn His love."

"That's a wonderful knowledge to have, isn't it? There's a Bible verse we've been going over in the women's study group I'm a part of." Sophie thumbed through a stack of papers on the table that was full of kids' artwork. "I thought I had my notes here some-where." She pushed the papers away. "I can't find the study sheet but the gist of it was that God never for-sakes those who trust Him. The Bible mentions that truth many times. It's almost as if God knew we would need to hear it over and over before we believed it." Sophie smiled across the table. "God has not left you, He has not forsaken you and He will see you through this. Hang on to that."

Macy sighed. "God might be willing to ride this bumpy train with me, but what if Rhett's not?"

"I wouldn't lose faith in Rhett if I were you," So-phie said. "Give him time to absorb whatever it is he just learned about. Right now, be there for him in ways you can."

Macy's sharp laugh held no humor. "I don't think he wants me to be there for him at all."

"Nothing is stopping you from praying for him." Sophie winked. "And you're resourceful so I'm sure you'll think of other ways too." They cleared the table and both headed for bed but Sophie caught Macy's arm before she could turn toward the guest room. "Can I pray for you?"

"Of course." Macy took the other woman's hand. They bowed their heads and both ended up praying for Rhett and the ranch and each other.

"And thank You for never forsaking us. Never leav-ing. Thank You for loving us just as we are." Sophie squeezed Macy's hands. "Amen."

However, even after Macy was tucked away in the guest room for the night she was restless. It wasn't even late yet but the kids had an early bedtime and

Jack had stumbled to his bedroom after tucking the kids in, saying he was running on empty. Macy put on her pajamas and got into bed but turned the light back on a few minutes later. What if Rhett or Shannon had sent an email? She dug through her things for her phone and her laptop.

She had a missed call but it was from Gabe the intern, not one of the Jarretts. "So, I know things aren't great right now," Gabe said in the message. "But I have an idea to help the ranch get back on its feet. Do you still have Clint Oakfield's number? Call me, okay?"

It wasn't late yet, but her throat was sore from talking with Sophie so she decided to call Gabe back in the morning. Gabe's call and her talk with Sophie worked together to shove Macy's brain into hyperdrive. Sophie was right; she didn't have to be at the ranch to help and support them. And she didn't need Rhett's approval to help. God had placed Red Dog Ranch in her life and she would fight to rebuild it however she could.

Macy opened her laptop and did a quick internet search for crowdfunding sites. She let her cursor hover over the top site for only a heartbeat before she clicked it. *Do it. Do it before you can think better of it.* It took her fifteen minutes to set up a page asking for donations; most of that time was spent typing out a passionate and heartfelt plea in which she detailed the storm's destruction, as well as all the amazing programs the ranch offered free of charge to foster families. She mentioned Rhett's desire to train therapy dogs, as well. She prayed her love for her favorite place shined through. When it was done she pressed for the page to go live before she could convince herself not to. With two clicks she linked the donation page to two of her social media accounts and then slammed her laptop closed.

Macy flipped off the lights and curled back into bed.

Had she just made another colossal mistake? Would her actions serve to drive Rhett further away? No, she'd done what she knew was right, what God would want her to do, and she could live with that.

Macy loved Rhett. No matter what happened, she always would.

But if the past few weeks had taught Macy anything, it was that she couldn't build her life on one person or one place or even one mission. She could only build her life on God and what God would have her do.

And that would be enough.

Rhett—
I'm writing this because Macy keeps insisting you deserve to know and you deserve answers. I suppose if this is in your hands then you moved your mom's painting and I'm sure you have a heap of questions. Why would your mom and I keep something like this from you? Why did we work so hard to ensure you wouldn't discover the truth? You have every right to be upset and angry. I don't blame you for either. I do hope you can find it within you to forgive an old fool.

You and me have been at odds ever since we lost Wade, and I don't know how to put that to right. I think if I would have told you the truth about your adoption I might have lost you too, and I couldn't have borne that.

Years ago your mother and I were volunteering at a youth group when we met your birth mom. She was scared and alone and she knew she couldn't keep you, but she loved you with such a protective love. I want you to know that, Rhett—you have never lived a day when you weren't fiercely loved by your birth mother, by me and your mom and by God. She had grown up in the system and it had failed her. A family had adopted her, but they'd always made her feel secondhand and more as live-in help than a branch in their tree.

She dreamed bigger for you. You've always reminded me of her in that way. When we told her we wanted to adopt you, that you were an answer to our prayers, she made us promise to treat you as our flesh and blood. We would have anyway, but the promise was important to her, and your mom and I are people of our word.

Perhaps I should own up to a more selfish reason too. From the first day you were in my arms you were my child, Rhett. I never saw you as anything but a Jarrett. I was a sentimental fool who wanted it to always stay that way. When you chose to leave us I told myself that you would have left sooner had you known, so then I guarded the secret even more doggedly.

For that I'm sorry.

Now you know our secret, but I can't go any further. We promised your biological mother if you ever did discover you were adopted, we would still protect her identity. She gave you the red stuffed dog you loved so well. You carried that thing everywhere your first few years.

If you haven't figured it out by now, your mom and I walked away from the life we had once we adopted you. We used Grandpa Jarrett's oil money to purchase this ranch. I didn't know a thing about cattle! But I did know I wanted to help kids. You opened my heart up to this life— to all of life. Every choice after that was made because of our great love for you. You filled our hearts and our lives with so much joy it over- flowed. We wanted to give that joy to others, so we created a safe place for foster children to en- joy—a place that could feel like a second home.

Red Dog Ranch has been and always will be a symbol of our love for you. You made us parents. You made us a family. We are forever grateful for the gift of you. I'm so proud of you and the man you have become, son.

With all the love in my heart,

Dad

Each time Rhett reread the letter he felt something different. At first it was anger and betrayal but that faded into shades of acceptance tipped with disap- pointment.

Was it possible to track down his birth mother?

Did he want to?

Rhett hardly knew.

Folding the paper back up, Rhett tucked it into the pocket on his shirt where it would be close to his heart. He rested his hands on the edge of his belt as he looked out the newly installed floor-to-ceiling windows of the family room. Moonlight rippled over the large lake that sprawled behind the Jarrett family home. They had dredged the last of the debris from the lake yesterday morning and Rhett found he was glad he had moved that task up the prioritized list. The lake was a special place for him.

Red Dog Ranch has been and always will be a symbol of our love for you.

A lump formed in the back of Rhett's throat. He rubbed a fist over his collarbone to try to dispel the feeling, but it lingered. Maybe it always would.

He had been so bitter over this place, so wrong.

His phone vibrated in his back pocket and as he fished it out he wildly hoped it was Macy. Rhett owed her an apology. He was still upset about her keeping such a huge secret from him, but he shouldn't have pushed her away.

When he asked her to go, he had meant he needed a few hours to himself. When Shannon told him Macy had left the ranch, Rhett had figured she had wanted some space too and he had respected that by not bothering her with calls. But when her car hadn't appeared today, Rhett had started to worry. Had his words driven her away?

Rhett didn't know where she was staying. The few times he had worked up the nerve to call her today, her phone had been off and her voice mail was oddly full.

He would find her at some point and he would ask her to come home. He couldn't run the place without her. He wanted her around, near him.

He glanced at his phone screen: Boone.

Boone blinked at him over the face-to-face connection program on their phones. Rhett had talked with most of his family about being adopted, but he hadn't been able to catch his brother yet.

"How's the ranch doing?"

"It's a mess." If only he was exaggerating.

"The pictures you sent of the damage turned my stomach. We wish we were there to help," Boone said. "Oh, and before I forget, I'm supposed to tell you June and Hailey say hi."

Rhett's brother Boone had met his wife, June, in high school. They had always joked about their names rhyming and had teased that they would pick their kids' names to rhyme, as well. When Hailey was born there was speculation about what her name would be... Thankfully they went against the rhyming scheme.

Rhett's watch showed that it was after eleven in Maine where Boone and his family lived. He chuckled softly. "I'm sure they're both long asleep by now so tell them hi in the morning for me."

"We keep late hours in seminary." Boone's yawn followed quickly.

Rhett glanced over at his mom asleep in her recliner and Kodiak snoozing near his mom's feet. "There's something I need to tell you." Rhett plunged right in and told Boone about discovering the shoebox in their dad's office and explained what he had found inside.

Boone was quiet when Rhett paused, but finally he let out a low whistle. "Wow. That's a lot to deal with all at once. How are you holding up?"

"Boone." Something had been bothering Rhett since he had learned about being adopted and he had to get it off his chest. "You're technically the oldest Jarrett. Dad's will names you as the heir in the event that something happens to me or if I'm unable to serve as director." Rhett heard Boone make a disgruntled noise on the other end of the line so he rushed on. "This inheritance… I know you said you don't want to run the ranch, but if that ever changes, if you ever want to take this from me—"

But it wasn't Boone who answered Rhett first. It was their mom.

"Why, that's the daftest thing I've ever heard you say." His mom pounded her hand on her armrest. Evidently she hadn't been sleeping all that deeply after all. Kodiak's head swung up. She sleepily blinked in Rhett's general direction.

Rhett turned up the volume on his phone. "Mom's on with us."

Their mom curled her finger, a silent command for Rhett to draw closer. He obeyed. He crossed over to her and knelt at her feet.

She cupped his cheek in her weatherworn hand. "You are my firstborn son. It doesn't matter that someone else bore you—you were my first child, my first little love." She ran her thumb in a light caress over his skin. "God knew you were the brother Boone, Wade and Shannon needed. And He knew you were the son who would first make me a mother. No secret, no hurt can make any of those things untrue."

Rhett swallowed hard.

"This family has loved you and prayed for you and cheered for you since before you were even born. You are ours, child. Ours," his mom continued more firmly. "And you always will be."

Boone's face lighted up Rhett's phone screen. "I'm one hundred percent going with Mom on this one."

"Smart boy." Their mom beamed at both of them.

The front door opened and Shannon tiptoed in. She started when she spotted them in the family room. "Way to scare a girl silly! You guys are still awake?"

"Join us." Rhett motioned for her to come over. "We're on with Boone."

"Aww, Boone! My favorite middle brother." Shannon shrugged off her purse and skidded across the wood floor to sit beside Rhett. She tossed an arm over his shoulder and reached to hold her mom's hand in her other. Rhett eased back so he was sitting on his ankles. He kept the phone so Boone could see all three of them.

Rhett took a deep breath. "Since I have most of the family here I'd like to ask for some advice." They were missing Cassidy, but she and Piper had their own house on the property and they would be asleep by now.

Mom's brow bunched together. Her gaze darted around the room as if she was searching for a lost item. "Where are Brock and Wade? Do we need to wake them?"

Boone's focus went to Rhett and Shannon. "I, ah, I think this is plenty of us for an opinion."

Rhett had worried that the family gathering might confuse his mother. He needed to be more careful with how he phrased things.

"As everyone here knows, the ranch suffered heavy damages. Besides our barns, Camp Firefly—mainly the cabins—was the hardest hit part of our land." Although that didn't mean a whole lot. The tornado had carved a path from one end of his property line to the other. As if the storm had wanted to wage a war on Rhett specifically. Much of the ranch looked like it had been walloped with a meat tenderizer. "Now we need to decide what we're going to do."

Shannon's fingers tightened on his shoulder. "Wait. You're not planning to rebuild?"

Rhett looked away from them and worked his jaw a few times. "We don't have enough money. Insurance only helps to a point and even if they end up helping more, it won't be quickly enough to host camp." He spoke slowly, evenly delivering the information so everyone understood what they were facing. "At the least, I think we need to consider cancelling this summer."

"We can't." Shannon sat up a little more, letting go of their mom's hand in the process.

"If God wants our mission to continue, He will find a way." Their mom rested her hands in her lap. "You'll see."

Rhett rubbed his jaw. "Everyone made it through the storm safe. I think we should be grateful with that huge blessing from God and not expect a bunch more."

"Do you think there's a cap to how much love God can shower on us?" Their mom laughed gently. "Do you think He ever says, 'Oh, that's enough, I'll stop showing them my love'?" Mom leaned forward and whispered, "God delights in loving us. Don't forget that."

Shannon bit her lip and sought Rhett's eyes. "What about the family holdings?"

"That money is for the family to live off of." Rhett

sliced his hand through the air. His heart had changed toward the foster programs, but he was still firm in his belief that the business account shouldn't mix with the family's personal money. "That's the legacy I want to leave to my nieces."

Boone spoke up first. "Legacy isn't money—you know that, right?"

"Boone's right." Shannon's fingers drew across his back as she leaned away from him. "The Jarrett family legacy is this ranch and what this ranch stands for."

Rhett knew that. He did. But he also knew that he had some tough business decisions ahead of him.

"Your nieces don't need you to worry about leaving them with a nest egg." Boone straightened in his chair. Rhett had to bite back a smile because he could tell Boone was about to launch into what they called his pastor mode. Boone had always been the bookish one in the family.

"The Bible talks a lot about treasures in heaven," Boone said. "Meaning we should be doing things that please God instead of amassing things here on earth." His hand came into view. "Now, I don't think that means that we don't take care of our family or make sound business choices. But I do think when we use the word *legacy*, as Christians it should only ever be in the realm of a legacy for the Kingdom. What are we devoting our time and energy and resources on earth to? Things that matter in eternity or not?"

"You do know you're not a minister yet, right?" Shannon teased.

They laughed and the conversation turned to catching up, but Rhett was unable to keep his mind from wandering. It wasn't the first time he had considered how people would remember him after he was gone someday. As morbid as it sounded, it was something that had crossed his mind often since his father had passed away.

How did Rhett want to be remembered?

As a man who took care of his family or someone who ran a successful business? Why couldn't he be both? But as the voices of his family—the family God had chosen for him—drifted over him, Rhett knew his answer was neither of those things. It didn't have to be one or the other.

Rhett would choose God.

He would trust God with the ranch and with his family.

He would hand it over. All of it.

Chapter Thirteen

"Rhett!" Shannon pounded on his bedroom door. "Rhett Jarrett, you need to get out of bed this instant and come downstairs."

Rhett groaned and sat up slowly. After they had hung up with Boone last night Rhett had headed outside to pray and clear his head. He had ended up staying up until past two in the morning and was not yet ready to handle any amount of his sister's exuberance.

Although it was nice to catch a glimpse of the old Shannon again. She was still dating Cord, and Rhett was praying about how he should deal with their relationship. Rhett knew for sure that Cord was no good for his sister, but his sister was an adult and he couldn't force her to break up with someone either.

He glanced at his clock and discovered to his embarrassment that his family had let him sleep until noon.

"Open up now, Rhett. I mean it." She kept knocking. "Or I'll barge in and pour water over your head like when we were kids."

"I'm up," he muttered. He raked his hand down his

face then rose. "And if I remember correctly, you got in trouble for that."

"Worth it," she called through the door.

Rhett grinned and crossed the room. Good thing it was only his sister because he usually wouldn't wander out of his room in his old sweatpants and undershirt. He pulled open the door and had to shield his eyes against the sunlight streaming into the hallway through the wide glass panels in the window seat. "So where's the fire?"

Shannon latched onto his wrist and tugged him over the threshold. "The place is swimming with reporters. They're all asking for you. I tried to hold them off but they keep showing up."

Reporters?

That didn't make any sense.

Rhett caught the ridge of trim around his door so she couldn't tug him forward anymore. "Slow down. What are you talking about?"

"Downstairs." She trained both of her pointer fingers downward. "Some from the papers and a couple from the internet. There are even ones out there with camera crews and they all want to see your pretty mug." She let go of him and pursed her lips. "Oh, you need to change. Maybe shower too?" She pulled a face. "No, that will take too long." She put her fingertips on his chest and gave him a push back toward his room. "Go make yourself presentable."

"Call me slow, but I'm not following any of this." Rhett crossed his arms. "Why would reporters have any interest in talking to me?"

Shannon gave a long suffering huff and tapped on

her phone. She pulled open a webpage and shoved the phone in his face. "This is why."

Rhett jerked his head back and snatched the phone from her so he could hold it at an angle where he could see the screen. A picture of Sheep and Romeo was splashed across the top of the page.

Fund-raiser by Macy Howell: Red Dog Ranch

The bar showing donations was already past its goal and a small flag in the corner announced that it was a trending fund-raiser. The page went on to talk about all the lives the ranch had touched and changed, Macy's included.

This place is home not just to the generous family that runs it free of charge to participants, but it becomes home to every foster child who steps onto the ranch. It's the only taste of home some kids ever know. When I was a lost child it became my home too.

She went on to explain all the free programs offered at Red Dog Ranch, followed that with detailing the destruction wrought by the tornado and ended with a call to action.

I've known the ranch's amazing owner, Rhett Jarrett, all my life and he's the one who taught me long ago to dream big, impossible dreams, so I've placed the amount we need to raise high. There are only weeks left until camp starts. Will you dream big with us?

Rhett's throat burned with emotion. "I need to find her."

"What you need to do—" Shannon grabbed his shoulders, turned him slightly and guided him all the way into his room "—is change and deal with all these people waiting in our dining room."

"You're right." Rhett crossed to his closet and pulled a fresh shirt off a hanger. "But when I'm done with them, I'm going to figure out where she went."

"Macy?" Shannon cocked her head. "Oh, she's over at the Donnelleys'."

Rhett's mouth was probably wide open. "Jack told you but not me?"

"No." She batted the suggestion away. "It took me all of ten seconds of thought to realize that Macy literally had nowhere to go but the Donnelleys' unless she went to one of the hotels. I guessed." Shannon shrugged. "I went there a few hours after she left and sure enough, there she was."

Jack hadn't said a word. Not that Rhett had told his new friend that he was trying to find Macy, but it was curious that her staying at their house hadn't come up. Then again, Rhett hadn't confided in Jack about what had happened between the two of them. Additionally, Macy very well may have asked the Donnelleys not to tell anyone she was staying there and the Donnelleys would have honored her request.

Just like his parents had honored his birth mom's request.

Still, Shannon had figured out Macy's whereabouts when he hadn't put two and two together. "I can't believe I didn't figure that out."

Shannon didn't even attempt to hide her eye roll. "Seriously, Rhett, where else would she have gone?"

Nowhere.

The thought gutted him.

Red Dog Ranch was her home—her world. And he had unintentionally shoved her out in the cold.

"I need to apologize to her."

Shannon's answering laugh was quick and sharp. "Oh, you need to do a lot more than that."

He scrubbed his hand down his face. "I never told her to leave the ranch. It was a miscommunication."

"And then some," Shannon said.

"Point made." He held his hands out.

"My advice?" She sauntered into the hallway. "A lot of groveling, some pleading and definitely kneeling down when you beg that woman to marry you, okay?"

Rhett swallowed a few times and then nodded. "I will."

"Get her back, Rhett. She's family."

He smiled at his sister and then he shut the door so he could get ready.

The afternoon flew by in a blur of interviews and phone calls. Not only had Macy's online fund-raiser gone viral, but Clint Oakfield had penned a blog entry about his experience at the ranch when the tornado hit and he had shared it everywhere he had an online presence. He expressed how he cared about the vision of Red Dog Ranch and he implored his fans to stand behind the rebuilding efforts. People in the comment section were offering to donate supplies or put together teams of free labor. Clint ended his post with a promise to host a benefit concert with all proceeds going to support the ranch's foster programs. He pledged to partner with Rhett and the ranch for as long as they would let him.

Once the first interview aired they had to forward the office line to the house phone and Shannon was flooded with incoming calls.

"How does Macy handle this all day? I can't answer these fast enough." Shannon set the phone down to re-fill her water. "Everyone wants our address so they can send checks. People are planning workdays and wanting to coordinate the best way to help. Our voice-mail box has already reached capacity!"

Cars started showing up in the driveway full of people who wanted to hand Rhett a check or drop off construction materials. There were crews lined up to begin rebuilding the cabins starting next week.

Rhett had never said thank-you so many times in his life. It was overwhelming.

God delights in loving us. Don't forget that.

He should have known better than to doubt his mom's wisdom. God's love had no cap, no end. Rhett felt like he was flooded in blessings, but instead of wondering like usual when it all would end or if there would be a trade-off, he was simply thankful.

Uncle Travis had reminded Rhett about the Bible verse that said to whom much is given, much is re-quired. At the time Travis had been talking about Brock's will. But Rhett had been given an inheritance far greater than three thousand acres of gorgeous Texas Hill Country. God had given Rhett an inheritance of love—the deep and abiding, never-giving-up type of love that no man could ever hope to deserve. He had been given much and he would spend the rest of his life making sure every person who stepped onto his property got to experience the same love too.

And he needed to start with Macy.

Macy had spent most of the day staring at her computer screen in shocked awe as she witnessed the donation amount grow. She hadn't expected it to catch fire overnight quite like it had. Of course it was a good thing—Red Dog Ranch would have an opportunity to rebuild faster and return more quickly to being a safe haven for hurting kids.

Macy slammed her laptop closed and slung her purse over her shoulder. It was time to go to the ranch. She wasn't going to sit around waiting for three years like last time.

Macy burst out the Donnelleys' front door and charged directly into a solid chest. Hands took hold of her arms, steadying her. Rhett's handsome face—his strong jaw and shocking blue eyes—came into view and her heart squeezed. She loved this man.

She needed a little space so she would be able to say the things she had planned to.

Macy shrugged out of his hold. "Jack's not home."

Rhett eyed her. "I'm here for you."

Trying not to let his words derail her, Macy gripped on to her purse strap as if it was a lifeline. "I'm going to take an educated guess and assume you know what I've done?"

Rhett took off his hat and worked it around in his hands. His hair stuck up in the odd, adorable way it always did. "If you mean I need to thank you for single-handedly saving the ranch, then yes, I know about that. And I'm forever indebted to you for doing so." He looked down at his hat. "I wouldn't have acted that swiftly or even thought to take that measure." He peeked at her with a tentative smile on his face. "You sure know how to take on the world and win. I'm glad I have you in my corner…that is, if you still want to be."

It took every ounce of her restraint not to close the gap between them. "I should have told you about being adopted. I should have told you when I first found the paperwork. I'm so sorry, Rhett. You have no idea how sorry I am."

"Why didn't you tell me?"

She wove her fingers together. "I looked up to Brock so much. I think I had him on a bit of a pedestal. He was there for me when I had no parents." She shrugged. "A part of me felt like I owed him for letting me live here and giving me a job and basically giving me a family too. Selfishly I didn't want to jeopardize that." She rushed on, "And you and I weren't speaking, and when you came here we avoided each other so I convinced myself it wasn't my secret to tell—that you wouldn't have wanted to hear it from me anyway."

He nodded his understanding.

Macy sucked in a breath. "And I didn't want to drive you further away from your family either. Brock was really afraid of that happening." She took a half step closer. "I should have said something when you got back to the ranch."

His eyes searched hers.

"But I held on to this idea that I had to honor Brock by keeping the secret. As if it was even more important since he was gone. That probably sounds stupid, but I feel so much loyalty to him and I'm sorry. I'm so sorry and I don't know how I can even ask you to forgive me for keeping something so huge from you, but I am. Is this something we can get through?"

He reached toward her, slipped a piece of hair behind her ear. He left his hand there to cup her face as he said, "I'm pretty sure we can get through anything as long as we're together."

Macy pressed her cheek into his hand. "I thought about telling you so many times and I came close but—"

"But you're a woman of your word—one of the many things I love about you—so you kept a promise to a man who was like a father to you." Rhett's voice was full of tenderness. "I see only someone doing something admirable. You have nothing to apologize for." He splayed his other hand over his heart. "I'm sorry I told you to leave."

"You had every right."

The muscles along his jaw stretched taut. "I only wanted an hour to collect my thoughts. I never thought you would take it as me asking you to leave the ranch. Please." He rested his forehead against hers. "Don't ever leave again."

"Never," she whispered.

He stepped back, set his hat on and thumbed toward his truck. "I brought someone else who wanted to see you." He whistled and Kodiak's head popped through the window. Her tail wagging was evident from where Macy stood.

Macy couldn't help but smile at seeing Kodiak. "How's she doing?"

"Good, but she misses you." Rhett stepped into her line of vision again.

"Wait. Rhett." Macy grabbed his arm. "I forgot to tell you. There's this organization in California that specializes in training therapy dogs and they caught wind of our fund-raiser. They reached out to me with an offer for you. They want to fly you out there for a week or two this fall so you can learn their methods and connect with their trainers. I think it would be amazing."

Rhett's mouth opened, closed, opened again. "I feel like this is the right moment to say I finally understand the phrase 'my cup runneth over.'"

Macy held out her hand. "Should we head home?"

"Well, we actually need to talk about that." Rhett took her hand. "See, I don't want you back as the assistant."

Macy's heart plummeted. Had she heard him wrong? "But, Rhett, I—"

"I want to hire you as my codirector," Rhett said. "Equal decision-making power."

"Codirector of the ranch," said Macy, trying out the title. "Are you kidding?"

"I've never been more sure of anything in my life. I can't run the ranch without you. But more than that." He took a step forward and held out his other hand so they were facing one another again. "I need you in my life. I want you beside me in all things."

She slipped her hand into his. "Rhett."

He glanced at her lips and then met her eyes. "I can't

promise a perfect life or even an easy one, but I can promise to love you every day for the rest of my life."

"I never wanted perfect." She brought their joined hands up between them. Macy looked into his eyes and knew she wanted to wake up to the sight of him every morning. "I only ever wanted you."

He let go of her hands only to slip his fingers into her hair. "I love you, Macy."

Macy tipped her face up. "I love you too."

Last time his kiss had been slow and gentle, but this kiss was sure and full of tomorrows. This kiss proclaimed love and promises. He angled his head to deepen their kiss at the same time she tiptoed her fingers to the hair at the nape of his neck. When they finally came up for air they both just grinned at each other.

His expression instantly sobered. "Macy, I don't have a ring. I thought of a speech on the way over but I'm so nervous it's fled. Will you—"

"Of course I'll marry you." Heart full, Macy laughed and tugged him close for another kiss. It was a quick peck that left her wanting ten more. She moved in for another but then stopped. "I interrupted you again, didn't I? And in the middle of... I'm sorry, Rhett, I couldn't help it. I've been waiting to be able to give you my answer for years."

"A few more kisses and we'll call it even." He winked.

"I like your terms." She playfully jabbed him in the ribs.

They climbed into his truck but Macy only scooted so far as the middle seat of the bench so Kodiak could stay sprawled with her cast in the passenger seat. Kodiak laid her head on Macy's thigh and let out a long, contented sigh. When Rhett got in, Macy looped her arm through his. He pressed another kiss to her temple and pointed the truck in the direction of Red Dog Ranch.

Toward home.

* * * * *

THE TEXAN'S
SECRET DAUGHTER

Jolene Navarro

To Andrea Porter. She might not be a writer,
but she has created an oasis for writers
in Canyon, Texas. The West Texas Writers' Academy
is one of the highlights of my year. Thank you.

Acknowledgments

The West Texas Bangers—C.S. Kjar, Jenna Neal,
Kimberly Packard, Lana Pattinson, Linda Fry,
Linda Trout, for helping me through the
twists and turns of Elijah and Jazmine's journey
to their happy-ever-after. See you in June.

Pam Hopkins—the best agent a girl could wish for.

Emily Rodmell—I've said it before but it's true.
My stories are better because of your insight
and knowledge.

Peace I leave with you, my peace I give unto you:
not as the world giveth, give I unto you.
Let not your heart be troubled, neither let it be afraid.
—*John* 14:27

Chapter One

No. That couldn't be him.

Jazmine Daniels stood in the doorway of the food bank. The bags loaded with canned goods cut into her fingers, but she couldn't move. She understood now why deer froze in the middle of the road.

Walk in, turn around, run, hide.

The options tumbled over each other in her brain, confusing her body and making it impossible to pick one.

Elijah De La Rosa. It had been over six years since she'd seen her husband. Ex-husband.

His hair was a little longer and there was more red tangled in the dark strands, as though he'd spent a lot of time outdoors. He looked older, his skin weathered in a good way. A small groan formed in the back of her throat. How was it possible that he was even better looking now than the day she had first seen him? Not fair.

He laughed at something one of his companions said, and she forced herself to look away. Her mother and daughter would be following her any minute. She needed to leave before that happened.

Her eyes scanned the large open room for a fast escape. Colorful carved starfish hung on the walls while windows flooded the dining area with friendly sunlight. About twenty-five people gathered around the long tables, eating the lunch that the local mission provided to the homeless and needy.

Homeless? Her stomach plunged. He couldn't be homeless, but why else would he be here? The drinking must've gotten worse after she left. Had his family refused to help him or had he refused to accept their help?

His pride had always been bigger than his common sense. Not that she had blamed him. Her heart had wanted to fix all his hurts, but she hadn't been enough.

She shook her head and bit hard against the remorse. No. Her actions kept her and her daughter safe. That had to stay at the forefront of her brain.

The good times wanted to sneak in and melt her heart for the boy she had loved with every fiber of her being. That boy was long gone.

This was the reason her mother had told her to stay away from their beach home. Both of her parents had agreed that any kind of contact was dangerous for her. They had handled everything needed for the divorce.

She hadn't seen him again, only his signature on the papers that broke the vows they had made to each other.

No, *he* had broken those vows. She glanced down at the ugly white scar running from her palm to the underside of her wrist. It had been caused by her own careless mistake, but it was a was a tangible reminder of that night.

The night she had come face-to-face with the ugly truth of his self-destruction.

He had never hurt her, physically or emotionally, but his hatred of the world leaked into all his actions.

When her heart's memory failed her, one glance at the mark reinforced why she had left. He had refused her help and closed her out.

Her daughter's safety had been her priority. So, she had run from him without saying a word about the pregnancy.

Guilt was hard to live with. This last year, she had almost called him several times. Rosemarie had asked about her father. With first grade starting in the fall, it was time to let Elijah know about their daughter.

But only if he was sober. She refused to put Rosemarie in danger.

Eyes burning, she took a step back. This was not how she had imagined their first meeting. In a homeless shelter. Beautiful, proud Elijah with the quick and easy smile was eating a free lunch at a homeless shelter.

She glanced at the door. It wasn't that far. She looked back at him, then groaned. Too late. They had made eye contact. Her lack of decision had taken the choice out of her hand.

His eyes lifted, and the smile that used to make her heart flutter slipped into a frown. He tilted his head, as if he couldn't figure out what he was looking at.

The exit was just a few feet away. Maybe she could rewind, go right out the front and pretend she hadn't seen him. Her breathing came faster. Her feet were cemented to the cold floor.

"Jazz?" It sounded as though his throat was full of sand.

He stood. A worn T-shirt with the words Saltwater Cowboys stretched across his broad chest. There was a rip at the neckline.

One, two, three slow steps and he was around the table. Then he stopped, like he was afraid of getting too close.

His faded jeans were low on his hips and fit him perfectly, but they were threadbare and ripped at the knees. Small flecks of paint decorated the denim. Was he painting houses now, or were they second-hand clothes?

After growing up in hand-me-downs from church donations, Elijah had refused to wear anything someone else had thrown away. He'd started working at thirteen. Once he had a job, he had dressed immaculately every day, his boots constantly polished.

Even on his worst days, he'd still looked put together. Until he stumbled through the door late at night, drunk.

She lowered her eyes. Those boots looked worse for wear.

"Jazmine? What are you doing here?" Two more steps brought him close enough for her to see the unusual blend of color in his eyes. The color of Spanish moss, somewhere between gray and green. The exact shade of her daughter's.

Unable to talk, she lifted the bags of food she, her

mother and daughter had brought in to donate. To her horror, her arms started shaking.

"Here, let me get those for you." He reached over and took the bags, his callused hands brushing her wrist. His fingers touched her scar and she jumped back, ripping one of the bags and sending cans rolling over the floor.

The men who had been sitting with him rushed to help pick up the canned vegetables and junk food her mother had cleaned out of the beach house's pantry.

After a bit of fumbling and laughing, one of the older men brought a new bag, and they collected her donations.

"So, who's this lovely lady, Elijah?" The shortest one said with a grin. It was hard to judge their ages, due to the rough life that was written in every wrinkle and crease.

Elijah cleared his throat. "Guys, this is Jazmine..." He looked at her with a question in his eyes.

"Daniels. Jazmine Daniels." She couldn't look him in the eyes, afraid to see his reaction when he learned that she'd dropped his name. Holding out her now free hand, she made sure to smile. So, what if pieces of her world were crumbling around her? There was no need for them to know. "Pleasure to meet you. Thank you for the help."

They handed her the bags.

Her ex-husband started introducing the three men, but they all went wide-eyed. "This is Jazmine? Your Jazz girl?"

His? Had he been talking about her to these men? Her forehead wrinkled as she glared at him.

He closed his eyes and grimaced.

When he reached for the bags this time, she was ready. She held her ground without acting like a middle-school girl at her first dance.

"The food donations go in the pantry area. Through the door over there." He pointed his chin to the left, then walked in that direction.

She followed without thinking but stopped midway. No way was she going anywhere with him. She glanced over her shoulder. Then again, he was leaving the dining area where her mother and daughter could appear any minute.

With a deep breath, she went through the swinging door. She'd get his number and get out before anyone was the wiser. Three women were working behind the counter. Jazmine recognized two of them from the summers she'd spent at the beach. Their eyes went wide when they saw her.

"Well, I'll be. Jazmine Daniels De La Rosa, it's been ages." Kate glanced at Elijah, then back to Jazmine. "This is quite the surprise. So, what are you doing in Foster?"

"I'm at Port Del Mar with my parents. We're staying at the beach house, so my father can recover."

The other woman, Martha, nodded. "Sorry to hear about what happened. Y'all brought him to the right place to recover. The beach is so much better than that city. The salt air at Port D has healing powers. We'll keep him in our prayers. You should take him over—"

"Martha." Kate shook her head. "She's not here to jibber jabber." Smiling at Jazmine, she took the bags. "Interesting that you and Elijah brought these donations in together. We haven't seen you in what? Over six years? Your parents don't come as often, either." The women glanced between her and Elijah, waiting for an explanation.

Obviously, Kate wanted to talk as much as Martha. The news of her being in Port Del Mar with Elijah would be flying as if a town crier was dashing up and down the boardwalk. Another reason she should get out of here.

The way Elijah found out about Rosemarie needed to be well planned. The gossip mill was not how a man should discover he was the father of a five-year-old girl.

Elijah gave in to the silent pressure first. "I was as surprised as you when she walked in the door. I was just helping with the bags. Nothing interesting here."

"That's sweet of you." Martha looked as if she was about to ask more questions, but Kate interrupted her.

"Well, we need to take these to the back and start the dishes. Y'all have a good one. Tell your parents hi and that they're in our prayers."

They all smiled at Elijah as if he was a favorite son. Then they disappeared through the back door.

It shouldn't have surprised her that they still adored him, even if he had fallen on hard times. Despite his uncle's reputation in town as a mean drunk and cheat, Elijah had charmed everyone. Except for his uncle and Jazmine's parents.

She blamed his uncle for teaching him the family tradition of drinking. But then her parents had made his life even harder. They had all had a hand in destroying their marriage.

Shaking her head, she cleared her thoughts. They

might have made his life difficult, but she had promised to quit making excuses for him. He made his choices, and she was not going to feel guilty. She wasn't.

And if she said that enough maybe she'd believe it.

His decision to turn to the bottle instead of to her and God had been his alone. Elijah had put an end to their happily-ever-after. There was no going back once trust was lost.

He turned to her and ran his long fingers through his hair. He focused on the counter, not making eye contact.

"Well, by dinnertime everyone in Port Del Mar will know you're back and that we were seen together." Finally, he looked at her. The corner of his mouth twitched.

Her stupid heart fluttered and skipped a beat.

He took a step closer. "It's amazing that you're here. I was going to try to contact your parents again. I really have to talk to you."

Her heart hit her ribs in double time. Had he found out about Rosemarie?

He stared at her for a long, silent moment, then gave her that old half smile he used whenever he thought he was in trouble. Unfortunately, it had worked way too many times.

She had a long track record of giving in to his promises, promises that never survived forty-eight hours.

She was stronger now. Straightening her spine, she made sure to look him right in the eyes. "What is it, Elijah?"

Something on his fingernail became the center of his world.

"Elijah, I have to go, but if you give me your number, I'll call and we can…talk."

He took a deep breath and nodded. "I've practiced this speech for years, and now that you're standing in front of me all the words have disappeared. Jazz, you're the only person left on my list that I need to apologize to."

She frowned. "List?" Then she understood. "You're doing the twelve steps?"

Scrutinizing his features, she looked for any clue that he was lying. Would she be able to tell if he was sober?

He nodded as he stuffed his hands into the front pockets of those worn jeans. "Yeah. I started it a few years back, but well… I haven't been able to reach you. And I…"

"Momma! Look what GiGi got me!" Rosemarie, her five-year-old daughter—*their* five-year-old daughter—rushed through the doorway, holding up a fragile-looking doll in a Victorian dress and oversize hat.

Jazmine looked over her daughter's shoulder but didn't see her mother. Yet. "That's lovely, sweetheart. Can you go wait with GiGi for a minute? I need to take care of some business."

"But I thought we were going to—"

"Jazmine?" Behind her, Elijah's voice was even rougher than before. She dropped her head and shut her eyes. Putting a hand on Rosemarie's tiny shoulder, she turned to face him.

"Elijah. We need to talk—"

"Obviously." The word was barely audible through his clenched teeth.

The clicking of heels on the concrete flooring told her that time was up. Her mother was going to take this stressful moment up another level. It was like watching a collision about to happen in slow motion and not being able to stop it.

Gasps sounded at the doorway. "Jazmine. What is going on?"

Calming her mind, she waited a few seconds before turning to her mother with a smile on her face. "Mother, you remember Elijah?" She glanced at Rosemarie, hoping Azalea would take the hint. "He was having lunch and offered to help me with our donations."

"Jazmine, this is exactly why I told you to stay away." Azalea Daniels pinned a hard glare on Elijah. In a few quick steps, she had Rosemarie's hand in hers. She pulled the little girl closer to her side, staring Elijah down. "You're eating lunch at the food bank? Did you lose your home, too? Homeless. It shouldn't surprise me."

"Mother! Not helping." Jazmine rubbed her temple. A massive headache was climbing into her frontal lobe.

With an indignant nod, Azalea dropped her gaze to the five-year-old. "Papa is waiting. The nurse will be leaving soon, and I must talk to her." She gave a tight nod to Elijah before heading to the door. When Jazmine didn't immediately follow, her mother's spine stiffened. "Jazmine?"

"Mom, take Rosemarie to the car. I'll be right there, I promise." She made a point of looking at the innocent little girl standing there without a clue of the drama swirling around her. "Please."

"Two minutes." With tight lips and one last warning glare, Azalea walked out the door.

"That's my daughter. You—"

"Yes, she's your daughter and we need to talk."

"You not only left me without a word, but you took my daughter?" He stared at the door Rosemarie had just walked through, his chest rising and falling in rapid movements. "I have a daughter." He turned to her, eyes flashing intense heat. "Your parents knew. They knew."

"Yes. Like I said, we need to talk. I have to go right now, but I can meet you tomorrow—"

"Tonight. We'll meet tonight or I'm camping at the beach house door until we talk."

"Don't come to the house. That would upset Daddy, and we have to keep him calm. I'll meet you tonight at Pier 19. We can grab some coffee. Is the Painted Dolphin still there?" That was probably a mistake. Every wall was covered with memories of when they were dating and the early days of their marriage. The days that were filled with joy and laughter. When they thought they could conquer the world with their love.

The last thing she needed right now was all the could-have-beens from the good days before the drinking started.

He snorted. "Yeah, it's there. New owners reopened it last month." A grim expression shifted across his face. "What's going on with your father?"

"He suffered a heart attack while driving and crashed his car and wanted to recover at the beach house."

Elijah frowned. "I'm sorry. I know how close you are to your father. Is he going to be okay?"

"The heart attack itself was minor as far as these things go, but he was also injured when he hit a street sign. It didn't yield." She held back a groan. *Not an appropriate time for humor, Jazmine.* "Anyway, if we can convince him to follow doctor's orders, he'll recover fully." The acid in her stomach started climbing up her throat. "I also came because I knew it was time for us to come together and discuss a few things."

"Really? A few things?" he snarled at her. "About six years too late."

She took a step back. "This isn't something that can be done over the phone. I wanted to see how you were and…" She cut her glance back to the dining area. "I was hoping you were…"

"Sober?" His nostrils flared, a clear sign he was angry. "I've been sober for five years now."

Her eyes closed. If that was true, she didn't want to think about the time she wasted worrying about calling him. "I was hoping you were better. I didn't mean to meet you like this or for you to see her for the first time without…" She fluttered her hand helplessly in front of her, then looked at her bare wrist as though there was a watch there. The glimpse of her scar gave her new resolve, and she became businesslike once more. "I need to go. Rosemarie goes to bed at 8:30. I'll see you at nine?"

"Rosemarie? You named her Rosemarie De La Rosa?"

"She's Rosemarie Daniels. I did want Rose in her name, and since my mother's family has a history of naming the girls after flowers, I thought…" She needed to stop babbling.

His eyes went dark and hard. She took another step back. That was the expression of rage she had learned to fear. He had never deliberately hurt her, but that look had always made her wonder if the potential was there.

"Does she even know about me? Does she know who her father is?"

"Yes. She knows your name." Today he didn't resemble that boy at all. "How long have you been at the shelter? Never mind. I'm sorry. I need to go. I promise I'll answer all your questions tonight. And don't worry about the tab. I'll cover it."

He leaned back on the counter. For a second, he closed his eyes. He inhaled deeply, causing his chest to expand. When he finally looked at her, the flash of anger was gone, but his face was closed and hard to read. "I can afford a couple of cups of coffee."

He smiled, the kind of smile that was a bit forced. Like he had to remind himself to play nice. It showed off the long dimple on his left cheek, and the new lines at the corner of his eyes. "I'll even throw in some sopaipillas. I could actually get you one of everything on the menu if you want. I have an in with the chef."

"I'm sorry. I didn't mean to insult you. I just—" This was so much worse than she had feared. *God, please lead me in this and give me the words and strength I need to make this right for everyone.*

He straightened and walked toward her. When she backed away from him, he stopped and frowned. "Why are you acting as if you're afraid of me? I never hurt you." His hard gaze held her in place, studying her like an image he couldn't identify. "Did I?"

Forcing herself to stand still, she shook her head. "No. You never hurt me. I'm sorry." Why was she apologizing?

"Don't worry about it. It takes a lot more these days to upset me. Just be there." Each word clipped and tense. "If you're not, expect me at the house. I'll stand at the door until you answer."

Her phone vibrated. She glanced down and saw her mother's name. "I've gotta go."

"Jazz?"

His low voice made her knees weak. She could not afford to be weak. "Don't call me that. I'm not that naive girl anymore."

"You'll be there?"

"I'm not the one who breaks promises." With resolve, she pivoted and headed for the door.

"No, you only hide a child from her father."

She almost stumbled. That was a punch to the gut. And the worst part? He was right. And he had every right to be angry. But she was not going to regret what she did to keep her daughter safe. Not looking at him, she replied, "I'll be there. I'm also going to do whatever it takes to keep her safe."

Then she rushed out of the pantry area. Now she was going to have to explain all this to her daughter.

Chapter Two

Standing alone, Elijah tried to clear his brain. The hum of the commercial refrigerators gave him something safe to focus on, anything other than the curve of her face. The rust colored freckles that dusted her cheeks over soft mahogany skin. The need to reach out and touch her, to make sure she was real had been a punch to the gut. He buried his fingers in his hair and dropped his head.

For over five years, he had practiced his apology, holding each word tightly in his mind until the day he could tell her. He had written letter after letter, flooding her parents' mailbox with them. Not that she had seen any of them—her parents had made that clear—but he had been desperate to make things right. And now the day had come, and he hadn't uttered a word of his apology. He'd blown it. Anger soured his stomach.

Because she had stolen his child. Digging his fingers into his scalp, he dropped into a crouch, elbows dug into his knees. Did she actually believed he was homeless? He laughed. Alone in the pantry, he laughed out loud.

And then he stopped. Took a few deep breaths. Right now, he needed to be calm and steady. He couldn't afford to lose his grip.

The Daniels were powerful people in the state of Texas. Elijah couldn't imagine Judge Nelson James Daniels III ever being weak. The man ruled his world with an iron fist. There was only one person Elijah knew with a stronger will—Azalea Daniels, his wife, Jazmine's mother. She and her husband had hated him from the first moment he had stepped on their porch to take their daughter to a beach party to kick off the summer season.

He was only two years older, but at the time, his twenty to Jazmine's eighteen was too big of a gap for them. He wasn't in school or planning to attend. Plus, they knew his uncle.

Frank had stood in front of Judge Daniels's bench more times than Elijah wanted to think about.

The Daniels family had faced their own tragedy, losing a young son to a drunk driver. Elijah was an idiot. Leaning his forehead against the door, he planted his fist against the wall. This was 100 percent his fault. Why had he tried to overstep and reach for something he didn't deserve?

With his program and counseling, he'd finally been in a place to let it go, to let her go. Making amends and apologizing was all he'd had left, but everything had just changed.

Jazmine, the Daniels's only surviving child, had had a bright future. Even before her senior year had started, she had been accepted to three Ivy League schools on the East Coast. Elijah, on the other hand, had barely gotten out of high school.

He preferred the outdoors. On a horse, working with cattle, or on a boat out in the Gulf fighting the elements. Both of those were a thousand times more fulfilling than sitting behind a desk at the job Judge Daniels had gotten him.

He closed his eyes. That job had taken all the life out of him, but instead of talking he had started drinking.

Needless to say, her parents had not been happy when Jazmine had decided to stay and attend the local college, so she could stay close to him. They had done everything but disown her when they had gotten married.

Then his stupid De La Rosa weakness had to ruin it all, giving her parents the perfect opportunity to take her away from him.

He had never hurt Jazmine. Not physically. A hollow thud hit his gut. At least, he didn't think he had.

The night she had left was a foggy mess of impressions. No matter how hard he focused, that night, like so many others, was a blur. All he remembered was the bang of the thunder and blinding flashes of lightning.

When he had woken up, she had been gone and had never returned. Until today.

The huge ornate mirror her parents had given them had been smashed into hundreds of razor-sharp shards. There had been traces of blood on both the frame and his knuckles. He hoped the glass was the only thing he had broken. The thought of touching her in anger made him sick to his stomach. Even at his worst, he wouldn't do that. Would he?

The token in his pocket had a strip of paper wrapped around it. He pulled it out. This morning his meditation verse had been Second Corinthians 5:17. *Old things are passed away; behold, all thing are becoming new.*

When he had read his daily meditation scripture before the sun had risen over the Gulf this morning, God knew what this day would bring.

One of the first lessons he'd had to learn was that in order to control his life, he had to control his anger. Getting angry was never going to help. He had to focus on today and what he needed to do going forward.

He wanted to show Jazmine that they had all been wrong about him. He had become a successful businessman. Just a few months ago, he and his partner had added the Painted Dolphin to their line of restaurants here along the coast. They just added another boat to their recreational fleet. With God, he had become a new man.

Becoming new. But, boy, did that take on new meaning today. Elijah closed his eyes and rubbed the sobriety token between his thumb and index finger.

If he was going to get through this day, he couldn't go into the past. It would be like those long lines of dominoes he had loved setting up as a kid. One negative thought would trigger another until a tidal wave of guilt sucked him under. The alcohol used to help him silence the voices, but he couldn't give in now. He couldn't go back to that dark place.

There was a little girl who needed a sober father. The man he had been for the last five years could be that father. He would give her what his uncle had never given him.

Anger flared again. They had stolen five years of his daughter's life from him. Elijah took out his phone and called his best friend and business partner. One of the people who had helped him stay sober.

"Hey, Miguel. I need to talk."

"What's up?" The casual question was lined with concern. A door closed and the background noise vanished.

Elijah knew he had his friend's full attention. His throat went dry. He couldn't believe the words he was about to say.

"I just saw Jazmine. She's in town."

"Oh, wow. That had to be a surprise." There was a short pause, as though Miguel was struggling for words. "How are you doing?"

"That's not all." He took a deep breath. "I'm a father. She was pregnant when she left. I have a five-year-old daughter."

Silence fell.

"Miguel?"

"Yeah, I'm here. You didn't have a clue?"

"Nope." Suddenly his throat burned, and he beat back the tears. "I know I have to take responsibility because my drinking drove her away from me. She couldn't trust me, and she thought she was protecting our baby. But Miguel, every time I think about what I've missed the last five years, I want to explode. I'm not sure I've ever been this angry at someone, not even my mother or uncle."

"Yeah, losing people is one of the reasons you

stopped drinking, right? So the people you love can trust you. I have to say you also have a right to be angry, but that's not going to help. Are you at the ranch? I can be out there in the next fifteen minutes."

"No, I'm at the mission. I'll come to the pier. Are you there?"

"Yep. Come straight over, okay? I'll be waiting."

"I won't stop." Elijah disconnected the call. *Lord, You've gotten me through the darkest times. I trust You have a plan in all this. Give me the wisdom to know the right thing to do and the patience to wait for Your timing.*

He was going to need more wisdom and patience than he'd ever thought possible.

On the drive back to Port Del Mar, Rosemarie had chatted away about her new doll and the horse she wanted to get her. All her dolls had their own horses. She was oblivious to the silent tension between her mother and grandmother.

Driving down Shoreline Road, Jazmine didn't even take the time to appreciate the beautiful beach that lined the tiny coastal town. There were two main roads that ran parallel to each other. In some spots, the strip of land between the bay and the Gulf was less than a mile wide.

Her father had inherited the beachfront home that had been a staple of Jazmine's childhood. It was one of her favorite places on Earth. But her parents had kept her away since that night, not allowing her anywhere near Port Del Mar.

It had been six long years since the sounds of the waves and the feel of the salty breeze filled her senses.

This was her daughter's first trip to Texas.

She pulled into the long, bricked driveway lined with tall palm trees and large fuchsia flowers. The soft blue house trimmed in pristine white stood three stories tall. By the time Jazmine parked in the carport, Rosemarie was climbing out of her booster seat.

"Momma, unlock the door so I can show Becca to Papa."

"Remember he needs to be resting." She turned to her daughter. "Don't wake him if he's asleep. Can you be quiet?"

Rosemarie's dark curls bounced as she nodded. "I can be as quiet as a mouse." In a heartbeat, she jumped out of the SUV and leaped up the stairs.

Jazmine waited for her daughter to disappear inside the house before turning to her mother. "Thank you for not making a scene in front of Rosie. Go ahead. Out with it. What have you been champing at the bit to tell me?"

"First, I don't champ. Second, this is a mistake. She does not need that man in her life. You need to pack up and go back to Denver." Azalea's arms were crossed, and her face was set like stone.

"His name is Elijah. Not saying his name will not make him go away. She's his daughter. The least I can do is talk to him."

Jazmine looked at the organized walls of the garage. Everything fit in a perfect space. If it didn't, it was tossed out. No room for anything undesirable. "I'm not leaving you alone with Daddy. He's not a good patient. In less than a week, he will drive you crazy. You need me as much as he needs you. With Rosie around, he might be easier to handle."

"There is nothing easy about your father." The perfectly lined lip quivered.

Jazmine reached across and placed her hand over her mother's. "He's going to be fine. Dr. Brent feels good about a full recovery. It is going to take all of us to keep him from overdoing it. I'm not going anywhere. I can be just as stubborn as you."

With a harsh exhalation, her mother rolled her eyes. "You get that from your father. We can't tell him that Rosie…that…her father…" She shuddered. "I just don't like this. What if he causes problems? He was always good at that."

"Mother, what we did was wrong. He had every right to know about Rosemarie. I know I had to leave, but we should have told him." She pressed one arm over her middle, trying to ease the sick feeling. "I have to meet him. We should have never done it."

"Your father and I did exactly what we needed to do to keep our daughter and our granddaughter safe. I would do it all over again, with not a single regret." She rubbed the edge of her purse.

"That night you came to us, you were so scared, and you had that nasty cut. I can't get the blood-soaked towel you had wrapped around your arm out of my head. There is no reason for me to say his name." Her shoulders squared.

"I told you. He never hurt me. I got cut trying to pick up the shards of glass. My hands were shaking." Jazmine relaxed her grip on the steering wheel, revealing her scar again. "If you had been able to stop us from getting married, we wouldn't have Rosemarie."

Azalea sighed and dropped her head. "Okay, so I wouldn't change that part. But I would still send you and Rosie away. I'm not sure I believe the story about the glass. You had a habit of making excuses for him."

She dug into her purse and pulled out her gold tube of lipstick. Lowering the visor, she used the mirror to reapply the bronze color. "Sweetheart, it doesn't look good. I mean we found him eating lunch at Esperanza's Kitchen. You know that's for homeless people. He's fallen further than even I would have guessed."

Jazmine wanted to beat her head against the windshield. "We don't know why he was there. His family still owns the Diamondback Ranch."

"His family might own land, but they have major issues. If he's been kicked out of that family, he's really sunk low. You shouldn't go alone. We'll arrange to have him come to the law office. He can be reminded who he's up against."

"No. I'm not going to have this turn into a legal battle. That would just drag it out. Rosie doesn't deserve a messy court battle between her parents."

"What if he hasn't changed?"

Jazmine took a moment to stifle the words she wanted to scream at her mother. "Rosemarie's older. She'll be able to call me if she needs to. She—"

"You're not going to let him be alone with her!"

"Not right now, but when she's older. Keeping them apart is wrong."

"What he put you through was wrong. What would you do if Rosie was in the same situation?"

Jazmine bit her lips to hold in words of frustration. There was really no arguing with her parents. "They don't know each other, so any meetings we set up now will be with me. I'm not going to just drop her off with a stranger and leave."

"We need to get something in writing, some sort of legal agreement before you allow him to talk to her. We have to protect her and make sure he can't—"

Jazmine's fist hit the steering wheel. "Stop. She has as much right to know about her father as he does to know about her. We're meeting tonight, and I'll make a plan from there." She twisted and faced her mother. "You're going to have to trust me on this. Okay?"

Her mother sighed. "I'm not sure I trust you when you're in the same room as him."

"That love-struck girl has grown up. I'm not going to allow anyone to hurt my daughter. If he is sober, we'll come up with a plan that protects her."

"If I can't change your mind, then please be careful. I don't want to see you hurt again. And you have to think about that innocent little girl." She looked out the window. "With your father down, I just can't…"

Jazmine reached across the center console and threaded her fingers through her mother's. "I know. But if nothing else, this has reminded me that our lives can change in a blink. I can't put this off any longer."

"Rosemarie is so trusting."

"I won't let anyone hurt her. That includes her father." She gave her mother a hard look. "And her grandparents. Have you thought about the questions she'll have in a few years when she learns we kept her father from her?"

With a quick nod and a deep sigh, Azalea got out of the car and headed for the stairs.

Jazmine rested her forehead on the steering wheel. Her heart wasn't so sure she would be fine with Elijah being in Rosemarie's life, but for her daughter's sake, she couldn't hide behind her parents any longer.

Elijah was going to find how much she'd changed. The meek girl was gone. She was a full-grown mama bear now, and if she thought he would hurt Rosemarie in any way, she was walking out. Even if she left behind another piece of her heart.

Chapter Three

Jazmine arrived at the Painted Dolphin thirty minutes early. She wanted to be there before Elijah so she could pick the table where this meeting would take place. The seat of power had to be hers. She walked around the building, then went up the steps.

A few boats with lights strung over every mast and piece of rigging sailed by in the bay. A longing surprised her.

A young staff member in a tie-dyed T-shirt came over to her. "Can I help you?"

A nervous laugh slipped out. Why did she felt like a teenager sneaking out of her parents' house? "Yes. I'm meeting someone." She scanned the large room. Several life-size sculpted dolphins painted with bright patterns still hung from the ceiling, but everything else looked new. The place was a surprising mix of modern and bohemian charm. Elijah had said it had been reopened a couple of months ago.

"Ma'am?" The blonde, sun-kissed girl looked at her with concern.

"Oh, I'm sorry. I use to come here all the time. It looks different."

She smiled. "It looks great, right? So, do you want to sit inside or on the deck? The singer will be starting up again, so if you want to talk, then I suggest the deck. Sitting by the water is nice. It's my favorite place."

Jazmine nodded. "I always sat next to the railing." She glanced across the room at the long wooden serving counter and froze. He was already here.

Working? He shook hands with someone and laughed.

Then he saw her and his smile vanished. With a few words to the man, he left the register area and headed straight for her. The work-worn clothes were gone. A blue dress shirt was open at the neck, the long sleeves rolled up to his elbows.

Oh my. The beach bum cowboy cleaned up well. Very well.

He moved with the easy grace she remembered from the early days. Like he owned everything around him. The confidence that he had shown the world was always in conflict with his self-esteem.

Without a doubt he had always been gorgeous, and she had never understood what he had seen in her. All the local girls had wondered the same thing. Her parents said he had just been after her money and social standing, but she had never believed that.

As she watched him, she saw a difference in him. He seemed more...more *something.* What, she wasn't sure, but wow. Okay, so it looked as if he had a steady job. That was good.

"Hey, Jenny. I'll seat Ms. Daniels."

"Hi, Mr. De La Rosa. Oh." She looked back to Jazmine. "You're meeting Mr. De La Rosa."

"Yes. She's meeting me. We're going to be outside at table seven. Will you bring us some chips with guacamole and some lemonade?"

"Of course, sir. I'll have it right out." Her long blond hair swung as she turned to do his bidding.

With his most charming wink, he grinned at her. "You're early."

Caught. She glanced around. "I wanted to—"

"Get here first to get the lay of the land." He chuckled. "I'm not surprised." He lifted his right arm and gestured to the doors leading out to the deck. "Ladies first."

She glanced around as they walked under the giant garage doors made of glass. Two of the three were rolled up into the ceiling, leaving the restaurant open to the water. On a small platform, a man was strumming a guitar and softly singing. The dining area looked busy. "Will you get in trouble for talking while you're at work?"

With a half-hearted chuckle, he shook his head. "No. I'm good. I'm pretty tight with the owner." He pushed back his hair.

Her brain was trying to catch up. The Elijah she saw this afternoon was not matching up with the Mr. De La Rosa she followed now. "You work here?" Was he the manager? "You're not...why were you eating at Esperanza's today?"

Outside, they walked to the far corner of the railed deck. He pulled out the chair on the opposite side of the table and waited for her to sit before seating himself across from her. "I volunteer there, and I have a few men there I visit with whenever I get the chance."

"Oh." Her cheeks felt warm. "Are they in AA?"

He gave her a tight smile. "We're here to talk about our daughter."

"Of course." Opening her purse, she pulled out an envelope. "I printed these up for you. I can send you more if you want."

His hands shook a little as he picked up the pictures. Was he nervous or was it a side effect from all the drinking? The gentle lapping of the water against the pier was the only sound as she watched him.

He flipped through the pictures one at a time, studying each one as if devouring every detail. They started with the first hospital pictures and ended with a selfie they had taken yesterday while waiting for the car to take them to the airport. He looked through them again.

The only indication of what he was feeling was the flicker of muscle on his jawline and the bounce of his Adam's apple. Unable to watch any longer, she let her gaze follow the boats in the harbor.

The clearing of his throat brought her attention back to him. He held the envelope out to her.

"No. Those are yours."

"Thanks." He slid them into his shirt pocket. For a moment his hand rested there.

Needing to focus on something else, her gaze swept their old hangout. "It's nice. I like the changes. How long have you worked here?"

"About six months." He sighed. His gaze darted around like he was embarrassed.

"You have the look of a manager." She tried to keep

her face neutral, rather than judgmental, but she wasn't sure how successful she was. "So, you're not homeless? You run the restaurant? That's great."

He shifted to the side and opened his mouth, then clamped it shut.

There was something in his eyes that seemed off. Was he ashamed? "It's the perfect job for you. Outdoors, no sitting still. And you were always good with people. Working at a desk indoors everyday was not a good fit."

"What about you? Have you moved back to Texas for good?"

"No. I took family leave to help my mother. I'm an event planner for a large resort in Denver. I have eight weeks, and then we're going back."

"Eight weeks?" He popped his knuckles. "I have eight weeks to get to know her before you leave."

Nodding was all she could manage.

He leaned back, one arm draped across the empty chair next to his. The silky blue shirt pulled taut across his shoulders. He studied her, those intense gray eyes making her look away. She took in the boats. There were the normal charters and sailboats, but at the very end there was a new addition. A huge, old-fashioned ship bobbed in the water.

There had to be something safe she could talk about. "Is that a pirate ship?"

"Yeah. It's new. I've been out on it a few times. It's fun to watch it go by when I'm eating dinner on our deck at home."

Biting the inside of her lip, she shut her eyes. The

little beachfront cottage they had bought in the first months of their marriage.

It was on the opposite side of town. Her parents had given them the down payment to the fixer-upper. She had loved that place. "Our deck? I thought the house was sold in the divorce."

"They didn't tell you anything, did they?" This time his look of disgust wasn't directed at her.

"No. They thought it would be easier for me." Why was she suddenly afraid to hear what had happened to their little home? They had worked so hard together to restore the beach cottage until it was just the way she wanted it.

"Originally, they told me to sell it." He shrugged. "I wanted to keep it. We had put so much sweat equity into it. It was the first time ever I had a real home." He took a drink of his lemonade. "It looked like I was going to lose again. I didn't have the money to buy you out." His fingers ran along the braided leather brace-let he wore on his left wrist. "Then the hurricane hit. There was a great deal of damage. We wouldn't have been able to sell anytime soon, so I made an offer to buy your half at a discount. My cousin Xavier helped me out. I still live there."

She wasn't sure why the idea of him fighting for their house made her heart flutter, but she needed to move on to other thoughts. "Were you able to rebuild?"

"I discovered that I have a skill for rebuilding."

She turned her attention to the busy restaurant. "You always enjoyed being out on the water. You talked about owning your own fishing boats."

He looked away and waved to some people on a boat

gliding by. "I talked to my lawyer about child support. She's going to do some research and figure out how much I owe you."

"What?" The change of subject startled her. "No. I don't want your money. I'm fine."

His attention returned to her. Now his eyes were a steel gray. "It's not for you. I'm not a deadbeat dad."

"Elijah. You don't—"

His fist clenched. "I will not be my father." He took a deep breath and relaxed into his chair. "Buy her shoes or a pony or put it aside for college. I don't want her to ever think I didn't support her." He pulled a card out of his shirt pocket where he had slipped the pictures. "Here's my lawyer's information. She'll set up payment. Whatever is easier for you."

She nodded, but her stomach turned. If he was paying child support, he'd start thinking he could have more say in Rosemarie's life. She wasn't ready to share her.

An awkward silence fell between them. When they had first met, talking had been so easy. They would stay on the beach late into the night discussing family, horses, the plans he had for the ranch, the boats he wanted to buy.

Sometimes they just talked about silly things that didn't matter. All that counted was that they were together. He was only two years older, but she had been eighteen. The world had revolved around him and he owned it all. She never could figure out what he had seen in that shy, clumsy girl.

Leaning on his elbows and lacing his fingers together, he stared straight at her. "I'm really trying to understand. I know I scared you, but how could you keep her from me for so long?" The hard lines on his face and the white in his knuckles betrayed the anger he was holding in.

She shifted in her seat and looked away. It was hard to forget how strong her love for him had been in the early days. Then, a few months into their marriage, the drinking had started. That's what she needed to remember. "You had become too unpredictable."

"You didn't even give me a chance." His voice was low and harsh.

"I tried to help. When you had a difficult time with my parents or your uncle, I tried to intervene, but I know now that I only made it worse."

She had been so sheltered, and it had shocked her to see at firsthand how ugly people could be to the ones they loved. Elijah's uncle Frank had been a cruel, violent man who had no problem hitting someone small or weaker. The people he should have protected.

She shook her head. "I didn't have the life experience to help you. I couldn't imagine being abandoned by a mother and abused by an uncle. When it got worse, you started stumbling home hours after dinner. The one person I would have turned to for help was the one I was afraid for. I didn't know how to get you to stop drinking."

He grunted.

She knew Elijah had been suffering, but the more she had tried to help him, the worse the problems grew.

Looking down, she captured her hands and held them still. Her napkin was now an organized pile of neat shreds.

"The night I was going to tell you I was pregnant was the night you really seemed out of control. I thought about all the horror stories I'd heard about your uncle and the abuse. It overwhelmed me. I was scared of you." The cold seeped through her skin.

"I'm not my uncle." His voice was hard.

She wasn't sure if he was trying to convince her or himself.

If Elijah was truly sober, then she owed it to her daughter to let her know him. But it didn't mean she had to trust him.

He pulled out the pictures again.

With his attention on the photos, she had the luxury of studying him. His golden skin looked darker, but he had lighter streaks in his hair. The stubble from this afternoon was gone, leaving his skin smooth. Had he shaved for her?

With a heavy sigh, he looked up at the night sky. The string of white party lights highlighted his features. "I don't even know where to start. We had a baby. I still can't believe you left without telling me." Lowering his head, he stared straight at her.

Gripping the edge of the wooden seat, she forced herself to sit still. Despite the anger that radiated from him, his body language told her he was in control.

He had a right to be upset, but she couldn't back down. "The minute I found out I was pregnant, that baby became the most important person in my world." She allowed her brain to take her back to that night.

She would not regret her decision. "You were out of control. Each night was getting worse. I was waiting up later and later. When you finally came home, it was an hour of yelling and ranting before you passed out. The violence was escalating. That last night I was so scared."

"I never hurt you." His lips tightened as his hard jaw flexed. "Did I?"

He looked down, but not before she had seen anger mixed with loathing. And something else. Doubt?

She sat back. "Not physically."

"I'm not my uncle. I would never have touched you with violence." His voice was low and gravelly. "Why didn't you talk to me? Maybe if you had told me, I would've sobered up sooner."

Now her own anger burned. "Are you serious?" The words forced their way out from between clenched teeth. "I did talk. You had three modes." She held up one finger, keeping her scar facing her. "Drunk." The second finger went up. "Asleep." Then the third, the one she used to wear her wedding ring on. "Hungover. When was I supposed to reason with you?"

"You took my child and ran." He closed his eyes and rolled his shoulders. When he opened them, his gaze bored into her. He appeared calm, but clearly determined.

"When I spoke to my lawyer about child support, I also asked her to look into my rights as a father. I want to see my daughter. What does she know about me?"

Fear jumbled her insides into a big ball of mush. This was what she had been afraid of, the one thing she wanted to avoid at all costs. "I've never hidden you from her." Much to her mother's dismay. "I've shared a couple of pictures of us from when we were dating. She knows that her name is a combination of her father's family name and my grandmother's name."

"Why does she think I'm not around?" Tension reappeared in his shoulders. "Does she know you stole her?"

She leaned closer to him. "I did not kidnap my daughter." He needed to understand that her daughter, their daughter, was the most important person in this mess.

"I was protecting her the only way I knew how. You'd started drinking. I was not going to bring my baby into a house where objects went crashing into walls without warning or wait around to see if you got better." Over Elijah's shoulder, she saw the cheerful waitress heading to their table carrying a tray that held chips and guacamole, as well as a glass pitcher full of lemonade with fresh sliced lemons.

Twisting, he looked to see what had caused her to stop talking. With a tight smile, he thanked the blonde.

"Did you need menus, Mr. De La Rosa?"

He looked at Jazmine.

She shook her head. "No. I had dinner already." She wasn't even sure she could keep down the lemonade.

"We're good, Jenny. If I need anything else, I'll come in and let you know."

"Yes, sir." With one more perfect smile and a polite but curious look, she left.

Did Elijah bring dates here a lot?

That was none of her business.

It was back to the heavy silence. The discussion had derailed again. Years ago, she had put all the anger and bitterness behind her. Or at least she thought she had. "Elijah—"

"I want—"

Speaking on top of each other, they both stopped. His fingers ran over the surface of the envelope. Had she made a mistake?

The real question was, did she make it six years ago or tonight, like her mother thought?

He laced his fingers in front of him. With his head down like that, he looked as if he were praying. Maybe she should join him. The only thing she knew right now was that God had to be in control. Because she and Elijah had made a mess. She didn't want their daughter paying the price.

He cleared his throat. "Sorry. It's been a few years since I've had to go through this. I've forgotten how difficult it could be."

Confused, her gaze scanned his face, looking for clues to what he was thinking. He had always been good at hiding his feelings. "What do you mean?"

"Letting people air the hurts I caused them without getting defensive. It's part of the program, the twelve steps. The list I started telling you about at the mission, but we got a little distracted. I have to find each one and express my true regret for the damage I've done. The person I hurt gets to vent and I listen. No excuses, I just listen. You were the only one left on my list. The last one. The one who deserves the biggest apology." He reached across the table like he wanted to touch her, but then pulled back.

"I destroyed our marriage with my drinking. I... I know I did that. Those are the words that I've wanted to say to you, and I mean every single one of them. You had every right to walk out, but we have a daughter now and I'm at a loss as to what that means. It's another horrible casualty of my drinking, but the thought of everything I missed is killing me. I can't get back those years."

"That's why I'm here. But I have to be honest. Trusting you again is not going to be easy. I'm worried."

He nodded, then looked up and made eye contact. "I'm sober. Soon it will be six years. I can't fix the past, but we can move forward. I want to see her tomorrow."

Chewing on the inside of her cheek, she organized her thoughts before answering. "You might have been sober for years, but in my mind, it was just the other day that you…" She looked down. "It might be best if we wait a little longer."

He tossed his head back and stared at the night sky again. His chest expanded with deep, hard breaths. "Maybe it would be better for everyone if we finish this discussion in a courtroom. I'll call my lawyer in the morning."

His full attention was back on her. The eyes that she used to stare into for hours now looked at her with anger. Not filled with the love from the beginning or the drunk haze they held last time she saw him, but clear crisp determination.

Her stomach turned. "Elijah, I don't—"

"I'm not the poor ranch kid from six years ago. If we have to go to court, I will. I deserve to have her in my life."

She held up her hand. "No."

He put his hands on top of hers, gently holding it

to the table. Nerves tingled up her arm and down her spine. She stared at the hands that use to hold her with tenderness before the drinking. Clearing her head, she tried to pull away.

At first he increased the pressure, but then let her go.

"I won't—" His voice was low and calm, but she didn't doubt his iron will.

"Elijah, I didn't mean you can't see her. I just don't want to drag her through court. I came here tonight so we can work something out between us. Her parents."

Finally breaking eye contact, he propped his elbows on the table and rested his forehead on his palms. "What about your parents? Every time I tried to get in contact with you, they had restraining orders thrown at me. What makes you think they'll go along with this now?"

Cutting her gaze to the busy restaurant, Jazmine felt thankful to be in public. It would help them both keep emotions in check.

"You know your drinking was very hard on them. That might be the one thing they can never forgive you for. You know our family history." She blinked back the wetness in her eyes.

With a tight nod, Elijah acknowledged the horrible truth. Her parents had lost a child because of a drunk driver. His gut burned. There was nothing to say to that.

"I'll take care of my parents. I came here tonight because it's time Rosemarie met her father. But Elijah, it has to be on my terms. I know there's a whole family she needs to meet, but please give me time. It's been just her and me. Bringing you into her life is not easy."

He wanted to point out that she had made this hard, not him. "I want to see her tomorrow."

"Okay, but not alone. That's my stipulation. I can't trust you yet. Besides, she doesn't know you. To her, you're a stranger."

A sadness replaced the fury. "Because you took her from me." The words fought against the rawness in his throat.

She swallowed. "To protect her. She's very shy. If you come over for lunch, it will be a comfortable and safe way to introduce you."

"And she knows I'm her father, right?"

"In the abstract, which doesn't mean much to a five-year-old. I'll make sure she knows who you are."

He sat back. "Okay. Tomorrow at 11:30. Will that work?" Elijah dropped his gaze from his wife—his ex-wife.

She still hadn't said anything. This Jazmine was stronger. Surer of herself. But she couldn't keep his daughter from him. "Jazz? Eleven thirty tomorrow?"

She gave the slightest jerk of her head. "Elijah, you have to know this is hard for me. My last memories of you are... Well, they don't reassure my maternal fears. You've had years of being sober, but in my heart it all just happened."

The tension was back. "You really think I would hurt our child? That I would hurt any kid?" He wasn't that messed up.

Staying steady and calm was more important than his tattered pride. In the last five years, he had learned to listen and to wait before responding. It took time to process information and…ugh, feelings.

Even thinking the word to himself made him feel like an idiot. It was hard to completely erase his uncle's words from his mind. *Crybaby. Worthless. Weak. Waste of space.* How could a dead man still taunt him?

His uncle had spouted nothing but hatred and lies. He knew that now. But it was still hard not to get lost in the black hole of doubt that swirled in his brain whenever life hit him with an unexpected hailstorm.

In God's eyes, he was worthy of love. He was a child of God. That's what his sister, Belle, and his friend Miguel told him anyway, and if he was going to believe a lie, it was better to go with that one.

What did he know? One fact that was drilled into the smallest fiber of his being was that he would do whatever it took to have his daughter in his life. He didn't want to cause her any embarrassment or give her any reason not to claim him as her dad. *Dad.* He closed his eyes. He was someone's dad.

Daughter. Wow. He was prepared to face any of the consequences his drinking brought to his door, or so he thought. This, he had not seen coming. He opened his eyes and studied his ex-wife.

She was staring out over the water. She hadn't answered him, or he hadn't heard her.

"I wouldn't. You know that, right? I'd never hurt someone weaker than me."

"No. Not intentionally. But when you're drunk, your impulses and—"

"Which is why I don't drink anymore." Was he ever going to truly get away from his past? "Jazz, I know words aren't enough. Earning your trust is a task I'm up for. Let me show you."

Lips tight, she nodded. "That's why you're coming over. Rosemarie also needs time to get to know you." She looked at the sailboat outlined with cords of white patio lights, its reflection slowly dancing on the water as laughter floated through the air. Looking back at him, her eyes shimmered. "We'll see you tomorrow at 11:30."

Her face might have the grimmest expression, but he wanted to lift her up and swing her around. It had been a long time since he just wanted to laugh. She used to give him that. And then he had destroyed her light, pitching them both into darkness.

Now he had another opportunity. Lunch with his daughter was now on his agenda.

And just like that, the fear was back.

What if he messed this up? What if she didn't like him? He was a stranger to her. He twisted the leather at his wrist and repeated the words from his recent meditation verse, from John 14:27. He had needed an extra one today. *Let not your heart be troubled, neither let it be afraid.*

He needed to let the fear move on, through and out.

She stood, seemingly unaware of the turbulent sea of his emotions. "Now that we have that settled, I need to go home. I'll see you tomorrow. Mom will have Daddy at PT, so it will just be the three of us."

Pushing back the chair, he got to his feet and pulled out his business card. As he held it out, his work-hardened hands grazed her soft skin. The instinct to put her hand to his lips had to be locked down tight. "My personal cell is written on the back. If you don't want to go through my lawyer, let me know whatever you need."

"Thanks."

He wanted to keep her here longer, but couldn't think of any way to do it without kidnapping her. That wouldn't help with the trust issues. "I'll see y'all tomorrow. Do I need to bring anything?"

She swung the strap of her purse over her shoulder. "Just yourself."

He wanted to ask her if he would be enough, but he stopped himself. Did he really want to know the truth?

As they walked to the exit, the singer started to cover "Just the Way You Are." Jazmine jerked her head up to his, her eyes wide. "Did you—"

"No." The words to their song swirled around him. "Just a coincidence." Possibly a very cruel one. The memory of holding her while they slow-danced flooded his mind, and his body didn't seem to notice the time difference. He was there with her. Back when she still loved him. More importantly, she had trusted him.

Lips tight, she turned from him. "Bye. We'll see you tomorrow."

His eyes followed her until she vanished from his sight. He needed to take some sort of gift. There wasn't a thing about him that would make an impression on a five, almost six-year-old girl. *His* five, almost six-year-old girl. What did little girls like?

Pulling his phone out, he called his sister. It was time to let his family know. Belle was obsessive about family sticking together. He wasn't sure if she was going to be more upset with him or with Jazmine and her parents. Either way he was in for a lecture about family.

Chapter Four

Elijah slowly pulled his truck into the brick driveway. The looming, three-story beach house with its wrap-around porches and floor-to-ceiling windows always made him feel as if he didn't measure up.

Jazmine had laughed and said it was just a house. But that's what she didn't get. To her, it was just an ordinary vacation house. In his world, even the idea of a vacation house was extraordinary, let alone the design and size of this one.

His family had a ranch along the coast that included waterfront property, but they were considered land-poor at best. What was the point of owning land worth millions if you struggled to pay your basic living expenses?

Parking in front of the huge garage door that looked as though it belonged on an English carriage house, he tilted his head to look up. They had spent so much time sitting on the top balcony, staring at the stars, listening to the water. Those had been the best days of his life. Back when she had drowned out his uncle's voice.

Of course, when her parents found them one night, they had been fit to be tied. They didn't care that the most he and Jazmine had ever done was hold hands. In their mind, he was a De La Rosa and would contaminate their daughter. He hated himself for proving them right. This morning's devotional ran through his head again. *Don't be anxious. Stay in prayer.*

Easier said than done. His skin itched. Not the kind of itch that you could scratch, but under his skin. It was the kind that reminded him that he was an alcoholic, and that the minute he forgot it he would be in big trouble.

Stepping out of the truck, he centered himself before opening the door to the backseat. He hoped he hadn't gotten the gift wrong. A movement on the top balcony caught his attention. A mini Jazmine was looking over the railing. Her thick, dark, corkscrew curls framed her tiny golden-brown face.

All the blood left his body. When he'd seen her the first time, he hadn't known who she was. His brain hadn't had time to process that she was real. A little person that was part of him and Jazmine. He wanted to stare at her, take the time to make sure every detail was branded in his memory. But he needed to move, do something. He waved. "Hi, Rosemarie." His voice cracked. *Really?*

He was an idiot. *Great first impression, De La Rosa.*

She darted away. "Momma! He's here!"

A few seconds later, mother and daughter were looking down at him. Something he couldn't identify pushed at his insides.

"Hey," he called up to them. "Should I climb up the

side like the old days?" There was elaborate ironwork decorating the side of the house.

"Elijah De La Rosa, don't you dare."

Rosemarie studied him wide-eyed, then turned to her mother. "He can climb the wall like Spider-Man?"

He grinned. "Sure. I used to do it all the time."

"No. You stay right there. We're coming down to let you in."

He chuckled. Getting her riled had been one of his favorite things to do. Probably not a good idea now. By the time she opened the door, he was requesting wisdom and strength from God again.

Jazmine stepped back to let him enter the downstairs foyer. This was the plainest part of the house. It was designed to take water during heavy storms. The main living area was on the second floor and the bedrooms on the third.

With a hesitant move, Jazmine turned to the stairs.

His heart hit harder with each step, steps that brought him to his daughter. Most fathers had nine months to get used to the idea of having a child. A tiny wiggling infant was placed in their arms, and each month their baby grew into more of a little person.

Jazmine stopped on the last step. He was behind her but didn't see his daughter. His gaze darted to Jazz. She gave him a half smile. Had his daughter already decide she didn't want to meet him?

"She's very shy." She glanced toward the upper level. "Rosemarie? Come on down, sweetheart."

The worn leather of his bracelet was warm between his thumb and finger. He had already seen her, so why was he so nervous now? They would be in the same room.

He kept his focus on the top of the stairs. If his heart beat any harder, it might break his ribs. Licking his lips, he discovered they were dry. Then that sweet face surrounded by dark curls peeked around the corner of the wall.

There were people in his life he loved, but at this moment he was hit hard by a love so wild and raw that his knees almost gave out.

"Hi, there. Rosemarie, right?" His eyes burned. *No, no, no.* He took a deep breath and unlocked his jaw. The last thing he wanted to do was to scare her.

She nodded, moving toward her mother one slow, agonizing step at a time. She eyed him as if he was a coiled rattlesnake. Her hand stayed on the railing. The wall behind her was covered with photos. Rosemarie's pictures hung with the other members of the Daniels family, including the boy they had lost.

Jazmine had said she didn't have many memories of her older brother. He had been killed when she was only three. Sweat broke out across Elijah's body.

The family had to hate that their only surviving child had married an alcoholic. He had a lot to prove, but first he wanted to see his daughter smile. He lowered himself to a crouch, so he wouldn't tower over her.

Finally, she made it to her mother's side, and wrapped an arm around Jazmine's jean-clad leg.

"Hi, Rosemarie." He tried again, making sure to give her an easy smile. "I'm…" *Your dad, father, daddy.* Each word clogged his throat. None of them sounded right. "I'm so happy to meet you."

"You're my daddy, right?" Her tiny, bow-shaped lips twisted to the side.

He couldn't breathe for a minute. "I am."

"Momma calls Papa Daddy. Is that what I should call you?"

Everything below his neck locked up. He managed a nod and what he hoped was an encouraging smile. "If you want to. I like it."

Silence slipped between them again. What topics of conversation did a father have with a five-year-old daughter he'd never met?

Jazmine ran her hands over their daughter's head, pushing back her hair. "I think he has a gift for you." She raised her eyebrows and looked pointedly at the bag in his right hand.

"Oh. Yeah." He lifted the bright pink bag. "I brought this for you. My sister helped me pick it out. You can call her Tía Belle or Aunt Belle. She has a little girl about your age. You have a few cousins and a couple of aunts." Great, now he was babbling. He tried to laugh, but it sounded more like a cat caught in a trap. "Want to know a secret?"

She nodded but didn't step away from her mother.

"I'm a bit nervous." He leaned closer, stopping himself from reaching out to touch her. Nodding to the bag, he offered it to her again. "I hope you like it. If you don't, we can trade it in for something else."

Taking the bag, she smiled at him. He didn't know it was possible for a heart to hold a beat.

Rosemarie peered into the colorful wrapping his sister had chosen for him and gasped. He wanted to know if it was a good or bad noise.

"Momma, look! I'm naming her Zoe! She and Abby'll be best friends." She pulled out the dark-haired doll and hugged her. "Thank you." Turning to her mother, she held up the doll. "Can I take her to lunch?"

"That's a wonderful idea." Jazmine looked at Elijah. "She set her table for us. She wanted all her friends to meet you."

"Friends?" His gut tightened. "I thought..." Narrowing his eyes, he studied Jazmine. Her dark eyes gleamed like they used to whenever she messed with him.

"Yes!" Rosemarie interrupted his thoughts. "Mary has somewhere very important to go, so Zoe can have her spot." The little girl nodded somberly before skipping through the kitchen to the back door. Through the large glass panels, Elijah could see the ocean.

"Come." Jazmine followed her daughter. "She might not seem excited that you're here, but she set the table and helped my mother make fresh lemonade. I told her how we used to drink it during the summer while we sat on the pier and watched the waves. She planned the menu."

"You told her about us?"

"The good parts."

Swallowing the bitterness, he inhaled. He couldn't remember the last time he'd had to use his calming strategies so often in one day. "Your mother helped her? Will it be safe for me to eat?"

One hand on the door, Jazmine paused. For a moment she studied his face with a fierce intensity. Was she going to kick him out?

He held his breath as he waited for the verdict. "Sorry." He made a note to lay off the mother jokes.

"She's a little girl. A little girl who lives in a world where everybody loves her and cares for her. Please don't be her first heartbreak."

The first instinct was to deny he would ever do anything to hurt her, but then he stopped. He had blown his promises to honor and protect Jazmine out of the water. He had broken her heart.

Rubbing the back of his neck, he glanced to the little girl. She was talking to a line of stuffed animals and dolls. "I'm in a different place now. I don't know how to promise never to hurt her, but I'm going to do my best."

Their gazes stayed locked for longer than he could count.

He must have passed her test because she nodded, then crossed the threshold. To the far right, in the shaded area on the large balcony, was a mini pink picnic table. There were purple and green chairs at each end. They were a bit higher than the yellow benches on either side, but not by much.

Starfish, seashells and driftwood decorated the center, and pretty teacups and delicate plates were set at each place. The doll he had given her was in the middle of a militant line of other dolls and animals. She came over and took his hand.

"This is your spot." There was a pause. "Daddy." She stood next to the plastic chair at the end of the table. One brow up, he eyed the little polka-dot piece of furniture. Serious doubts flooded his brain.

With a huge smile, Jazmine took the chair opposite.

Slowly, he followed suit, easing himself down onto the fragile frame. His knees came halfway to his chest.

"So, these lovely ladies are your friends?"

"Yes." She went on to introduce him to each one, then picked up a small pitcher with both hands. "May I pour a drink for you?"

"I would love that. Thank you." He wanted to reach out and help her as wobbly hands tipped the pitcher, but he held back. He recognized that determined expression.

Her tongue stuck out at the corner of her mouth as she concentrated, and he felt his own mouth twitch. She looked just like his sister when she was focused on a task.

Rosemarie moved down the side of the table and poured a little in each small cup. As she served her posse, she told him how she had met each one.

No surprise that his daughter had a very vivid imagination. He had loved reading and making up stories. His sister and cousins had been participants in many of his imaginary adventures. Uncle Frank had called him a lazy dreamer.

The doll he had given her sat next to a royally dressed Abby. Apparently, she was the queen of all the other toys.

There was a bowl of chips and salsa on the table. Rosemarie offered him a small plate. "Would you like some appetizer?"

It took him a minute to figure out what she was saying. "Chips are my favorite."

He glanced at Jazmine, and she flashed him a proud smile. It was a good look. She wasn't his Jazz anymore. In the last six years she had grown up, became a mother.

Rosemarie finished serving everyone, then tucked her sundress under her as she sat. Just like a little lady. "For lunch we're eating flautas. Momma told me how you taught her how to make them when you didn't have enough money. She said you ate them all the time."

He frowned at Jazz. She had told their daughter he hadn't had enough money to feed them?

He smiled at Rosemarie. "I'm impressed you did your research." Elijah was pretty sure he had never eaten with a party of stuffed toys before. Not sure how to start a conversation, he took a slow sip of lemonade.

His daughter reached over to feed a doll, then looked at him. "Abby would like to know if you still have horses. She has a pony, but we had to leave it back home. Prince is a pretty palomino."

Before he said anything, a timer went off. Rosemarie popped up. "That's the flautas."

Jazmine got up from her chair.

"No, Momma. Stay here and talk with Daddy. I can get them."

Instead of sitting as her daughter told her to, Jazmine shook her head. "Rosemarie Daniels!"

"Momma, I'm a big girl. I want to make lunch. I don't need help." She pouted.

"You can't open the oven by yourself, young lady. It's dangerous."

With a sigh bigger than her small shoulders, Rosemarie followed her mother into the house. Elijah sat alone.

Well, not completely alone. All the little dolls glared

at him. He looked down, breaking eye contact with the toys, and stared at his intertwined fingers.

Daniels. It tore at his gut that his daughter didn't have his name. How did he fix this? His relationship with Jazmine might be beyond repair, but he had a second chance with his daughter.

His ex-wife and her parents were going to have to deal with the fact that Rosemarie had another parent who loved her too. There would be no doubt in his daughter's mind that she was loved by her father. She wouldn't grow up with his issues.

Now he just had to show Jazmine that he could be trusted with their daughter's heart. She had every reason in the world to doubt him.

Lifting his head, he found the dolls staring silently at him, judging him.

"Yes, I know," he whispered to the toys. On their wedding day he had promised to cherish and honor her. But in grand De La Rosa fashion, he had broken her.

The downstairs door opened and closed. Glancing at the clock, Jazmine frowned. It was too early for her parents to be back. Her mother had agreed to stay away for two hours. Slipping the round stone onto the cooling rack, she helped Rosemarie move the tightly rolled corn tortillas filled with refried beans onto a serving plate.

Rosemarie looked up at her and smiled. "Papa and GiGi are here! They can meet my father and eat lunch with us." Like a good little hostess, her expression changed to panic. "Do we have enough?"

"We're good. Take this out to your father." *Wow.* Words she wasn't using to saying. "I'll be right there."

What was her parents doing here? Jazmine snorted as her irritation grew.

There had been very loud complaints about her and Rosemarie meeting with Elijah alone. Her mother had wanted to be here, but Jazmine had insisted she could handle the meeting alone.

She glanced out the kitchen window to make sure Rosemarie was safe. Her heart still bounced at the thought of Elijah being with her daughter. She needed to start thinking of her as *their* daughter.

Rosemarie laughed. The sound was all joy, free of adult angst.

He was going to be a part of her life now. She sighed. Azalea would have to learn how to deal with it.

Elijah's broad back was to her, so she couldn't see his expression, but he was sitting at the kiddie table as though he did this all the time. When Rosemarie had first asked to serve lunch on her little table, Jazmine had liked the thought of making Elijah uncomfortable. To test him, see if he was ready to be a real father to a little girl.

Part of her would have been happy if he hadn't shown up.

"Did you leave her out there alone with him?" Her mother's voice was at its coldest setting.

"I had planned to be out there, but someone didn't stick to the plan." Jazmine twisted the corner of her mouth as she glared at her mother. Then she realized her father wasn't with them.

Her heart plunged. "Is something wrong with Daddy?"

With pursed lips, her mother shook her head. She

started removing her stylish blazer. "He's good. His friend Larry is with him, and they wanted to sit by the pool and visit. Larry will help him up the stairs in just a bit. Two hours is too long for him to be out. It was the perfect time to touch base and see how it was going."

Craning her neck to look out the window, she made a disgruntled noise. "It's a bad idea to have him here alone with you. He's an acholic."

"Mother, it's the middle of the day, and I wouldn't have let him in if he had been drinking." She picked up the purse her mother had placed on the counter and handed it to her. "Go. I told him it would just be the three of us for two hours. It hasn't even been thirty minutes yet. Don't turn me into a liar. They need a chance to get to know each other."

"He lost that chance when he picked up a bottle." Ignoring the elegant leather bag, Azalea walked past her toward the outside door.

Jazmine rushed to cut her mother off. "Rosemarie has a father, and we are going to learn to deal with that. Please go back to Daddy. I've got this."

A scream came from the balcony. Both women lunged for the door.

Chapter Five

Jazmine stopped when she saw Rosemarie jump up and down, then throw herself at Elijah. The force of her energy unbalanced his chair, throwing him backward. With one hand he caught himself and braced Rosemarie with the other.

Azalea was over him in a flash. She scooped up Rosemarie, pulling the little girl against her as if saving her from certain death.

"What's wrong, baby girl?" she fussed.

Elijah jumped to his feet and dusted off his pants. He gave Jazmine a guilty look.

She narrowed her eyes at him. "What happened?"

His gray-green eyes darted from her to the Gulf. "I kinda of…um. We were—"

"He's giving me a horse of my very own!"

"What!" Both women turned to him, eyes wide.

"You promised her a horse?" Azalea glared at him. "How irresponsible are you? You never grew up, did you? You're the same—"

"Mother. Stop." Jazmine turned to Elijah. "You promised her a horse?"

"A real one, Momma. He said I can pick it out. I want a palomino." Rosemarie craned back to look at her grandmother. "And he's a pirate. My dad is a real pirate."

"I'm not a—"

As one, the mother and daughter team turned their glares to him again. The displeasure on Azalea's face was tangible. "You told her you're a pirate?"

"He owns a pirate ship." Turning from her grand-mother, Rosemarie faced her father. "Right, Daddy? And fishing boats." With a huge grin, she touched her grandmother's face. "We can go fishing, and he said we could go to his ranch and pick out a horse."

"His ranch?" Sarcasm dripped like honey from Aza-lea's lips.

Jazmine cut her mother off before the insults started flying again. "Mother, could you take Rosemarie into the kitchen? Maybe eat one of the brownies we made."

"But we haven't finished lunch, and I made the brownies for Daddy!"

Jazmine's eyes started burning. She hadn't thought her daughter would bond this quickly to Elijah. Of course, she didn't know that he would give her a horse or tell her five-year-old he was a pirate. Between grit-ted teeth, she forced a smile. "Go with GiGi."

The small shoulders slumped. "Can I take Zoe?" The voice that had been so happy just a bit ago was now trembling. Big tears were building in those sweet eyes as she looked up at her father. "I made brown-ies for you."

Elijah stepped closer, then dropped down to one knee. "It's okay. I'm not leaving without saying good-bye." He picked up the doll and handed it to her. "Go with your grandmother."

It grated on Jazmine's nerves that he stepped in and acted like a parent. Closing her eyes, she took a deep breath. "He's not going anywhere, sweetheart. We'll be inside to have a brownie in a moment."

Her mother scoffed and turned away. She was not making this easier.

"Mother, be nice." She leaned in closer. "Please, keep your personal opinions to yourself."

Once they were alone, Elijah righted the chair. "Listen. I'm—"

"No. This is not the kind of thing you can just say 'Oops, my bad' and then go on your merry way. You can't make that kind of promise. And why are you lying to her about being a pirate?"

Tilting her head back, she looked to the sky for answers. *God, please help me here.* "Elijah, you don't have to impress her." She came back to his guilty face. "You're her father. She automatically loves you until you break her heart. Don't lie to her."

"I'm not lying. I do own a pirate ship." He stuffed his hands into his pressed jeans. "I don't captain it, so I don't think I can claim piratehood. I didn't tell her I was a pirate. I offered to take her out on the water. It's fun. The crew dresses up. Pretending to be a free and reckless pirate is a safe way to create an adventure. I told her she could be the brave daughter of a pirate. But no stealing. We don't steal." He winked at her, trying to lighten the mood, but his smile was sad.

He had stolen. He had taken her dreams, her heart. Falling in love with the bad-boy pirate had been exciting and fun. Each day had been a new adventure with him. It had been the greatest time of her life.

The last few months of their marriage? Not so much.

"I have a whole fleet. I'm living the life we used to dream about. Remember all those crazy plans for owning boats and running the ranch?" One hip propped against the railing, he crossed his arms over his chest and stared out over the water. "After I got sober, I made my dream of being a pirate cowboy come true. Crazy, right?"

She didn't even know how to respond to that. "You." She pointed at him. "You own a pirate ship?" Her mouth dropped open as she thought back to last night. "The restaurant? How?"

He took a deep breath as though he was going to confess a deep, dark secret and nodded. "I told you I wasn't a poor ranch kid anymore. You know how they say the storms of our lives can be blessings in disguise?" His Spanish-moss eyes burned with intensity, waiting for something.

She nodded, not sure what else to do. Elijah had never been a liar, not until he started hiding his drinking.

He shifted and braced his hand on the railing. "I lost my office job the Monday after you left. No one would take my calls."

She would not feel sorry for him. She wouldn't.

"My uncle was not an option. I went to the pier and took any job they'd give me. Working the recreational fishing boats, I met Miguel Valencia. We had an opportunity to buy a charter fishing boat, and he became my business partner. I always loved working outdoors meeting different people. I found my place." The smile on his lips contrasted with the sadness in his eyes.

"That sounds like a perfect career choice for you." He had hated working in an office. Even if it had been one of the nicest offices in the county.

On the water behind them, a boat was making its way to the bay. "We bought one boat that had been damaged in the storm and fixed it up. We put all our profits into the business. It grew." He pointed to the boat full of people. "That's one of ours. Now we have four fishing boats and a sightseeing boat. We opened the Painted Dolphin and just added the pirate ship. There are several other threads to our business, and now that my uncle is dead, I'm working with my sister and cousins to expand the income for the ranch. We might sell it, not sure yet. We're looking at hosting a fishing tournament and rodeo event as a huge community festival. We need to start small but...well, we tend to expand quickly."

"You own your own businesses and are developing community events?" This was so hard to compute. Yesterday morning she had thought he was homeless, only to find out he owned half the businesses on the waterfront. Her parents had to have known, but they hadn't said a word to her. "The Painted Dolphin is yours?" Her brain was having a problem recalibrating.

"Yep. We bought the pier. We're restoring a bit at a time. We have more than sixty people working for us now. The summer numbers are higher because of tourism." He turned away from the beach view and focused on her. "I talked to my lawyer this morning."

Her stomach clenched. He had the resources to take her to court. She had basically stolen his child.

He studied her. "She has the amount I owe for the past five—"

"No. I don't need your money. That's not why I came back."

"When she's older, I want her to know I was responsible. I also want to be a part of her life. On all levels. You had to know I would have strong feelings about supporting my daughter. Don't fight me on this." His lips formed a hard line. "I want to take care of her."

Nodding, she stepped back, away from the familiar scent that made her want to curl into him.

When they had been together, one of his favorite things to do had been to lean in close to her ear with one hand in her hair and the other on the center of her back. He'd hold her against him and whisper that he'd take care of her, like the princess she was.

Unfortunately, she had believed him until it had been too late. He hadn't even been able to take care of himself. Over the last five years, though, she had stepped out of her parent's shadow and stood on her own. She'd raised their daughter.

She bit at her lip. Back in the beginning, she imagined they were taking care of each other, but she couldn't really say that, either. She hadn't been strong enough to take on his struggle, to break the chains that held him to the past.

He had been fighting a fight she couldn't win for him. Moving to face the Gulf, Elijah braced his hands on the top of the railing. "Jazz, I'm sorry about the horse. But I meant it. We can go out to the ranch. We have a stable of very well-behaved horses that we use for beach rides."

"That's not the issue. You could have a hundred horses. We live in an apartment in Denver. We don't have the space or time for a horse. I'm her mother. You can't just start making promises without talking to me. That's basic parenting."

"When she started talking about how much she loved horses and had always wanted one, I got excited I could give her that. That's something I can do. My businesses are doing well." He paused. "I want to take care of you the way I should have for the last six years."

"You and I are over. All she needs is a father who will be there for her."

With a sigh, she glanced into the kitchen. Rosemarie was waving her hands around as she told her GiGi some grand story. "Now I'm the one who has to tell her 'No.' Don't make any more promises to her without talking to me first. Okay?"

He twisted his lips and squinted one eye.

That wasn't good. "What is it, Elijah? Just spit it out."

"I, um…asked her about her birthday. As we were talking about that, I kind of told her we could have a big birthday party on the pirate ship. That's how we got to talking about birthday wishes. She told me that every year of her life she wished for a pony and never got one. So, I—"

Jazmine couldn't help the chuckle that escaped. "No. No pirate ships. She's going to be six. So, her whole life thing is a bit dramatic. She loves theatrical statements. You should have seen the fits she could throw for the first three years. I'm happy to report the tantrums have been a thing of the past since she turned four."

He grinned. "You were never dramatic. Always even-keeled, the practical girl. The drama sounds more like my sister."

Tired, Jazmine sat. She rolled her head back, looking up at the clear sky. "Yeah, I remember that. My parents like to blame any hint of a bad character flaw on your family."

"Of course, they would. Unfortunately, they're probably right. I'm sure she takes after you more than me." He eased down on the chair next to her. "Speaking of my sister, Belle wants her to meet her daughters, Cassie and Lucy. Lucy is Rosemarie's age."

"I remember when Cassandra was born. Belle and Jared run the ranch?"

His mouth tightened. "They split up during her last pregnancy. Right after you left. She'd been running the ranch on her own for Uncle Frank."

"What about Xavier and Damian? You were always close to your cousins."

With a deep sigh, he rubbed his forehead. "Damian came back from a tour in Afghanistan. He's not doing too well. He's pretty much isolated himself in the back forty on the ranch." He paused, his mouth tight.

"Xavier." His jaw set, he took a deep inhale through his nose. "He returned from the Middle East, but then he took a security job down in Colombia. He didn't make it back. His team was ambushed. None of them made it out."

She sat up and grabbed his hand. "Oh Elijah. I'm so sorry. I know how close you were to him. Poor Selena. They were together since middle school. Do they have kids?"

"She found out she was pregnant, and a month later we got word that he was killed." His throat sounded rough. "He never knew they were expecting."

She studied his face, but didn't see anything but a clear expression, devoid of emotion. "I'm so sorry. That must be so hard."

"It was the closest I've come to ending my streak of sobriety." He looked at his hands before taking his gaze back to the Gulf. "Selena has triplets."

"Wow." She didn't know anyone who had triplets. "Are they here in town?"

"Yeah. I love playing uncle. But it's hard. They haven't started asking questions. They're too little. Xavier believed in me when I decided to fight to stay sober. He's—was—part owner of the business. If he was here he wouldn't allow me anywhere around his babies if I started drinking again."

Picking up one of the dolls, he fixed its little hat. "I'm sorry about the horse. I'll talk to her. And the birthday party. Tell her it was all my fault."

"By her birthday we should be back in Denver."

The silence fell with a heavy thud. All the unspoken words they were afraid to release swirled around them.

She finally stood. "Rosemarie is very excited about serving the brownies she made for you."

"You're the one who loved brownies." His features softened. "The gooey center."

The sweet memory warmed her. "You taught me to

go for the center. I didn't have to wait until the edge was eaten." She wrapped her arms around her waist and studied her daughter through the window. "I told her how you would bring me warm brownies you made yourself. You'd cut the edges off and give them to me on Monday, so I'd have them all week."

Watching a pelican dive into the Gulf, he braced his arms on the railing. "Did you tell her it was because I didn't have money for flowers or fancy dinners?"

"Elijah, it was never about money for me. You taught me that it's the little things in life that bring the most joy." She closed her eyes and swallowed. The burn in her throat could not be allowed to rise. She would not cry for everything lost. "I've worked hard to pass that lesson on to her, so stop the over-the-top gestures."

Before he could respond, she hurried to the door. "Rosie's waiting." As she opened the door, his hand stopped her. For a second she wanted to lean into his warmth, but she made herself step back, pulling her arm out of his grasp.

Distance. It was important that she kept distance between them. She couldn't afford any closeness, physical, mental or spiritual. Talking about his family had been a mistake. They had all been so close at one time. She turned her back to him.

His fingers gave a gentle squeeze. "Jazz, can I join y'all? For her birthday. I'll fly to Denver if you're back there."

Closing her eyes, she managed a shrug. "We'll see." She was his daughter. Opening her eyes, she faced him. Avoiding him would not make this better. "Do me a favor and don't say anything yet. I'll talk to Mom. I'm sure we can work something out."

He snorted, letting her know what he thought of that. If Azalea had her way, he'd never be a part of Rosemarie's life.

If she thought he would go away as easily as last time, she'd be in for a surprise. He wasn't the insecure poor ranch kid anymore, and now he had a daughter to fight for.

Chapter Six

Elijah watched Jazmine enter the house. Had he really thought the Daniels would allow him to meet Jazmine and Rosemarie without interference? Anger flared up, but he knew expressing it wouldn't do any good, no matter how righteous.

Mrs. Daniels smiled at Jazmine. "Larry settled your dad in the family room. I need to make sure he is in bed after his outing. This is not a good time for visitors."

"Mom, you agreed to give us two hours."

Arms around Rosemarie, Azalea glanced at Elijah, then moved on, like he wasn't even worth her time. She had made it clear he was not welcome. "This is our home. Your father needs rest."

Choices he made had created this mess, so he was just going to have to suck it up and smile.

Given time they would trust him. He'd been sober for five years now, but Jazz had reminded him that to them it was just yesterday.

He gave her his best smile. Being nice to difficult people was a gift that worked well for him in business, and he would use it now. There would be no pride getting in his way. His daughter was worth it.

"Mrs. Daniels, it's a pleasure. Thank you for letting me in your house."

"Daddy." Rosemarie jumped from the bar stool she sat on and darted over to a credenza. "Look!" She pulled out a realistic toy horse. "I want a horse just like Misty."

It was a prancing golden palomino with pink ribbon woven through the flaxen mane and tail. "That's a pretty pony. I might—"

Mrs. Daniels made a great show of clearing her throat. He sighed. Looking at the women, he knew he was on shaky ground.

She moved to stand in front of Rosemarie. Going down to eye level, she placed one hand on the small shoulder and gently took the horse with the other. "We've talked about this. Your mother doesn't have the room or time for a real horse. They need a great deal of care, and you haven't even had a dog yet."

"Mother." Jazmine's voice sounded tired or resigned. "I've already said no to a dog." She glanced at Elijah with a frown. He needed to be careful and not mess this up. There was so much he didn't know.

Tears started welling up in the little girl's big eyes. How did anyone say "No" to that? He sat on a chair next to his daughter and her grandmother. "We have dogs at the ranch. My sister's Australian shepherd had puppies. You could visit and play with them."

"Really?" The joy was back. Turning from her grandmother, she hugged him. He brought his hands around the tiny body. Her hair smelled like oranges.

Closing his eyes, he made sure to take in everything about this moment.

He'd do anything for this little being that was a part of him and Jazmine.

She stepped back. The huge smile and sparkling eyes were about the sweetest thing he'd ever seen. He glanced up to Jazmine.

There was no sparkle there, and her full lips were thinned by tension.

"An Australian shepherd? Are they aggressive?" His ex-mother-in-law crossed her arms.

"They're one of the best breeds around kids." He leaned forward. "A couple of years ago when my niece was about three, she had figured out that she could open the door if she used a chair. Belle, my sister, was working in the kitchen and had no clue that Lucy had escaped the house."

Both women gasped.

"Frog followed her out and barked until my sister came." He chuckled. "Belle said it was the craziest thing to see. Little Lucy was trying her best to get to the barn. She wanted to go riding. Frog kept herding her back, cutting her off every time she tried to go through the yard gate. She didn't stop barking until she saw Belle."

He patted Rosemarie's shoulder. "So, once you belong to a shepherd, they're yours for life. She is the mother of the new pups."

"I want one. I want one of Frog's puppies."

Mrs. Daniels frowned. If looks had energy, he'd be burned to a crisp. She looked at her daughter, silently telling her to do something about this interloper. Elijah rested his elbow on the glass tabletop. He stared straight at her, making sure she understood that he was not going anywhere.

Jazmine sighed. "This will be a family discussion tonight after dinner. Okay?"

"But Momma, I want a dog. If I can't have a horse, can I get a dog?"

Jazz gave him a look that promised they would be talking later and he might not enjoy the conversation. He doubted there would be any conversation going on, more like a full-on lecture. He wanted to defend himself and point out he had not offered to give her a dog, just the time to play with one.

A kettle started whistling. Mrs. Daniels went to the stove top and poured the hot water into a tall thermal mug. "Come here, sweetheart, your papa needs his green tea."

Tucking her horse under her arm, Rosemarie skipped to her grandmother. "Yes, ma'am."

"You also need to give him his afternoon healing kiss." After putting the lid on the silver cup, she handed it to her granddaughter.

Rosemarie carefully carried the tea with both hands and disappeared into the front family room.

Elijah checked his watch. "It looks like a good time for me to leave." He spoke directly to Jazmine, making a point to ignore Azalea Daniels. "Maybe we can pick a neutral place tomorrow."

Jazmine's mother stared straight at him. "I'm not sure there is a place for you in Rosemarie's life."

"Mother." Jazmine's voice had a new edge.

He shook his head. "It's okay, Jazmine."

Turning to Azalea, he held eye contact. "I hurt your daughter. I get it. But I'm not the man I was."

He needed to be up front and clear. "I know first-hand what it's like to grow up without a father. Thank you for taking care of my daughter when I couldn't. But I'm here. I'm sober and I'm not going anywhere. I know it'll take time to build trust. But I will."

Azalea's mouth went tighter. She didn't believe a word he said, but that was fine.

"The people in my life who didn't believe in me have outnumbered the ones who did. I proved them wrong, and I'll do the same with you."

He turned to his ex-wife. Right now, she was the only one who mattered. Her parents had interfered with their marriage, and he had used drinking to hide from the problems instead of dealing with them head-on. This time had to be different. He was a father, and he had to be strong enough to claim that right.

Jazz was guiding his relationship with his daughter, and he wasn't going to let his past insecurities stop him from being the kind of father his daughter deserved. "I'll go for now." He hoped he looked a lot calmer than he felt. "Call me so we can make arrangements."

"Okay." Jazmine rubbed her head. She knew that her mother was only trying to help, but she was making it worse.

A crash from the family room shattered the tense silence. It was followed by her father yelling. Rosemarie ran to the door looking scared. "Papa fell."

Azalea rushed out of the kitchen. Jazmine stopped

at the door and hugged her frightened daughter. Elijah stood right behind her.

"It'll be okay, baby." She took the small hand into hers.

Next to the hospital bed, her father lay on the floor, his tea running across the tile. He was pushing her mother away.

"I'm not an invalid, Lea. I can get up," he snarled at his wife.

Azalea ignored him. She had her hands under his arms, trying to lift him off the floor. "You almost died. You banged up your whole body, and you broke a couple of bones. So yes, for now you are an invalid. Deal with it. Where's Larry?"

"Woman, I can walk myself into the house." In the process of trying to free himself, he caused her mother to lose her balance, and she ended up on the floor beside him.

"Ugh. Stubborn man. What is your problem?" She sat up, shaking the liquid off her hands. "At this rate you're going to end up back in the hospital. Is that what you want?" She slipped off her heels, then stood over him with her hands on her hips, watching him as he struggled to sit up.

He leaned against the bed, looking defeated.

"Daddy, what are you doing? You scared Rosemarie. Why didn't you call for help and wait for one of us?" Going to the cabinet, Jazmine pulled out a roll of paper towels and cleaned up the mess. Her mother straightened the rumpled blankets. Elijah remained next to Rosie, his hand on her shoulder.

"I just wanted to watch the fishing show sitting in a

chair. Is it too much to want to sit in a chair? I should be able to walk across the room and sit in a stupid chair."

"The doctor said that rest is the most important thing you could do. Do you want to die?"

"If I can't even sit in a chair? Maybe," he grumbled.

Her mother gasped. "Nelson James Daniels. Don't you say that!" Tears hovered on the edge of Azalea's dark eyes.

Rosemarie stepped away from Elijah. "Papa, why do you want to die?"

"Oh, no, sweetheart." He held his hand out to his granddaughter. "I'm just being a grumpy old man."

Elijah followed her and crouched so that he was shoulder to shoulder with Rosemarie. "I don't think the issue is sitting in the chair, but you might need to let them help you get to the chair."

Azalea took Rosemarie's hand and led her to the living room door. "Elijah, this is a family matter. You were leaving."

Rosemarie shook her head. "Not yet. Please don't go."

He glanced at Jazz, then her. He didn't say anything, waiting for them. Azalea sighed. "We'll go make you some more green tea. Maybe your papa will find his way into the bed where he should be resting." She lowered her chin and stared at her husband. "I guess you could do that in the chair just as well. When we get back, I expect you to be in the chair, so you can have tea with your granddaughter. Then you can say goodbye to…your father." Back straight, barefooted, she left the room.

After cleaning up the spilled tea, Jazmine went to

the small sink that sat in the wood bar and made herself busy. He needed privacy and space to recover his pride, then she would offer to help him up before her mother returned.

She grunted. At this rate, if her mom didn't let up, her parents were going to kill each other.

From the corner of her eye she noticed Elijah sit on the floor next to her father. She turned to intervene. This was the last thing her father needed. He glared at the wall across the room, his eyes hard and cold. Elijah's voice was so low she couldn't hear him.

She moved closer, not sure if it was her father or her ex-husband she needed to protect. Before she could interrupt, Elijah spoke again, his voice steady and calm. "I know you don't like me but let me help you up. I've been in a worse place, and I wouldn't have made it if there weren't people who picked me up. No shame in needing a hand to get back on your feet."

The Judge's lip went tight, and he narrowed his eyes, still refusing to look at the man beside him. This was not going to end well. She stepped closer, intending to send Elijah on his way.

But then the hard jaw wobbled and her father's eyes watered. She froze.

One hand rubbed his face. Her father gave Elijah one quick glance before putting the stern judge expression back in place. "I know you have every right to be here." Each word sounded as if it had to climb over gravel to reach the air. "To see your daughter. I might be weak, but I'm keeping an eye on you. I won't let you hurt them again." He winced as he tried to pull himself up.

She turned away, unsure what to do. Judge Daniels

had always been the strongest man she knew. Seeing her father like this made her feel lost.

Hand out, Elijah continued. "I know, and I completely understand. I'm the last person you'd ever take advice from, but don't let pride stop you from asking for the help you need. The consequences aren't worth it. When you have time, I would like to speak with you. I owe you an apology, but the debt I owe your daughter is more than I can pay, so I've turned it over to God. Now, are you going to let me help you up, or will we still be on the floor when your wife and granddaughter return?"

Her father lowered his head.

Elijah went on in a low voice. "Asking for help doesn't take anything away from you. A man who loves his family will let them help. They need to help."

Okay, that turned her lump into a boulder. Turning away from them, she cleaned the counter and checked the mini refrigerator for water.

Her father leaned his head back, eyes closed like he hadn't heard a word Elijah had said.

"Judge Daniels, I'm sure with just a little help you can be in the chair by the time they come back. And then I'll leave. That should make your wife happy."

Jazmine could hear the weary smile in Elijah's voice. Holding her breath, she heard the rustling of movement, followed by slow, heavy footsteps. Her father's recliner popped up and the TV came on.

"So, what are we watching?" Elijah asked. His question was followed by a long period of silence.

"The MLF Championship Cup. Major League Fishing. It's the first round," her father replied in a gruff voice.

Elijah gave a good-natured chuckle. "Yes, I'm aware of that. I know a couple of the guys from Texas. We've been working with the league to get a qualifying event here in Port Del Mar."

"We? Are you back on your family's ranch?"

"My partner, Miguel, and I own the Saltwater Cowboys. We charter fishing trips and tours of the Gulf. Now that my uncle is gone, I've been working with the ranch to expand our reach."

Her father studied his former son-in-law for a bit before asking, "What kind of boats do you have?"

Elijah went into details about his boats and the fishing in the area. Then the men fell silent, watching a high action scene on the TV.

Her father had always been obsessed with sport fishing, a passion she and her mother didn't share. It was one of the reasons he loved the beach house. She quietly made her way to the kitchen and met her mother and daughter heading to the living room.

"Mom, he's watching a fishing show with Elijah. Maybe we should just let him be for now."

"Let him be? The doctor said he needed to rest. How can watching TV with—" she glanced down at Rosemarie "—with your ex-husband be good for him?"

"They're talking boats and watching some deepwater fishing show. He's relaxed. Give him room. If you go in all bossy, you'll only upset him."

Her mother lifted her chin and scoffed. "Please forgive me for wanting him to live."

"Mother."

"I'm going to the office to plan our meals for the week. I found a new list with a better variety of approved foods for heart patients. Rosemarie, would you take this fresh tea to your grandfather?"

"Come on, sweetheart." Jazmine put her hand on her daughter's shoulder. "Let's take your papa his tea."

"I don't think he likes tea." The little girl frowned.

"It'll be fine. He loves you, and we'll drink tea all together."

"What about Daddy? Will he want some tea? I can give him GiGi's cup." She glanced over her shoulder. "I don't think GiGi likes him."

"GiGi is very protective of you. She just wants to make sure you're not hurt."

"She thinks he's going to hurt me?"

Ugh. She was making this worse. "No. With Papa being sick, she's just on edge. It'll be okay."

Rosemarie gave a solemn nod.

"It's going to be okay, sweetheart." Together they entered the man cave.

She paused in the doorway. Her father was laying back in his recliner.

"Daddy, Mom went to organize menus."

Her father grumbled something she couldn't make out.

Jazmine decided to ignore him and placed the tea set on the small table between the chairs. Rosie stood next to him.

Elijah stood. "Time for me to go."

"No. You can stay and have tea with us. Please. I have a cup for you too."

His tall frame relaxed back into the large chair, but his nervous gaze locked with hers. "I'm not sure."

She nodded. "Rosemarie helped make the tea. You should try it."

He nodded.

"I want coffee," her father protested.

Rosemarie took a cup from Jazmine and hesitated. Elijah leaned forward and took the cup from her. "Thank you." The smile he gave Rosemarie just about melted her. He took a sip. "Judge Daniels, this is really good."

"Papa, do you want a cup? GiGi says it's good for your heart."

He smiled at his granddaughter. "Then I should drink every drop, right?"

She smiled. "Yes!"

Her father's hand reached out for the cup she held. "Thank you, sweetheart. Oh, look at that big boy." With his good arm, he pulled Rosemarie up into his chair, and she laid her head on his shoulder.

"That's a big fish. What kind is it?" she asked.

Over the last week, she seemed to have acquired her grandfather's love of fishing. Jazmine glanced at Elijah. She'd forgotten how obsessed he had been with the sport. Maybe her daughter had gotten that gene from both.

The three kept their eyes focused on the screen as her father explained everything to her daughter. Jazmine started stripping his sheets and cleaning the area, hoping they would keep him distracted and calm.

Who would have thought that having her ex-husband in the house would have this side benefit? Gathering the sheets to wash and the dirty dishes, she glanced over at the three sitting in front of the big-screen TV.

Her father chuckled at something and Rosemarie giggled. It was the first time she had heard her father laugh in the last three weeks. "Hey, guys." All three pairs of eyes turned to her. "I'm going to take this up and get clean sheets. Do you need anything from the kitchen?"

"Coffee." Her father was quick to reply.

It was best to just ignore the request so she left the room. In the upstairs office, her mother was tapping away on her laptop. She turned away from Jazmine and wiped her face.

Setting everything down, Jazmine went to her mother and wrapped her arms around her. Azalea had always been a tower of strength. Always in control, never showing any weakness.

Her strong mother crying terrified Jazmine more than anything else since she'd returned home. "Mom? How did the doctor appointment go? Was there bad news?"

"No. No, everything's fine." She slipped out of Jazmine's arms. "Well, the doctor made the mistake of telling him his recovery was going amazingly well."

"Mom, that's great."

"Your father took it as to mean he can do whatever he wants. He is so stubborn. It's like he won't acknowledge he is human and could die. This is the worst time for your ex to worm his way back into our lives."

"Mother, it was time. And you should see them right now. All three are watching some fishing show. Daddy was smiling. He didn't look upset at all."

"Oh. So, you're saying I'm the one who's bad for his heart?"

She sighed. "No. That's not what I'm saying at all, and you know it. You love Daddy and you're worried about him. I am too, but hovering and being overprotective isn't going to help."

She slipped her arms back around her mother. "I love you both so much. Let me help."

Patting Jazmine's hand, Azalea nodded. "I know, sweetheart. If I could, I'd wrap my family in a warm blanket of love and keep the world out. I just want you all to be happy and safe." She twisted and kissed Jazmine's arm. "Will you be okay if I go to the store?"

"Yes! Go. Maybe get your nails done. I'm here so you don't have to do it alone. I know you like being in charge, but you have to take care of yourself if you're going to take care of Daddy."

A few more words and Jazmine left. She gathered up the soiled sheets and went to the laundry room at the end of the hall.

As she went back to the kitchen with the clean sheets, a slight snoring floated from the front room. Jazmine paused at the door. From this angle, she saw Rosemarie hanging on the arm of Elijah's chair. He was leaning in. Their heads were close. She always thought her daughter looked like her other than her eye color, but profile to profile, her resemblance to Elijah startled her.

Jazmine's father was fully reclined and sound asleep.

"Is his heart going to stop working? GiGi said if he didn't listen to her, he was going to drop dead."

Jazmine covered her mouth. Rosemarie had heard her mother's rants.

"I think your GiGi gets mad when people don't do what she says," Elijah replied.

Her daughter nodded.

"It's scary when people we love get sick. Do you know anyone who broke a bone, like an arm or leg?"

"My friend Clare's sister broke her leg on her skate-board."

"She had to wear a cast, right?"

Rosemarie agreed.

"While it was healing, she had to protect it. Then when she got the cast off, she had to rebuild muscles. It took time. That's what your grandfather needs. His heart needs a little rest, a little exercise and a little time. My guess is you might be the best medicine for him."

"But GiGi told me to stay away and not bother him." She frowned and glanced over at her grandfather.

"When he's sleeping let him sleep, but I would say that sitting quietly with him is better than any medicine. Do you do puzzles?"

"I'm good at puzzles. I'm almost six, but I can do some of the grown-up puzzles."

"I remember your grandfather liking puzzles. He likes solving problems and keeping his brain busy. When I see you tomorrow, I'll bring some puzzles that you can give him, and y'all can work on them together."

Jazmine closed her eyes. She and her mother had been so worried about her father's heart that they hadn't thought about him being bored. Rosemarie leaned over the chair arm and whispered something. Elijah brought his head low. He smiled, and Jazmine's heart melted.

She shook her head and went into the room. Going straight to the bed, she popped the new sheet over the mattress. "Sweetheart, it's time for your nap." She kept her voice low so as not to wake her father. Her baby was outgrowing naps, out growing too many things.

"But Momma, Daddy is visiting."

Elijah stood, then knelt in front of Rosemarie. "I have to get back to work. But this has been a great afternoon. Thank you for everything."

Rosemarie glanced at her mother, then lowered her eyes and faced her father again. "Thank you for the doll. I love her. Can I go see your horses? Momma said I couldn't have one, but I could visit them, couldn't I?"

"Rosemarie!" she warned through gritted teeth.

He chuckled. "Of course." He raised his eyes to Jazmine and kept his voice low. "I'll talk to your mom about a time." He nodded and stood. "Okay. Well, this has been a great afternoon. I'll see you soon."

He looked as if he wanted to hug her but shifted uncomfortably. "I'll call later to set up a time."

Moving to stand behind her daughter, Jazmine took her small hands. "If you're willing to wait just a little bit, I'll tuck Rosemarie in with a few books and meet you on the porch."

A moment away from him before they talked about the next visit was what she needed. Rosemarie's interacting with Elijah was pulling at her heart in ways she hadn't expected. He couldn't hurt her more than he already had, but what if she had to watch their daughter go through the same agony?

She rubbed her head, attempting to ease the throbbing pain.

Chapter Seven

One foot on his front bumper, Elijah flipped his keys through his fingers. He tried to relax against his truck as he waited for Jazmine, but it wasn't happening.

He couldn't tell if the day had gone well or not. His sister's girls were chatterboxes who bounced everywhere they went. Rosemarie seemed far too serious for a five-year-old. He couldn't read her. Other than the moment he offered her a horse.

Then she had called him Daddy. He blew out a gust of air. He had thought his brain was going to implode, or maybe it was his heart. Pushing his hair back, he took a deep breath and tried to stop his shaking hands.

It had been so long since he'd dealt with these kinds of emotions. He snorted and looked upward. A few clouds dotted the light blue sky. Who was he kidding? He had never dealt with anything like this.

That beautiful little girl with the huge eyes and the serious look was his daughter. He shouldn't be a stranger to her.

The door opened, and Elijah shot his gaze to Jazmine.

She stopped in front of him, a frown on her face. Had he done something else wrong? He swallowed. Fear prevented him from asking.

She crossed her arms over her chest, looking everywhere but at him.

"Jazmine." He bent his head, trying to make eye contact.

She sighed. Meeting him eye to eye, she pinched her lips. "Elijah, I'm sorry."

Sorry. His stomach sank. "Why?" He hated the feeling of not being in control. He'd just met his daughter, but she could be taken away at any time and he had no say in the matter.

"I don't think you coming here is going to work."

His throat locked up. "I...did Rosemarie say anything? Did I do something wrong? I'm sorry about the horse. I can tell her—"

"No. That's not it." A car went by and honked. She gave them a tight smile and a small wave.

The town was already flooded with rumors that Jazmine was back with his unexpected daughter. The gossips were divided on who was to blame for this scandal. He hated that they were talking about Jazz and Rosemarie.

"Let's go to the back." Without waiting for him, she went around the corner of the house. At the edge of the back deck, she leaned on the railing and looked out to the Gulf. The breeze blew her hair back. A few seagulls flew low and called out, waiting to see if they were going to throw out any crumbs.

"I'm sorry about my mother. I had asked her to stay away until after lunch, but it seems I can't trust her to give us space."

"I could have told you that. For the last six years, they've been fiercely protective of you." He gritted his teeth, not adding that they also kept him from his daughter. Bitterness and defensiveness wouldn't help.

She rolled her bottom lip between her teeth. The moisture in her eyes took the edge off his anger. She was trying to fix this, and it had been his weakness that set it all in motion.

The desire to stroke her cheek was overwhelming. "We'll just have to work around her. She's never going to trust me." He braced his hand on the custom deer guard and leaned back. "What about you?"

Her forehead wrinkled. "Me? I'm doing my best. I'm just stressed right now. Seeing Daddy so weak has turned my world upside down. But we're not talking about me. I came out here to talk about tomorrow. I also promised Rosie that I'd talk to you about the horse." She cut a hard glare his way. "You realize she will be obsessed until she sees one."

"She can do more than see one. I'm not the broke kid you married. I was serious about getting her one. But it's up to you." He shrugged, hoping to look casual. "We have about twenty on the ranch. More if you count the ones Damian has rescued. There are about twelve we use for the beach rides. All of those mounts are super calm and trustworthy."

Rolling his shoulders, he focused on relaxing and letting the tension move out. "I can set up a ride. We can go out on the ranch or ride along the beach. Your mom can come along." He grinned. "She seems to think I'm going to kidnap Rosemarie. You tell me where and when, and I'll have the horses there." He needed to stop talking.

After a few seconds of silence, she nodded. "We could meet up with you and go riding. For now, we need make it clear she is not getting a horse." Lowering her chin, she glared at him with her best librarian look. "She is not getting a horse."

"What about a dog?" He hesitated to say anything, but he didn't want to be outmaneuvered by her mother. The woman had hated him for too many years to give up now.

She made a noise somewhere between a chuckle and a groan. "You and my mother are going to push my sanity right over the edge. Please don't turn this into a competition between y'all. I can't take any more right now."

Tears welled in her eyes. She opened her mouth but closed it again. Blinking, she turned to the beach and pulled her shoulders forward.

Her pain tore at him. Not touching her was no longer an option. Standing next to her, he wrapped his arms around her and pulled her close.

At first, she tensed, but then she relaxed and leaned into him. The years slipped away, and she fit next to him as if she was his missing piece.

But he had driven her away; there was no going back. He set his chin on the top of her head and watched the waves. Laughter from kids playing somewhere down the beach mingled with the water hitting the sand.

He felt wetness through his shirt. His arms tightened, and he held her closer as she fell apart. She was crying. When she had been his, he would have done anything to stop her tears.

Well, not the one thing that mattered the most. There had been too many nights when she had cried, asking him to stop drinking. That had made him mad. In those days he denied he had a problem.

"It's okay," he whispered. He wanted to tell her he would protect her, but he'd lost that right. He bit back the promises he wanted to make, promises she would see as hollow. Just like the first time he gave them to her.

Closing his eyes, he gently stroked her familiar curls. He prayed for wisdom and strength. "It's going to be okay." Weak, but they were the only safe words he could say. "Your father's strong. He's going to be fine." He brushed his lips against the corner of her temple.

She pulled back, wiping her eyes. A weak smile on her face, she looked up at him. Her dark eyes were bright. He leaned forward. He didn't try to resist her pull.

His gaze stayed deep in hers. Her soft breath mingled with his. The fierce beat of his heart roared in his ears, louder than the crash of the ocean. The world disappeared. The years of destruction vanished. They were young, innocent and in love.

Before he let fear control him instead of faith.

He lowered his head.

Her hand came up and she stepped back, breaking their contact before their lips touched. He let her go.

The sound of the car in the driveway reached him, and Elijah's heart sank. Azalea was back.

Idiot. Where was a concrete wall when he needed to smash his head? He wanted her to trust him, and he did this? He'd never had a strong sense of survival.

Jazmine had moved to the far end of the deck. Her look of horror was a punch to his gut.

Her expression reminded him that it was not his survival at stake. Right now, everything went back to having a relationship with his daughter.

It had to. He wasn't going to be his father; he wasn't going to abandon his family. He would break the family tradition of fathers abandoning their families.

His cousins had made a pact it would stop with them. Xavier was dead, and Damian was so wounded he didn't go to town or make any contact with other people. That left him to break the cycle, and he'd do it no matter what it took. With God as his strength, he could do this.

Being a lousy father was one of many family traditions stopping with him.

His daughter deserved better.

The car engine shut off, and the car door opened and closed. Time was running out.

"Jazmine, I'm sorry. That won't happen again. I'm just here for Rosemarie, I promise. Can I come by for lunch again tomorrow?"

She shook her head. "Why don't we go to the pier? It's public, so my mom won't have any excuses."

"I can make arrangements for us to eat on the upper level. It's for private events. Tell me what she likes for lunch, and I'll have it there."

She blinked a couple of times like she didn't believe him. "Okay. Anything with broccoli and strawberries. They're her favorites. She loves mac and cheese, too. Does the Painted Dolphin still make that?"

He laughed. "Our mac and cheese is the best on the coast. You brainwashed her on broccoli, didn't you?"

She grinned, looking more relaxed. "It never worked with you."

"I've been known to load up on a side of the green stuff every now and then."

"Really? I tried hard enough. I think I experimented with hundreds of recipes, so you would eat healthier." She crossed her arms and looked down. "Elijah, thank you for answering Rosemarie's questions. I had no clue she was worried."

"Sometimes kids don't want to upset the adults they love, so they don't ask. Since she doesn't have to worry about my feelings, I'm safe."

"Thank you for handling it the way you did. It's so hard finding the balance between truth and protecting."

He nodded. Unfortunately, he was one of those ugly truths in his daughter's life. For now, he would focus on what he could control. "So, about the horse. I'd like to tell her our plans tomorrow. Will I be able to take her riding?" He wanted to do something that made his girl smile at him.

The back door opened, and Azalea Daniels stepped onto the deck. "I'm surprised you're still here."

He made sure to smile. He would not let her rile him.

"Mother." There was a warning in her voice.

Great. He grimaced. He loved that Jazmine stood

up for him, but he also didn't want to cause friction between mother and daughter.

"We made plans for tomorrow, and we were talking about the best time to go riding at the ranch." She looked back at him. "We just got into town, and she's never been around horses. Let me look at the calendar."

The keys flipped around his finger. "Just tell me when. I have to get back to work. I'll see you tomorrow at eleven."

She nodded.

He tilted his head to her mother. "Thank you for allowing me to visit. I appreciate it."

With another flip of his keys, he turned and got out of there as fast as he could. It hadn't been perfect, but it was a start, and he wasn't going to overstay his welcome.

Jazmine watched him walk away. He had twirled that key ring around the fingers of his left hand. That had always been a sign that he was agitated. Whatever was bothering him, he hid it well. She used to know everything about him. She rubbed her head.

"Are you okay? Did he do something to hurt you? Did he threaten you?"

"No. He was a perfect gentleman." Well, other than almost kissing her, but that had been as much her fault as his.

She turned on her mother. "You promised to keep your distance for this first meeting. I don't want you confusing Rosemarie or making her feel she has to pick sides. It's not fair to her."

Her mother sighed. "I know. But then I started

thinking about the night you came to us. You were scared, bleeding and pregnant. My motherly instincts are not going away just because he says he's sober. His family doesn't have a good record."

"I'm not going to let him hurt Rosemarie."

Her mother laid a hand on her arm. "You're a great mother. I'm so proud of you. But you got really good at hiding his drinking from us. I just don't want to see you fall back into that pattern, baby. It's hard to tell your heart to stop loving someone."

"I don't love him anymore." Why did saying that hurt so much?

She turned away and looked at the endless horizon. She understood why her father wanted to come here to heal. Port Del Mar had always been the one place that felt like home, where she belonged. The beach cottage she'd restored with Elijah would always be in her heart.

"Sweetheart." Her mother stepped closer and tucked a loose strand of hair behind Jazmine's ear. "Are you sure he didn't do anything to upset you?"

"No. He just asked to take Rosemarie out to the ranch. He wants her to meet her cousins and go riding." Was she lying to her mother already?

He had almost kissed her. She had almost let him. Was she covering for him again? She couldn't trust herself to be alone with him.

From now on, someone would be with them or they would text. "I'm good, Mom. I think we're just not used to the idea of sharing Rosemarie."

"I'm not sure you should let him take her to the ranch. His family is out there."

"They also happen to be Rosemarie's family. I think

it would be nice for her to meet them." She gave her mother a look that made it clear this was not up for discussion. "You know I always wanted…cousins to play with." She had almost said brothers and sisters, but she had had a brother. Even if she didn't remind her mother, it would always be painful, and she had caused enough pain. "He can give her that."

"Yes, well, I think this might be too much for her. It's moving too fast. Too many changes. It has to be hard for her."

She wrapped her arms around her mother's small frame, noticing that she'd lost weight. That couldn't be good. "Change is hard." She leaned her head to her mother's. "If we're truly honest with ourselves, she's going with the flow. We're the ones with all the hang-ups. We're strong and God is holding us. It's going to be okay." Now if only she could believe it.

Chapter Eight

Belle gripped the dashboard. "Elijah, I think she would be perfectly fine with any of our stable horses. They have the best disposition and can be trusted with any level of rider."

It had been a week since his first meeting with his daughter, and each day he got to know her a little better. At first it had been hard to get her to talk. Now he knew all he had to do was mention horses or fishing and the conversation would take off.

Jazz was still dragging her feet about coming out to the ranch, but he wanted to have everything ready when she said yes.

He hit another rut in the old dirt road, and they bounced to the right. He and Miguel had just finished their business meeting with his sister. She had been buzzing with ideas. They'd sell the full Texas coastal ranch experience. Renting a cabin on a working ranch, cattle drives, riding on the beach at sunset and deep-sea fishing. A Big Texas Experience.

He still thought selling the land would be for the best, but his sister was being stubborn. A family trait.

Their uncle's laziness combined with that stubbornness had put the ranch in financial trouble, but Belle had worked hard to keep it going. After her girls, it was her whole life. Elijah, on the other hand, could've walked away without a single regret. He had nothing but bad memories.

When she had approached him about the partnership, he had one condition—that he could take a sledgehammer to the shed.

She hadn't asked which shed. She had known.

The old wood shed had turned their childhood into a series of waking nightmares. On the nights his uncle was at his worst, he would put them in the shed. Needless to say, they learned to play in silence and stay out of his sight.

Elijah's daughter would never know that the monsters in fairy tales were real. He glanced at his sister. Back then he hadn't been strong enough to protect her, but things were different now. And he needed to keep his head in the present.

After the meeting, he'd told her about Rosemarie's dream of having a palomino of her own. They didn't have one in their line, but Belle thought Damian might be rehabbing one. Their cousin was the true owner of the ranch since Frank had died, but they had grown up more like siblings. Old Frank had been just as mean to his own kids.

Damian was more like a brother, not that it mattered now. Since returning injured from overseas, he didn't seem to care about anyone or anything other than his wounded horses.

Miguel grumbled from the backseat. "Last time I came out here, your cousin shot at me. This is a bad idea. Are you sure he doesn't have a phone?"

Belle laughed. "If he did, he wouldn't answer it. And he didn't actually shoot at you. He would've hit you if he'd been aiming at you. He never misses."

"Oh, that makes me feel better. I know you want to impress your daughter, but she's five. I think she would love that big gray or that little paint pony."

As they pulled into the dirt road leading to the isolated cabin, a tall figure came out and sat in an old farm chair. Tilting it, Damian balanced it on the back two legs, a rifle casually resting across his knees, his beat-up cowboy hat pulled low over his eyes.

Miguel whistled. "How is it a man missing half an arm and leg looks so threatening? Even without the gun, I wouldn't want to tangle with him."

Elijah sighed. "Yeah, he was always the most like his father, but Afghanistan pushed him over the edge."

"No!" Belle turned on him. "He's nothing like Uncle Frank. Just like the rest of the De La Rosas, he's struggling through shadows. He'll find his way if we give him time and support. Just like you needed."

"Point taken." Cautiously, he opened the door and walked to the front of the truck. Miguel and Belle joined him.

"Hey, Damian. Wanted to talk to you about a horse." Small talk would irritate his cousin.

They all stood in silence. The former soldier didn't move, not even to blink.

Belle stepped closer. "Elijah has a daughter who wants a palomino. He wants to surprise her. The other day you had that beautiful mare out in the pasture. She looked perfect. Her previous owner was a young girl, right?"

Damian gave a short nod, then turned his gaze to Elijah. "Since when do you have a daughter old enough to ride?"

"I just found out about her. She's almost six."

With a thwack, the chair legs hit the boards of the old porch. "Six? You got another woman pregnant while you were still married to Jazmine?" Anger filled every syllable, and his one hand tightened around his rifle.

"No!" All three responded vehemently. Elijah glanced at his sister and friend. It was nice that they had his back.

"Jazmine is her mother. She left without telling me about our daughter, Rosemarie."

Damian frowned and shook his head. He'd been the first one to congratulate them on their wedding. He left for Afghanistan right after Elijah and Jazmine had married, and by the time he'd gotten back, Elijah had been sober again. He'd missed the ugly years.

"While you were gone, I, um, developed a drinking problem. Jazmine decided it wasn't a safe environment for a baby. That's when she left."

Relaxing and leaning back again, he nodded. "Smart woman." He lifted the brim of his hat and looked straight at Elijah. "You sober now?"

"For five years." Elijah wanted to point out that if

his cousin bothered to come out of hiding every now and then, he might know what was going on.

One quick nod was all the response he got before Damian hid his face back in the shadow of his hat. "Why me? Why not one of her horses?" He thrust his scarred chin in Belle's direction.

"My daughter wants a palomino. Belle said you have one. If you've trained her and say she's good with kids, I'll pay top dollar for her. I'm not expecting a freebie."

Before Damian had enlisted, Elijah had counted him as more than a cousin. They'd been friends, brothers. They had formed a tight-knit family to protect each other from Uncle Frank, Damian's father.

Now they were strangers. Damian had made it clear he didn't want to reconnect. Didn't want anything to do with people, period.

Like his sister said, the De La Rosas had issues. Some might even call it a family legacy. And this was the family he had to offer his daughter.

"I'm working really hard here to earn father points." He didn't need to mention he was still working on Jazz, but he would have everything in place when she finally agreed. He just didn't know what else he had to offer his daughter. "Is the horse available and good with kids?"

Damian stood, slipping the sling of his rifle over his shoulder like it was part of his arm. Seeing his cousin without the lower part of his left arm still startled Elijah. And by the way the former solider moved, he would never have known the bottom half of his left leg was gone also.

Without a word, Damian stomped across the yard

toward the barn. Elijah shot Belle a questioning look, but she just shrugged and followed.

Miguel began walking in the opposite direction, back to the Ranger. Elijah called out to him, but his friend shook his head. "I'll wait by the car. I don't think your cousin likes having people around. I have emails to check." He waved his phone and turned away.

Elijah caught up with them at the tack room. With a bucket of feed tucked into the crook of his arm, Damian gestured at the end stalls. "Don't go near those guys."

Out in the pasture he rattled the bucket, and three horses trotted over. He talked in a low voice to each one as he gave them their treats, then, putting the bucket down, slipped a halter onto a pretty palomino mare.

"She's a little shy and might not ever be trailer ready. Perfect for light pleasure riding, though."

Elijah gently scanned the mare with the palm of his hand. Several areas of her coat were marked by scars. Her front legs were the worst. "What happened to her?"

Belle shook her head. "She was a top prospect with outstanding bloodlines. Poor thing was in a four-car accident. A large truck T-boned the stock trailer she was in. The other two horses had to be put down on the spot. Williams, the owner, was going to put her down, too, but she's his daughter's horse. The little girl was there. She'd been hurt, too. She made her father promise to take her to the vet. They did surgery, but when they informed him she wouldn't be able to perform or carry a foal he said she was useless. Dr. Ryan called Damian. They had to sedate her for the trip to the ranch."

Worried, Elijah studied the sturdy little mare. She

rubbed her head against Damian as he talked to her in a low voice. "Is she stable? I don't think Rosemarie has any experience."

Tossing the lead rope over the fence, Damian shook his head. "She's good. If you don't put her in a trailer, she'll be fine. She likes kids."

"Williams just dumped her?"

Damian's hard nod radiated anger, and he petted the mare's forelock.

"She's perfect, just like the horse my daughter showed me. What's her name?"

"Bueno Bueno Sonadora. They called her Dreamer."

"Just like my boats." He stepped back and took a couple of pictures of her. "Nice. Can we move her to the main barn at the ranch house?"

Damian nodded. "I'll ride her over tomorrow and see how she reacts. You got the proper gear?"

"I'll get it."

He moved her to a stall and headed out to the opposite end of the barn, leaving Elijah and Belle standing alone. "I guess that means he's done with us."

"Yep." She squinted at him. "How are you doing? You seem to be taking fatherhood in stride. You are getting legal papers drawn up, right? You have rights as her father. Rights that were stolen."

He sighed and started moving to the door. "Jazmine and I are working this out between us. She'll be in town for seven more weeks. That will give us time to work something out without upsetting Rosemarie."

His sister snorted. "You can't trust her or her parents. They think they're better than everyone else. Or at least better than us."

"She's stronger than she used to be. I had lunch with them every day this past week. We're going to the beach tomorrow."

She stopped and looked up at him, then threw her arms around his middle. "I'm so proud of you. You're a good man and will make a great father. I know you're already an awesome uncle. When will I get to meet my niece?"

"We're working—"

"—it out. I know. Brother, you need to get something in writing. She can sue you for back child support."

He really didn't want to talk about this right now. Moving to the truck, he adjusted his hat. "I've already talked to a lawyer about child support. I'm going to support my daughter." It made him angry that Belle would even thing he'd try to wriggle out of his responsibilities. She should know him better than that.

Letting go, she punched him on the shoulder. "Stop being a grumpy grump. I know you're going to do what's right. I'm just so mad they think they can keep her from you and then make you pay."

"No one is making me pay. Jazz has already told me not to buy her any more gifts."

She laughed. "And the first thing you do is get her a horse? This is going to be fun." She sighed as they stopped at the front of the truck. "Why wasn't I smart enough to fall in love with a good guy who wants to be a part of his children's life?"

"Don't go there. You're a great mother." His gaze went to the scar on her face. She hated the guilt he carried for her injury. He hadn't protected her when she needed it. "He doesn't deserve the three greatest females on the planet."

His words didn't budge the deep sadness in her eyes.

"These females want to meet your special little girl. She's part of the tribe now."

He let out a long breath. "Maybe they were better off without me. She had good reason to run. Why burden them with the De La Rosa legacy?"

She took a step closer and placed her hand on his forearm. "Now it's my turn to stop you there. We can change the legacy. It starts with us. My girls aren't going to grow up scared and fighting for survival. All they know is love, ours and God's. You have so much to give your daughter." She cupped his face. "You lost Jazmine. But she's giving you this opportunity to be a father, and you're going to be a great one. Our daughters are blessed."

He nodded, but the heaviness in his gut didn't let up. Could he really out run his uncle's legacy? Was it buried in his DNA along with the alcoholism?

Chapter Nine

Elijah slowly guided his truck through the hordes of people that had descended on the beach. These days the tourists were outnumbering the locals.

A few of the beachgoers recognized him and waved. This would be the most public place he had taken Rosemarie and Jazmine. All the lunches had been in private areas, out of the way. How could it have been such a short time since his daughter entered his world? It was a world he never expected, but he was anticipating the new adventure.

He tried to imagine if he had been a part of her life from the start. When would he had taken her on her first beach day? She would already know how to boat and sail. Or was she still too young? She certainly could be using the boogie board like a pro. He was by her age.

He had already been riding and deep-water fishing. He didn't really remember learning to do any of that; it had just been part of his life. And it should have been part of his daughter's.

He closed his eyes and ran the morning's verse through his mind. He had to stop thinking about all the "what-ifs" and just enjoy the moment.

All he could do was make this day the best he could. Today Jazmine had agreed to bring Rosemarie to the beach for their lunch meeting, but they were going to meet earlier than normal so they'd have time to play in the sand and water.

A couple of his staffers set up a canopy with chairs, and a cooler full of drinks and food at his favorite spot near the pier.

From the top step leading to the beach, he scanned the area for his ex-wife and daughter. Did Jazmine still wear oversize floppy hats? She had hated the freckles that popped up across her nose whenever she got in the sun. Despite her mahogany skin, any outing would leave her with scattered sun kisses. He had loved them.

She had blamed it on her Irish grandfather.

Her father's parents had always liked him. They'd been the only ones in the family who had welcomed him with open arms.

They had to be in their early nineties by now. Were they still in Austin? He hadn't thought about Jazmine losing her grandparents. A lot could happen in six years. He'd lost his uncle.

Not that the man was missed. But he had also lost Xavier.

He closed his eyes and shot up a quick prayer. Thoughts like that could send him into a bad mental place.

He headed down the steps to the boardwalk over the dunes, looking up and down the beach.

He glanced at his phone. It was still a few minutes early. They might not be here yet. He needed to relax.

But then he saw a huge hat with a yellow lemon print scarf fluttering in the wind. They stood at the bottom of the steps, holding hands.

He relaxed. They were here.

Calling to get their attention, he waved as he made his way through the sand. Rosemarie twisted around and waved back.

She stepped closer to her mother and gave him a tentative smile. He had to remind himself that he was still a stranger to her. He couldn't expect her to feel a sudden father-daughter bond just because he did.

It shocked him how much he craved something that he'd never even thought about.

"Hey." He went down to one knee, so they were eye to eye.

"Hello." It was a bashful greeting, but he took the smile as a good sign. It was the same shy smile Jazmine had given him when they first met.

It might be corny, but both females had taken his heart the minute his gaze had fallen on them. There was no getting it back, ever.

Even if Jazz didn't want it.

The love he had for his ex-wife was powerful, but it was nothing compared to the swelling of his heart as he looked into the eyes of their daughter.

This had to be made right. Clearing his throat, he stood and gestured toward the shelter he had his employees set up. "We have everything for a great day on the beach. Shade." He pointed to the oversize bright orange canopy, complete with back drape. "Drinks, food." He gestured to the two coolers. "Sunblock and other essentials. And…" He looked at the large mesh bag. "I wonder what that is?"

"Elijah?" Jazmine gave him a warning look. He could hear the no-more-gifts lecture already starting. But he had five years to make up for.

"What? There are no gifts here. Just essential beach day stuff. Plus, I just arrived, and it was already here. Whose name is that?"

"That's my name!"

He made an act of examining the tag. "Yep. It says property of Rosemarie."

"Elijah?" Jazz didn't sound happy.

He glanced at her. She had her hands on her hips, one brow up and her chin down. Oh man, that glare. It shouldn't make him smile. Smiling was not appropriate. He turned to his daughter, so Jazz's view was blocked.

"It's mine?"

A lightness he couldn't explain came from his core. "Looks like it. Maybe your grandparents sent it."

"Elijah. My parents didn't send it." She looked down at her daughter and tucked a strand of loose hair back in the clip. "Your father is messing with us. He had all this set up for you."

"Really? For me? Can I look inside?"

With excitement bubbling off her, she glanced between Jazmine and Elijah. It was as if she wasn't sure who could grant permission. He wasn't sure either, so he looked at Jazz. She nodded.

He rubbed his hands together. "Okay. Dig in and let's see what kind of activities we get to do today."

With a low shriek, she fell to her knees in front of the bag. Elijah noted with amusement that it was slightly bigger than she was. A gasp of joy erupted as she started pulling out shovels, buckets and molds to build castles. With an exclamation, she held each item up. "Look at this. Oh, look at this one."

Next came a set of horses and little figures, ranging from princesses and pirates to cowboys, all ready to live in the sandcastles. "Wow. There's more." She kept pulling out beach paraphernalia: Frisbees, water goggles and snorkels. "Thank you so much."

Jazz looked at him with one brow raised. He knew it was too much, but Jazz had to understand growing up he hadn't had money to buy even the cheapest plastic shovel.

He held her gaze. "I have so much to make up for. Not just the five years, but everything I never got to give you." He lowered his voice. "I hated not having money to buy you nice gifts. For never being able to get my sister the things other kids took for granted. I don't know what else to give her."

Her eyes softened. "You're enough. I never missed those gifts."

Rosemarie gasped, and they both turned to her at once. "Surfboards?" The toys were spread out around her, and her eyes went big.

He went to his knees in the sand next to her. "They're boogie boards. When you're ready, I'll show you how to use one. We can use them right here on the beach. We don't have to paddle out, so I thought your mom would be happier about that."

She nodded. "Yeah, Momma likes me to stay close." Her head swiveled as she looked at her loot.

"So where do you want to start? Eat first, then play, or play, then eat? We can build castles or play in the water. It's your day, so you tell me where you want to start."

Her eyes were huge. She stared at all the stuff he'd had delivered and looked frozen.

Jazmine went to Rosemarie and sat down beside her. "Sweetheart, I know it's a bit much and it's hard to know where to start, so why don't we eat a little lunch and make sure we drink plenty of water before we start playing in the sun. I think you should start with your dad showing you how to build a sandcastle."

Pulling Rosemarie into her lap, giving her a sandwich then applied sunscreen. "When we were younger, he built some of the biggest I ever saw. Once he made a giant mermaid riding a seahorse for me. When you get hot, he can take you to play in the waves and show you how to use the board."

She nodded. "Okay. Look, Momma, there are three boards. There's one for you, too." She tilted her head up to Jazmine and gave her an unreserved full-on smile.

Elijah caught his breath as a yearning settled deep within him. It hurt. How did he become part of the mother and daughter family?

He didn't have a clue how a real family behaved. He'd never been a part of one. As close as he was to his sister and cousins, they never had a normal experience. Damian had always hated people in general, even before he'd enlisted. He'd never even had a girlfriend. Belle's husband had left before their second child had been born, and Xavier had started off strong, just like Jazmine and him, but never got a chance to finish.

They were a mess. Maybe the Judge and his wife were right, and Rosemarie would be better off without him. Right now, he was an outsider without a clue how to join the circle. Nothing new there.

"Thank you, Daddy." Rosemarie's gentle voice pulled him out of his spiral of negativity.

She smiled at him. It wasn't as big or open as the one she'd shared with her mother, but it was a smile.

He hadn't thought it possible to fall love even deeper. The time was going too fast. How would she remember him after they went back home so soon? In a short time, she had managed to change his life in ways he could have never predicted. She changed him.

"It's like an early birthday." Picking up a horse and shovel, she looked ready to attack the sand.

Turbulence rocked the pit in his stomach. He didn't know the day she was born. Where had he been while…he closed his eyes. "When's your birthday?"

"August seventeen."

He stopped breathing. Three weeks after his. They would be gone by then?

Stay in the present.

"This is not a birthday gift." He flashed a worried glance at Jazmine. "It's not even a gift. Just some stuff everyone needs on the beach. Let's say it's for all of us. So what do you want to do first? Your mom can rest here in the shade if she's too tired to play."

Crossing her arms, Jazmine rolled her eyes. She had always done that, right from the first day he'd met her.

Grabbing a cold bottle of water out of the cooler,

he tossed it to her, then handed one to Rosemarie. "The sun is high today, so make sure to drink plenty of water." He jutted his chin toward one of the chairs. "Sit, relax, enjoy the view. We're going to build a giant castle for your royal highness." He winked at her.

Rosemarie ditched the horse and grabbed a bucket. "I want to build a castle in the sand. Will you help me?"

"That's why I'm here. That looks like a good spot to build. What do you think?"

With a nod, she ran to the area and dropped to her knees. He turned to Jazmine. "Are you going to join us?"

She shook her head. "I'll guard the mother ship. You have fun with her."

He looked at Rosemarie already digging and making a pile, then back at Jazz. "Has she said anything about me?"

"Go build the sandcastle. You're good at being a big kid. I'm giving you this time to spend with her. Do what you do best. Go play."

He glanced at his daughter, then back to his ex-wife. "Why don't you come play with us? You look like you could do with a little fun." Judging by the look on her face, that was the wrong thing to say. *Smooth move, De La Rosa.*

She shifted in her chair and glanced at their daughter. "Being responsible for another human being is serious business, Elijah. Spend time with her. Talk to her. Listen to her. I'm going to read, but we will be leaving in two hours. Use your time wisely. Get to know your daughter."

"You were always too serious."

"And you always needed to grow up."

He bowed in defeat. He headed out into the sun, then stopped and turned back. "I've made arrangements for us to go horseback riding on the ranch. There's a horse that's perfect for her. Would Friday work for you?"

"Elijah, I'm not sure she's ready to go horseback riding."

He snorted. "She's a De La Rosa. She was born ready to ride a horse."

"We're here on the beach to spend time with you. Right here, right now. We'll talk about future plans later."

"I don't want to break any promises to her. Please don't make me a liar."

"You told her about getting a horse before talking to me." The wind snapped her hat back. As she went to grab it, her paperback fell off her lap.

He stooped to pick up the book. She reached for it at the same time. Instead of grabbing her book from the sand, he held her arm and looked up at her, then back at the scar running from her palm to the underside of her wrist.

His brow furrowed. That hadn't been there the last time he saw her. A knot squeezed his gut. His thumb softly traced the jagged line. It had been cut with something uneven. "How did you get this?" His brain screamed at him to not ask. He didn't want to know. After a long stretch of silence, he forced his chin up and held her gaze. "Jazmine?"

Pulling her bottom lip in between her teeth, she broke eye contact with him.

Sand clogged his throat. "Jazz?"

She glanced at him, then swung her eyes to Rose-marie. "What do you remember from the night I left?"

He had to fight the urge to go out and get lost in the waves. Facing his past actions, his mistakes, was never easy.

No matter how much the denial screamed in his skull, he had to hold steady and listen. He took a deep breath. "Not much. When I woke up, I was on the sofa. My laptop was in the yard. The front window was broken. Chairs were turned over and..."

That was the worst day of his life. Waking up to the mess he knew he had made but couldn't remember how it had all played out. He could only imagine. "The table was turned over, dishes broken on the floor. The big mirror you loved was shattered into a million pieces. There was blood, but I had a few cuts and bruises, so I thought it was mine." He tightened his fist and looked down, recalling the bloody cuts across his knuckles.

Please, tell me it was mine. He sat back on his heels and ran his fingers through his hair. "It wasn't mine, was it?"

She shook her head, a sad smile on her face like she was apologizing. "I had made a special dinner to give you the news about..." A tear slipped down her cheek.

He didn't want to hear this. "That night. You knew you were pregnant?"

Head down, she gave him a quick nod. "Yeah. I had called you to make sure you were coming home. You said you'd be home in less than an hour. I waited. A storm blew in, and I was so afraid you'd stopped off at the Watering Hole. I knew if I could just get you home, the baby would give you a reason to stop drinking.

"A few hours went by and you hadn't shown. The storm got worse. I was worried about you being out. I called several times, but it went straight to voice mail. I didn't bother to leave a message. I fell asleep on the sofa."

"Oh, baby. I'm so sorry." He wanted to cry for the pain he had caused, the joy he had destroyed. All the time he had lost.

The worst part? He didn't even know what had been so important that night that he hadn't gone home to her. There were a few bars he had visited. The people were faceless, nameless. He'd given himself to them instead of to the woman he had promised to love and cherish. The mother of his daughter. His gut hit a new low.

"About two you stumbled in, mad about something. I couldn't understand what you were saying. I was upset because this had become your normal. I told you to leave. That if you wanted to spend your nights with Will and Tristan, you could spend your days with them, too."

He wanted to touch her. To give her the comfort he hadn't given her that night.

"I told you the drinking had to stop. It was out of control. You were out of control. The anger was so intense. Then you turned your back to me."

She took a deep breath and watched Rosemarie. "I was standing right behind you. Reaching out, I touched your shoulder." She closed her eyes. "That's when you clenched your fist and smashed it into the mirror. On the reflection of my face. I was shocked. I'd never seen you violent. You know my parents never even yelled. I was so scared."

She had only been nineteen, and pregnant. His gaze went to their daughter, blissfully playing in the sand. Because of Jazmine, none of his ugliness had touched their innocent little girl. She was an incredible mother.

"I told you to stop. Instead, you went on a rampage. You hit the wall again. That was your blood on the walls there. You flipped the table, and then you threw your laptop through the front window. You were yelling that my father had ruined your life. I ran to our room and locked the door. You banged on the door, yelling at me to unlock it. I told you to leave. For about thirty minutes—it seemed so much longer—you ranted. Elijah, for the first time ever, I was afraid of you."

He couldn't hold back any longer. He placed his hands on her knees. "Jazz, if there was any way in the world I could go back and change that night—that year—I would in a heartbeat. There is no way I could ever express the..." He lifted his head. "There are no words, nothing I can do to erase that night." He ran his thumb over the bunched scar tissue. "How did this happen?"

She shifted a little away from him and watched Rosemarie play for a while before continuing.

"You finally passed out. After I was sure, I opened the door and crept into the living area. You were face down on the sofa. I think I was in shock. The mirror. A present from my parents. The rage I saw in your eyes right before you smashed my reflection was something I had never seen and didn't ever want to see again."

Tears landed on his skin. He wasn't sure if they were his or hers.

"All I wanted was to put the pieces back together. I

went to my knees and tried to gather the broken shards of glass. Somewhere inside I thought if I could fix the mirror I could…" She shook her head. "The tears started falling so fast I couldn't see. You made a noise. I jumped, thinking you had woken up. I cut myself. The blood was all over. I couldn't stop it. I got a towel from the kitchen and went to my parents. I didn't know what to do. Elijah, I had never been afraid of you before, but with your uncle's history…"

Lifting her chin, she looked at Rosemarie. Their daughter was pressing sand into molds.

He nodded. "I get it. After my aunt died, my uncle got worse. We decided to send Gabby away to her mother's sister. She was only eight, but it was the only way we knew to protect her."

"Gabby?"

"Yeah, she's the baby of the family. Xavier and Damian's little sister."

Tears hovered on her bottom lashes. All the pain in those eyes had been put there by him. "I hated my uncle. I wished I could have sent my sister away. You did what you had to do to protect our daughter."

Now he looked at the tiny little human he had helped create. She stood and danced to the other side of the mountain of sand. A few other children stood close, like they wanted to play but didn't know how to ask.

She caught his gaze and waved at him, her smile open and honest. There were no clouds of pain or hurt in her eyes. He realized at that moment that he had to let go of all the anger he had been holding on to.

He looked back to the mother of his child. "You did what you had to do to protect her. You are an incredible mother. She has no clue how blessed she is to have you. Is there anything I can do to... I don't know? I want to make your life better. I can't do enough to make this up to you and her."

"Elijah, you don't have to work so hard for her to like you." She closed her eyes and leaned her head back on the chair. "Go be with your daughter. I need to be alone right now. We'll talk about the horse later."

He glanced down at the book in his hand before handing it to her. "So, you haven't stopped reading your romance novels. Does that mean you still believe in love?"

"It's fiction." The lack of emotion in her eyes tore at his heart. He was the reason for the emptiness there. She took the book. "It's an escape that my heart needs. My daughter is my focus."

He nodded. "I want her to be my focus, too. Please let me put Friday in the books. Belle can have everything ready at the ranch. There'll be a horse for each of you."

"Your persistence must be why you've been so successful at your business."

"Sorry. I just need to do something, and she wants a horse ride." He wanted to tell her that the business didn't mean anything to him; it had just given him something to do. He had been so lost without her, but it wasn't fair to her to lay his pain and guilt at her feet. "I want her to meet her aunt and cousins. They want to meet her."

With a heavy sigh, she glanced over at their daughter. "Be at the house, Friday at 5:30. A short ride.

Maybe just around the barn. She's never been on a horse before. So small steps. Okay?"

"Okay," he quickly agreed. "After we ride, we can make ice cream with peaches at the ranch house." He smiled, remembering all the nights he had made her ice cream with fresh peaches. She had joked that the treat was the reason she had fallen in love with him. He'd given her too many reasons to fall out of love. Pushing out a hard breath, he looked at the sky and cleared his thoughts.

"I'd like her to see the family place."

An unladylike snort escaped Jazmine. "You hated your family's ranch."

"It's better with my uncle gone. There's not much to give her when it comes to my family history, but it's a part of her history, too."

She glanced at her phone. "You're wasting time talking with me when you should be talking to your daughter. Go build a castle. Friday we'll go riding with you."

"Daddy! Come help me."

He needed to stay focused on his daughter. The days were flying by in a rush. The limited time had to be used wisely, to make a permanent bond with his daughter, so that when they went back to Denver he'd still be a part of her life.

Jogging over to her, he went to his knees.

"Daddy."

"Get ready to make the biggest castle ever." Picking up a shovel, he pushed it deep into the sand. His heart absorbed the sound of her joy, and he thanked God for the gift he had been given. He needed to enjoy the moment and not think about the things he couldn't change.

Jazmine had done what she had needed to do, but now she was back, and he was sober.

God had given him a second chance. He might not deserve it, but he wasn't going to waste it.

He invited the kids who had been hovering to join the fun. He knew the parents of one of the boys. The girls giggled in agreement when Rosemarie explained how the cowboy had to be saved by the princess.

He glanced at Jazmine. Her eyes were focused on her book.

She had been his princess, but when she had tried to rescue him, he had pulled her into the riptides instead.

He thanked God that her parents had been there to get her out of his mess. They deserved his respect and appreciation.

Jazmine stared at the pages of her book, but the words just floated. Glancing up at the small group of children that had gathered around Elijah, she saw her shy daughter laughing as she played with children her own age. She looked like she belonged, instead of hanging around the edges watching the fun.

Elijah had done that for her. His charming, easygoing playfulness came so naturally to him. Early in their relationship she had told him he'd be a great father. Even now, she remembered the look of horror on his face. The thought of having children had terrified him.

Looking back, she had probably added to his stress every time she'd mentioned wanting children.

He'd been so afraid of becoming his father or uncle. But she had assured him that he was so different from them. To her, he had always been a man of honor, one who loved deeply.

She had to take her gaze off the man. Instead, she turned her eyes to the endless horizon. The Elijah she needed to remember was the one who had started drinking.

Not the boy she fell in love with, the one who taught her to embrace life and dive into the water, to jump from the pier and dance with joy. She had lost him to alcohol. The addiction and his family legacy had swallowed him in their undertow.

Watching him with the children, with their daughter, she saw the man she had thought he could be. With the castle high, his little fan club added shells to the turrets and towers. A couple of boys finished the moat and let the water come in with the tide. A cheer erupted from the group, who laughed and clapped as the water rushed in and surrounded the grand castle.

Rosemarie ran to the canopy. "Momma, did you see it? It's the biggest one ever!" She grabbed the bag with the rest of the toys. "We're going to put the other people and horses in it, then Daddy's going to show me how to stand on the board. Are you going to do it, too?" She bounced with excitement as she gathered up all the toys Elijah had bought her.

"No, sweetheart. I'm going to watch from the shade." Jazmine picked up a bottle. "Before you go, let me put more sunblock on you."

"It was nice of Daddy to get us shade, wasn't it?" Rosemarie lifted the curls off the back of her neck, so the lotion could be reapplied.

"Yes, it was very thoughtful of him. Now go play—you only have an hour left before we leave."

"But I don't want to leave. I have new friends."

"No arguments, or we can leave now." She looked over at the other kids. "I'm sure your father knows some of their parents, so we can invite them over."

"Can I invite them to my birthday party?" She sounded like her father.

By then they might be back in Denver. "We'll talk about it later. Go play."

With a heavy sigh, Rosemarie bounded off to her father and new friends.

Jazmine prayed her daughter wouldn't get hurt when it came time to go back to Denver. Would Elijah still be so eager when they were out of sight and the newness had rubbed off?

Elijah ran to the water, waving for the kids to follow. His laughter had all the children running along with him. Her heart seemed ready to jump back in, but she was smarter this time and wouldn't follow.

If he had really found his faith and left the drinking behind, maybe she could stick a toe in to test the waters.

Every child deserved a chance to have a loving father in their life. She closed her eyes. *Please God, protect my baby girl's heart.*

If she was honest, her heart might be at risk, too.

Chapter Ten

Elijah gritted his teeth. Miguel had called from one of their boats out in the Gulf. Ben, one of their best captains, was in trouble. He'd been sober for eighteen months, but now he was drunk at the Watering Hole and was trying to drive himself home.

The owner had called Miguel instead of the cops, and in turn Miguel had called Elijah. He'd done this before.

With a quick glance at his watch, he calculated how much time he had before he was scheduled to pick up Rosemarie and Jazmine. He could get Ben home, then take his daughter out to the ranch for her first ride.

Crossing the threshold to the old dive had his skin crawling over his muscles. The dim lights of the bar hid the grunge and sadness. The smells turned his stomach. *God, let me get in and out as quickly as possible.*

More than five years had passed since he had been a patron. There was nothing pleasant or temping about his old hangout. This place had distracted him from his real life. The pressure from her family and his uncle had been his focus instead of Jazmine. He had hated the life he thought he was supposed to be living. But the beautiful parts had been lost too, because of fear.

He spotted Ben by the jukebox, arguing with Patrick, the owner. When the short man saw him, relief flooded his face. "Elijah! See, Ben, I told you he would come and get you home. You don't need to drive."

Ben's red-rimmed eyes glared at him. "You said Miguel was...coming." He tried to turn away and fell against the jukebox. "I don't need no help. I can...drive just fine." He stumbled in the other direction.

Patrick shook his head. "He won't give me his keys."

Elijah nodded and put his hand under Ben's arm. "Come on, buddy. Let's get you home. When Miguel gets off the boat, he'll stop by for a visit."

"I can't go home. She won't..." The man started crying. "I promised—" He fell to the side.

"I'll take you to Miguel's place, okay?"

The older man nodded.

At first it went smoothly. Ben followed him to the parking lot. When Elijah opened his passenger-side door, the older man fell apart. Deciding he was being kidnapped, Ben made a run for his car, yelling and screaming.

With a heavy sigh, Elijah went after him.

Arms wide, Ben tried to swing at his rescuer.

"Ben, I'm here to help you."

Another swing.

Elijah managed to duck, then tackled the man against the car. "Give me your keys so we can go home." Not knowing where the man's keys were, he was carefully guiding him toward his Ranger when Ben's fist punched him in the center of his gut.

Being so unsteady on his feet, the older man didn't create much of a threat. Even so, he managed to get another shot in, right on the bridge of Elijah's nose. *Great.*

Miguel and Ben owed him big-time.

A patrol car pulled into the lot, blocking Elijah's vehicle. He sighed. This was just getting better and better.

Officer Sanchez approached them. "Everything all right?"

"Oh, peachy. Just trying to get ol' Ben to Miguel's place safely."

"Sounds like a good plan. Need help?"

Ben finally relaxed and let Elijah take him to the passenger's door again. "Thanks, but I think we got it."

This time he was able to open it as the drunken man leaned his head against the side of the Ranger. He was clearly giving up the fight.

Pulling out his phone, Elijah checked the time. Not too bad. If he could get the older man home, he'd be only a few minutes late. One arm braced against Ben's chest to hold him in place, he scrolled and found Jazmine's number.

A strange noise came from the man next to him. Before he realized what was happening, Ben had leaned into him and lost his last meal.

With a yelp, Elijah leaped back, dropping his phone, but it was too late. His shirt was covered. Bending down to rescue his phone, he gagged. Lying on the filthy pavement, his phone was even in worse shape. The screen was broken.

Officer Sanchez laughed. "No good deed goes unpunished."

"Thanks," Elijah growled. There was a towel in his backseat, but it wasn't much help.

Ben leaned into Elijah. "I'm so sorry," he mumbled.

Sanchez went to his car and returned with a plastic bag and a T-shirt. "Here. Put your phone in here. The shirt might be a bit small for you, but it's clean."

"Thanks." Elijah made a fast job of taking off his once favorite tee and tossed it in the plastic bag with the useless phone. It was history. He'd have to get a new phone in the morning. "Come on, Ben, let's get you home. I have a date with a very special lady."

Sanchez raised an eyebrow. "Really? And you came here to save this old coot?"

"Yeah, he wanted to drive. Not going to let that happen."

As Elijah buckled Ben into his passenger seat, Sanchez clapped him on the shoulder. "I don't care what anyone says, you're a good man, De La Rosa." The officer laughed at his own joke.

Elijah grunted. This was a good reminder of why he was sober. He had a date with his daughter. That lifted his heart.

He waved to Officer Sanchez, then glanced at Ben, now snoring against his window. He'd drop him off, then head over to pick up his family.

Hopefully, he wouldn't be too late.

Thank you, God, for the reminder and the opportunity to be that little girl's father.

Jazmine placed the dry dishes in their proper places and resisted the urge to look at the time again. Elijah had worked too hard for this day to show up late. He owned several businesses now, so maybe something had happened. Bracing her hands on the edge of the granite counter, she dropped her head.

Did she really just start making excuses for him? He had a phone.

"Momma! What time is it? How much longer until he'll be here?" There was the sound of a truck outside. Rosemarie ran to the window and looked out. She turned around with a pout. "Did he say what kind of horse I was going to get to ride?"

"I think he wants to surprise you." She broke and glanced at the clock. Fifteen minutes. Her heart plummeted. He had been early to every appointed time.

No. He said he would be here. She wasn't going to panic. He'd be here. She was just on edge because she was going to have to tell him something that would upset him. "Do you have a change of clothes?"

"Yes." Rosemarie bounced and twirled. "He said my cousins would be there. I've never had cousins before. Did you know I have five, but three are babies? They're triplets, like twins but there are three of them. Zoe and Claire are twins, but there are only two of them. Three at one time. I've never seen triplets. Have you?"

"Only on TV." There had been a time it was challenging to raise one baby by herself. But triplets? She couldn't even.

Elijah and Xavier had been so close. It had to be difficult to know he wasn't coming back to his children.

"It'll be fun to have cousins." Rosemarie had gone back to her perch on the window seat.

Jazmine went to the window and stood behind her

daughter. She had worked so hard to protect her. If he did anything now to prove her mother right, she'd… well, she wasn't sure what she'd do, but he would regret it. No one hurt her baby.

And he was going to have to deal with her and Rosie going back to Denver sooner than expected. It wasn't going to change anything other than the daily lunches. She was doing the right thing taking her daughter back home. Getting back into a routine was good for a young child.

Restless, Rosemarie ran to pick up her horse and pack it in her bag. "Maybe my horse will be a palomino." Zipping up the bag, she skipped around the table, excitement bouncing off every part of her body. "Maybe it'll be black, like Black Beauty."

Tires crunched the crushed gravel in the drive. With a squeal, her daughter ran to the window. "Oh." Her tiny shoulders dropped, right along with the excitement in her voice. "It's just GiGi and Papa."

"How about we pack some snacks and make Papa's tea?"

Rosemarie skipped to the pantry and pulled out her favorite snacks. "Should we get some carrots and apples for the horses?"

"I'm not sure." The door slammed downstairs. She had hoped they'd be gone before her mother and father arrived. She made the tea, trying to keep her heart from pounding with each passing minute.

After a minute her mother's heels hit the stairs, but before she reached the top she hollered up. "Jazmine, come down here. I need to speak with you in private."

She closed her eyes. Dread filled her. After giving

Rosemarie a task to keep her busy, Jazmine gave the clock one last glance, then made her way to her mother.

"What's up, Mom?" Her mother's tight face didn't ease her anxiety.

"I saw him. It's not good." Azalea crossed her arms.

From his recliner, her father scowled. "Jumping to conclusions is a waste of time, honey. We should have stopped to see if he needed help."

Eyes rolling high into her brows, Azalea shook her head. "I know what I saw, and you needed to be home to rest." Her gaze bored into Jazmine. "Has he called?"

"No." Jazmine hated the hesitation she heard in her voice. "Did you see him?"

With a nod, Azalea narrowed her eyes. "In the Watering Hole parking lot. He couldn't stand straight. Looked like he was fighting with someone. The police were pulling up as we sat at the red light. It didn't look good."

Her gut twisted. All the old memories of waiting for him swamped her.

Hearing the Ranger outside, they both turned toward the door. Her mother crossed her arms. "Do you want me to tell him to leave?"

"No. I'll talk to him." She had made a promise not to run and hide behind her parents. She met him at the door. His hair was disheveled, and the shirt he wore was too small. It was obviously not his.

"I can't believe you drove here."

Frowning, he looked at his truck, then back to her. "How else would I get here?" He walked closer to her. "So sorry I'm late. Are y'all ready?"

"Do you really think I'm going to let her go with you like this?"

"What?" His eyes went wide. "Wait. You think I've been drinking?" He stepped closer to her.

She stepped back, repelled. The smell. It was as if they had slipped back in time to all the nights he had showed up late and lied to her. But it was worse. He was lying to their daughter now. He was making their daughter wait.

She forced herself to step out of the house and close the door. "I can't believe you would come here like this. And you drove."

He blinked, a look of confusion on his face. The exact same look he used years ago to pretend he hadn't been drinking. "Jazmine, I haven't had a drink. I had… Well, I went to help a friend. I didn't think it would take this long, but it got complicated. And even if I was drunk, I'd never drive. You know that."

"I don't know anything." She waved her hand. "This situation was so complicated you couldn't call or text?"

He reached out to her, his eyes burning. "Baby. Listen to me, please. I haven't—"

"Don't." She wrapped her arms tight around her middle. She had been so stupid. "I know that smell all too well. I'm not doing this. I'm not putting my daughter through this."

Biting the inside of her cheek, she willed back the tears. Crying over him was in her past. It wasn't going to happen again.

"Jazz." He looked up to the balcony, then back to her. "I'm not drunk. I know how—"

"Stop. For all I know, you've gotten worse. Maybe

you even drove back then. I was so naive I believed anything you told me. I won't go there again."

Taking his cowboy hat in his hand, he slammed it against his leg.

She jumped.

"Right." He dropped his head and pinched the bridge of his nose, then winced.

Was that a bruise?

He took a deep breath and looked back at her. "There was an emergency. I couldn't just ignore it. Yes, I went to a bar. The Watering Hole. I had to go inside. Someone got sick, and I had to borrow this shirt. I didn't go home and change because—"

"Daddy?" They both looked up to the balcony above them. "Can I come down? Are we leaving?"

With a big intake of air, Jazmine forced a smile. "So sorry, sweetheart. There's been a change of plans."

"Jazz, please don't do this." His voice, low and gravelly, made her want to believe him. Forgive him. "I'm less than thirty minutes late."

"Your dad just dropped by to tell me he doesn't feel well."

"Jazz." He closed his eyes and gritted his teeth for a moment before putting that wide smile on his face. "So sorry, sweetheart. We can't go today."

He was blinking, and his breath was coming in quick pants. "I promised her."

She would not, could not give in to him. "Don't make promises you can't keep." She forced each word from between clenched teeth.

He put his hat back on and ran the back of his hand over his eyes.

His eyes were cold. And, she realized, clear. There weren't glassy or hazy, but stone-cold clear. Without breaking eye contact with her, he spoke loud enough for Rosemarie to hear. "We will be riding on the ranch before the month is up."

Her mother joined Rosemarie on the railing. "I'm so sorry. I thought she was in her room. I'll take her inside." She put a protective arm around the small shoulders. "Goodbye, Elijah."

His eyes went colder. "She saw me at the Watering Hole, didn't she?"

"Don't blame her. She wouldn't have seen you there if you hadn't been there."

"So instead of asking me why, you jumped to conclusions." He took a step back. "I'm not going to argue about this. If you can't listen to me right now, I need to walk away. But I promised Rosemarie a ride, and we are going to make a new time and date."

He turned and walked toward his truck.

Why did she feel like she was in the wrong? He'd been the one to break promises. "You can't just make plans without my approval. Before you do anything, call me."

He paused but didn't turn around. "I've lost your number. Call the Painted Dolphin and leave it with them so I can put in my new phone."

"New? What happened to your phone?"

He opened his door. "I'm sure you wouldn't believe me. I'll have my lawyer contact you. We can set up all future dates through her."

"Are you threatening me?"

"No." There was a deep sadness in his soft voice. He finally turned. "I'm setting boundaries. We both need to come from a place of respect, and if we can't, a mediator might be a good idea." He paused at his opened door. "I'm leaving now because I'm not going to fight with you. I'm not going to try to make you believe something you don't want to believe. But I want to be very clear about this—I am not walking away from our daughter."

Slipping into the truck, he shut his door and backed out of the drive.

Everything in her told her to run after him and… what? Apologize? She didn't have anything to be sorry for. He had slipped into his old ways, and she wasn't going to be an enabler this time. She had done her own coddling. Without knowing it, she had helped his addiction. She was smarter now, stronger.

But his eyes had been clear, part of her brain insisted. It didn't matter, she argued with herself. Even if he was sober by the time he drove out here, it was obvious where he had been. She couldn't afford to disregard the warning signs and explain away his actions.

She should feel strong, so why did she want to throw up? She glanced at the balcony where her sweet, innocent daughter had been standing. Her fears had come to life. Elijah was so easy to love when he was sober. But what she remembered the most was the waiting.

All alone at their house, waiting late into the night. Waiting for him to reach out to her when she had moved to Denver. All the waiting had hurt her so deeply.

Now her daughter was hurt.

* * *

Elijah gripped the wheel. His jaw hurt, and his breathing was short and shallow. Did he really expect her to trust him?

Yes. Without trust, how would they be able to parent Rosemarie together?

He'd jumped through all her hoops. Then the first time he'd been a little late she'd slammed the door in his face. The urge to stand and fight, to yell until she listened to him, was strong.

But he had done the right thing. He slammed the steering wheel. He wanted to show her the phone. Wanted to drag Sanchez up there so he could explain. He wanted her to believe in him. But he couldn't force her.

Even now, he wanted to go back and say more. The words he wanted to scream swirled around his head. He wanted to force her to listen. But force was never the right answer.

She didn't trust him, and he couldn't make her feel something she didn't. His knuckles twisted.

If Miguel hadn't called him to get Ben... *No.*

He wouldn't start the blame game. Pulling into the barn area, he rested his head on the steering wheel. *God, how do I fix this?*

His gut hurt.

His sister stood at the barn door and waved with a huge grin. Her girls came out and ran to the truck. They were excited to see Rosemarie. Family was so important to his sister.

But there was no Rosemarie. His eyes burned. No way was he going to cry, but the pain was deeper than any he had felt in a while. He had already missed too much of his daughter's life. There had to be a way to fix this before they left, but if Jazmine wasn't going to have any faith in him, he was fighting a losing battle.

Confusion marred the faces of three of the most important people in his life. They glanced into the truck and then back at him.

"Where's Rosemarie?" his older niece asked.

"Elijah?" his sister asked, her hands resting on his open window. "Where are they?" She frowned. She leaned in and sniffed. "And why do you smell like…" Her nose wrinkled. "Is that cigarette smoke?" Horror flared in her eyes as she stepped back. "Girls, go inside."

Leaning his head back against the headrest, he closed his eyes. *Great.* Not only had he upset Jazmine and disappointed Rosemarie, now he had upset his sister and nieces.

Lord, help me change the things I can, accept the things I can't and give me the wisdom to know the difference.

"Elijah, what happened? Tell me, please, because right now I'm scared to death."

Opening his eyes, he studied the face of his beautiful sister. Together they had been through so much. Life had taught them early on that the people you love had the greatest power to hurt you. And yet here she was, still willing to love him.

He looked into her eyes as the story spilled out, swallowing his raw emotions. Here was the one person in his life who would believe him and be there without question, the way family should.

All he wanted to do was love his daughter the way his sister loved him. Loved her girls. Now all Rosemarie knew was that he had broken a promise.

Had he been an idiot to think Jazmine might ever trust him again? She had once, and he had crushed her.

Chapter Eleven

Jazmine caressed her daughter's hair as they watched a movie with her parents. She shoved down her desire to go to her room to cry for Rosemarie's sake.

A pounding on the door jerked all their attention from the TV. Moving Rosemarie to the side, Jazmine rose and went downstairs to answer it.

Outside stood Elijah's sister, Belle. Her eyes were red. Fear spiked Jazmine's stomach. Stepping out of the house, she carefully closed the door behind her.

"Is Elijah all right?" What if something had happened after he left? Maybe she had read him wrong and he hadn't been in any condition to drive. She should have called someone to pick him up.

"No. He's not all right."

Jazmine gasped. Her hand flew to her mouth. All the blood dropped to her knees.

"You made him break a promise to his daughter. You kept her from him for her whole life. And now you…you take away a day that he's been planning with so much detail. He's been working so hard to make sure everything was perfect for her."

Relief flooded her body. "He wasn't in a car wreck?"

"No! But you might as well have run over him."

Pressing her palm to her forehead, Jazmine closed her eyes. She wasn't in the mood for this. "Belle, this is between Elijah and me. I'm not—"

"Stop. He told me not to get involved, but after everything he's gone through, everything he's fought through, I'm not going to let you hurt him where it matters the most. I'm going to tell you that he's a great uncle, and he'll be the best father ever. You don't have the right to take that from him."

Belle jabbed her finger in the air. "He was keeping a drunk off the road. He might not be used to fatherhood, but people in this town count on him."

"What?"

"He has become a depend—"

"No, no. What was he doing tonight? How can he be keeping a drunk off the road if he's the—"

Belle threw her head back and grimaced at the sky. When she brought her chin down, a fire was burning in her gray eyes, so much like Elijah's. "You punished him for doing the right thing. He hasn't touched a drop of that stuff in over five years." With a sound of disgust, she turned away and looked at her phone.

The door opened. Jazmine jerked around, afraid of seeing her daughter. Instead, her mother stood there. She wasn't sure if that was any better. "Mom, please go back inside."

Her mother's face made granite look soft. "No. His family doesn't have the right to harass you."

Belle turned back, her chest expanding as she stepped closer, her finger pointed. "You don't have the right to keep his daughter from him." Her eyes grew moist. "She has a whole family that wants to know her and love her."

Azalea sniffed. "A family that can't be trusted."

Elijah's sister stood taller. "He is not our uncle." Her chin lifted. "You don't know my daughters or... you don't know us."

"Mother, stop. Insults are not going to help. Belle, I'm sorry."

Jazmine turned to her mother. "She was saying that Elijah was at the bar to stop someone from driving drunk."

Belle nodded. "His phone was ruined in the shuffle. I can tell you that he's never late, and he hasn't had a drink in years."

"Mom, you said you saw him fighting with someone and the police were there?"

Taking a deep breath, her mother closed her eyes and lowered her head. "The police were pulling up. I assumed." She raised her head and looked at her daughter. Her skin had lost some of its color. "I... He was struggling with an older man I didn't recognize." She pressed the back of her fist to the bottom of her chin, her eyes darting as if she was looking for something. "Your father warned me about jumping to conclusions. If he was stopping someone from driving drunk, why didn't he say that?"

Jazmine groaned. "I didn't let him, and what he did say I refused to believe. I didn't want to..."

Azalea crossed her arms. "I just don't want to see

my daughter hurt again. And Rosemarie is so innocent. As a mother, you should understand that."

Belle's stance softened. "I do. But I've seen Elijah work so hard to overcome our family's past. He knows how personal it is to your family. He'd never allow anyone to get on the road if they've had anything to drink. He never has, even at his worst."

Azalea glanced at Jazmine.

She nodded in agreement. "It's true, Mother. He'd walk home on the nights he…" The memory clogged her throat. She swallowed. "I'd go get his car in the morning while he slept it off. He never drove."

Belle reached out, the fire gone. "Your first instinct is to protect your baby. But you don't have to protect her from Elijah." She smiled. "I might have also gone a little mama bear protecting him. He asked me to stay out of it, but I told him I had to run to the store."

Azalea stepped closer and put her arm around Jazmine. A girl was never too old for her mother's hug. "Is it too late for Jazmine and Rosemarie to go for that ride?"

"Elijah is at the barn with my girls."

"I'll call him." Jazmine's heart picked up as she reached for her phone.

"You can't. His phone was ruined. Believe me, it's a complete goner." Reaching into her back pocket, Belle pulled out her cell. "My oldest has a phone. We can call her." She dialed, and they heard the ringing through the speaker.

"Hey, Mom. What's up?"

"Tell Tío Eli that I ran into Jazmine and she wants to speak with him."

They heard a gasp. "Are they coming?" Excitement colored each word.

"Hand the phone to your uncle."

"Izabella, I told you to stay out of this." Elijah's voice had no give in it.

"Do you want to take your daughter for a ride today?" She looked at Jazmine with a tight smile. "Talk to her and don't be *terco*."

"I'm not being stubborn." His sigh was heavy. "Is she there now?"

"I'm here. I'm sorry about earlier. I should have at least given you a chance to explain." She was proud of herself for keeping her voice calm and steady.

"Oh, hi. Sorry. I thought I was still speaking to Belle." Unease lined his voice.

She couldn't help but chuckle. "Yeah. She handed you to me. So, she explained the situation to us. I'm sorry we jumped to conclusions. I should have known you wouldn't have driven to the house if…well, you know." Fire ants attacked her stomach. "Would it be okay if we followed Belle out?"

"We're at the barn, and if you get here in the next twenty, we should have enough daylight."

"Good. We're on our way." Her throat was dry. "Elijah—"

"You need to head out now if we're going to get to ride. We'll talk later."

"Okay. We'll talk later. See you in a bit."

She handed to the phone back to Belle. "Looks like we're going riding."

Her mother nodded. "Let me get Rosemarie. I know

she did a good job of hiding her disappointment, but this will make her very happy."

Belle moved to her Jeep. "As soon as y'all are ready, we can head out."

Jazmine nodded. She wasn't sure she was ever going to be ready to have Elijah back in her life. Her emotions were too unpredictable.

He had taken a shower in the tack room. His skin scrubbed clean, Elijah smiled at Lucy and was about to answer one of her many questions when Belle's old Jeep came into view. It was followed by a small, shiny SUV. He hadn't allowed himself to believe they were actually coming.

After the showdown in front of her house, he'd thought it was over. That he would have to fight with a team of lawyers to see his daughter again.

But she was here. Somehow his sister had made this happen. His throat tightened. After all the years of him being a walking mess, she had fought for him. Even at his lowest, she had been there ready to kick him out of his wallowing self-pity. She had been an unabashed example of tough love.

Now she was bringing his daughter to the ranch. She was his role model for parenting, not the man who raised them.

Her girls clapped. "Rosemarie is here!"

He grinned. "Where should we take her? To the pasture or the beach?"

They both jumped up. "The beach. The beach."

His sister stopped the Jeep right next to him. She

hopped out of her vehicle and grinned at him like she'd brought in the winning catch.

He leaned close to her ear. "I told you to stay out of it."

Not a hint of guilt or apology touched her face. "And if I'd stayed out of it? Your daughter wouldn't be on the ranch. You've worked hard to get your life right. They can't treat you like dirt. Not as long as I'm around."

"Not only do I not have credit with Jazmine, I'm digging myself out of emotional bankruptcy. I owe her. She has every right to do whatever she thinks is necessary to protect her daughter."

She reached up and tugged at his ear. "Your daughter. How long are you going to punish yourself?"

He started to reply but shut his mouth. She wouldn't accept his answer. The sweetest sound saved him from having to think up another response.

"Daddy!" Rosemarie yelled, as she plowed into him. "We made it! Are you better?"

"Yes, and I'm so glad this worked out. Are you ready to meet my new horse I just bought?"

"She's yours? Yes!" She screamed and clapped. "What's her name?"

"Bueno Bueno Sonadora."

She made a face. "Good Good something? That's a strange name."

He laughed. "Sonadora means dreamer. You know Spanish." That surprised him.

"I'm learning at school. Why does she have two goods in her name?"

"Bueno is very important in the quarter horse bloodlines and she has it on top and bottom, so they put it in twice. That's the name on her official papers. I'm thinking of giving her a new name. What do you think? The little girl who had her before called her Dreamer."

Her little nose wrinkled. "Top and bottom?"

Laughing, he lifted his hand above her head. "The father's side of the family is listed on top." Then he tickled her at her waist. "Her mother's family is listed on the bottom of her papers."

She flung her arms around him again, erasing all the unpleasantness of the past few hours. He forced himself to stay in the moment. No worries about the future or guilt about the past.

Jazmine joined them.

Rosemarie turned to her mother and clapped. "Momma, did you hear? Daddy has a new horse. Where is she?" She was bouncing with barely controlled energy.

Cassie and Lucy each grabbed one of her hands. "She's in the barn." The girls took off running.

"Slow down," all three adults yelled at the same time. Belle rushed ahead to take the girls into the stables.

Picking up the pace, Elijah followed, but a warm touch on his arm stopped him. He looked down at the stern face of his ex-wife and gave her his best smile. "I've got the horse covered. It's been a long time since I've had my own horse. She's going to stay on the ranch, and I'll share her with Rosie. Please, Jazz, let me do this." His gaze sought out his daughter. "The only good moments growing up were with the horses." He came back to Jazmine's eyes. "It's the only thing I have to offer."

Her fingertips brushed his chin. "Not true. And that's not the point. You said you were going to find a horse she could ride, not buy a new one. Why do I have a feeling you will never ride this horse that you didn't buy for your daughter?" She sighed.

He took her hand and walked to the barn doors. Her hand fit into his so naturally. "Let me tell you her story. Her owners wanted to put her down, but Damian saved her." He gave her all the details. "She's a sweet horse, a bit shy, but with a great deal of love to give. She just needs the right little girl. They're a perfect match."

Stopping, she pulled him around. "Elijah, how am I supposed to say no to that?"

On impulse, he kissed her forehead. "You're not." *What was he doing?* Taking a quick step back, he released her hand, then turned to follow the girls.

The three cousins were standing at the far end of the breezeway. His heart paused. They were here as a family. He stood behind them, his hands on the tiny shoulders of his daughter.

Belle led the mare out of her stall and Rosemarie went still. She seemed to stop breathing and a strange sound came from her. Had he done something wrong?

He bent down and pulled her against him so that her back was pressed against his chest. "What's wrong, baby?"

She shook her head. "She's beautiful. Just like in my dreams." Twisting, she looked up at him. Wet with tears, the gray eyes looked violet. "Is she really ours?" The small voice was filled with awe.

"What are you going to call her?"

"Dreamer."

The Texan's Secret Daughter

"That's perfect because she knows it already."

She sank further into his chest. "What if she doesn't like me?"

He couldn't imagine anyone not loving his girl. "You belong to her now. She needed a little girl just like you. She was in a bad accident and has scars, but she's all better. I bet she's nervous about meeting you."

"Think so?"

"I was the first time I met you. Remember?"

And today he'd almost lost her. One mistake and he would lose everything again, but this time there was more at stake. It wasn't about him, or even Jazmine.

He glanced up and made eye contact with Jazz. He had to be strong and make the decisions that were best for his daughter. And Jazz. No matter how much he loved them, he had to put that aside and do what was best for them.

Chapter Twelve

Jazmine hung back. This was the kind of moment a little girl would remember for the rest of her life, and Elijah was making it happen. He had always been that way. Zeroing in on a person's dream and making it feel like it could come true.

Belle stopped in front of them and smiled. "Dreamer, this is Rosemarie." The pretty mare lowered her head, and the little girl gently touched the soft muzzle. The horse made a rumbling noise in her throat. Rosemarie giggled.

"Ready to saddle up? Girls, get your helmets." Belle was all business.

Out back, several other horses were already saddled and waiting. Elijah went step-by-step, showing Rosemarie how to saddle a horse and take care of it. Lifting her into the saddle, he explained each action before leading her to a large round pen. Belle and her girls followed on their horses.

"Your Tía Belle is an excellent horse trainer and riding instructor. One of the best in the state. She's going to help you before we hit the beach. I'll take your mom to get her horse. You okay?"

She nodded, a huge grin on her face. She leaned forward on her mare and hugged her neck.

As they started through the doors from the barn to the arena, they saw Damian standing at the other end.

"Wow. I wasn't expecting to see him," Elijah said. "Hey, Damian. What brings you out?"

He tipped his hat. "Wanted to make sure the transition went well for Dreamer and Rosie."

Smiling, Elijah turned to Jazz. "The only person better with horses than Belle is Damian."

"Hey!" His sister's voice carried across the arena. "I heard that." Belle sidestepped her horse to open the gate and lead Dreamer into the arena. "I mean, it might be true, but you don't have to say it in front of me and my girls."

"It's okay, Momma." Lucy urged her mare into the arena. "We already know Tío Damian is the best with horses, but you're better with people."

Elijah laughed. "Out of the mouths of babes."

Belle shook her head. "Whatever. Go get yours and Jazmine's horses. I've got this covered."

"Yes, ma'am." He patted Rosemarie's thigh. "Relax. Have fun and listen to your *tía* and *tío*. Your mom and I will be right back with our horses, and then we'll all head to the beach."

He turned to Jazmine. "You want to stay here with her? I'll go get our horses."

"No. I'll go with you."

"Are you sure? I know you don't like Rosemarie out of your sight."

She snorted. "First, I'm within shouting distance. Second, your sister is raising two girls on her own, and they seem well-adjusted and happy." She winked. "Remember who taught me how to ride? She was one of the best back then, too."

"True." His sister had the trophies and ribbons to prove her skills.

"Anyway, I need to talk to you."

He paused as he slipped the halter off the buckskin's ears. "Talk about what?"

She took a deep breath. The comforting smell of hay and salt air soothed her. "Daddy is being an over-achiever, as usual. The doctors said his recovery is ahead of schedule."

"That's great news, right?"

"Yes. Absolutely. But I think that means it's time for Rosemarie and me to go home."

He leaned on the saddle he'd just cinched and looked at her, his eyes wide. "What? I thought we had more time?"

"I want to get her home and back into a routine before school starts." That sounded weak even to her own ears. Was she just running again?

Without a word, he picked up the other saddle and placed it on a bay's back. His muscles bunched and moved across his shoulders. "Is this because of the bar incident? I thought we were good."

"No. I was going to tell you today." She waited for him to say something.

He wasn't responding. Of all the scenarios in her head, his silence was not one of them.

"I'm missing work. I don't want her to lose connec-

tions with her friends. Elijah? What are you thinking?"
Did she really want to know? She put a hand over her
stomach, trying to calm it down.

He had his back to her. hands were braced on the
saddle. "We're supposed to have more time together."

"You knew we would be going back."

He shook his head. "At the end of summer. She's
just getting comfortable around me. You're worried
about her forgetting her friends in Denver. What if
she forgets me?"

"She's not going—"

"I'll move to Denver. I'll get a condo."

"Elijah, you can't just leave here. Your dreams have
always been tied to this place, and now look at you.
Those dreams have become reality. You've worked so
hard. This place is in your DNA, just like the color of
your eyes. It's a part of you."

He finally turned. "She's a part of me I didn't even
know was missing. Building up the business has kept
me focused on something other than everything I lost.
She's bigger than all of those put together and there is
so much to make up for. I don't have to be here every
day to run the business."

Her stomach twisted. She hadn't thought of him
moving to Denver. He'd be part of their daily lives.
He walked the horse over to her and handed her the
reins. His hand brushed hers and she wished the moment could last.

Standing in front of her, he studied her face. There
were so many unidentified emotions pinging through
her head.

"You don't trust me. I got the message loud and clear

today." He turned from her and, in one quick motion, mounted his gelding. "Or is it that you don't want to share her? You've had her to yourself for almost six years. Are you running again? I understand why you don't trust me, I get it. But how much of you leaving is to keep control of my relationship with Rosemarie?"

"What happened earlier today was not fair to you. You have been nothing but trustworthy." To the point that she was having a hard time remembering why she needed to stay away from him. Maybe she was running. It would be too easy to give her heart to him again, but could she trust him? Could she trust herself?

Stepping into the stirrup, she swung her leg over her horse's back and settled into the saddle. The bay shifted under her.

The truth? She had left her heart with him, and her parents knew it. That was the reason they had worked so hard to keep her away from him.

But if all the changes she had seen in his life were true, there was no reason to run from him again. He was right. She had run last time, and she was about to run again.

Offshore, thunder rolled. The sunny day disappeared fast as storm clouds were propelled in from the Gulf. They had made it only a mile before the weather changed on them. Announcing they needed to head back, Elijah was met with a chorus of groans.

After rubbing down and stalling the horses, they ran for the screened porch that covered the back of the ranch house. They almost made it before the heavens opened.

Belle pulled out towels for everyone as lightning flashed across the sky. The girls laughed and recapped their ride, not realizing how dangerous the weather had become.

Elijah jumped as he felt a heavy hand on his shoulder. Turning, he found his sister. Belle's brows were pulled tight.

"Everyone's fine and we made it safely to the porch." Taking his hand, she squeezed it between both of hers. "I know the storms bring back the worst memories, but he's gone. He can't hurt us anymore. Don't give him the power." She pointed her chin toward the girls, now sitting with Jazmine. "Relax and have fun."

They would never know the fear of being locked outside during a storm or sleeping in the mud as rain poured into the shed they were locked inside. Their childhood would be filled with joy, love and adventures. Storms wouldn't bring the monsters out of the shadows, because they wouldn't have monsters there to begin with.

"Knock, knock!" His cousin's widow, Selena, opened the screen door from the kitchen. "Room for a few more?" She carried one little boy on her hip, his straight dark hair falling over his gray eyes. Two more with identical wild curls toddled out ahead of her as she guided them like a mother with three arms. The two on the ground squealed when they saw Cassie and Lucy.

"We heard a rumor that I have a new niece, and the boys wanted to meet her." She tried to set the one she held on the floor, but he clung to her and buried his face in her hair.

Selena hugged Jazmine with her free arm and intro-

duced her sons. Elijah went into the house and helped
Belle gather the ingredients to make ice cream. Cassie
and Lucy showed Rosemarie how to add each item
to the ice cream maker. Female voices and children's
laughter filled the porch as the rain hit the metal roof.

Selena cut a bowl full of fresh peaches.

Elijah sat back. The women in his family were so
strong. He was the weak link. Ben was an ugly but
true reminder of who he was at his core. He had failed.
When Jazmine and Belle had needed him, he had been
drunk.

He was one drink away from being that guy again.
He wasn't two separate people, the good guy versus
the jerk. They both lived in him.

Rosemarie ran to him with two ice creams in hand.
"Did you see? We made real ice cream. Here's yours."
She took a bite of hers, and her eyes rolled back in bliss.
"This is so good, Daddy. Momma said this is why she
fell in love with you."

Jazz bumped him until he scooted over. Sitting next
to him, she nodded. "How can a girl say no to a man
with homemade peach ice cream and a barn full of
horses?"

Rosemarie giggled, then ran off to join her cousins.

They sat next to each other as they watched the kids
play on the porch. Two of the triplets kept trying to run
out into the storm. The other was forever hiding his
shoes under something. Selena finally gave up on covering his feet, but she refused to let the children out.
They turned their attention to the litter of half-grown
pups in a playpen. The girls took the pups out and total
complete joyous chaos ensued.

"Jazmine."

Her large eyes turned to him as she took another bite of her ice cream.

"Thank you for making sure Rosemarie…" He didn't know how to put what was in his heart into words she would understand.

"Elijah?" She lowered the ice cream cone as she looked directly at him. "What is it?"

"You've given Rosemarie a childhood and home that is full of love. You made sure she was safe. Thank you."

"It's what any mother would do."

"No, it's not. I didn't even know what a home was until you made one for us. I'd never belonged anywhere. My mother didn't stay around to make sure we were okay."

He'd had a tough childhood, but… "I knew your mother left you, but you had a home. You had your sister and cousins. Despite your uncle, y'all seemed so close."

"We were. We needed each other to survive." Another roll of thunder vibrated the house as lightning flashed.

She held his hand. The warmth anchored him. The kids laughed and crawled into the daybed with the puppies.

He couldn't look at her. "I never wanted you to see me as less because of the way I grew up. I didn't have a bedroom. Most nights I wasn't allowed to stay inside the house."

She gasped. "You never said anything about being forced to sleep outside. That's child abuse. Why didn't anyone intervene for y'all? Where did you sleep?"

He shrugged and kept his voice low. "We were De La Rosas. We were written off as damaged goods." His jaw hard, he looked down, then tilted his head back and scrutinized the ceiling as if it held the answers. "On a good night we slept here on the porch or in the barn. Sometimes he wouldn't let us stay there, either. Storms made him worse. We made sure to stay out of sight during storms."

All the moisture left her mouth as she sat next to him, perched on the edge of the bench they shared. His worst nights had been during storms.

"When we disobeyed orders, he had a toolshed he'd lock us in for periods of time." He turned to face her. "I'm not telling you to make you feel sorry for me. I just want to be honest about everything. Part of the reason I drank was the shame…"

Instinct made her tuck his arm against her and pull him close so there was no space between them. The need to comfort him drowned out all other worries. Her fingers wrapped around his. "But that's your uncle's shame. Not yours."

A rough grunt was followed by a lopsided grin. "At the very least it was embarrassing. You came from such a perfect family."

"Elijah, no family is perfect. A child is not responsible for the actions of the adults in his life." Running her hand up his arm, she squeezed. "There was no way you had done anything to deserve that treatment."

"In my head I know that. But here—" he tapped his chest "—is another story. That's part of what I had to learn. I'm dealing with it."

"You hated your uncle, so why did you stay in Port

Del Mar? You had to fight my parents and him to build a life here."

Rolling his shoulders back, he shifted away from her. "I've always liked a challenge." His sarcasm wasn't missed.

"Some might call it stubbornness." She let her dry tone match his but followed it with a wink.

"Yeah. That's a trait the De La Rosa family had in abundance."

"Hello, have you met my mother? Poor Rosemarie didn't have a chance. There were times I wasn't sure if we'd survive the terrible twos, and then she hit the threes." Both of their gazes went to their daughter. "Man, those made the twos look easy. She was awesome at saying no, but if anyone dared say no to her, she could bring the roof down with her fits."

He frowned. "She was difficult? She's so sweet and shy." His expression had relaxed. Rosemarie was letting a puppy lick her nose as she giggled.

"Will you tell me more about her as a baby and toddler?"

Jazmine smiled. "She's my favorite topic. Around new people and places she is very shy, but once she's comfortable, watch out." She told him of the period when Rosemarie refused to wear clothes. Then about the battle of eating anything other than chicken nuggets. Her obsessions with horses and purple. He asked questions and laughed at the more outrageous stories.

The smile on his face was warm and relaxed. "Okay. So, she's sweet, shy, smart and stubborn. All the best *s* words. I wish I could have been there."

"You're here now, and you'll be there for her in the years to come."

Years? The thought of a forever promise terrified him. Another spiderweb of electricity flashed through the clouds as thunder rolled over the land. The girls jumped and screamed, then fell into bouts of laughter.

While they were on the beach, the storm had come in unexpectedly. What if he hadn't gotten them back to the house in time today?

Damian might have the right idea. His family was safer with him watching from the perimeter.

If he made a mistake or a misstep, the collateral damage would be too high. Should he even get a house in Denver? Jazmine's instincts had been spot-on the first time, so why was he trying to stop her from running now?

Chapter Thirteen

Jazmine took a deep breath as she let the quiet of her car soothe her. Ten minutes ago, she had pulled up to the beachside cottage she and Elijah had bought just months after they had married.

With Jazmine and Rosemarie leaving for Denver soon, Elijah had wanted to make dinner for them tonight in the home they had built together.

The home they built together. The words had bumped around in her head since he said them. They had made promises to each other, and the only thing that stopped them had been his drinking, which he acknowledged and turned over to God. So, what was stopping her now?

For over twenty-four hours, she'd rehashed the same dialogue with herself. Her heart pounded as she sat in the car looking up at the warm lights shining out. This was where their love had grown and died. The best and the worst had all happened here.

Since she'd been back, God had shown her the best could still be theirs if they both trusted Him. Now she was about to change their course again, if Elijah agreed.

To her surprise, her father supported her. Her mother hadn't said anything one way or the other but had agreed to keep Rosemarie tonight so that she could talk to Elijah about their future.

She'd even bought a new sundress in his favorite color.

Her barely there sandals hit the first step, and she looked down. The wooden deck and all the old loose boards were gone, replaced with all-weather decking. There hadn't been enough money for upgrades back in the day.

The seaside cottage sat high on the exposed pilings. It was smaller than her parents' beach house, but the first time she saw it from the beach she dreamed of making it her home. Before they were married, she had told Elijah it should be theirs.

She had fallen in love with the wraparound deck. The turquoise blue she had picked out looked fresh. It was a bit of a shock to see he had repainted the deck the same color. The corners of her mouth went up, easing some of her dread.

It had taken her a while to convince Elijah that the color was perfect. It still looked good on their little beachfront house. The white trim had recently been redone, too.

Her knees shook so hard she had to slow her pace. When her parents said the house had been sold in the divorce, she had cried. It made the end of their marriage more real than anything else.

The outside looked the same, but the inside had to

have been changed. Had other women picked out furniture or rearranged her dream home? She stopped.

This had been a mistake. If other women had been in her home, she'd be sick. Maybe she should meet him somewhere else.

It had been six years since she had left him, but she had never really thought about Elijah moving on without her, never thought of him building a new life inside the shell of their old one. It should have been expected, though. He was young, good-looking and now a successful business owner.

Laying her hand on her heart, she tried to calm its rapid beating.

This was their house, where their family belonged.

The idea of restoring their relationship had been planted in her brain that day on the ranch. Or maybe it was in her heart. Her heart had gotten her in trouble before. But her head also told her they could have the future he'd promised her over seven years ago.

Standing on the deck wasn't going to get anything done. Closing her eyes, she cleared her head. *God, I'm turning this over to You. I know through You all things are possible, and if he has put You first, then we can do this. We need You to guide us through these choppy waters.*

She stood and smoothed out the nonexistent wrinkles in her soft pink summer dress, then adjusted the starfish necklace.

The windows glowed with warm light. Her heart slammed against her chest. This time, they could get it right.

Raising her fist, she paused. Her bracelets slid down

her wrist. On the anniversary of their first date, he had given her a bracelet made of natural stones. He had promised to give her one each year.

She smiled at the pretty pieces of jewelry. Six were missing. But those six years might be the most important to their future. They had needed that time to grow up and find the strength to trust in God.

Before her knuckles hit the textured glass. Elijah opened the door and stepped back, a huge smile on his face and a dish towel in his hand. "Sorry, I didn't hear a knock. Have you been here long? Come in." He looked behind her. Frowning, he stepped onto the deck and looked around. "Where's Rosie?"

"I left her with my parents."

He closed the door, confusion on his face. "But I thought we were having dinner together. Is something wrong?"

She played with the bracelets on her arm. "No. I just wanted to talk with you alone. Talk about our future."

"Our future? With Rosemarie? I don't understand." He rubbed his palm against his worn jeans. A look of deep fear burned in his eyes. "Have your parents—"

"No. No. It's nothing like that. I think this is good news. I hope it's good news." Now she wasn't so sure of herself. This had seemed so much easier in her head. Needing to center herself, she scanned the living area that used to be her home. The fear of seeing changes had made her avoid really looking around.

What she found startled her. "It looks the same."

It was a large open room that flowed into the white kitchen. An island anchored the space between the rooms. The four stools she had found at an estate sale were still there, waiting for the family she had always imagined.

The cream sectional was new, but the same style. The pillows had been replaced, too. But they were still the fun, tropical colors and patterns she had y spent hours selecting.

She turned slowly, taking in every detail. "You haven't changed anything."

As she took in their old living space, her hand went to her heart. There had been a few new additions that brought tears to her eyes.

Photos of Rosemarie were framed and placed around the living room. The drawing their daughter had made for him after their horse ride hung in the dining room.

Even the lopsided ceramic cup that she had made at Sunday school was on the island holding scissors and measuring spoons. Seeing her daughter's work in the home she had decorated so many years ago tightened her heart and twisted it into a lump of emotion.

Moving to the island, he draped the town over the edge of the sink and kept a wary gaze on her. "I loved everything you did here. Growing up, well, you know. For the first time, I had somewhere I belonged." He looked at her. "A place that was made for me."

Until he had told her the horrible events of his childhood, she hadn't really understood his need for a home.

"For you and our children." Sitting on the stool across from him, she reached over and took his hand. "Is this why you stayed here instead of leaving? You could have started over somewhere new." Like she had done. Instead, he had stayed and fought for the dreams they had shared. Now she knew without a doubt she was ready to fight alongside him.

He stood, walking to the sink. "I couldn't leave. Too many people needed me. Belle's husband left her. Then we lost Xavier. Selena discovered she was pregnant with triplets." One hip pressed against the edge of the counter, he turned to the window, as if studying something out in the darkness only he could see. His shoulders tensed as though the weight of the world was getting too heavy.

"They needed me. Honestly, I had thoughts about leaving." His gaze sought her. "There was a part of me that was hanging on to the idea that you might come back. I had to let that go. There were times I thought I'd be better off selling and starting over."

His chest expanded as he inhaled deeply. "The absolute truth? When we first started dating, I didn't think I deserved you. I thought that once we were married I could relax. You'd be mine, right?"

She slipped onto the stool and nodded.

"But even then I was afraid you would realize I wasn't worth the hassle. Fear drove me to hide in the alcohol. Your parents wanted me to be more. They made that clear when they got me the job in the law office. I hated every minute of it. But I couldn't tell you."

"I never expected—"

"I know. I'm not blaming you or them. It's just what was in my head at the time. You needed someone better than me. I tried and, as we know, it didn't work out so well."

Both of her hands went to her mouth. "Elijah."

With a sigh, he crossed the kitchen, out of her reach.

"I fought to keep the house because of you." He ran his hand over the butcher-block countertop. "The house was a reminder that you saw something in me you could love, even if it was for a short time. I lost control of my life, and I lost you because I was living in fear and hiding—or trying to hide." Bracing his hands on the edge, he lifted his head and studied her for a minute.

His half-cocked grin melted her heart.

"Reclaiming my life was not easy. During the darkest days of my battle, the house became a touchstone. When my uncle's voice got too strong, our home reminded me that, through God, I was worthy of love."

There was no stopping her tears as his honest emotions tore at her. Needing to gather herself, Jazmine turned away from him to do something, anything, to get control of her heart and brain. Heading to a cabinet by the front door, she paused. The world shifted under her feet.

She couldn't be seeing what was there, propped against the wall, tucked safely between the two tall cabinets. The mirror.

Fingers outstretched, she touched the hand-carved frame. Lightly stained wood surrounded the six-foot mirror. It was warm under her touch. Her parents had commissioned the custom mirror as a wedding gift.

She looked up and met Elijah's steady gaze. Silently, he had crossed the room. Now he stood right behind her, just like that night. Instead of being lost in a haze of alcohol and rage, she found concern and doubt clouding his beautiful face.

"How?" The word came out as a strangled whisper. "You destroyed it that night." Breaking eye contact with him, her attention went straight to the front window he had broken during his fit. There had been a fierce storm that night. She focused on him again. "It was shattered."

His throat worked for a second. "Yeah, I wanted to fix the original, but…" He shook his head. "I took it back to Omar, and he did the best he could. It needed new glass."

Caressing the smooth wood, she allowed her thoughts to travel back to their wedding day. The joy, the endless promise of a future full of love. Then she noticed the new inscription. Jazmine dropped to her knees to trace the letters. "Psalm 40:3. What verse is that?"

Elijah lowered to his haunches, next to her. "'And he hath put a new song in my mouth, even praise unto our God.' I had to learn a new song. That's why I put it here, by the door, so I see it every time I leave."

Silence fell between them. He reached over her shoulder to touch the frame next to her fingers. The warmth of his skin was so familiar, even after six years. His scent surrounded her.

One slight move and she could bury herself in his arms. With a tilt of her chin, she looked up at him. His lips were so close. His gaze lowered to her mouth. All breathing stopped as her heart pounded hard.

The back of his knuckles gently caressed her cheek. Tears. He was wiping off tears.

His fingers moved up into the curls of her hair, and the years between them slipped away.

The warmth of his hand rested on the back of her

neck as he pressed his lips to the small area between her ear and jaw. He knew all her sensitive spots. He knew her. He brushed her hair from her shoulder and trailed soft, gentle kisses to her chin.

Finally, he reached her mouth. She leaned in and, for an instant, their lips touched. Her hand went to his arm to balance herself and pull him closer.

Instead, cool air hit her. He was gone.

Opening her eyes, she found him standing a few steps back.

"Elijah?" She waited for an explanation. Something. Anything.

Heavy wrinkles marred his brow. "I'm sorry, Jazz. That can't happen. I promised myself I wasn't going to do anything to complicate our relationship. Once something is broken, there's no getting it back. Rose-marie is the most important person in this scenario, not our old feelings."

"What if they're new and stronger?"

A pained expression crossed his face. With a hand in his hair, his arm rested on the top of his head. One pivot and all she had was his back.

"Elijah?"

He groaned. "Feelings are not my strong point."

"But that doesn't mean you should ignore them."

"Parenting is the only thing between us from here on out." The timer went off, and she was ignored as he set the roasted chicken on a cooling rack. In silence, he pulled a couple of plates down and fixed them. Sliding a plate in front of her, he sat on a bar stool one space over. He stabbed a piece of broccoli. "So, you came here without Rosemarie, but you claim I have nothing to worry about." He stared into the night, chewing with too much energy. "Just so you know, I kind of worry all the time now."

So many emotions were whirling around her heart and head she couldn't sort them out. He had built a new life without her. Just like she had in Denver.

The only reason he had let her in now was because of their daughter. The daughter she had kept from him. Was that too big for him to really forgive?

What if she had gotten this all wrong and he didn't want her, just Rosie?

Chapter Fourteen

Blinking her eyes, she cleared her thoughts and focused on what he was saying.

He adjusted his napkin. "God had to start from the ground up with me. There isn't a day that's easy."

The jellyfish were back in her stomach. She pushed the chicken around. That night six years ago was so clear in her head, but how had the following days played out for him?

She had been in survival mode, allowing her parents to take care of her and all the decisions. She had focused on her baby, on creating a new life for them in another state. At nineteen she had still been a child playing house.

Letting her parents remove any means of contacting Elijah had eased the stress and uncertainty that surrounded her decisions about him. They knew his voice alone would soften her. What if she had been strong enough to reach out to him a month or two later?

He grinned. "What are you thinking?"

"How did you... I mean when did..." She took a

deep breath. "The next morning? What happened after you woke, when you found me gone?"

He stood up, his gaze focused on the wood floors.

"Do you remember?" She slid onto the stool closer to him, but he shook his head and moved farther away.

Dinner forgotten, he went to the sofa and sat, his arms resting on his thighs, his head down. "I remember every detail."

His head came up and his gaze crisscrossed the room, as if he were replaying the morning in his head. "At first I rushed through the rooms. The times before, no matter how late I came in or what I did, you were still here. I was terrified. No matter how hard I concentrated, I couldn't remember anything after leaving the bar.

"I panicked until I noticed all your things were still here. Your hair stuff and makeup littered the bathroom. I thought maybe you'd gone to get more coffee. Or you went to get my car. You did that a lot, too."

His gaze stilled on her. "I took it for granted you were just cleaning up my mess again. I was so self-centered."

He closed his eyes and leaned his head back on the sofa.

A long moment of silence let the images of that night sink into her thoughts. "All I did before I left was cover the window. The rain was coming in hard and pooling on the floor. I didn't want our new floors to be ruined."

His attention stayed on the white beams above them. "It looked as if you'd be right back. So, I thought I'd help." He grunted. "The great Elijah started sweeping up all the scattered debris and broken glass. Could I have been more of a clueless idiot?"

She bit her lip, holding back a snort. "I might have thought the same thing a few times."

He nodded and gave her a half-hearted smile. "I assumed you just needed cooling-off time. After an hour or so—" he gave a hard, self-deprecating laugh "—I tried calling, but you didn't answer. Then I called your parents. At first they didn't answer, either." He searched her eyes for a heartbeat. "Did you ever get my messages?"

"No. I gave my phone to Mom and told her not to let me answer. Monday, they gave me a new phone and number."

Moving across the room, she sat on the wicker chair next to him, she reached over and took his hand. "I'm s—"

Brows knitted, he frowned at her. "Don't say you're sorry. I'm the one who put you in a place where you were forced to do that."

Leaning forward, she lightly squeezed his fingers. His free hand started tracing the old scar at her wrist. Instinct told her to pull away, but she held still.

"Your mom finally answered and made it clear I shouldn't call again. You weren't my business anymore. I was sick to my stomach thinking of how I had treated you. I understood that you needed time away from me."

He stood, breaking their contact. Behind the sofa he began rearranging the colored glass bottles on the smooth driftwood shelf. "I put everything back in order and waited for you. Monday, I went to work."

He moved to the bookshelves. Parenting books and

children's books filled the two lower shelves. Pulling out one, he flipped through it. "No one would make eye contact with me. I was fired with a yellow Post-it note. I tried contacting your father. He told me that you'd be filing for divorce."

Book back in place, he braced his hand on the middle shelf and dropped his head. "I don't know if he told you about our conversation."

"No." She had begged her father to let her know what was going on, but he said it was all fine. "He told me that you wanted a divorce."

He made a strangling sound, as if someone were choking him. His spine stiffened, and his jaw went stone hard. Stomping across the room, he threw his long body into the other wicker chair and tilted his head back. "I told him I'd go to counseling. I begged him with everything I had to let me talk to you just once."

She gasped, her intertwined fingers pressed against her mouth. He was such a proud man. His pride wouldn't have ever allowed… "Oh, Elijah."

"I promised to stop drinking, but he rightfully reminded me that I'd said that before." He leaned forward, elbows braced on his knees. "He was right. But I still held out hope that you'd come back. You had always come back. I mean, your shampoo was in the bathroom."

Both hands went to his hair. "I went to their house to see you, but they put a restraining order against me."

He shot up like a jack-in-the-box unlatched. There was a hard crease between his eyes. "Did they know you were pregnant? That night, did they know?"

She couldn't say the words, but her silence was

enough. The distress in his eyes at that realization hit her hard.

A depth of grief she had never seen filled his eyes. "That whole time I was pleading to speak with you, they knew. They knew I was going to be a father." He pressed his palms against his eye sockets.

Her heart hurt for all the lost moments, but she needed to focus on the future, on what they could be together going forward.

He dragged his hands down his face, then paced. "They were trying to protect you. I get it. Just like I'd protect Rosemarie. Like I protected Gabby and eventually my sister." He closed his eyes and a deep painful groan came from his throat. "My daughter and wife had to be hidden from me."

"Elijah, they went too far." Standing, she cupped his face. "Have you been sober since the night I left?"

He shook his head, as if confused. "No. I was determined to be sober for you so that when you came back you'd see I could be a good husband. I went to my first AA meeting. A few weeks went by and still no word from you, then the restraining orders and the divorce papers arrived. I lost it. I didn't know how to deal with all the emotions, so I fell right back into old habits." He sat on the sofa with his elbows on his knees, and he watched her.

Sorting through all this new information was putting pressure on her head. "Right before I signed the divorce papers, I asked my parents to let me see you. They said you were worse than the last time I saw you. Were they telling me the truth?"

He dropped his head, his long fingers interlocked behind his head.

"Elijah? How long were you…"

"I don't remember anything about the week after I signed the papers." He still hadn't raised his head.

Was she hearing him, right? "One week? And you've been clean ever since?"

He nodded.

He'd been sober when their daughter was born and during most of her pregnancy. "What changed?"

"Xavier. Basically, he told me I had a choice to make. I could wallow in self-pity and have a miserable life and prove the Judge and your mother right. Or I could turn it all over to God and figure out my purpose. He said if I wanted to be like our fathers, I was on the right track."

She sat beside him. "Oh, Elijah. I know how much you respected your cousin's opinion."

He nodded. "He was right, as usual. I miss him so much."

Putting her fingers under his chin, she lifted his face to hers. "Even through losing him and finding you have a daughter you've stayed sober. You're so strong. He'd be so proud of you."

Moisture shimmered in his eyes. "Not me. God is my strength."

She didn't bother to point out that trusting God was what made him strong. But her gut told her it was time to change the subject. Or maybe her heart couldn't take any more arrows. "How'd you become a successful businessman in such a short time? You've impressed my father."

One dark eyebrow went up. "That heart attack must have affected the Judge's brain."

She laughed. "Maybe he sees the world a little clearer now." Leaning back to give him room, she tried to look relaxed. "So how did Saltwater Cowboys happen?"

"I couldn't get a job. I even went to my uncle, but he refused to let me on the ranch. I started working odd jobs on the pier. I'd bus tables at the restaurants, clean out the boats, whatever anyone would let me do. I started going out on the fishing boats more. That's where I met Miguel. He had business experience. I had grown up here, on the water. We make a good team."

He popped his knuckles. "Before I knew it, a year had gone by without a drink, and I realized I liked life better without the haze of alcohol. I started taking AA seriously. Xavier had one boat, so we went to him with our plan. I was able to use our house as collateral."

A heavy sigh escaped his lungs, and he fell back against the sofa. "One of the hardest periods of my recovery was letting go of you. In order to heal and move on from the past, I had to give up on the idea of you and me together."

His gaze roamed the living room and kitchen. He gave her a sad grin. "I'm pretty sure there's a part of me that tucked you away and held on."

She nodded. "A part of me stayed with you. My parents knew. That's why they fought so hard to keep you out of my life."

The sadness that always hovered in the edges of his eyes swallowed them. Putting a pillow on her lap, she studied his face.

"You had a part of me with you," he whispered.

"Yes. She was my strength when I was at my lowest. When I look at her, I see the best of you and me. I'm so sorry my parents kept—"

"Don't." His large hands covered hers on the pillow. "I told you no more apologizing for protecting our daughter."

"I went through counseling, too. In one of the group sessions, I was asked if I would do it again. Would I marry you if it had to play out the same way? I said yes without hesitation. I would say yes, every single time."

He nodded. "Because of Rosemarie."

"She's one reason, but also because of you." She sat back and smiled. "Loving you was a great adventure. When you were sober, it was the greatest joy of my life. You taught me to enjoy the little things in life and to not always play by the rules. Like eating the center of the brownie first. Without the alcohol, you're the greatest man I know."

He made a rude noise. "Your father is the Judge. *The Judge*. That's what everyone says, with respect and honor. Sweetheart, there is no way—"

She pressed her fingertip against his lips. "Don't argue with me. My father is a great man and so are you. The real you. Not the man trying to be someone he's not. You're not my father. You're your own man, and I think you've found him."

He took her hand in his and kissed her palm, then her knuckles. For a moment she couldn't breathe, but then he dropped her hand and sat back. "But I also broke your heart."

"Yes. It was the biggest heartbreak of my life. But I

grew up and wove my heart back together. It's stronger than ever. We can do the same thing. We can weave our broken life back together and be unbreakable."

"What do you mean, 'we'?" He narrowed his gaze, distrust written all over his face.

Excitement bubbled through her limbs. She was going to do it, take the plunge. "So much time was lost, time we can't get back. I want to come home."

"You're moving back to Texas?" He looked down, nodding. "Austin's not that far."

"Not Austin. Here."

His eyebrows scrunched, making hard lines in his forehead. "Port Del Mar? That's not a good idea."

"This is what I wanted to talk to you about." Leg tucked under her, she shifted to face him. "We're both in a better place now." She took his hand. Willing him to understand.

"You taught me to take chances. You showed me there was more life beyond the books and my parents." She grinned. "Don't get me wrong, I love my parents, but they kept me in a tight little box. You opened the world up to me in a way I would have never experienced it."

"Your parents had good reasons to protect you. Just like you should protect Rosemarie. She'll be exposed to the rumors about my family."

"We'll teach her the truth and how hurtful gossip is. You have nothing to be ashamed of." With a nervous laugh, she shook her head. "We can do that together. I want Rosie to grow up here. With time maybe we can even reclaim our dream of having a family."

Horror filled his face. "Jazmine, you can't be serious." He yanked his hands out of her grasp and stood.

"I'm so proud of everything you've accomplished. I should have come back sooner."

His jaw dropped and all the color left his face. "No." He stood and moved behind the kitchen counter.

She was offering him everything, and he was walking away. She didn't understand. Her brain scrambled for a way to make him see that this was what they both needed. Her nails cut into her palms. She would not cry. He just didn't understand.

She tried to make eye contact, but he turned away.

He stared out the window. "We have a plan. It's a good plan for everyone. I'll visit Denver during the year, and on holidays and in summer you'll come here with her."

"But what if I want more?" Each word had to be pushed past the sand in her throat.

"I have no more to offer."

"I'm stronger now. I know what I want. I... We can get it right this time." She followed him, needing him to understand.

His forehead was deeply creased. "And if we don't? You were never the problem in our relationship, you understand that, right?"

"I have accountability in this, too." She circled her arms around her waist. "I expected you to know what I was thinking and feeling. Instead of dealing with the real issues, I ran and hid. We've learned so much, and both of us are stronger in our faith."

She moved around the counter and put her hand on top of his, not letting him get away this time. "You were my world. I thought we would just love each other enough and the problems would go away. I loved you so much. We could have that again."

He pulled away. "I destroyed your world."

"You won't do that again. I won't let you." The lopsided cup caught her eye. Picking it up, she traced the uneven surface. "This cup isn't perfect, but our daughter made it with perfect love. Just like that mirror, we can build a new world. A better world. A world that can survive the storm."

"I don't want you or Rosemarie anywhere near me if that storm hits again. It's never far. If you're in Denver with her, you'll be safe."

"That's what you want? For me and Rosemarie to be over a thousand miles from you?"

He wouldn't look at her. "I can be a good weekend dad. I didn't cut it as an everyday husband." He started pacing. "You want me to pull out my family history? Your parents had it right. You and Rosemarie need to be as far away from the De La Rosa family as possible."

"She is a De La Rosa," she whispered. She wanted to grab him and make him face her, stare into her eyes until he understood that he deserved to be loved. "Elijah, please."

"No. You made sure she was a Daniels. Which might be best in the long run. The De La Rosa legacy will not be hers."

"You can't let Frank define who you are."

"I'm not, but some things are facts."

"I don't believe it."

He dropped his shoulders, as if the fight had left his body. He rubbed his fingers hard against his forehead.

She stood on the edge, waiting for him to join her. Needing him to join her. Everything she ever dreamed of was in front of her if he would only take her hand.

Elijah forced himself to step away from her. It would be too easy to grab the hand she offered and hang on. But he knew better. Her eyes sparkled with excitement. He didn't want to be the one who took that away. Not again.

"You really want her to grow up in a town where she'll be known as one of those De La Rosas? And don't you dare lie to me. You wouldn't even give her my name, and you were all the way in Denver."

"I regret that. You and your cousins have changed the legacy of your family name. I'm proud of you and I want Rosemarie to see that, to be a part of your life, here in Port Del Mar."

Loser. Worthless. Drunk. He didn't want his daughter to hear those words about him. He couldn't breathe. Turning sharply on his heels, he went through the double doors to the back deck. The waves crashed against the shore.

He felt her hand on the center of his back, circling in a soothing motion. He closed his eyes. Longing for everything he lost swirled in his head. The desire to give in. To tell her yes.

Her touch was as soft as gentle waves. "Some of the best moments of my life happened right here. We could have the future we dreamed of if you have the faith."

Gently, he stepped back, disconnecting them. Turning, he held her arm, palm up. His fingers traced the jagged scar that sliced her palm. "I did this to you."

402   *The Texan's Secret Daughter*

"You didn't cause my injury."

His head tilted back. He closed his eyes. "I should have been your safe place."

"We were young and made mistakes."

"Sometimes letting go and moving on is the best second chance we can hope for."

"No. You apologized, right? Everything about your life since I left shows you meant it. You don't think you deserve to be happy."

Blinking did not ease the burn behind his eyes. How did he answer that? His jaw locked.

"You don't, do you?"

He felt raw. It was like she was gouging his chest, exposing all his weakness. "I'm happy with my life. What I don't deserve is your trust. I'm toxic. I live one day at a time. I can't promise you a future. I can't promise that in one month or ten years I'll be the man I am today."

He ran his hand through his hair to stop himself from grabbing her. "I'm one drink away from being Ben, drunk in the parking lot fighting with a friend who's trying to help me."

"I'm not the same pushover. We belong together. Our daughter deserves to grow up in the home we built. You're my husband. In my heart you always have been, even after I signed the papers." Her gaze scorched him. "Elijah, could you grow to love me again?" Fear and doubt etched each word.

His face tightened. *I love you so much. I've loved you forever.* The words fought to get past his lips, but they wouldn't budge. They lodged in his throat. He needed them to stay buried.

"The question was never whether I loved you. Do I love you enough to walk away, to protect you? I'm one drink away from being the man that chased you away. He's still inside me. Lurking."

"God has you."

"Jazmine, I'm an alcoholic. My life happens one day at a time. That's all I have. All I can offer. It's not good enough."

Her lips parted.

"There is no cure for what I have. We can't do this to Rosemarie." Tears were running down his face, but he was powerless to stop them. "If I go down again, I'm not pulling you with me. Don't trust me."

"I trust God."

An exasperated huff of air escaped his lungs. "Stop being stubborn." He took a deep breath, calming himself, then lowered his voice. "I'm doing this for you. What if our love isn't stronger than the addiction?" He shook his head. "I can't risk losing control and her seeing that side of me."

"Do you regret marrying me?" The hard edge of her voice softened.

He couldn't answer that. She was his life. The world was a better place with her in it. He was a better man because she was in his world. He swallowed, not blinking, as their eyes stayed locked.

"Okay." Head down, she smoothed the pretty pink skirt that floated around her legs. She had been so innocent when he first met her.

"You deserve better than me." He needed her to get that it was about saving her, not hurting her. "So does our daughter, but she's stuck with me as her father. I'll do the best I can, but I can't promise anything long-term."

Her breath hitched, and her body stiffened. "You're a coward." It was a harsh whisper between clenched teeth.

He was doing this for his family. He was going to be a man of courage for the first time in his life. "If that's what it takes to keep you both safe, then I guess I'm a coward. Go back to Denver, Jazz."

Back straight, she lifted her chin. Her eyes searched his face and her mouth opened, as if she had more to say. He braced himself. He couldn't be weak now.

"It's over, Jazmine. Let me go."

She swung around and walked out the door. This time, she wouldn't be coming back. The urge to yell at her, to beg her to keep fight for him, hit him like a tidal wave taking him under. Pulling everything out, leaving him hollow.

The door clicked shut behind her, and he fell to his knees and prayed. Tears fell hard. He wanted to reach inside and rip his heart out. He just needed to stop the pain. His elbows hit the ground, and he buried his fingers in his hair. "Please God. You're my strength." With her light gone, the darkness threatened to overtake him. This time he wouldn't let it.

He scoured his mind for a verse. John 12:46. "'I am come a light into the world, that whosoever believeth on me should not abide in darkness. I am come a light into the world, that whosoever believeth on me should not abide in darkness.'"

On the floor, he repeated the verse over and over again.

Chapter Fifteen

The moon looked as if it hung right above her parents' house. Pulling into the shadow of the tall, three-story home, Jazmine parked her car. She rested her head against the steering wheel and sobbed. She had been able to hold the worst of it back as she drove, but she was safe in her parents' driveway now.

A tap on the window caused her to jump right along with her heart. Her mother stood in the dark. Hand on her chest, Jazmine opened the door. "What are you doing? You scared me half to death."

"I'm sorry, pumpkin." Without another word, Azalea pulled her grown daughter into her arms and rocked her like a child.

After a few minutes of crying until her throat and ribs hurt, she sat back and wiped at her face. "Mom, what are you doing out here?"

"I was waiting for you on the balcony, but when you didn't get out of the car I got worried." Tucking a loose curl behind Jazmine's ear, Azalea laid her forehead against her daughter's. "It didn't go the way you wanted? You were gone a long time."

"No." Jazmine stepped back and rubbed the back of her hand across her face. A stupid sob escaped.

Her mother took her by the hand and pulled her to the back door. "Let's go sit on the balcony. I have lemonade and brownies waiting for you."

The crying started all over.

Once on the top balcony, she settled in and allowed her mother to pamper her. Jazmine noticed the Bible open on the table. "What have you been reading?"

"My Bible study group has been discussing Romans. This week, Romans 5:8 was part of our reading, and it stuck with me. I was praying over it while you were gone."

Jazmine leaned back in the rocker and sipped her drink, trying to let the stress float past her. "What does it say?"

"'But God commendeth his love toward us, in that, while we were yet sinners, Christ died for us.'"

The corner of her mouth curled. "You've concluded that God loves Elijah."

"Oh, it's much more personal than that. God loves me despite my own sin, yet I sit here judging Elijah for actions from the past. What does the last six years tell me about him? It's the plank in my eye while I point out your splinter. Don't get me wrong. Getting you out that night? I would do it again. But the following months should have been handled differently. He has to hate us, but he's been very patient."

"We talked about that tonight. He understands why you hid us. He did the same for his family. Part of his healing has involved letting go of the past and the anger and taking responsibility for his actions."

Her mother sighed. "So, why the tears?"

Her throat burned. If she spoke, the tears would start all over again.

Azalea slid into the large rocker next to her. "What happened?"

"He doesn't want us to be close."

Warmth surrounded her as her mother pulled her into her arms. The crying started all over again. When the sobs finally subsided, she leaned back, focusing on the stars so far away.

"Tuesday, we'll be leaving for Denver." With a slight turn of her head, she looked at her mother and gave her the best smile she could manage. "The message was loud and clear. Not only is there no future for us as a family, he thinks we should go back to Denver. As far from him as possible. That should reassure you."

Azalea didn't let go of Jazmine's hands. "No, baby. All I ever wanted was for you to be happy. I thought you were happy in Denver, but after watching you the last few weeks, I realize you were just surviving. You're a great mother, but I think a part of you was missing. Maybe it's time for you to come back."

Jazmine frowned. "Rosemarie and I are fine in Denver. She'll get to see her father every other weekend and spend summers with her grandparents."

Azalea put her arm around her daughter, resting her chin on the top of Jazmine's head. "I know I've tried everything in my power to keep you from Elijah. But some things are in God's hands. These last few weeks there's been a joy in you I haven't seen in years. I think you belong here, with Elijah."

"Mom?" She pulled back and looked at her mother, stunned. "What have you done with my mother?" Sighing, she shook her head and rested on her mother's shoulder. "You might have changed your opinion, but it doesn't matter. He doesn't want me in his life."

"That man loves you. He always has. I've seen how he treats Rosemarie. He's a good father. If I truly believe that God can change people, then I believe the evidence in Elijah's life. Not just this summer, but what he's done since you left. You wanted to fight for him after that first weekend, but you were so hurt and lost. It was easy for us to take care of everything and send you away. Are you strong enough to fight for him now?"

Fresh tears made their way up from the bottom of her heart. "I don't know."

"He tried everything short of breaking down our door to get to you, and that was before he knew about Rosemarie."

Jazmine sat up. "It's true? You and Daddy lied to me." She closed her eyes. The betrayal hit hard. She had based so many decisions on the lies her parents had told her. "You told me he wanted the divorce. When I asked how he was doing, you said his drinking was worse."

"It was." The words were sharp and defensive. Azalea dropped her head. "The time I went…" She looked back up at Jazmine, her eyes softer, regret deep. "It was the week after he signed the papers. I went to the house and, well, it wasn't pleasant. That was the last time I saw him in that condition or heard about him drinking."

"He told me he had one setback when he realized I wasn't coming home."

Her mother took her hands in hers, and Jazmine saw tears in her eyes. "Oh sweetheart, I'm so sorry. We just wanted to protect you. It's not an excuse, but I didn't know what else to do. I was so afraid I'd lose you. I'd do anything to keep you safe. We went too far."

Pulling away, Jazmine stood and went to the railing. The moon hung low in the night sky, the reflection dancing on the waves. "You know he said that? He said he understood why you did what you did. He's trying to protect us." She turned back to her mother. "From him." The tears started falling again.

Coming to her side, Azalea wrapped an arm around her. "You're a good mother. You'd never put Rosie at risk. He's proving to be a good father. If you think the best place for you both is with him, I'll support you."

"Are you sure?"

Her mother's gentle hand on her cheek took her back to childhood. "In my need to control, you might not notice this, but I do trust you. I also see the world a little differently these days." She kissed her temple. "I almost lost your father. I'm working on trusting God more. That's not easy for me. Elijah is surrounded by the good choices he's made since you left. You need to stay true to your heart. God has you, follow Him."

"It's that easy?"

"Yes and no. Nothing of true value is easy." Her mother cupped Jazmine's face. "You're strong, my beautiful daughter. God will show you the way. And I'll support you."

Did she know the right thing to do for all of them?

Jazmine looked at the time. Elijah would be here bright and early to take them fishing. He didn't trust himself, and she had only reinforced that by not allowing him to be responsible for Rosemarie.

She needed to prove to both that he was trustworthy.

"Mommy! Mommy! Wake up."

Jazmine groaned at the weight bouncing on her bed. Forcing one eye open, she peered at the time. It was almost five o'clock. Why was Rosie…? She shot up. "Your father!"

With all the drama last night, she'd forgotten to make sure her alarm was set. She rubbed her face.

"Daddy said to be ready by five. You're not ready."

Blinking her eyes, she focused on her daughter. Rosemarie was wearing a Painted Dolphin T-shirt, jeans, and the pink and purple waders Elijah had bought her. And a purple tutu. Oh, to be five and wear whatever struck your mood.

The tutu matched her new fishing pole. She was even wearing Jazmine's oversize hat.

"What do you think about making this a day with your dad and cousins, a De La Rosa trip?" She needed to prove to Elijah that she did trust him. Plus, spending all day with him in the confines of a boat might prove too much for her right now. Her emotions were still raw. And she had a great deal of praying to do.

"But you're coming. You don't want to fish?"

"It's not really my thing. Anyway, I thought you might like a little time alone with your father."

Rosie plopped onto the bed. "We could talk about you." She giggled.

Before she could ask what, they would talk about, there was a knock on the door.

"He's here! Mommy, you're still in your pajamas."

Her pajamas consisted of an oversize Jim's Pier T-shirt and yoga pants. Slipping out of bed, she threw her robe on. "Go get your fishing pole and backpack."

Then she stumbled down the steps, trying to push her hair into some sort of civilized shape.

Opening the door, she came face-to-face with the same Painted Dolphin logo that Rosemarie had picked out to wear. Elijah's fit a little tighter, stretching across broad shoulders. Very broad shoulders.

She blinked a couple of times, trying to escape the sleep fog that clouded her thoughts. Moving her gaze up, she was trapped by her favorite set of eyes. This morning they seem to dance in between shades of gray and green.

She frowned. The look of hesitation and doubt she found in them hurt her heart. With a shake of her head, she glared at him. He had no right to be all sad. He was the one who had rejected her.

Last night she had gone to him, and he had turned her down. Why was he looking like the kicked puppy?

"Do I have the wrong day?" He glanced around, as if the date was written in the air.

"No."

"We're going fishing, right?"

"Yes." *Brilliant, Jazmine.* It seemed as if one word at a time was all her brain could manage.

His gaze dropped to her bare feet. "I wouldn't recommend going barefoot."

"Oh, I'm not going. I'm not feeling well, so I decided today you can take her without me."

He closed the distance between them and put the back of his hand on her forehead. "We can reschedule."

She stepped back. "No, no. I'm not that sick. Just didn't sleep well last night."

The crease in Elijah's brow deepened. He searched her eyes. What was he looking for?

"Just her and me? You're going to let me take her? Out on a boat?"

This should have happened so long ago. She covered her face with her oversize terry-cloth sleeve. She was not going to cry again. Forcing a smile, she nodded. "It's time."

"Jazmine, I'm sorry. I know last night wasn't what you had expected." He stuffed his hands in his back pockets, stretching his shoulders wider. "I'm so tired of letting you down. It seems it's all I ever do."

She took a step closer but made sure not to touch him. Yelling at him to be brave and take a chance with them, was not a viable option this morning. She had said all the words last night, and it hadn't made a difference.

He lowered his chin until their foreheads almost touched. "Please, don't look at me like that. This is the first time in my life I'm not taking the easy way out. I'm doing this for her. And you."

Rosemarie's excited footsteps bounced down the stairs, and they jumped apart. Their daughter hopped off the last step and ran to Elijah. He went down to her level and opened his arms.

Hugging her tight, he pretended to be knocked off balance. "You're so strong!"

"Careful, sweetheart. You're going to hit someone with that fishing pole."

Elijah laughed. "Here, let me take it. I have a special place for it in my truck."

"Will you keep it there, even when Mommy takes me back to Denver? We can still fish every week, right?"

"Rosie." She put a hand on her tiny shoulder. "We can't come back every week. It's too far away."

The child's body stiffened, and a hard scowl took over the sweet face. She took in a lungful of air. Jazmine had a feeling Elijah was about to get a first-hand experience of stubborn Rosemarie. "Then I don't want to go to Denver. My fishing pole won't be there or my horse or GiGi and Papa." She took a breath. "I want to stay with Daddy. I want to live on the boat."

Elijah took a step back.

He had been the one to say no, and now he wasn't going to say a word. She gathered her daughter's wild curls and put them in a ponytail. "Sweetheart, we've talked about this, but if you want to throw a fit, you're more than welcome to go to your room. If you want to go fishing with your daddy, you need to put on a smile. We can talk about this later if you want to, but not right now. Do you want to go fishing or throw a fit in your room?"

"Fishing."

"Good." Jazmine looked at her ex-husband. He had the deer-stuck-in-the-headlights look. "Elijah, are you ready?"

Elijah looked a bit lost as Rosemarie stood, fishing pole in hand. Clearing his throat, he dropped to one knee in front of their daughter. "I'll be coming to visit at least once a month. We'll have a great time when I'm there. You can show me your school and all your friends. You miss them, right?"

Rosemarie scowled.

Jazmine wanted to explain to him that a five-year-old didn't have a good grasp of time and distance. But Elijah stood, and those beautiful lips kicked up on each end.

Her heart skipped. There was the carefree boy she had fallen in love with so long ago. He offered his hand to Rosie. "You want to go fishing, or what?"

Rosemarie took it, her scowl vanishing.

Elijah glanced at Jazmine, his face suddenly serious. "I'll have her back before noon."

She crossed her arms. "It's okay if you want to take her to lunch."

"That's seven hours. Without you or your parents."

"You've always been good at math." Serious again, Jazmine tilted her head. "I trust you with her."

He gave a solemn nod.

"Daddy, we're going to catch big fish, just like on the TV." Rosemarie pulled at him, moving to his truck.

Jazmine smiled. "Save some. We can have them for dinner tonight. Papa needs to eat more fish. And take pictures to show me."

"Okay! Love you, Mommy!" Rosie yelled over her shoulder, eager to go off with her father.

"I love you too, sweetheart." The urge to cry burned her eyes. Was she going to stay and fight, or was he right? Would it be best for their daughter to keep things as they were?

He paused. Turning away from Rosemarie, he studied her.

Did he know what she was thinking? "Elijah?"

His eyes looked teal right then. "Do you want to join us for lunch?"

She shook her head. "I wanted to go to Dad's doctor visit."

"Daddy! Hurry, so we can sneak up on the fish before they wake up."

The left side of his lips curled. "Duty calls."

Jazmine laughed. "She's always been a morning baby. Up early and ready to attack the day—or the fish. She's all your daughter this morning." She yawned. "Sorry."

He grinned. "We'll see you this afternoon. Go back to bed, princess."

Rosemarie bounced beside the truck, excited about her new adventure.

"Don't forget to make her wear a life jacket."

Elijah strapped Rosemarie into the backseat of his truck. He had a booster chair all ready. He saluted Jazmine and winked. "Yes, Mom."

She stood and watched them disappear.

Six years ago, she had run without looking back. She was so tired of running. She needed Elijah to see the future she saw when she looked at him. But if he didn't, why was she fighting him? Putting her family back together wasn't something she could do on her own; he needed to want it too.

Chapter Sixteen

Elijah sat back in the shade of the canopy as the boat headed to land. Rosemarie had crawled into his lap and was chatting away about the fish she'd caught.

He couldn't believe he had her all to himself. Jazmine had actually allowed him to take their daughter out into the Gulf. With the curiosity of a five-year-old, she had asked tons of questions about the boat, and it was obvious she had a love for being outdoors. He wanted to do this with her every weekend.

"Could I work on the boats with you, Daddy? Tío Miguel said I would be a great second mate." Rosemarie had picked up that Belle's girls called his best friend "Uncle" and had started doing it, too.

"You would make the most excellent second mate." But she was going to be in Denver. He closed his eyes and leaned his cheek on the top of her head.

Someone sat down next to him. Opening his eyes, he found his sister staring at him. She looked as if she was about to cry. Alarmed, he lifted his head. "What's wrong?" He glanced down at his daughter and discovered the reason the chatter had stopped.

Mouth hanging open as if she had stopped in midsentence, she was sound asleep, her cheek pressed against the purple life vest. Shifting so he could pull her closer, he glanced back at Belle. Her smile was back in place.

"Are you okay?" he asked. Everything in this moment was perfect. But if his sister needed him, they would deal with whatever had to be done.

"I'm fine. You're the one I'm worried about. Are they still going back to Denver?"

He nodded. If he put real words to what was going to happen, he might lose control of his emotions. His arms tightened around the little body in his lap, as if that simple action would keep her in his life.

"Have you thought about how you're going to feel with her living in another state?"

His jaw flexed, pushing down the words that wanted to escape. *Every moment.*

Belle tugged at the bottom of her T-shirt. "I'm sorry. Of course, you've thought about that."

"How did one little person become such an important part of my everyday life? I want her here, but that's not fair to her." The sway of the boat usually calmed him, but it wasn't working right now. He'd give anything to change his history. But his history was always going to be part of him.

Belle leaned in close and stroked back a wild curl. A sad smile pierced his heart, and she looked up at him. "Have you thought about asking her to stay? I've seen y'all together. You're a new man and she sees that."

Eyes closed, he tilted his head back against the side of the boat.

She didn't allow him to hide in silence. Gripping his arm tighter, she leaned in. "Ask her to stay."

Inhaling deeply, he shook his head. "Last night she came to the house to tell me that she wanted to stay in town. Give us a second chance."

Belle gasped, her eyes bright with excitement. "Oh, Elijah!" She covered her mouth, trying to stay quiet.

"I told her no."

Confusion replaced her excitement faster than he blinked. "What?"

"She wanted to see if we had a future as a real family." Great. Now his eyes were burning, and he didn't have a free arm to wipe his face.

"How can you tell her no? You can have everything you've worked for. Her, your daughter and your business. I don't understand how you could walk away."

"Here's the deal, Belle. That guy who made her worry and wait until the early hours of the morning, the one who tore up our house? He still lives in me. He's part of me and always will be. She wants a commitment to a future that I can't give her. I can't do forever. I can't do six months. I have to live day by day. That's all I have to offer her."

"That's not true." Belle stood, her arms tight across her chest. She turned to him, about to say something, when Miguel came down the ladder.

He looked from one to the other. "What's going on?"

"Mr. Brilliant over here turned down the best offer he's ever going to get."

Miguel's brows went up. "Jazmine?"

"Yes, Jazmine. She wants to stay to give them another chance. He sent her away. *Terco.*" She tapped the side of his head.

"I might be stubborn, but that doesn't mean I'm wrong."

"Why would you reject her?" He looked at Belle.

She twirled her finger next to her head. *"Loco."*

"Shh. Don't wake her up." Elijah wanted out of this conversation. "You're both messing with my live-in-the-moment moment. Go away."

"Listen." Miguel ignored him and sat on the opposite chair. "You have every reason to say yes to her. To them. To this moment." He indicated the child innocently sleeping in Elijah's arms. "Why are you punishing yourself?"

Elijah glared at Belle. "Did you tell him to say that?"

She rolled her eyes. "No one has to tell anyone to say that. We all see it."

The walls were closing in on him. Breathing became harder. "I'm always one drink away, Belle. One drink away from being Uncle Frank."

"No. Even at your worst, you couldn't be him. It's not in you."

"I don't think there's any way to get through that thick *cabeza.*" Miguel sighed. "I came down to take your daughter to see a pod of dolphins. They're ahead of the boat. We have a great view from the upper deck. Cassie and Lucy are up there with Carlos."

Elijah gently shook Rosemarie. "Hey, sweetheart, you want to see a family of dolphins?"

She was on her feet and looking around. "Where?"

Miguel held out his hand. "One thing your Tío

Miguel can do better than anyone else is find dolphins. Want to see them?"

She grabbed his hand and nodded. "Can I, Daddy?"

"Of course, you can. It's why we're out here."

Belle moved closer to her. "We'll be up in a minute."

With a smile and a nod, they were gone.

He shook his head. "There's nothing else to say. I'm not going to let the woman I love and my daughter ever live in a house with the monster I could become."

"You never drove drunk. You never physically harmed her."

"Woo-hoo!" He twirled his fingers in the air. "Give me the husband of the year award." His gaze went to the scar along the left side of her forehead, near her eye.

She got right in his face. "Don't go there. You are nothing like either one of those men."

"Just because the scars I gave her are all inside doesn't make it better. You know as well as I do that emotional injuries can be more damaging than the ones everyone can see." His finger traced her jagged scar.

His sister wrapped her fingers around his hand. "Even at your worst, you never hurt someone weaker than you. Not even verbally. Without you, I wouldn't have survived. I'm so tired of watching you punish yourself. You asked for forgiveness. God forgives you, Jazmine has forgiven you, so why can't you forgive yourself?"

"How can they forgive me?" That was the question that had rattled around in his head from the start. The question he shouldn't ask if his faith was good enough. "I shouldn't doubt God's word, but how can forgiveness be so easy? It doesn't make sense."

"That's what faith's all about. Believing what doesn't make sense in this world. It's God's kingdom. God's love. It's way beyond our feeble understanding. You have a gift that has been beautifully wrapped. Take it and treasure it."

He dropped his head. "I can't."

"Have you stopped loving her?"

"Loving her isn't the problem. I've always loved her. Even when I moved on from the divorce, I couldn't think of dating someone else." He looked out into the afternoon sky. "She's it for me, but I can't risk—"

"Stop right there, Elijah Gilbert De La Rosa. You love her. She loves you. Why are you wasting time being such an idiot?"

"Hello. Alcoholic." He held his arms out wide and pointed to himself. "And I've seen guys sober for years lose it all in one glass. When they fall off, they tend to fall off really hard."

"So, you're cutting her and your daughter out of your life. Too bad, so sad, Rosemarie doesn't get a father." Belle clenched her teeth and paced. "I know you think you're doing the heroic thing, but you're denying them your love as much as you're denying yourself theirs. You're letting fear win."

"I'm protecting her. I want her in my life. But if she's in town, people will tell her what a loser her father is. A drunk. If they're in Denver, she won't be hurt if I fall."

Stopping, Belle turned and stared at him, eyes wide, mouth open.

He rolled his eyes. "Close your mouth, you're letting flies in."

With a thump, she flopped into the chair next to

him. "You really believe if you fall off the wagon, living in Denver will save her feelings? You're her daddy. This little girl loves you. No matter where she lives, what you do will affect her."

Wetness hovered on her lashes. His gut curled. Why was he always making the women he loved cry?

She reached over and gently touched his cheek. "She loves you, and you'll be the best dad because you'll wake up every morning and promise her another day. You'll commit to her one day at a time, every single day. That's how you got sober. The same way you built your business. Look at what you've accomplished, one day at a time."

Something inside him shifted, hard. He couldn't let that happen. He had to keep it there, because if he... He popped his knuckles. "What if I lose my sobriety?"

"You get up and you fix it. You're not protecting her by sending her away. Listen to me." She grabbed his ear and forced him to look at her. "It doesn't matter how far away you send her. If you fall, it's going to hurt her. Jazmine knows what she's doing. She said she loves you, and she wants to commit to a future with you. Trust her and love her and lean on God to take care of the rest. Can you picture a life without her?"

No. "I can, but not one I want to live."

"Do you trust God?"

Oh, that was harder. "With her heart? It's not God I don't trust. It's me."

"Then you've already hurt her. You're only giving her little parts of you. That's never going to be good enough. Your daughter and your wife need all of you.

The good, the bad and the imperfect. You're a good man, and they deserve all of your love."

Could he say yes to Jazmine? He shook his head. "I can't."

"You won't."

He sighed. "I have a few days left with my daughter. I'm going to watch dolphins and do anything else she wants." He moved to the steps, then stopped in front of her. His knuckle traced the edge of her scar. "You didn't do anything to deserve this, Belle. If anyone deserves to be fully loved, it's you."

"We don't always get what we deserve. I've got everything I need—my girls, a family I can count on, a business I love and God. What else do I need? A man? No, thanks. Anyway, who would I date? All the men around here know my past. Jazmine knows us. She knows you, all of you, and she still believes in you. Think about that. Now, go be with your daughter."

He nodded and swung around, jumping up the ladder. His stomach tightened, but he couldn't focus on the days ahead. Right now he had Rosemarie, and he wanted her to have good memories of her father.

The kind to let her know he loved her even if he falls.

His sister was right. Giving her the childhood he never had could happen one day at a time.

Each morning he could wake up and promise to love them through the day. Day that could make up years.

Was it too late? Had he pushed Jazmine past the point of forgiving him ever again?

Chapter Seventeen

The sun was peeking over the water as he drove to the three-story beach home. To Jazmine. He was not going to let them get on that plane tomorrow without laying his heart on the line like she had done for him. He had been a coward that night.

Stepping out of his truck, Elijah looked to the top of the three-story beach house. He closed his eyes. *Please, God, give me the words and the strength I need to do this work.* For the last few days, he had gone back and forth on and circled every word his sister had said.

Letting Jazmine go had not been for the good of her and their daughter.

He could give her one day, each day. Together they could watch the sun rise and make a new vow each morning to love one another. The same as he vowed to God each morning to turn his problem over to him.

He stood at the door, wiping his hands over his jeans. Had he waited too long?

Before he knocked, the front door opened. "Elijah?" Jazmine's mother stood on the threshold.

"Yes, ma'am."

She stepped farther out and closed the door behind her. "They're not here."

All the blood drained from his body, and his head went blank. They couldn't be gone. "No. It's too early."

"She got a call yesterday. There was an emergency at work, and they asked her to come back. They left on the next flight out. Didn't she call you?"

"I had a missed call from her and a message she wanted to talk, but..." She hadn't want to tell him over the phone. "I had Lane cover my charter today and came over to talk." It seemed she had decided to move on just like he told her. What did he do now?

He looked Azalea in the eye. "I love her. I love them both."

"I know."

"You also know I don't deserve her." He stood before her with his hat in his hands.

"My daughter loves you. She never stopped. I don't want to see her hurt, and I trust you want the same. That's what I've seen this summer, anyway. In God I trust. If you do the same, this will be good for everyone."

There was a new lightness in his chest. "I won't take her for granted. I need to talk with her."

"Wait here a moment." She wasn't gone long and when she returned, she handed him a box.

"A ring box?"

"It's her great-grandmother's. It has an incredible love story attached to it. The world didn't think they belonged together, but they proved everyone wrong by loving each other for over fifty years and filling their days with happiness." She picked up his hand and wrapped his fingers around the box.

"You're giving it to me?" He had no clue how to react, what to say.

"I'm not saying you should give this to her right now. You probably have a few things to talk about, but I can't imagine anyone else giving this to her. She asked for it the first time you got married. I didn't think you were right for her, so I refused to let her have it. Of course, that didn't stop her from marrying you."

Tears gathered in her long eyelashes. His own chest felt as though a vise grip was squeezing his ribs. "We rushed the first time. It was a mistake."

"No. The alcohol was the mistake, not the marriage. You told Jazmine it was fear that led you to drinking. That's the reason you lost her." Azalea placed her hand on his shoulder. "I've had my own recent lesson. Fear is a lie you believe. That lie will mess up your future."

"Being an alcoholic is not a lie."

"You didn't beat the odds because of luck, but by faith. Leaning on God, you've fought hard to stay sober. The man standing at my door decided he wanted to own the largest fleet of boats in Port Del Mar, and he made it happen."

She clasped her hands in front of her and took a moment to search his eyes, her gaze firm and intense. "You wanted a real relationship with your daughter, and despite my best efforts—" a chuckle softened her words "—you're not just her biological father, you're the daddy she loves. You even won over a mother-in-law who was letting bitterness blind her. With each goal set, you've not only achieved, you've exceeded."

"I didn't do it alone."

"No. None of us survive this life by going it alone."

Elijah looked down. A few more arrows of doubt hit him.

"She's seen you at your worst and knows you at your best. She's willing to put her trust in God that together you'll make the family she has always wanted."

Raising his head, Elijah took a deep breath and rolled his shoulders. "I think God's been trying to talk to me. And, as usual, I've been stubbornly ignoring Him."

"God's good. He won't give up on you. And I don't think she will, either." Sincerity softened Azalea's dark brown eyes.

"I'm starting to see that." God had put so many people in his life who had helped him find the right path. "I keep hearing Jazz, Miguel, my sister, all telling me the same thing. God might be bringing in the big guns to pop me on the back of the head."

"Me?" Her eyes twinkled.

Elijah nodded.

"I hope you're listening."

"You think I should go to Denver?"

She rolled her eyes. "Why are you still standing here?"

With the tip of her finger, Azalea patted the corner of her eye. "Go get her. Love them like they're the most precious things in your life."

"They are." Certainty pulled every nerve taut. On impulse, he hugged her. "I'll always protect them, even if it's from me."

She nodded against his shoulder and patted his back. "I know."

He was ready to lay it all out there. As he pulled out of the drive, plans started forming in his head. He would do whatever it took to prove to her that he was worth the risk. Would it be groveling or a big gesture? Maybe a little of both.

Hopefully, she still wanted him.

Chapter Eighteen

Jazmine looked around the decorated ballroom covered in soothing ocean blue. There was that little something extra missing for the fund-raiser, but it could have been much worse. The event had been on the edge of disaster. Her boss had called her when the man who had covered her position left without notice and they discovered he had done next to nothing with the plans she had left him.

"Ms. Daniels." One of the interns rushed in with a large box. She was followed by two others carrying the same kind of box.

The use of her maiden name tugged at her heart, which was ridiculous. Elijah had made it clear he wanted to move on. So three days ago she had returned to Denver, and for her daughter's sake she was going to have to get over this deep sense of loss. She was not part of the De La Rosa family. But her daughter was. She needed to talk to Rosie about adding Elijah's name to hers.

Elijah. She blinked back unwanted tears. They had

been playing phone tag, but not actually saying anything in their messages. Irritated with herself, she focused on Claire's excited face.

"These were just delivered to you. I think they're exactly what you were looking for to finish off the tables. I love the wooden starfish. You were holding back on us. There have to be over three hundred."

Paul, the newest intern, picked one up. "They each have a tag that reads, 'One at a time.'"

"I didn't order these." She looked on the box for any clues. They were from a gift shop in Del Port Mar. Oh, no. The stupid tears were trying to escape again. She needed to make herself busy.

Claire pulled more starfish out of the boxes and arranged them on the table. "These will be perfect gifts to the donors. Let's scatter them on the tabletops."

Not understanding how this was happening, Jazmine lifted one out of the box, a light turquoise starfish. "Do you know the story?"

Paul shook his head.

Claire laid a couple on another table. "It's about the boy walking along the beach?"

Jazmine nodded. "Yes. He was throwing the stranded starfish back into the ocean to save their lives. When an older man laughed at him and said there were too many for him to make a difference, he gently put another on back into the ocean then smiled and said—"

Someone cut her off by clearing his throat. She turned expecting her boss but froze in place when she saw Elijah. "He said, 'I made a difference to that one.' One at a time."

In a well-cut suit, he stood with his hands clasped in front of him. Her mind went blank.

"Hi, Jazz." He walked across the room.

"What are you doing here?" Then it hit her square in the center of her head. "Rosie. I'm sorry about taking off like that I tried calling but—"

This time he cut her off with his thumb on her bottom lip. "I know." He glanced over her shoulder.

"Um. Sorry. Claire, Paul and Monica are interns." She waved in Elijah's direction. "This is Elijah De La Rosa. He's Rosie's father."

There was a chorus of "ohs." Claire had a starfish in her hand. "Did you send these? There's a bunch."

He grinned. "Yes. Three hundred and sixty-five to be exact." His gaze found Jazmine again. "One for each day of the year. It's been pointed out to me by several people that I've accomplished some pretty good stuff with my one day at a time philosophy."

He had done more than some good stuff, but she couldn't seem to find any words.

Leaning in, his lips were so close to her ear that she could feel his breath. "Is there somewhere we can talk?"

"My office." She nodded, then gave final instructions to the interns before taking him to her private office. Closing the door, she leaned against it for support. "I can't believe you're here."

One hip on her desk, he crossed his arms. "I messed up, Jazz. You thought we had a future in Port D and I…well, I was stupid and scared." He stood and stalked toward her. "Tell me what's going on in that brilliant mind of yours."

She couldn't comprehend this man. Words tried to organize themselves in her head, but before she could get them out into the air between them, he closed in. Taking all her personal space.

Sharing space with him was something she had always loved. His scent comforted her in ways nothing else ever could.

He leaned in and pressed his mouth to hers, cutting off any words. The feel, taste and scent of Elijah De La Rosa consumed her.

At this moment he was the only thing in her world. She liked her world.

She never wanted to leave this world.

His hands cupped her face and she leaned deeper into his warmth. But then cool air touched her lips as he pulled back.

She tried to follow, but he held her in place. With his hands still holding her, he put space between them. Her hands went to his wrists, making sure they kept contact. The word *no* fought its way up her throat, but she bit it back and waited.

His fingers gently dug into her hair. "I got ahead of myself. Everything I said about letting you go and moving on was a lie."

"What do you want from me? You told me to return to Denver, and I did. You send me hundreds of starfish after you gave me a hundred reasons why I shouldn't stay in Port Del Mar. You come in here and kiss me like you have a right to. You're in a suit. And I don't—"

One corner of his mouth curled up.

She frowned at him. "What's so funny?"

"You get really wordy when you're nervous." He

moved in again, pressing his forehead to hers. "Are you done?"

"I don't know."

He chuckled. "While you're thinking of other things to tell me, I have something I need to say to you."

His face was so close she could see all the beautiful colors that made up his eyes. The ring around his irises was an indigo blue. That was new.

He cleared his throat. "I went to your parents' place to tell you something I should have said at our house the other night when you offered me everything I ever dreamed of. Things I didn't think I deserved. This morning, Romans 11:29 was a part of my morning devotionals. Do you know what it says?"

With a shake of her head, she waited.

"'For the gifts and the calling of God are irrevocable.'"

The intensity of his eyes anchored her to him. "For the first time ever, I really understood what people meant by having an epiphany. It was like parts of my brain opened and God's words filled it. I might've gotten off His path, but God kept righting me."

His eyes glowed with excitement. "I had been given the most precious gift, and then it was multiplied. God's been working on me even if I didn't trust Him the way I should."

He sighed. "You're a gift that can't be revoked or replaced. By turning you away, I *was* being a coward. Telling God I didn't trust His word."

With her thumb she wiped the single tear that had fallen from his eye.

He caught her hand and held it there. "Five years

ago, I committed my life to serving Christ. When you came back with Rosie, I was overwhelmed and dealing with new emotions. I have a hard enough time dealing with the old ones. I didn't know what to do, so I waited for something bad to happen instead of accepting the gift and treasuring it like I should have. I failed you again."

She needed space to process all his beautiful words. Breaking contact, she went to her desk.

He joined her. Not getting too close, he held out his hand. She didn't hesitate. One hand in his, she picked up a ceramic starfish painted with the exuberance of a three-year-old who loved purple. It had been a Christmas gift from Rosie.

Squeezing Elijah's hand, she looked him in the eye. "One starfish at a time or one day at a time. We can make a difference. I want to make a difference in Port Del Mar. With you. I wanted to honor—"

He crushed her to him, holding her so close it was difficult for air to get in her lungs.

His lips pressed against her ear. "I love you so much. I love you. I should have told you that sooner, but I'm saying it now and I want to say it every day. I can move to Denver if you want." His hold on her relaxed. He moved his lips to the corner of her forehead. "But, honestly, I want you and Rosie to come back to Port Del Mar. Come home and let us figure out our future." Hands slid down her arms, fingers entwining with hers, then flexing. "Please, don't let go of me."

She wrapped her arms around him. "You're mine. I'm not giving you back. I love you, Elijah De La Rosa. I always have, and I always will."

They might have messed up the first time, but it had shaped them into the people they were now. With God's grace they would figure out the future, of that she had no doubt.

Epilogue

Elijah adjusted the red scarf and flipped the bead-covered dreadlocks over his shoulder. Lane needed a raise for wearing this for every pirate trip. The boat swayed.

For the hundredth time, his hand went to his pocket. The ring was still there. This time he was asking with her parents' blessing. They would be here with his family and all the families in Rosie's first grade class.

He had to get this right. But he was having major doubts about the plan. He'd been dragging his feet, wanting it to be perfect, but the need to tuck Rosemarie into her bedroom at his house, their home, was driving him crazy.

"Daddy!" The reason he was wearing this ridiculous get-up wrapped her arms around his neck. Zoe, the doll he had given her on their first meeting, had a red bandanna wrapped around her black curly hair. "I knew you were a real pirate." She giggled and climbed into his lap and started playing with the colorful beads in the wig.

"Where's your mom?"

"She and GiGi are doing last-minute stuff. Papa brought me, so I can help you."

He chuckled. Jazmine had always been good at managing people without them even knowing.

"So, do I get a sword?" Judge Daniels joined them.

"Yes!" She slid down and pulled two plastic swords from a barrel. "This is going to be the best day ever." She jumped in place. "Daddy! You're doing it, right? For my birthday."

"Doing what?" her grandfather asked, as he pretended to be stabbed.

Elijah sighed and eyed his daughter. "For her birthday she only wants one thing from me."

Rosie twirled. "I want Daddy to marry Mommy for my birthday. I always wanted a sister, but that takes more time if you don't order ahead."

The Judge laughed, and some of the tension drained from Elijah's shoulders.

Standing, he picked up his daughter. "Crazy idea, right?"

"Asking Jazmine to marry you?" The older man crossed his arms and leaned on the edge of the faux ship. "Or proposing at a six-year-old's pirate party?"

His father-in-law sat down and propped his deck shoes on a short barrel. "This is going to be a great show. You can't back out now, boy. Lea told me she gave you my mother's ring. You got it?"

"Yes, sir." His throat went dry.

"Good." He winked. "Girls like that kind of thing. And I can tell you from experience that telling your daughter no never gets easier."

"Elijah!" Jazz called from below.

"Yes?" He went to the edge. Jazmine stood on the dock, boxes of cupcakes and a bundle of flowers in her arms.

"My mom needs help unloading the car," she called up to him.

"Got it."

That was the last moment not swamped in controlled chaos.

As they pulled away from the dock, he watched Jazz laughing and interacting with everyone.

Several times she caught him staring and smiled at him. Occasionally he worked his way over to her to steal a quick kiss. Like any good pirate would do.

The afternoon flew. The sun was setting, and they were heading back to the dock. It was time.

The young second mate distracted everyone with an outrageous song, so Elijah had time to climb up the platform. He unhooked the rope.

This might be the worst idea he had ever had while sober.

Lane winked up at him, then made his move. Drawing his plastic sword, the second mate held it to Jazmine's throat and told her he would be taking all her jewelry. The kids screamed and ran to her rescue. But the crew held the kids back, and they all laughed as they played along.

Jazmine looked confused. Her gaze searched the boat. She was looking for him.

"Argh!" he roared, and jumped from the platform, swinging across the deck. His boots landed on the box anchored to the floor specifically for this scene, one they usually played out for tourists.

The kids and parents cheered. His sister might have been the loudest. "Hands off the lady, you scoundrel!" Elijah used his best pirate voice.

Lane turned, and they lunged back and forth, slashing at each other with their plastic swords. Backed into the corner, Lane went to his knees and surrendered. He might have done a bit of overacting, but the kids loved it.

Dramatically, Elijah sheathed his sword. Swaggering across the deck to where Jazmine stood, he took her in his arms. For a moment he stopped and looked into her eyes. This might be over the top, but he wanted her to see him. To see the love he had for her.

Slowly, he lowered his head and kissed her as hoots and hollers surrounded them. Pulling back, he grinned at her.

Smiling, she raised her eyebrows. "What if this lady plans on saving herself?"

He removed his leather gauntlet and cupped her face. Leaning in, he kissed her nose. "She is more than capable, but this is what our daughter wanted. And I wanted you, so it works out." He winked, then twisted to face Lane. "Bring in the treasure so we can share our bounty."

The shrieks were higher than his ears could gauge as Lane and Carlos carried a wooden chest onto the deck. Elijah kneeled before the ancient-looking lock and, with a flourish, broke it. A hush fell over the kiddie crowd. The water hitting the sides of the boat was the only sound heard.

He lifted the lid. On top of the costume jewelry, chocolate coins and brightly colored beads sat a small velvet box. Closing his fist over it and pressing it to his chest, he turned on his heel and strode over to the love of his life.

She tilted her head, her eyes narrowed. He grinned. This would be something they would always remember. This was a good plan. He hoped.

One of the dreadlocks dropped across his face, and he yanked off the wig and bandanna. He wanted this to be real.

Her fingers went to his hair, trying to bring some sort of order to it.

In front of her, he dropped to one knee. She gasped.

"I've asked you before, and I broke those vows." He swallowed against the dryness of his throat. "You have no reason other than faith to be my wife again. Life without you is nothing but a gray mist. You fill every day with beautiful color. I want to give you all the love you deserve." He lifted the box and offered her the ring. "Will you marry me again?"

Her hands pressed against her mouth. "That's… That's…" Her eyes flashed to her mother before coming back to him. "You have Mama CiCi's ring." Slowly she went to her knees in front of him.

Her hand cupped his. Her eyes stayed on him. "What took you so long?" Her voice was low and hoarse. Tears glistened in the kindest eyes he had ever looked into.

"I wanted to make it perfect."

Tears overflowed her dark lashes. "I've never much

liked perfect. I love you and our life together. Yes, I'll marry you as many times as you ask."

He slipped the ring onto her finger where it belonged. It felt like going home again, but this time with the support and love of their families. Standing, he pulled her up with him and brushed his lips against hers.

A small body slammed into them. "Are you married now?"

They laughed. "No, sweetheart. We're engaged."

"When can we move in with Daddy? I want a puppy and a baby sister."

He swung his daughter up against his shoulder. "Give us a little time, sweet girl. You get to help your mom plan a wedding."

With a nod, Jazz kissed Rosie's cheek. "A very small wedding that will take less than a few weeks to organize."

He slipped his hand into the woman's who had always owned his heart. Lane and Carlos passed out the loot and the party favors. They docked, the families chatting as they disembarked. By the time the sun slipped out of the sky, his family stood alone on the deck.

Belle hugged him and whispered in his ear, "I'm so happy for you. You're the best guy, and you deserve to be happy."

"So do you, sis."

Stepping back, she shook her head. "I am happy. Now that you have your wife back, don't start matchmaking."

Selena laughed. Holding one of the triplets, she

leaned in for a hug, too. "Don't worry, I've got the perfect guy for her." She laughed at the horror on Belle's face.

Azalea helped with the other two triplets as they made their way off the ship. With just the string of party lights breaking the shadows of night, Elijah stood with his soon-to-be wife again and his daughter, and waved goodbye to everyone.

For a moment he wanted to fall to his knees and thank God for a life he had never even dared to dream of.

Rosie's eyes fluttered shut, and her head fell against his shoulder. Jazz pressed her cheek to his other shoulder and sighed.

With a yawn, Rosie snuggled closer to him. "Who knew life on a fake pirate ship could be so perfect?"

He kissed the top of her head. "Stick with me, babe, and the adventures will only get better. I love you."

"I love you, too, Daddy." The sleepy voice interrupted his thoughts. "Now that we're engaged, are we going home with you?"

"Not tonight, sweetheart, but soon. Very soon I'll take you home."

He felt Jazz's smile as her hand went to Rosemarie's back. "It won't be long before we'll be going home together."

His heart clenched, and he tightened his arms around his world, holding them close. He had been waiting for them, and he would be taking them home soon.

Jazmine stretched to her toes and kissed his cheek.

"Elijah De La Rosa, you're my home. I love you, always will."

His hand in hers and his daughter on his shoulder, they walked the plank. Together.

* * * * *

SPECIAL EXCERPT FROM

🌿

LOVE INSPIRED
INSPIRATIONAL ROMANCE

*Arleta Bontrager's convinced no Amish man will
marry her after she got a tattoo while on* rumspringa,
*so she needs money to get it removed. But taking a job
caring for Noah Lehman's sick grandmother means
risking losing her heart to a man who has his own
secrets. Can they trust each other with the truth?*

Read on for a sneak preview of
Hiding Her Amish Secret,
the first book in Carrie Lighte's new miniseries,
The Amish of New Hope.

Arleta had tossed and turned all night ruminating over Sovilla's
and Noah's remarks. And in the wee hours of the morning, she'd
come to the decision that—as disappointing as it would be—if
they wanted her to leave, she'd make her departure as easy and
amicable for them as she could.

"Your *groossmammi* is tiring of me—that's why she wanted
me to go to the frolic," she said to Noah. "She said she wanted to
be alone. And if I'm not at the *haus*, I can't be of any help to her,
which means you're wasting your money paying me. Besides, her
health is improving now and you probably don't need someone
here full-time."

"Whoa!" Noah commanded the horse to stop on the shoulder
of the road. He pushed his hat back and peered intently at Arleta.
"I'm sorry that what I said last night didn't reflect the depth of my
appreciation for all that you've done. But I consider your presence
in our home to be a gift from *Gott*. It's invaluable. Please don't
leave because of something *dumm* I said that I didn't mean. I was
overly tired and irritated at—at one of my coworkers and… Well,
there's no excuse. Please just forgive me—and don't leave."

Hearing Noah's compliment made Arleta feel as if she'd just
swallowed a cupful of sunshine; it filled her with warmth from

her cheeks to her toes. But as much as she treasured his words, she doubted Sovilla felt the same way. "I've enjoyed being at your *haus*, too. But your *groossmammi*—"

"She said something she didn't mean, too. Or she didn't mean it the way you took it. If I know my *groossmammi* as well as I think I do, she felt like you should go out and socialize once in a while instead of staying with her all the time. But she knew you'd resist it if she said that, so she turned the tables and claimed she wanted the *haus* to herself for a while."

That thought had occurred to Arleta, too. "*Jah*, perhaps."

"I'm sure of it. I can talk to her about it when—"

"*Neh*, please don't. I don't want to turn a molehill into a mountain." Arleta realized she should have spoken with Noah before jumping to the conclusion that neither he nor Sovilla wanted her to stay. But she'd been so homesick yesterday, and she'd felt even more alone after she'd listened to the other women implying how disgraceful it was for a young woman to work out. Hannah's lukewarm invitation to the frolic contributed to her loneliness, too. So by the time Sovilla and Noah made their remarks, Arleta already felt as if no one truly wanted her around and she jumped to the conclusion they would have preferred to employ someone else. She felt too silly to explain all of that to Noah now, so she simply said, "I shouldn't have been so sensitive."

"*Neh*. My *groossmammi* and I shouldn't have been so insensitive." Noah's chocolate-colored eyes conveyed the sincerity of his words. "It can't be easy trying to please both of us at the same time."

Arleta laughed. Since she couldn't deny it, she said, "It might not always be easy, but it's always interesting."

"Interesting enough to stay for the rest of the summer?"

Don't miss
Hiding Her Amish Secret *by Carrie Lighte,*
available May 2021 wherever
Love Inspired books and ebooks are sold.

LoveInspired.com

LIEXP0421

LOVE INSPIRED

INSPIRATIONAL ROMANCE

UPLIFTING STORIES OF FAITH, FORGIVENESS AND HOPE.

————————————

Join our social communities to connect with other readers who share your love!

Sign up for the Love Inspired newsletter at **LoveInspired.com** to be the first to find out about upcoming titles, special promotions and exclusive content.

————————————